Stealing Gold

by

Michael Balkind

This book is a work of fiction. Names, characters, places and incidents are either the product of the author's imagination or are used fictitiously. Any resemblance to actual persons, living or dead, or to actual events or locales is entirely coincidental.

STEALING GOLD

Cover Designed by Telemachus Press, LLC

Cover Art:
Copyright © iStock/1159636118

Published by Telemachus Press, LLC
7652 Sawmill Road
Suite 304
Dublin, Ohio 43016
http://www.telemachuspress.com

ISBN 978-1-956867-00-8 (eBook)
ISBN 978-1-951744-99-1 (Paperback)
ISBN 978-1-951744-98-4 (Hard Cover)

Version 2021.11.01

What Readers Are Saying About *Stealing Gold*

"With sharply drawn characters and a plot as twisty and dangerous as a Super-G race on an icy course, Balkind's *Stealing Gold* gives new meaning to the term a slippery slope."
—**Reed Farrel Coleman**, New York Times Bestselling author of *Where It Hurts*

"From the first chapter to the last, I was hooked. *Stealing Gold* has plenty of action—it was impossible to put down. I was able to feel what the characters felt."
—**Melissa Harring**

"Engaging and exciting … Flows effortlessly … Evokes a range of emotions, from fear and anxiety, to laughter and relief. A truly great story."
—**Tim Parker**

"Enjoyable and interesting. Not just about sports or a mystery but a fascinating look into what can happen in any sports venue. Details on the Olympic skiing were great!"
—**Sheri Anderson**

"*Stealing Gold* is a fast-paced, enjoyable read, with an exciting finish. You don't need to be a skier to enjoy this ride."
—**Deica Ruiz**

"Balkind gets you involved with his characters right from the starting gate. A fast paced, fun read. Really enjoyed it!"
—**Mark Jeffers**, President of Marsar Sports & Entertainment

"I loved the book. The twists and turns kept me glued from start to finish. An Awesome read."
—**Brian Summer**

"A wild ride!"
—**Melissa Libutti**

"Michael Balkind is a proven master of weaving a suspense filled story through the exciting world of sport. *Stealing Gold* introduces readers to the world of competitive skiing at the highest levels, while unveiling the potential dangers lurking in the shadows of competitive sport. The readers will find a comforting sense of relief as familiar characters from other novels in Balkind's outstanding series, arrive to lend their skills and expertise in hopes of solving the mysteries that unfold in *Stealing Gold*."
—**Professor Andrew Gillentine**

"*Stealing Gold* reads like a roller coaster ride, except this ride starts out quickly, becomes addictive, and then concludes with explosive excitement."
—**Steven Peltz**

"Favored to win Gold for the U.S. Ski Team, Peter Buckar is mid-flight on the alpine downhill racecourse in Chamonix Mont Blanc, out of control, about to crash! Balkind spins an adrenaline laced tale of a beloved athlete's shocking kidnapping just prior to the Winter Olympics. Tension builds as the plot line takes as many twists and turns as a slalom course. A heart pounding, entertaining read for sports and mystery fans alike!"
—AJ Friedman

"It was a great read!! Moves the reader along like a downhill ski course with more twists and turns than a Slalom. I enjoyed every minute."
—Warren Groner

Dedications

I have lost some people who were very special to me since my last novel was released. I'd like to dedicate this book to four of them who were all very close to my heart, as well as a friend's young child who was taken way too early in life.

My father-in-law, Morton Mann. Mort was unquestionably the most caring and giving human being I have ever met. Anyone lucky enough to have called Mort a friend, a brother, a husband, a father, or a grandfather knows there was no one quite like him. He was happiest when he was helping others and he was so good at it. He lived a very full, very rich life. While he was very successful in business, to Mort true wealth was more about friends and family, than it was about money. Mort, or rather, Dad, you are very missed.

I also lost one of my dearest and longest friends, Larry Schreier. We shared so many good times together. Larry, I can never thank you enough for introducing me to my best friend of 40 years, and my wife for 33. I hope you are resting peacefully, my brother.

Another longtime friend, Bill Dinaso, passed on suddenly while this book was in its final copy editing stage. Bill was 57, way too young to leave us. He enjoyed just about everything life had to offer. He was the ultimate family guy, the ultimate entrepreneur, and the ultimate friend to so many people. I will miss our regular phone calls, usually I'd hear from him as he was driving out to his house in the Hamptons. I always smiled and answered quickly when I saw his name on the screen of my phone. Whether I was having a good day or bad, Bill had a knack for lifting my spirits. I will miss you tremendously, Billy. Rest easily, my friend. Bill had gotten a kick out of the fact that a character in this book shared his name—Vilhelm Dinaso. I'll never forget his words when he called me, laughing, after reading his part in the email I had sent him. "Swedish? Really, Mike? Me a Swede? How the hell did you come up with that?"

Trucker Dukes, another character in this novel, was named after a little boy who also left us way too early in his life. Rather than my writing about him, here's what his mother, Shauna had to say about him: "Trucker boy had the biggest little life. He was sweet, goofy, fun, funny, and had a larger than life personality considering most of his life he was going through cancer treatment. He wasn't quite sure why he was a big deal everywhere he went, but he was, everyone loved him and he owned that role. In just 3 short years he touched the hearts of more people than most will do in a lifetime. I was blessed to be his mamma."

Finally, I lost my biggest fan, my mom, Joan. Mom loved it when I visited, or called her, and read to her from whatever manuscript I was working on. She enjoyed when I asked for help with an idea, or a character's name, or just about anything having to do with my books. In spite of enduring many devastating losses, (two husbands and a daughter,) Mom enjoyed her life. I once asked her if she was angry about losing two husbands, she answered, "Of course it saddens me, but then I think how lucky I am. How many people can claim that they've had two wonderful twenty-five year marriages." I never realized just how strong she was until that day. I love you, Mom, and I think of you every day.

Memorial

A memorial in honor of those who did not survive their battles with COVID-19. Below are names of loved ones submitted by some of my readers. A small representation of the millions who were lost to the pandemic. May each of the victims named below, as well as all the other victims of this horrible virus rest peacefully. My condolences to their families and friends.

Mary George
Pete George
Helen Dodys
Nick Dodys
Sophia George
Peter George
Charles Dodys
Michael Gatto
Ralph Caprio
Arnold Berman
Dorothy Potter
Betty Ray
Christine (Teena) Heim
Gregory Paterno

Victor Paterno
Lucille Paterno
Joe Logan Diffie
Annabelle Clayton
Steve Ravitz
Don Love
Susan Love
Gadi Avrahami
Joseph Mangione
Concetta Prisco
Donato Napoli
Claudio Cotza
Connie Franco
Richard Marchione
Marco P Bisceglia
Josephine Corigliano
Carmen Edith Roa
Charlotte Vaughn
Dwayne (from Telluride)
Robert Joseph Anderson
Ralph Caprio
Robert Smith
Memo Morales
Marie Tedeschi
Sally Tilles
John LaNunziata
Gina LaNunziata
Jim Kelly

Stealing Gold

Chapter 1

DAMN, THIS IS gonna hurt, thought United States Ski Team racer, Peter Buckar as his body twisted wildly through the air. His arms and legs flailed as he flew eight feet above the alpine Downhill race course on Mont Blanc's La Vert Piste des Houches in France's Chamonix Valley.

Peter's run had been fantastic until he had caught the inside edge of his left ski in a deep, icy rut just before the steep Goulet drop-off.

Flying out of control through the air was nothing new for Peter. But new or not, at over eighty miles per hour, the thought of his helmet hitting the ice and his tangled body bouncing repeatedly against the rock-hard surface nauseated him. *Stay loose,* he thought, *tightening up will only make it worse.*

The closest platform television camera zoomed in as Peter landed hard on the ice. Viewers throughout the world cringed in excited horror as his body twisted and flipped over, and over, down the steep grade. Luckily for Peter, the second smash of his helmet against the ice had knocked him unconscious. He continued to tumble and slide for seventy yards, before barreling through the first safety net, then being abruptly stopped by the second wall of netting. If not for the long, red mesh fence, Peter's body would have been mangled by the rocks and trees that lined the race course.

The crowd groaned as another camera captured a closeup of his limp, crumpled body.

Medics rushed to his side and checked him over. He was unresponsive, yet, miraculously, he had no obvious broken bones.

"*Incroyable*, it's like he's made of rubber," a French medic said to one of the American coaches who had skied over.

As ski patrols approached with a toboggan, the medic closest to Peter waved them away. Then, as he spoke into his radio, the medic raised his free hand and spun it in the air, signaling that he was calling for an airlift.

Pre-Olympic races are famous for spectacular crashes. World Cup racers ski every race as fast as possible. But those just before a Winter Olympics, like today's Super Combined, Kandahar event, were a proving ground. Competitors pushed themselves beyond their limits to give the world a preview of what was to come in the highly anticipated Olympic Downhill.

Alpine ski racers are a rare breed. Some say they have a death wish, but it's not so. They live for the adrenaline rush derived from racing down intensely steep vertical drops at insanely high speeds, with hopes of edging out their competitors, usually by only fractions of a second.

Peter's typical racing style was so aggressive even his colleagues often cringed when he attacked a racecourse. They watched now in dismay as his excessive speed had gotten the better of him.

***

Two days later

Stan Williams, the United States Ski Team head coach, strolled into Peter's room in the Chamonix Hospital at 6 a.m. only to find an empty bed. *They must have taken him for more tests,* Williams thought with a shake of his head.

Brain and body scans during the last day-and-a-half confirmed that, physically, Peter was okay. He had no broken bones and no obvious muscle, cartilage, or ligament tears. His problem was head trauma. While the severity had yet to be determined, he had not regained consciousness since his crash.

Brain injuries were Williams' biggest fear when his skiers crashed. While most bone and muscle injuries would mend within a year or so, trauma to the brain often had longer-lasting, sometimes permanent, effects.

He had watched the video of Peter's horrible crash over and over again until he knew exactly how many times Peter's helmet made contact with the ice and the severity of each blow. The knowledge was probably worthless, but Williams held himself responsible for his racers. If the doctors asked questions, he always wanted to be ready with answers.

Williams tossed the grease-stained, brown paper bag of croissants he'd brought onto a table. Always the optimist, he had hoped Peter might be awake and hungry. He walked out of the room and down the bright, fluorescent-lit hall to the nursing station.

"Do you know where Peter Buckar is?" he asked while removing his ski team hat and hand combing his parted, light brown, straight hair. At just over six-one, Williams towered over the nurse behind the counter.

"*Pardon, je parle un peu l'anglais,*" the heavy set, middle-aged nurse said. "*Attendez, s'il vous plait,*" she mumbled as she picked up the hospital phone, pushed aside her shoulder-length, gray hair, and tilted her head, sandwiching the handset between her pale jowl and shoulder. After a few quick words, she hung up, looked up at Williams, raised her short, thick index finger, and repeated, "*Attendez.*"

Remaining in place, drumming his long fingers on the counter and fidgeting—Williams' patience quickly waned. Just as he opened his mouth to question her again, another nurse approached from down the hall. She was petite with a big, bright-white smile that contrasted with her very dark skin. "May I help you?"

Williams' head tilted slightly.

"My accent? I'm from Haiti," she said, answering his unasked question.

Williams' head bobbed.

"Now, what can I do for you?"

"I'm looking for Peter Buckar."

"*Monsieur* Buckar is resting comfortably in his room," she said, pulling back a multitude of long, dark braids and tying them in a ponytail.

Williams' brow raised. "No, he's not."

Expressing little concern, she sauntered around the counter, casually picked up a digital tablet, tapped the screen, and glanced at it. "*Oui*, he's there, *monsieur*. His vitals were recently checked. His chart shows he's doing quite well."

With his arms now crossed and his brown eyes bulging, Williams said, "Look, I'm telling you, I just came from the room, and he's *not* there!"

"He's probably in the toilet."

"On his own?" Williams said irritably. "Are you telling me he's regained consciousness?"

She looked at the chart and frowned. "Hm. No, he has not. Let's have a look." She turned and quickly started toward Peter's room.

"There is nothing to look at, dammit!" he barked while chasing her down the hall. "If he's not somewhere in the hospital getting tested, then you better call security right now."

She entered the room and glanced around. The bathroom door was slightly ajar, and she pushed it open. "*Monsieur* Buckar?"

Receiving no answer, she poked her head in, looked around, then turned abruptly, and, with a look of desperation, ran from the room with Williams at her heels. He was surprised as she broke into a full-speed sprint back to the nursing station.

Grabbing the closest hospital phone, she pressed its buttons then spoke rapidly in French. Her eyes widened. Apparently, Peter was not in any of the testing areas. She frantically repeated the process, but this time she yelled into the handset.

Williams only caught two of her words, but they were enough. He recognized *manquant* (missing), since French ski coaches used it when talking about racers missing a gate on the course, and the word "police" is similar in many languages.

Red emergency lights began flashing in the hallway as the hospital went into full alert. Soon security personnel were checking every room.

They found no sign of Peter. He was officially missing.

Williams felt sick. He was queasy, and his head was spinning. Feeling foolish for waiting this long, he scrolled through his contacts on his cellphone, tapped the screen, and put it to his ear.

"DiBetta," a gruff voice answered. Gus DiBetta handled the U.S. Ski Team's security whenever they were in Europe.

"Gus, it's Stan. Peter is missing."

"What?"

"I'm at the hospital. They're looking everywhere. The last time anyone saw him was when a nurse checked in on him a little while ago. He's not here." Williams' voice was shaky. "They've called the police. How fast can you get here? I'm going to call Buck Green."

"Buck is Peter's agent, he won't know what to do? Call Jay Scott."

"I have to let Buck know. He'll handle it. Just get here quickly, okay?"

"Jesus, Stan, this is crazy."

"Yeah, I know," Stan said with a sigh.

"Okay. I'll be there in about fifteen minutes."

Williams ended the call. Feeling jittery, he scanned the hallway and noticed a metal folding chair next to a closed door. He headed toward it and sat. Shutting his eyes, he breathed in deeply, then let out another long sigh. Moments later, as his nerves began to settle, the loud "ping" of the elevator bell startled him. He watched three uniformed hospital security officers hastily approach the nursing station. A tall officer with a trim beard spoke to the nurses, who were huddled together nervously.

As the men turned and walked to Peter's room, Williams checked the time on his phone before dialing Buck Green. He thought, *6:34, that makes it …12:34 in New York.*

"Yes?" Green's voice was groggy.

"Buck, it's Stan Williams. Sorry to wake you but we have a problem. I'm at the hospital in Chamonix. Peter is missing."

"What do you mean, missing?" Green murmured, more asleep than awake.

"That's just it. They don't know. Hospital security checked everywhere. The police are on their way. I just talked to Gus DiBetta, and he's coming too."

"What are you talking about?" Green asked sharply, obviously now fully awake. "How can they not know where he is? Patients don't just disappear!"

After a moment of silence, Williams asked, "Buck? Are you there?"

"Yeah, Stan, I'm thinking. Do me a favor, text me the address and phone number of the hospital as quickly as you can. I have to call our Security Chief, Jay Scott."

Chapter 2

SITTING ON THE edge of his bed, bleary-eyed, Buck texted his good friend, business partner, and client, Reid Clark, *Come over right now. I'll explain when you get here. It's urgent.*

His stocky frame clad only in navy blue, silk pajama bottoms, Buck walked into the kitchen of his rustic, contemporary styled house at the edge of the AllSport campus in the Catskills, a woodsy region of New York. He opened a cabinet, reached for a container of coffee grinds, and began removing the plastic lid. Yawning, he stared out the window, beyond the railing of his wraparound deck. Mesmerized by the quarter moon's perfect reflection on the mirror-like surface of the lake, he fumbled and dropped the can. Coffee grinds spewed everywhere as the can bounced from the granite counter to the tiled floor.

"Shit!"

Consumed in frustration, he kicked the can with his bare foot, spraying the remaining grinds all over the floor. "Ow. Damnit!" The rim of the can left an ugly dent in one of the mahogany cabinets. Disgusted, Buck walked away from the mess, only to have his irritation heightened when dry coffee grinds stuck to the bottom of his feet. He snatched his cell phone from the counter and called Jay Scott.

As he sat at the breakfast table, the back door opened, and Reid Clark walked in wearing an old, frayed, black, AllSport warm-up suit and equally tattered, unlaced, black high-tops. He kicked off his mud-covered sneakers near the door. The Nike swoosh was barely visible through all the splattered mud from his 100-yard walk on the dew-drenched grass and dirt trail through the woods that separated his house from Buck's.

Reid covered a yawn as he silently surveyed the mess on the kitchen floor. He plunked down on a chair across the table from Buck. After pushing back a strand of his longer than usual, dark brown, wavy hair, he scratched his cheeks through days of unshaven stubble and listened to the call.

"Jay, it's Buck. Sorry to call so late. Give me a second. Reid just got here. I'm putting you on speaker, so I only have to say this once." Buck pressed the speaker button, put his phone on the table, and reached for some paper napkins.

"I'm all ears," Jay's voice boomed through the speaker.

"We have a big problem," Buck said, mopping beads of sweat from his bald head with the napkin.

"They are the only kind I seem to get, Buck. Fire away."

"Peter is missing. He must have been kidnapped."

Reid's eyes went wide. He murmured, "Oh my God!" and covered his face with his hands.

Looking at Reid, Buck continued, "I just got off the phone with Stan. Let me explain everything to Jay so he can get things in motion, then we'll talk." As he spoke, Buck was using another napkin to wipe the coffee grinds from the bottoms of his feet.

After a moment of silence, Buck said, "You there, Jay?"

"Yeah, Buck. First of all, Peter who?"

"Buckar. Sorry, I just figured you'd know who I was talking about. You've met him here at AllSport. He's on the U.S. ski team.

He's one of my clients, and he trains here when he's not at the team's facility. He crashed badly at a World Cup race in France a couple of days ago."

"Peter Buckar, yes, I remember meeting him. I didn't realize he was your client. I saw replays of his fall on TV. That was the Kandahar race, wasn't it?"

"Yeah. He caught an edge at about eighty miles per hour in the downhill race. He's lucky to be alive."

Jay let out a quiet whistle. "Eighty, huh? He is lucky."

"Well, his luck ran out. His coach called a couple of minutes ago. He went to visit Peter in the hospital, but he wasn't there. The hospital staff has no idea where he is."

"Why all the alarm? Maybe he just walked out. He's crazy enough to be a downhill racer, so leaving the hospital without getting discharged is probably no big deal to him."

"No, he couldn't have left on his own, he's been unconscious since the crash. He had to have been taken," Buck said.

Reid let out a loud, "Damn." He took a deep breath, "Listen, Jay, Peter isn't just Buck's client. He's a close friend of mine—he and I grew up together. He's also engaged to my sister, Hunter. We have to find him, Jay." Reid's voice sounded unsteady.

"Okay, I get it. I'll get someone over there immediately. I need some info. What's the name of the hospital?"

"Peter's coach is texting it to me." Buck sounded completely drained. "I'll forward it to you as soon as I get it."

"Good. Send me his picture and his bio, too. Any idea why someone would want to kidnap him?"

Buck sighed. "I can think of a few. It's only two weeks till the Olympics. Peter is the favorite for gold in two races, and he should win silver or bronze in two more. There could be a lot of people who don't want him to race."

"Right. Send me the names of the other top contenders he is competing against in those races. We'll find him, gentlemen," Jay said confidently. "Just get me that information quickly."

"Okay."

Buck hung up, looked at Reid, and sighed deeply. "Here we go again."

Chapter 3

AS CO-FOUNDERS OF the Inner City Sports Foundation (ICSF), Buck Green and Reid Clark had been through a lot over the years, namely the death threats and attempted murder of Reid during his first Master's Tournament by the brother of an athlete who Reid had kicked out of AllSport. Then, a few years later, the murder of Reid's best friend and CFO of the foundation, Bob Thomas. His killer had been hired by the ICSF's Accounting Director after Thomas caught him embezzling funds and threatened to have him arrested. Reid and Buck were becoming way too familiar with criminal investigations.

The ICSF's mission was to recruit hard-luck, inner-city youth who showed high-end athletic potential in almost any sport and help them reach a professional level in that sport. It provided them with world-class training from pro athletes who donated their time at AllSport, the ICSF's training camp. Many of the young recruits, though talented, had been hardened by living in very tough neighborhoods. A lot of them belonged to street gangs. AllSport had three rules: no fighting, no weapons, no drugs. Break one of those rules, and an athlete's AllSport opportunity was over. For many of the athletes, leaving their violent street instincts behind was difficult; for some, it was impossible. During AllSport's first few years, nasty fights were commonplace. It took Jay Scott and his security staff tremendous effort to maintain the peace on the beautiful campus. Scott, a Private Investigator, and Security Consultant, as well as a former Navy Seal commander, had been originally hired to protect Reid when he had received his death threats. When the violence at AllSport deemed it necessary to employ full-time security staff, Scott and his team were the obvious choices.

AllSport produced world-class athletes at a staggering rate, and Buck, one of the top sports agents in the country, helped many of them achieve extreme wealth and fame. Buck had a sixth sense when it came to connecting his clients with the right products for endorsement contracts.

Buck spent a lot of time on the AllSport campus getting to know, groom, and nurture many of the young athletes. When they made it to the professional level, although tough as nails when negotiating for them, he was a sentimental pushover when it came to their health and wellbeing.

Buck had started his Sports Agenting business during his senior year of college. Like most Division One college basketball players, he had dreamed of playing in the NBA. But, at five-foot-eight, he was realistic enough to know that despite his agility and his excellent three-point shot, his chances of an NBA career were slim. When a teammate asked Buck to review the contract an NBA team had offered him, Buck jumped at the opportunity. Within hours he blazed through the long contract and found a few areas that he thought his friend could negotiate.

"Will you do it for me?" his friend asked.

"Do what?" Buck asked.

"Negotiate with them."

"Seriously?"

"Hell yeah, Dude. You're like the smoothest talker I've ever known, and you'll charge me way less than the agents that are hounding me. Right?"

Buck stared for a moment as his friend's request sunk in. Then, he grinned and reached to shake hands. "Right!"

With the help of one of his business school professors, Buck put together and rehearsed his script for the negotiation meeting.

The meeting went well, and while Buck did not accomplish all he wanted for his friend, he did get him a much better deal. Soon the top players on the basketball and football teams were asking Buck to negotiate their pro contracts. News of Buck's newly found expertise spread quickly, and a slew of top athletes from various schools began clamoring for his help. After graduating, Buck's business soared, and years later, he reached the pinnacle of the Sports Agenting industry.

When he and Reid originally came up with the idea of the Inner City Sports Foundation and AllSport, while not his main goal, Buck knew that if the concept worked, he would garner a steady flow of new clients for his business.

Reid, Buck's most famous client, had also become his good friend and business partner. Reid had hired Buck early during his professional golf career. When Reid survived the attempt on his life during the Master's Tournament and went on to win the Green Jacket, Buck skillfully used the issue to help skyrocket Reid's endorsement earnings.

Since then, Reid had become an American sports icon.

Reid had introduced Peter to Buck years ago. Coming from a solid and loving family in the upscale suburbs of New York City, Peter did not fit the mold of the average AllSport athlete. Yet, he loved training on the facility's ski simulation system. While on it, he could ski just about any racecourse in the world, virtually. The system gave him the distinct advantage of getting virtual practice on the Olympic downhill course as soon as the hosting site was chosen by the International Olympic Committee. Peter divided his off-season time between the U.S. Ski Team's official training sites and AllSport.

Chapter 4

BUCK TAPPED THE end-call button after another quick conversation with Jay Scott, then turned toward Reid. In less than an hour, plans were falling into place. "Jay has an investigator in Paris named Philippe Varnet. He is putting together a team to find Peter. They are going to begin the search in Chamonix. I'm going to meet Jay down at Kennedy Airport, and we're going to fly to Geneva, then on to Chamonix. Why don't you come with us? It will save time if we fly over in your jet."

"I don't know if that's a good idea. Let me talk with my wife and figure things out. She wasn't expecting to head to St. Moritz for another two weeks for the Olympics."

"So, why don't you come with us now, and Shane can join us when the Games start."

Reid bit his lower lip as he thought for a moment. "No, things are going to get difficult when I tell Hunter about this. She had asked if I could fly her over as soon as we heard that Peter had crashed, but then her job got in the way. The Philharmonic had a big performance scheduled, and Hunter's replacement piano player has the flu. They begged her to stay. She's going to insist on flying over immediately, and I'm going to need Shane with me to help keep her calm. Hunter is going to be a wreck until we find Peter. Buck, we have to find him."

Buck nodded.

Reid sighed and folded his arms. "I guess my son can stay at Johnny's. He was going to stay there during the Olympics anyway. I'm sure Cindy won't mind having him for an extra week or two."

"Mind?" Buck said. "Are you kidding? She'll love it. Johnny is a great kid, but, let's face it, he's a handful. Casey will keep him out of Cindy's hair. I'm surprised she isn't going to the Olympics with Joel, though. In fact, I'm surprised you guys weren't planning to take Casey and Johnny too. They always go to big events like this with you."

"Yeah, well, that's exactly why they're not coming this time. Between the World Cup and the Super Bowl, they've missed too much school this year already. Shane and Cindy both insisted that the boys stay home this time."

"Makes sense." Buck nodded.

"I'll meet you in Chamonix with Shane and Hunter as soon as possible. You and Jay can take my plane. I'll call my pilot now." Reid let out another sigh. "I'm really not looking forward to telling Hunter."

Buck nodded, then looked down in silence.

"You okay?" Reid asked.

Buck looked up. "No. I'm not. Not even close. It's all coming back to me again. First, it was the threats and attempt on your life, then Bob's murder, and now this. We've been dealing with a major crisis every few years. I don't know how much more my nerves can handle."

"Look, maybe it's all just a mistake. Maybe they took him to another hospital, or, maybe, as Jay said, he just woke up and left on his own. You know Peter. It takes a lot to keep him down."

Buck shook his head. "No, a nurse confirmed he was still unconscious when they checked on him just before Williams got there, and they would obviously know if he was transported elsewhere. Someone had to have taken him. Someone wants him out of the Olympics. I have a rotten feeling about this."

Reid nodded. "Maybe you're right, but we need to stay positive for now. Getting down doesn't help anything."

"I know, I know," Buck said, rubbing his face and sighing. "Come on, let's get out of here."

Chapter 5

PHILIPPE VARNET, A tall, wide-shouldered, black man with an air of confidence, arrived on Peter's floor at the hospital with three of his investigators. He took note of the small army of officers already searching the area and questioning the hospital staff.

"Marvelous," he mumbled to his men. "Want to bet these clowns have already contaminated Buckar's room?" He turned toward a passing officer. "Excuse me, where is your captain?"

"That's him, right there." The officer pointed toward a uniformed man conversing with a doctor.

Varnet quickly sized the man up. Mid-fifties, fit and trim, stern-looking with a clean-shaven face, and short black hair, peppered gray at his temples. Everything about him portrayed power, except his height. He was quite short. Varnet was quite tall. *This is going to be difficult*, he thought. The captain stood stiffly, chest inflated, shoulders high and wide. *Probably feels the need to compensate for his lack of height*, thought Varnet.

Varnet turned to his men. "Go mingle, see what you can find while I try to make peace with the locals." He approached the captain, who was deep in discussion with the doctor, and waited at a safe enough distance so as not to irritate the man.

As their conversation concluded, the captain turned to walk away. "Excuse me, Captain," Varnet said.

The captain looked back. "Yes?"

"I am Philippe Varnet. I am here representing Jay Scott, who will be here shortly," Varnet said.

"Yes, Monsieur Scott. We were informed he'd be working on this case. Why don't you have a seat over there and wait for him." His tone was filled with chilled confrontation as he pointed to a distant sitting area.

"Actually, I'd like to get started and check out Buckar's room."

"No, Monsieur, what was your name?"

"Varnet. Philippe Varnet."

"Well, Monsieur Varnet, I would appreciate it if you would have a seat and wait for Monsieur Scott. When he arrives, we can all talk and see who *will,* and who *will not,* be working on this case."

"Pardon?" Varnet contained his growing anger. "Captain, with all due respect, if we all work together, maybe we'll find Buckar a little faster."

The captain's right eye twitched. A protruding vein that meandered from the corner of his eye to the graying hairline just above his temple began pulsating. "I don't think so, Monsieur. As you can see, we already have teams examining the hospital. If we haven't found the victim by the time Monsieur Scott arrives, maybe you and your team can join the search then. Until that time, you will kindly stay out of our way."

Biting his tongue, Varnet forced a slight smile. Lashing out would be counterproductive. Besides, he could see that his team had already begun working discreetly amongst the plain-clothed and uniformed officers.

Varnet sat quietly, watching the captain's eyes shift between him and the various officers and hospital employees. Fed up after about fifteen minutes, he took a deep breath and began walking toward the captain, preparing for an argument.

"Ah, there you are." A deep, bellowing voice stopped Varnet in his tracks. He turned and saw one of his investigators, Vincent Jarden, approaching along with a dark-haired, burly man.

"Phillipe, this is Gus DiBetta. We just rode the elevator together." Jarden said.

"Vincent tells me you're with Jay Scott," DiBetta said. "Pleased to meet you." His thick Italian accented, baritone voice resonated through the hallway. His enormous hand wrapped almost completely around Varnet's as he gave him a bone-crushing handshake. "I provide security for the U.S. Ski Team whenever they are in Europe." He made eye contact with the captain and waved him over. "Let me introduce you to Captain Pompard. It will be better if we all work together."

Varnet gave a skeptical nod.

Pompard approached, looking a bit hostile. DiBetta put his hand on the captain's shoulder. "George, this is Philippe Varnet. Philippe, this is Captain George Pompard. Philippe works with Jay Scott. You know of him, don't you, George?"

Not hiding his irritation, Pompard said, "I have heard plenty about Monsieur Scott. I do not know anything about Monsieur Varnet as we just met a little while ago. I have no problem having your team join mine on this case, but I must warn you, as I will repeat when Monsieur Scott arrives, there will either be mutual respect between our people, or else—well, let's leave it at that. I have heard how Monsieur Scott works, and I will not tolerate any disdain for my men, nor will I allow him to take over this case. If that is understood, I think we can all work together."

"Captain Pompard," Varnet said. "I understand your concern. You have my word that our people fully appreciate the need for teamwork and mutual respect. We must all work as one unit to close this case quickly. Dissension will not only hurt our prospects but potentially help whomever we are up against. Our only goal is to find Monsieur Buckar before any further harm comes his way."

"Agreed," Pompard said.

"Good," Varnet said. "May I suggest that we all meet for a quick discussion when Monsieur Scott arrives."

"Again, agreed."

"Until then, we will work alongside your team." Varnet's tone was matter-of-fact, yet respectful.

Pompard's eyes moved from Varnet to DiBetta, then back again. He finally gave a quick nod.

Chapter 6

PETER AWOKE IN absolute darkness and was immediately overwhelmed by chills, cold sweat, and a pounding headache. He felt cold air on his legs. He was in some kind of gown. A hospital gown? He'd been in those often enough to know how they felt. Despite his discomfort, he began his standard, post-crash self-evaluation to confirm his condition, from fingertips to toes. Attempting to raise his arms, the tug of restraints immediately sent his mind reeling. *What the hell?* he thought. He strained to lift his head to evaluate the situation. He realized there were also restraints around his chest, pinning him to whatever uncomfortable thing he was lying on. *It might be a wooden board? Or, maybe a very stiff twin bed.* The pain in his head became intense, and he could feel himself start to panic.

Where the hell am I?

His eyes darted every which way, but there was only blackness. Not even a sliver or pinhole of light existed. *Am I underground? Was I buried alive? Why the hell am I tied down?* Fear surged through him. Every inch of his long, sinewy torso tightened. He closed his eyes tightly as the pain in his head reached an unbearable level. A deep breath in followed by a long exhale. He knew the only way to relieve the pain was to relax. Then, after inhaling deeply again, he heard something and tried to focus on it. Something touched his leg.

"Who's there?" he yelled. He felt something moving on his bare leg. "Cut it out." The restraints kept him from thrashing. Still, he tried, but it only sent intense pain throughout his body. Shaking his restrained leg as hard as he could, he heard a squeak.

The sound of the rat pushed Peter's mind to its edge.

Again, he tried to move his entire body. The pain was unbearable, but the thought of rats crawling on him was worse. He felt himself fading into unconsciousness again and fought it. Having lost and regained consciousness more often than most kids scraped their knees on the playground, he could often sense when it was about to occur. There it was again, a squeak. Peter could feel tiny claws scamper up his bare leg, his constrained body filled with one more convulsive surge of energy just before he passed out.

Chapter 7

WEARY FROM TRAVEL, Buck Green was edgy and irritable as he and Jay approached the reception desk in the hospital's lobby.

"It is of no concern to me who you are," said the skinny, uniformed hospital staffer. Dark tattoos snaked just above the buttoned collar of his oversized white uniform, and nickel-sized, black ear gauges adorned his earlobes. "I have orders not to let *anyone* past this desk. This is of no use here," he said and tossed Jay's ID back to him with a flick of his nicotine-stained fingers. Jay and Buck watched in amazement as it slid along the thick marble countertop and fell to the floor. The young man's arrogance and his black fingernail polish were more than Buck could tolerate.

"You son of a bitch! Who the hell do you think you are?" Buck lunged at the guy, reaching over the counter between them.

Wide-eyed, the attendant shoved his wheeled office chair backward, barely avoiding Buck's assault.

Jay grabbed Buck's shoulder and pulled him back. "Whoa there, big guy." Looking at Buck's reddened face, Jay said, "Take a deep breath. I'll get us in."

The attendant was rubbing the back of his head. He had pushed his chair back so hard and fast that his head hit the edge of the thick, glass shelf on the wall behind him.

"What's going on here?" asked a rapidly approaching uniformed police officer who had been standing guard by the elevator doors.

Jay introduced himself and handed over his passport. "I am here on an official investigation on behalf of the U.S. ski team and the victim's family. My colleague and I have just flown in from New York. And I apologize for any undue tempers. It's been a long day." Jay's face remained completely still; his dark brown eyes fixated on the officer who was studying his passport in silence. The thin scar between Jay's strong jawline and chiseled cheekbone moved slightly as he clenched his teeth and tightened his jaw.

"You want my driver's license or military ID?" Jay maintained a respectful tone, despite his growing impatience. He reached for his wallet.

The officer finally looked Jay in the eye, handed back his passport, and said, "This is fine, Monsieur Scott. Come with me. Captain Pompard is expecting you."

Still rubbing his head, the attendant watched the men enter the elevator. Just before the doors shut, he raised his free hand in a fist and extended his middle finger. Buck's chuckle reverberated within the brushed metal walls as the elevator doors closed.

***

They exited the elevator and approached Captain Pompard.

"Ah, Monsieur Scott," Pompard said. "I recognize you from your picture in the newspaper. You have worked other cases in France, no?"

"Yes, Captain Pompard. It is a pleasure to meet you," Jay said as they shook hands.

"Your men are dispersed throughout the building, searching for evidence, as we speak," Pompard said.

"Thank you, Captain. I appreciate your allowing us to assist on this case. I'd like you to meet Buck Green, Peter Buckar's agent, and manager. Buck will be working with us as well."

"Monsieur Green, I am familiar with your name, but I am not sure where from."

"Buck is the co-founder of the Inner City Sports Foundation," Jay said. "You may know of it."

"The Inner City Sports Foundation?" Pompard's brow furrowed as he shook his head. "No."

"How about AllSport?" Buck said. "Our facility in America where we recruit and train talented yet troubled inner-city youth, to hopefully become professional athletes or Olympians."

Pompard nodded. "Ah, yes, AllSport." After a moment, he added. "If I remember correctly, although the program has merits, there have been many problems on your campus, including a murder."

"Yes. We have had our issues. It is difficult for some of our young athletes to leave their gang-related behavior completely behind. But I have found nothing more gratifying than helping kids who were destined for jail, become professional athletes and live productive lives."

"Hm, sounds very interesting," Pompard said. "I'd like to hear more. Maybe when we finish with this investigation, you and I could have a drink. AllSport sounds like a concept that might work here in Europe too."

Buck nodded. "We've thought about expanding. Maybe it's time."

Jay was impatiently waiting for the pleasantries to end. He desperately wanted to get moving on Peter's trail, but he held back the urge to ask Pompard for a briefing. Experience had taught him that pushing his agenda on a police captain too early in their relationship would only create trouble.

"Gentlemen," Pompard said, looking at his watch. "It's getting late. I think we should hold a quick meeting so our teams can bring each other up to speed. Let me find a room and round up my team."

"I'll do the same," Jay said, happy he had kept his mouth shut.

***

The investigation teams sat around two rectangular dining tables shoved together near the rear entrance of the hospital cafeteria. The overwhelming aroma from the *gateau de viande* (Meatloaf Special) intertwined with the stench of an overused rag a janitor was using to scrub sticky remnants from the table.

Buck pulled his black leather cigar case from the inner pocket of his blazer and removed two Cohibas. Holding one horizontally just under his nose, he offered the other to Jay.

"You're not going to light that, are you?" Jay whispered.

"Of course not, but even unlit it helps mask the nauseating smells in here." Noticing Pompard's harsh stare from the head of the table, Buck raised his cigar and said, "Don't worry, I'm not going to light it."

With a slight nod, Pompard said, "Do you both understand French, or will you need one of us to translate?"

"Je comprends," Jay said.

All eyes moved to Buck.

"I hate to be the ugly American who wants everything his way, but can we please hold the meeting in English? Peter is my client, and I need to understand everything we are dealing with. I'm afraid I may miss something in translation."

Pompard's head slumped, and he mumbled something under his breath. He sighed, then hesitantly said, "It's okay with me, as long as everyone else agrees."

Receiving no objections, he rolled his eyes and proceeded in English, "I'd like you each to introduce yourself and give a brief statement concerning any evidence you have uncovered." He looked to his immediate left. "Jacques, why don't you begin?"

"Excuse me," Buck said. "Sorry to interrupt, but I figured Peter's father would be at this meeting with us. Dan travels to almost all the World Cup races. Does anyone know where he is?"

"He's back in the states," DiBetta said. "I asked Peter about him just the other day. He and his wife are hosting a big fundraiser for their foundation. They were planning to come over immediately after it."

"Has anyone told them that Peter's missing?" Buck asked.

"I have not," DiBetta said.

"Nor have I." Pompard shook his head.

"How about Stan?" Buck asked, looking at DiBetta.

"I'm fairly sure he hasn't either. He was pretty shaken when I got here. I told him to go back to the hotel and make sure that no one on the team, nor any of his staff, come here to visit Peter."

Buck nodded while looking at his phone and moving his finger on the screen. He tapped on it and put it to his ear. "Hi, Dan. It's Buck. Please call me as soon as you get this message."

He glanced at Jay, then looked at Pompard and shrugged.

Pompard nodded and said, "Let's continue the meeting. Go ahead, Jacques."

"Okay," Jacques Ferrer said in a raspy smoker's voice. He cleared his throat as he stood. The sleeves of his tight black sports coat were pushed up, exposing his pale, sinewy forearms. His narrow, black leather tie sharply contrasted with his plum-colored shirt. His long, ebony hair was pulled into a tight ponytail. A soul patch below his lower lip and sparkling diamond studs in both ears were like exclamation points shouting let's finish this meeting so I can get back to practicing with my band.

Buck leaned toward Jay and whispered, "Lead or bass guitar?"

"Neither. Look between his fingers," Jay murmured out the corner of his mouth.

Ferrer's hands were moving. Buck shook his head with a questioning look.

"Drumstick tattoos."

Buck squinted, then grinned and gave Jay an elbow nudge.

"I'm Jacques Ferrer, a detective here in Chamonix. My team has been interviewing doctors, nurses, and other hospital staff. So far, we've uncovered two things. The head nurse said the kidnapping had to have happened just before Buckar's coach entered the room. Another nurse had checked on him only nine minutes earlier. His vitals were strong, but he was still unconscious." Ferrer paused, then continued, "We also spoke with an orderly on the first floor, who, during an earlier cigarette break, saw two men wheel a patient on a stretcher out of the hospital and into an ambulance. He said he didn't think much about it until he heard about Buckar's disappearance. He then checked the discharge log and saw that no patients had been released at that time. He said the vehicle was one of those large vans from a private ambulance company. He remembered that it was white with blue lettering and a big blue star, but he had no idea what the company's name was." Ferrer sat and added, "That's all I have for now."

"Merci, Jacques," Pompard said. "Monsieur Varnet, you are next."

"Thank you, Captain." Varnet casually pushed his chair back and stood. "My name is Philippe Varnet. I am a private investigator from Paris, and I am here with Monsieur Scott." He glanced at Jay, who returned a quick nod. Turning toward Pompard, he added,

"As you requested, my men and I did our best to stay out of your team's way until this meeting."

Pompard's head bobbed.

"We spoke with the hospital security staff as well as the Director of Human Resources," Varnet continued. "It appears that the kidnappers had a man working here at the hospital. A guard, who was hired about a week ago, vanished around the same time as our victim."

"Hold on a second," Jay said, with his brow furrowed and head atilt.

"It made no sense to me either at first, Jay. How could they know that Buckar would end up in the hospital? One possibility is that it was a backup plan in case he crashed. Hospitals are a frequent destination for downhill racers. Another possibility is that they were ready to grab anyone, and Buckar became the unlucky victim."

"You don't believe that any more than I do," Jay said.

"Excuse me, gentlemen," Pompard interrupted. "I have no problem with using English, but you must speak slower so everyone can understand."

"Sorry, Captain," Jay said before turning back toward Varnet. "Chances are your first scenario is correct. This was probably their backup plan in case Peter got hurt. We need to-" Jay abruptly stopped speaking and looked at Pompard. "I'm sorry, George. The meeting is yours."

With one eyebrow flared, Pompard curtly said, "Those are interesting thoughts. Maybe we'll discuss them *after* we hear from everyone else. Danielle?"

The tall woman sitting next to Varnet sneered at Jay as she uncrossed her muscular arms, pulled an elastic band from her wrist, and twisted her dirty blond hair into a tight bun. With her jaw clenched and lips pursed, she stood and said, "Danielle Maldonado."

Buck shot a sideways glare at Jay, who maintained a poker face. Both men realized that Jay's authoritative manner, intentional or not, had offended Maldonado, Pompard, and probably others at the table as well.

"My team has been dusting Buckar's room, as well as all the building's entrances and exits," Maldonado said. "We are searching for fingerprints and footprints both inside the building and out. The good news is that the perpetrators could not avoid leaving footprints in the fresh snow. The bad news is the snow is falling so fast that it's covering the prints almost as quickly as they are made. We are bringing in large fans, which at the right speed will only blow away the newest snow, exposing the impressions that were left earlier. It will not be a quick process, and it will be almost impossible to determine which prints are from the perps. There is a lot of foot traffic at the emergency room doorway, and it is partially covered by a," her eyes shifted to the ceiling, and she shrugged. "I don't know the English word for a *porte cochere*."

"Portico," Jay offered.

After a slight nod, Maldonado continued, "It would have taken a lot of nerve for them to use that door anyway. Chances are they used a quieter exit," She looked at Ferrer. "Jacques, did the orderly tell you where he saw them?"

"I'll check." He raised his phone and typed.

"Sorry to interrupt," Buck said. "But, is there a reason no one is mentioning the video system? There are cameras all over the place."

"The video system has been down for almost a week," Pompard said. "Probably the doings of the recently hired security guard who disappeared. I was told that all the technicians from the company that services it have been working over at the mountain. They were hired to help film a documentary about the Kandahar race. They're scheduled to fix this system next week."

"That figures," Varnet said with a quick chuckle.

Pompard gave a nod and shrugged.

"We should check out whoever hired them to do the documentary," Jay said. "Too strong a coincidence for my liking."

"Oui," Ferrer said.

Everyone nodded, including Pompard and Maldonado.

"Continue, Danielle," Pompard said.

"Si tout va bien pour ne pas être vu …"

"English, please," Pompard reminded her.

"Right, sorry," Maldonado said with a sour glance at Buck. "Well, hopefully, the perps were smart enough to leave through a seldom-used door. If we're lucky, there will only be tracks from one stretcher, making it easier to find the kidnapper's footprints."

"The footprints may help," Pompard said. "But we should concentrate on fingerprints."

"Do you want us to stop looking for footprints? It is tedious work. Do you prefer something more productive?"

"If I may, Captain?" Jay interjected.

"Yes, Monsieur Scott. Go ahead."

"Determining the shoe's tread could be extremely valuable. Most boot and sneaker manufacturers use unique tread designs. Some even print their brand names into the soles. Determining the manufacturer may help, especially if it's a small company that only sells its shoes in specific countries or regions. If we can determine the point of sale, it might help reduce our list of suspects. Once we have a list, that is. I know it's a long shot, but it could prove to be useful."

"Good point, Monsieur Scott," allowed Pompard as a couple of the men crossed their legs and looked at the soles of their shoes.

"Captain, please call me Jay."

Ignoring him, Pompard said, "Danielle, have your team continue."

Buck thought, *Well, at least he accepted Jay's evaluation of the search. Funny, it's the same everywhere, business, sports, politics, the military, even law enforcement. Life is just one big power struggle.* Ultimately, he believed that Jay would take the lead on the case. It was only a matter of doing it diplomatically, so as not to undermine Pompard and cause him to lose face.

"Monsieur Green, Peter Buckar was," Pompard raised his fist to his mouth and momentarily closed his eyes before continuing, "Pardon me, *is*, your client. Do you wish to add anything that may help us find him?"

"I think I'll defer to Jay. He and I discussed everything as we flew over here, and obviously, he has a better understanding of these things than I do."

"Okay, but before we give Monsieur Scott the floor, I'd like to ask you one question. What are the chances that this is all a big mistake? Is it possible that Monsieur Buckar regained consciousness and left the hospital on his own? Maybe he's sitting in a restaurant as we speak?"

Buck's eyes flared. It was one thing when that scenario was suggested by Reid or Jay, but coming from Pompard, it infuriated him. Seething, he said, "If I felt that was even a possibility, I would be out searching your streets right now instead of wasting my time here. There's no way in hell he'd walk out of a hospital without talking to the doctors to learn the exact nature of his medical condition. The Olympics are in one week. Peter trains harder than any athlete I know. He would never jeopardize his chances at a medal. The Games are everything to him." Buck took a deep breath while glaring at Pompard. He felt Jay give him a calming pat on his leg under the table.

"I'm sorry," Pompard said. "I didn't mean to offend you. I only wanted to get a better understanding of who we are dealing with. I know he has an excellent reputation, but obviously, I do not know him personally. We've all heard stories about professional athletes who live recklessly and like to party. However, I feel better after hearing your assessment. Especially due to the passion of your delivery. You have my word, my team and I will work nonstop until we find him."

Buck let out a long breath and waited a moment for his fury to wane. "Fair enough. I apologize for my outburst."

"No apology necessary."

Buck nodded.

"Okay, Jay, it is your turn," Pompard said. "Obviously, you know more about Buckar than we do. With your knowledge of him and ours of the area, our combined efforts should be much more efficient."

Jay nodded, somewhat pleased that Pompard had addressed him by his first name.

Chapter 8

A TICKLE ON his neck woke Peter and made him flinch. He instantly felt the restraints holding him down. *Where am I?* He wondered. It was still pitch black. All he knew was that he was drenched in sweat and was shaking from the chills. He desperately needed to wipe what he thought was a drop of sweat trickling down his neck behind his earlobe. The irritating sensation caused his shoulder and neck to twitch, which in turn brought a squeal from the rat whose whisker had been tickling him.

His tension surged from head to toe as the rat scampered away. Restrained convulsions from his fever sent other rats scurrying off various parts of his body. Revulsion and nausea consumed him. Shivers elevated to spasms, and his pain spiked. Another squeak near his ear was more than he could tolerate, and once again, he passed out.

Chapter 9

BACK AT THE meeting in the hospital cafeteria.

After reading through his notes, Jay rose from his chair and looked into the questioning faces of the investigators around the table. "Look," he said. "Narrowing down the long list of possible culprits is going to be cumbersome. We should concentrate on skiers who are known to have a good chance at beating Peter, as well as their family members, fans, and possibly government officials from their countries. The current top contenders are from Austria, Sweden, Croatia, Finland, and Norway, and, of course, we need to look closely at the French and American racers." Jay eyed Pompard. "Hopefully, whoever kidnapped him hasn't taken him out of the surrounding area yet. I'm sure you have roadblocks in place?"

"Of course," Pompard said irritably. "It was the first thing I did when I heard about the abduction. I have roadblocks all around the hospital and on every road out of town. I also have teams who have been knocking on every door in the area all day long."

"How about helicopters?" Jay asked.

"We have four of them in the air, and we're searching every aircraft before takeoff. I also have air traffic control watching the skies for any unidentified aircraft."

"Excellent," Jay said as he pulled two eight-by-eleven photographs from his briefcase. One, a headshot of Peter, displayed his pale, freckled skin, short, blond hair, and piercing blue eyes. The other was of Peter standing next to Buck just after a race. Peter held his skis vertically in the crook of one arm, and his helmet tucked tightly under the other. He looked especially lean and lanky in his tight racing suit standing next to Buck, who resembled a marshmallow in his puffy down jacket.

Jay slid the pictures over the table to Pompard. "Can you scan these and have them sent to as many police departments as possible? I really would like to increase the search area to all of France, Italy, Switzerland, Austria, Germany, and Belgium."

"Why not all of Europe?" said Pompard with a touch of sarcasm.

"That would be perfect," Jay said, casually crossing his arms.

After a snarky chortle, Pompard said, "This is not America, Monsieur Scott. Our colleagues in surrounding countries don't always jump when asked. I'm sure it's different in America, but getting cooperation here can be very difficult, sometimes impossible."

Pompard stared hard at the photos. With his arms crossed tightly, his right hand squeezed and released his left bicep continually in almost perfect unison with the pulsations of a protruding vein near his temple. After a moment of uneasy silence, he uttered, "Let's just move on."

Jay nodded.

"I've got Interpol standing by," Pompard said. "And a Europol agent should be here momentarily. It's difficult to get everyone working together. The fact that this is an international Olympic issue will help. It also helps that the Games are imminent. But be prepared for some friction." Shifting his eyes back toward Jay, he said, "Chances are the Europol agent will not be happy that you are involved."

"Because I'm American?"

Pompard nodded.

"That's ridiculous."

"Put yourself in his shoes. How would you feel if a foreigner came to the states and interfered with one of your cases?"

"Interfered?"

"Helped, interfered, call it what you wish."

Staring into Pompard's eyes, Jay breathed in deeply, then slowly exhaled. Once his nerves settled, he said, "Point taken. I don't want to piss off Europol any more than I want to upset you. I just want to be of assistance."

"Fine, but when he's here, he won't be as tolerant as I am."

A few of Pompard's men chuckled.

He scanned the table with a look that could melt ice. "Whoever thinks this is funny, should leave. And I mean right now."

The laughter ceased.

After another stretch of silence, Jay said, "Would you mind if I toss out an idea?"

"Go ahead," Pompard said.

"I have a network of private investigators throughout Europe. Many of them have good relationships with their country's authorities. It could help if we used them. But, not if you feel that it will interfere."

Pompard scratched his chin while looking at Jay. "You want to give them a try, fine, do it. But-"

Jay put his hand up to stop Pompard. "I will keep anyone I bring in on a short leash. If you don't like them, I'll get rid of them immediately."

"Fine," Pompard said. "We both want the same result. If there is anything you can offer that may help to find Buckar, don't wait for my permission. The only thing that I *will* mind is if you hold back information. It won't offend me if you are the one who finds him."

Jay nodded.

"So please enlighten us," Pompard said. "What else is on your mind?"

"Okay, but instead of just *my* thoughts, how about if we brainstorm a little. We have some very intelligent, experienced people around this table. I'm sure everyone here has things on their mind that may help. You never know what thought, idea, or question can trigger something in someone else's head. Let's spend a few minutes tossing out random thoughts. If any of you have something to add, no matter how irrelevant it may seem, just speak up. No one will laugh or think any less of you for it. You never know what may help."

Pompard nodded.

Jay let a moment pass, then placed his phone on the table and said, "I'm going to record everything, but will one of you please take notes too?"

"I will," Ferrer said, reaching for a notepad and pen.

"Thank you, detective," Jay said before looking around the table and adding, "Once again, just say anything that comes to mind."

Silence followed with everyone just looking at each other until Buck blurted out, "Peter's main competitor is Frank Arnot, an Austrian. If Peter doesn't race in the Olympic Downhill, Arnot is sure to get the gold."

"And the Swede, Vilhelm Dinaso. He is hoping for gold in both the slalom and giant slalom," Gus DiBetta said.

Ferrer finished writing and said, "How about the Italian who just won the race that Buckar crashed in. Does anyone know his name?"

"Lupinacci, Alex Lupinacci, they call him Loopy," Pompard said. "I know his father, Luigi. He's a detective in Torino."

A loud cough caused everyone to turn toward the doorway.

A large man with red, puffy, weathered cheeks noisily approached the table. While removing his overcoat, scarf, and beret, he said, "How about the American skier, Jarrett Eschmann? I heard he and Buckar argue a lot. He clearly stands to gain with Buckar out of the picture. Chances are he'll win more races which will increase his endorsement opportunities." The man carelessly tossed his outerwear on the back of an empty chair and sat. He leaned as far back as the chair allowed, clasped his massive hands together, and rested them on the thick, tightly stretched cable knit sweater that hugged his abundant gut. Returning the stares he was receiving from around the table, he obnoxiously demanded, "Well?"

With arms crossed and a slight shake of his head, Pompard said, "Everyone, this is Pierre Barden, a Senior Specialist at Europol. Pierre, we are creating a list of things that may help our search. You have thoughts to contribute. You can continue now, *or wait your turn*?"

Barden smirked, and without a hint of remorse, he leaned back further in his chair. A loud snapping noise from somewhere below the seat caused him to wince and quickly bring his weight forward.

Buck coughed into his hand, trying unsuccessfully to mask his chuckle. Looking around the table, he noticed that his amusement was shared.

Barden slowly leaned back again, testing the chair inch by inch until he was satisfied with its stability. Then, stretching his legs under the table, he nonchalantly said, "I'll wait."

"Arrogant schmuck," Buck whispered in Jay's ear.

Jay grinned. "Worse than me?"

They both snickered.

"Jay, I believe the floor is still yours," Pompard said.

"Thank you, George." Jay glanced at the notes on his phone. "As I said earlier, our list of possibilities is quite long. We need to look at the skiers and coaches from any country that will have a better chance at medaling if Peter does not compete."

"Ultimately, that's all the competing teams," Pompard said.

"Yes, as well as their families and fans. And while it may cause an uproar, we should also look at each country's government officials and their Olympic Committees." He paused while looking around the table.

Receiving none of the pushback he expected, he continued, "On our flight over, Buck informed me of two other situations we should investigate. Peter has recently been stalked by a woman. We don't know much about her yet. I'm told she looks to be around thirty years old. While she hasn't made any threats and is probably just an adoring fan, we have quite a few pictures and a couple of videos where she is standing in the crowd near Peter and staring at him. It appears that she has been following him for the last few months. She has approached him a couple of times, as fans often do. While she has not tried to hide, nor has she done anything aggressive, she needs to be checked out. My team back home is emailing me a recent picture of her standing behind Peter after a race at Vail. I have a team searching for her in the States, but obviously, we need to look for her here too. I'll send you her picture as soon as I have it."

Pompard nodded.

"The next lead will be a little tricky," Jay continued. "In a recent interview, Peter may have offended the head of a mafia crime family back in the States."

Barden's loud guffaw drowned out the mix of chuckles and groans around the table.

"I know. Not a very smart move. I know the guy he pissed off. His name is Sal DiGiacomo. Sal and I have helped one another out on occasion."

A few eyebrows rose.

Raising his palm to stop the objections before they began, Jay said, "While I do not approve of DiGiacomo's business dealings, he has helped me solve some big cases. He is an avid sports fan and a good skier. He recently made a public statement about financially backing the U.S. Ski Team. Even though neither the team nor the U.S. Olympic Committee would accept his dirty money, Peter was asked, during a live television interview, how he felt about being funded by the mob. He said that if DiGiacomo's money was accepted, he would quit the team. While I don't believe Sal would retaliate by kidnapping Peter, I'll speak with him."

"A mob boss wouldn't waste his time with something like this," Pompard said.

"I'm sure you're right, but you never know what might set them off," Jay said. "Sal is usually even-tempered, but I saw him fly off the handle once when a waiter brought his pasta with red clam sauce instead of white. The poor waiter was trembling when Sal finished berating him."

Barden chuckled.

"I know it sounds ridiculous, but if something so trite could rile him up like that, you never know how he might react to what Peter said on television."

Barden gave a skeptical nod.

"Anyway, that's enough from me. Let's move on. I'm sure we all want to pursue some of these leads."

"Pierre, do you have anything more to contribute?" Pompard asked.

"No, but as I said earlier, it is a known fact that Buckar and his teammate, Jarrett Eschmann, have had problems with each other. Someone should check him out. And as absurd as it sounds, I'm going to follow up on Jay's friend DiGiacomo. If he had anything to do with this, he probably used a European organized crime connection to handle it."

Barden stood, yanked his scarf from the chair, and tossed it around his neck. Then he grabbed his hat and coat and walked toward the exit. At the doorway, he looked back at Pompard. "Keep me informed, George," he said just before walking away.

"Au revoir," Pompard said, with a few additional words muttered under his breath. Then, looking at the team around the table, he added, "Nice guy, huh?"

As many in the group smirked, Pompard continued, "Well, unless anyone has more to add, I'm going to assign each of you areas to investigate." He took the notepad from Ferrer's extended hand, glanced at it, and said, "I'm amazed. I can't remember a meeting like this in recent years where 'terrorism,' or 'ISIS' weren't even mentioned. While I don't think ISIS would target an individual athlete, you never know what some terrorist cell might believe is important to their cause. *I* will pursue that angle with Interpol's assistance."

Looking down at the notepad, Pompard continued, "I want each of you to follow up on the racers, as well as their families, coaches, and any overly adoring fans in the regions I assign. And, as Jay said, look at members of the Olympic Committees and governments. If you receive any resistance, let me know immediately. Understood?"

Everyone nodded.

"Monsieur Varnet, you will handle Germany and the Netherlands."

Varnet raised a thumb.

"Gus, you'll investigate the Italians and the Swiss."

Gus smiled. "*Molto bene.*"

"Jacques, you will deal with our Scandinavian friends."

Ferrer shrugged. "No problem."

"Danielle, I trust you're okay checking out the Canadians?"

"That's fine," Maldonado said.

Pompard turned toward Jay. "I'm sure you already have more people on the way to work with you?"

"I do."

"And I'll guess you would like to handle as much of the investigation as possible?"

Jay gave an appreciative nod.

"Okay, you will investigate Arnot and the Austrians as well as Croatia and any other Eastern European country that has worthy skiers. You will obviously deal with your friend DiGiacomo, and the American stalker, as well as any other American possibilities. Good enough for now?"

"I'm also going to add Hector Vasquez to our list," Jay said. "He's a Columbian-born boxer who lives in Miami. When AllSport's CFO was murdered a few years ago, Peter informed us about a suspicious-sounding phone call he had overheard Vasquez on. We investigated and cleared Vasquez as a suspect but as you can imagine, he was pretty angry with Peter. I don't think he has anything to do with Peter's disappearance, but I want to make sure."

Pompard pursed his thin lips and nodded.

"I know what I'm about to say is obvious," Jay added. "But if a ransom demand is made, it will probably come to either Peter's parents or Buck." He looked at Buck. "When his father returns your call, I want to speak with him to make sure he's prepared, in case it's him they call."

Buck nodded.

"We need to keep this thing out of the media's hands for as long as possible," Pompard said. "For some reason, when celebrity kidnappings become public knowledge, the deviants of the world rear their ugly heads and begin calling in bogus leads, which are a complete waste of time. Where is Buckar's coach? We need to make sure he doesn't tell anyone until we're ready."

"I sent him back to be with his team earlier," DiBetta said. "I told him to keep it quiet and to make sure the team is busy with meetings and training, so none of them come here to visit Peter."

"Good. Thank you, Gus," Pompard said. "Jay, you and Buck should inform the team and their staff as quickly as possible."

Pompard handed Jay a bunch of his business cards. "You can give these to them. If the kidnappers contact them and they can't reach you, let them know to call me."

Jay nodded.

Pompard continued, "It's going to be difficult to keep the hospital staff quiet. My guess is some of them have probably told their family or friends already. When this goes public, the news is going to travel fast."

Pompard stood, and in a firm, but quiet voice, addressed the group, "The command center for the case will be in my office in the heart of Chamonix. We will hold meetings and press conferences nearby at the Hotel Mont Blanc. It is a nice place to stay if any of you have not made reservations yet. They usually hold rooms for me at a discounted price."

Jay said, "We'll need at least four, maybe more. How about you, Philippe?"

"I will need three for me, and my team."

"My assistant will let the front desk know to reserve rooms for you all," Pompard said as he passed more of his cards around the table. "I'm heading back to my office. If you can't reach me on my cell, call my assistant, Harrison LeBlanc. Please check-in as soon as you obtain any evidence, or if you determine the guilt or innocence of any potential suspect. I will be investigating the French team and the other French possibilities while you are pursuing your assignments." After a quick look at all around the table, he said, "I guess we're done here unless anyone has something to add?"

"Does anybody know where we can get a decent meal?" Jay asked. "Buck and I haven't eaten since we left New York."

"There is a small bistro across the street," Ferrer said. "Their *Croque Monsieur* and *pommes frites* are very good."

"Thank you."

"All right, everyone," Pompard said. "We all have work to do. Let's find our man quickly and unharmed."

Chapter 10

WHEN PETER HAD awakened for the third time, the lights were on. While dim, the bare bulbs were just bright enough for him to evaluate the musty-smelling room. Unpainted concrete walls. Wood planks, steel beams, and exposed pipes overhead. It was probably a basement, but where?

Straining his neck, he raised his head to look at what they had tied him down with. The effort almost made him cry out in pain. He laid his head back down on a soft but firm surface. *At least I can move my head.* His legs, torso, and one arm were held tightly to a bed with locking, nylon tie-down straps. After a couple of unsuccessful attempts to release the one strap he could almost reach with his free arm, he gave up. Dismayed, he lowered his head onto the thin, lumpy pillow.

As the pain in his head subsided, he looked to his right. To his amazement, he saw a plate with fried chicken and french fries on a small nightstand within reach of his free hand. *Ah, that's why they left my right arm free,* he thought. His stomach growled fiercely. Reaching for a chicken leg, he thought, *hmm, no rats.* He sniffed the warm chicken, then took a small, skeptical bite. He waited a moment, not quite sure what to expect. *I guess they're not going to poison me,* he thought. *If they wanted to kill me, they would have done it already.* Satisfied with his rationalization, he quickly consumed the entire plateful of chicken and fries, then guzzled one of the bottles of water on the table.

The one small paper napkin near the plate wasn't nearly enough to absorb the river of grease running from his lips and down his chin. Being a bit of a cleanliness freak, this typically would have bothered the hell out of him, but he obviously had bigger issues at the moment.

Suddenly, he heard noises coming directly from the floor above him. Peter strained to listen. He heard voices of two or three men. He could not make out what they were saying or the language. He heard heavy footsteps. Then, the unmistakable sound of someone urinating in a toilet followed by the flush. The rush of water in the pipes behind him stirred up an urge in his bladder. He thought about calling out to the voices above him. But the thought of meeting his kidnappers scared the hell out of him. *What do they want? And what if they don't get it?*

The pain in his body had subsided, but his head was still pounding. Often, after a bad crash, his head would throb for days. But this pain was worse than he had ever had before.

Attempting to assuage his urge to urinate, he thought hard about his crash. He remembered catching an edge during his downhill run, then flying sideways through the air. He remembered slamming hard on the ice and trying to remain limber as he tumbled and bounced down the mountain, but his memory ended there. He knew that even with a helmet's protection, when he hit his head hard, amnesia often erased most of his memory of a fall, if not all of it.

Over the years, Peter's many concussions made him extremely curious about amnesia. Research taught him that mild amnesia was one of the body's self-defense mechanisms. He knew it could completely erase the memory of a dreadful occurrence.

But he did recall some of his fall, even if he had no idea how he ended up wherever he was now. Waking after a crash without a friend, coach, or one of his parents nearby was unnerving. He thought about the many times after a ski accident when he awoke in a hospital room to find his dad, and often his mom there. Sometimes his coach was in the room, and of course, for the past four years, Hunter, the love of his life, was usually in a chair next to his hospital bed. God, what must she be thinking? Or any of his family. His dad rarely missed one of his races, and if Peter crashed badly, his father was always present when he woke up. Everyone knew Dan Buckar was his son's biggest fan and protector. Peter smiled, wondering how many hours his father must have sat by his side after every bad fall.

Somewhat ashamed, Peter thought, *Why did it have to take something like this to make me realize I've never really thanked him for his love and devotion. I need to tell him when I see him—If I ever see him again.* He sighed and closed his eyes.

Chapter 11

THE HOTEL MONT Blanc was a stately establishment in the center of Chamonix. Its elegant interior resembled a 19th-century palace.

After an early morning workout in the hotel gym a quick breakfast, Jay and Buck sat in brown leather armchairs in the hotel's lobby. Jay ended his phone call with Pompard and looked at Buck.

"They found the ambulance used in the abduction. It was left in an old, vacant warehouse about twenty miles from the hospital. Get this, it was called in by a couple of homeless squatters who are living in the building. They said they had been out looking for food, and when they returned, the vehicle was there. They actually complained that it was in their way, and since there was no bed inside, they had no use for it."

Buck shook his head.

"Crazy, right? You just can't make this crap up. Anyway, Pompard had it towed in, and it's getting dusted now. I'll bet the only prints they find are from the vagrants."

"He's having the whole area searched, right?" Buck asked.

"Yeah, but my guess is that they had another vehicle waiting near the hospital. I'm sure they transferred Peter into something less obvious to get through the roadblocks."

Another nod from Buck.

After a brief pause, Jay said, "I'm going up to up to change into some jeans and head over to the mountain. I want to speak with that U.S. skier who they said argues with Peter all the time."

"Eschmann. He's a piece of work," Buck said.

"So, you know him?"

"Yeah. He wanted me to represent him when he heard about the endorsement contracts I was getting for Peter. I had mixed feelings about him, and I had too much on my plate already, so I turned him down. Now that I'm thinking about it, I remember he got upset after I told him 'no'. He kept trying to convince me. Then, as he was leaving my office, he said that I had chosen the wrong guy and added, 'you'll see' as he walked out. I figured he was just another petty athlete with a chip on his shoulder. I didn't think much of it." Buck stood up and stretched.

"I guess you deal with a lot of that?" Jay asked as they walked to the elevator to get to their floor.

"You wouldn't believe how often."

Chapter 12

SITTING IN THE living room of their hotel suite, Jay was already dressed in his jeans and flannel shirt. While he waited for Buck, he tapped the screen of his cell phone, raised it to his ear and gazed around the room. His eyes settled on an oil painting of cows grazing in a field under a cloud scattered, blue sky. He glanced at his watch, wondering why Buck was taking so long to change.

"Hello."

"Hi Sal, it's Jay Scott."

"Jay. How are you, my friend?"

"I'm well, and you?"

"*Molto bene, grazie.* Where are you? You sound like you're a million miles away?"

"Chamonix."

"Ah, how beautiful. A ski vacation? I didn't know you skied."

"I do, but I'm not here to ski. I'm on a case."

"Ah, so this is a business call?" Sal's tone changed.

"Yes, Sal. I'm investigating the disappearance of Peter Buckar, the U.S. Olympic skier."

"I just saw him on the news. He crashed in a downhill race. Looked bad. I figured he would be in a hospital. Those racers are crazy. They have bigger balls than most of *my* crew."

"Well, he was abducted, Sal. As of this moment, all we know is that he was taken from his hospital room in an ambulance, and most likely transferred into another vehicle. You wouldn't happen to know anything about this, by any chance?"

"Abducted? That's terrible." Sal paused, then yelled, "Wait a second. You son of a bitch! You think I had something to do with it?"

Jay was silent.

"You bastard! I thought you knew me better than that."

"Look, Sal, don't take this personally. You know I have to look into every possibility. I was just thinking that Peter's statement about you during his television interview must have infuriated you."

"Yeah, it did. Here I am offering to back the entire team, and that punk thinks he's too good for my money. I had to respect the kid though. He's got some set of *cogliones*. Not only does he race down a mountain at inhuman speeds, but then he's got the nerve to publicly stand up to me. Not the smartest thing he could do, but it took *cogliones gigante*."

"Indeed it did. So, are you going to tell me you had nothing to do with his abduction, and you didn't ask a favor from a family member anywhere over here?"

"Jay, you know I'm a big sports fan. The Olympics are sacred to me. There's no way I'd jeopardize America's Olympic medal count. In fact, I'm gonna put the word out that I want information, regardless of whether it was a family job or not."

"Will you let me know?"

"Listen to you, first you accuse me, then you ask for my help."

"What can I say?"

"How about, *mi dispiace*."

"You're right. I'm sorry, my friend."

"Yeah, yeah. With friends like you …"

Jay laughed. "Please call me if you hear anything."

"I will, Jay. *In bocca al luppo!*"

"Grazie, Sal. I'll probably need some luck on this one." Jay hung up and shook his head.

Buck had emerged from his room toward the latter part of the call. He pulled at the tight collar of his white turtleneck and then adjusted the zipper on his brown fleece pullover. "Sounds like you don't think DiGiacomo has anything to do with it?"

"No, I don't. In fact, he says he's going to help us. It will be good to get someone questioning people from his side of the law. His colleagues will obviously be more comfortable speaking with him than us."

"Good point."

"Are you ready?" Jay stood, shoved his phone in his pocket, and picked up his ski parka.

"Yeah, let's go."

Chapter 13

CHAMONIX'S HOMETOWN FAVORITE, Thierry Paquet, was a few feet off the ground, his body in the perfect, tight tuck, as he attacked the final steep section of the Super G. The only person in the crowd not cheering for Paquet, was the father of Sweden's top racer, Vilhelm Dinaso.

Detective Ferrer could not have chosen a worse time or place to question the man. The father was screaming at Ferrer and was getting more furious by the moment. Jay and Buck approached the hysterical father just in time to help escort him away from the crowd before the cheering subsided and his yelling could be heard by all.

Unbeknownst to the French Detective, Gustav Dinaso had a reputation on the racing circuit as a bit of a lunatic; he was excessively aggressive and loud. Most of the other families of the downhill skiers kept their distance from the obnoxious father. His son Vilhelm Dinaso was very much the opposite. His complete focus on racing earned him the nickname "Ice." He rarely spoke to anyone except his coach, and even with him, few words were exchanged. He never spoke with his father before or after a race.

Detective Ferrer had not intended to stir up a confrontation. Merely mentioning that he needed to speak with the senior Dinaso about Peter's disappearance had set the man off in a psychotic fury. As serious as the situation was, Jay and Buck had a hard time holding back their amusement. Dinaso's rants and raves combined with his Swedish voice inflections were almost comical.

"Reminds me of that Sesame Street character," Jay said, grinning.

"Oh yeah," Buck said with a chuckle. "The Swedish Chef muppet. You're right."

Attempts to stop his maniacal outbursts only fueled them. Like it or not, they had to let him get it out of his system. That or gag him, which although tempting, would probably only reroute his tirade from verbal to physical. Both Dinasos, father and son, had muscular builds, fair complexions, and lots of bushy, dirty blond hair.

As soon as Dinaso began to settle down, Ferrer said, "If you can calm yourself for a moment, we can discuss this like civilized human beings. We just want to know if you or your son have heard anyone talking about bringing harm to Peter Buckar."

"So, I am not a suspect?" he asked.

"Should you be?" Ferrer asked with a hint of accusation.

As if a switch was thrown, Dinaso's face flared rage-red, and he lunged, reaching for Ferrer's throat. Luckily again, a roar from the spectators drowned out the obscenities emanating from the madman. Ferrer easily dodged the attack leaving Dinaso stumbling toward Jay. With fluid movement, Jay reached for Dinaso's wrist, then, with the grace of a dancer, spun him until his arm was behind his back and up near his shoulder blade. Very calmly, Jay applied pressure with his free hand to an immobilizing pressure point near Dinaso's neck.

Dinaso's eyes bulged but otherwise, he was perfectly still. A quiet, ugly groan seeped through his lips.

Jay spoke softly into Dinaso's ear. "If you remain quiet and calm, I'll release you, and we can discuss things. If not, I will increase the intense pressure you feel right now until you pass out. It's your choice.

Jay momentarily increased the pressure just enough to convince Dinaso to make the *right* decision. After another brief grunt, Dinaso nodded with clenched teeth.

"Atta boy," Jay said, releasing his grip. "Now, let's take a walk." Jay turned toward Ferrer. "I think we should go somewhere where we can sit down and get Mr. Dinaso something to drink, don't you agree?"

"*Bien sur*," Ferrer said sheepishly, obviously embarrassed at the scene he caused. "There's a café just past the Kitsch Inn."

"The kitchen?" Jay asked curiously.

"No, Kitsch, K, I, T," Ferrer stopped spelling and said, "Over there." He pointed past the crowd to a funky restaurant with loud music playing and smoke rising from a barbeque.

"Very good," Jay said. "C'mon Gustav."

Dinaso must not have been cooperating because suddenly he lurched forward, trying to free himself from Jay's grasp, and yelled a Swedish curse, "*Ow. Din javal!*"

Jay leaned close and quietly said, "Maybe you didn't understand me. You can make this very easy or very difficult. I don't care one way or the other. Either way, we will get what we need from you. I recommend the easy way." Once Dinaso settled, Jay added, "Now, why don't you be a good chap and walk across the street without giving me any further problems." It took another arm-wrenching shove to get Dinaso moving.

A grin broke out on Buck's face as he watched Jay handle the man with little effort. "Good to know you've still got it."

"Did you doubt it?" Jay asked.

"Well, you're not exactly in the shape you were in when we first met."

"Why don't you shut up and smoke another cigar, old man. You're telling me I'm out of shape. Look at you."

"What? I'm in shape. Round is a shape."

Jay rolled his eyes, and Ferrer snickered.

"What is this anyway?" Buck asked. "I give you a compliment, and you ridicule me?"

"Well, it was a pretty twisted compliment."

"I didn't mean it to be."

"No? Well, then, thanks."

"A little late for that, isn't it?"

"*Herregud*," Dinaso grumbled. "If this is your way of psychologically breaking me down, it's working. Let me answer your questions so I can get back to the race."

The tantalizing aromas of strong coffee and sweet chocolate mingled in the air as they entered the charming cafe. Buck ordered four café au laits at the old, heavily stained butcher-block counter, then they sat on stools facing one another around a small, round, counter-height table in the corner. After taking a sip, Dinaso started to answer their questions. It became obvious that although the guy was psychologically unhinged, neither he nor his son were involved with Peter's disappearance.

"Of course, I want my son to medal, but it has to be a righteous win. *Bega ett brott*," Dinaso said, then thought before continuing in English. "It would discredit the win even if no one ever found out. Neither Vilhelm nor I could live with that!"

"Bagel-what?" Buck asked.

"*Bega ett brott.* Committing a crime," Jay answered.

Gustav nodded, a little surprised that the American knew Swedish. He smiled and finished drinking the last drop of his coffee.

Chapter 14

JAY AND BUCK walked back to their hotel as the late afternoon light threw a dark blanket of shadow on the already treacherous racecourse. No doubt the last racers of the day were relieved to ski over the finish line intact.

When they walked into the lobby, they found Pompard sitting alone, drinking coffee in the crowded bar. He had texted them earlier asking to meet.

"Why don't we go up to our suite," Jay said loudly enough to be heard over the din. "It's way too crowded in here."

Pompard nodded, grabbed his coat, and followed them.

***

Buck offered drinks as he poured himself a scotch from the bar in their suite. Jay and Pompard declined as they sat, facing one another in armchairs.

"I haven't got much more to add since we found the ambulance," Pompard said. "We asked those who lived in the area, but no one admitted seeing anything. And the only prints we found on the ambulance were from the two vagrants. I hope you've had a more productive day?"

Jay took note that Pompard seemed unperturbed. It was puzzling. *He called us off the mountain for this? He must be holding back. He's worried that I'm going to take over his case. I'll appease him for a day. Hopefully, that'll be enough to win him over. We don't have the luxury of time, and I'll be damned if I'm going to let his pride get in the way of saving Peter's life.*

"We bumped into Jacques Ferrer while he was questioning Gustav Dinaso, the Swedish racer's father." Jay quickly explained their discussion with Dinaso, leaving out Ferrer's poor decision about when and where to question the lunatic. He thought, *Stirring things up between Pompard and his team might strain our relationship.* He informed Pompard of feedback he received from his own team, regarding their dealings with some of the other skiers. Nothing worthwhile had been uncovered by his team either.

"The press is asking questions about Peter's condition," Pompard said. "It's a miracle that the news of the abduction hasn't leaked out to the media, not even a tweet about it. I'm sure it will break in the morning news, if not sooner."

"That will probably bring the FBI into the picture," Jay said.

"Hm. I have not dealt with your FBI. Are they as difficult to work with as I've heard?"

"Let's just say that they like to receive information more than they like to share their knowledge."

"I've had similar issues with both Interpol and Europol—the police arm of the European Union. They often make me wonder if we're on the same team," Pompard said.

Jay couldn't hold back a slight grin and chuckle. "I find it's best to get what I need from them before I give up any information."

"Good to know."

Jay smiled, thinking, *Are we both just playing the same game with each other?*

Chapter 15

BUCK WALKED OUT of his room early the next morning to find Jay working on his laptop at the small kitchenette table. After pouring a cup of coffee, he watched as Jay lifted a newspaper from the chair next to him and waved it in the air before slapping it on the table.

Buck walked over and saw Peter staring out from his picture on the front page. He was standing on the top step of a podium with a big smile. Skis in one hand and gold medal raised high in the other. The headline read: *"Le garçon d'or de l'Amérique disparaît."*

"It says, America's golden boy disappears."

"Oh shit!" Buck said. "Well, it was bound to get out, right?"

"Right."

"Now what?"

"There are two ways to look at it. The good news is we can stop pussyfooting around. Now that the cat is out of the bag, we can question everyone much faster and more openly. The problem is, now that the word is out, we're going to get more bad information than good."

"Why bad?" Buck asked.

"Because when a kidnapping goes public, especially a high profile one, the wackos of the world tend to come out and play. People call in all kinds of fake leads."

"Why the hell would anyone do that?"

"Who knows? It just happens. Human nature can be very weird. Why do some of your clients take the chance of blowing multimillion-dollar contracts or endorsements just because they get angry with someone in a bar who smiled at their girlfriend?"

"Good point," Buck said.

"It is a little different. In the case of your athletes, it's probably due to temper and, or, low IQ. With people calling in false leads, it can be anything from a dumb prank to an extortion attempt. The problem is, we now have to try to confirm the validity of every lead before we take the time to investigate it. Inevitably some of the bad ones will get by us. It's all a big waste of time."

"As if things aren't difficult enough already," Buck said.

"Yeah, well, there's nothing we can do about it now. I just hope Pompard can set up an anonymous tip line with enough people to handle the influx of calls. I better call him. It's time to see how he *really* feels about my suggestions."

Chapter 16

A WIND-SWEPT mix of ice and snow pelted the racers as they waited to be called to the starting gate. Waiting for their turn during an ice storm was akin to torture. Leg muscles would knot up and cramp unless constantly stretched and massaged. Remaining anxiety-free was a challenge.

Jarrett Eschmann was being stretched by David Colodny, one of the American assistant coaches. Eschmann was lying on a blanket, looking up at Colodny, who was on one knee, leaning over him. Slowly, yet forcefully, Colodny pushed the calf of Eschmann's long, vertically extended, massive right leg toward the racer's torso, stretching his hamstring. A past gold medal winner himself, Colodny knew what it took to win. He was of average height, thin and sinewy. Lacking in the weight department, he compensated with his strength to push Eschmann's leg. Pushing as hard as he could till their faces were close, Colodny said, "Your hams are tight as a drum."

"Yeah, I feel it," Eschmann said, grimacing.

"You better win today. As upset as we all are with Peter's situation, it kind of opens a door for you."

With a gleam in his eyes, Eschmann said, "I know. It's my turn now. It is time to prove myself. I'm going to show Stan, the team, the whole damn world what I'm worth." The tone of his last four words was almost evil.

Colodny's eyes opened wide in surprise. He released the pressure on Eschmann's leg and subtly looked around to see if anyone nearby had heard.

With a raspy laugh, Eschmann said, "What's the matter, coach? You know me better than to think I'm going to get upset over that righteous bastard's disappearance."

Disgusted, Colodny quietly hissed, "You son of a bitch. We don't even know if he's alive. He's never done anything to you except beat you on the racecourse, and you have the nerve to badmouth him?" Colodny aggressively shoved Eschmann's leg aside.

"Ow. What are you doing, you idiot?"

"Stretch yourself, you bastard. Better yet, go pull a muscle." Colodny stood and stormed away.

Some of the nearby racers and coaches looked over at Eschmann curiously.

Eschmann stared back at Alex Lupinacci. "What are you staring at? Mind your own fucking business, and maybe you'll win a race."

Everyone looked away except Lupinacci, who smiled and flipped Eschmann the bird before resuming his stretching.

Chapter 17

REID CLARK'S FLIGHT to Chamonix on his Gulfstream had been a little boring for him. While he preferred to fly the jet himself with his captain as co-pilot, he didn't feel quite ready for trans-Atlantic flights, especially with passengers aboard. Although he often took chances on his own, he would never put his wife, Shane, or his sister, Hunter, at risk.

When Reid had informed Hunter of her fiancé's disappearance, she had insisted on coming, as he knew she would. Her orchestra had backup pianists who were eager to fill in for her, and she had already been scheduled to take time off to watch Peter race in the Olympics the following week anyway.

Reid was happy to see how Shane was able to console Hunter. He overheard them talking about the odd role reversal. Not too long ago, Hunter and her sister, Betsy, had helped Shane deal with Reid's death threats and the attempt on his life.

Reid sighed. He recalled his own harrowing ordeal. Life in the public eye could be difficult. When it turned you into a target, it became unbearable.

Both women had fallen silent. Hunter tucked her legs under her, curling her petite body into the large, comfortable, leather seat. She spent the next half hour staring at the same page of *Pianist*

Magazine. She then closed the magazine, leaned back, and gazed at the sky through the small circular window.

Shane nodded to Reid, reading each other's mind that they should let Hunter have some quiet time.

When they arrived at the small private airport near Chamonix, they saw the snow falling heavily onto the tarmac. Reid was pleased to see a waiting SUV.

Chapter 18

AFTER CHECKING INTO the Hotel Mont-Blanc and putting their luggage in their room, Reid immediately noticed the blinking light on the room's hotel phone. After listening to the recorded message, he turned to the girls and said, "Buck and Jay have left the police station and are over at the mountain, waiting to speak with the team coaches. I'm going to join them. You guys can either come with me or stay around here. I'm sure there are some nice shops close by."

"What?" Hunter snapped. "Shopping? Are you serious? There's no way I'm going shopping. I'm coming with you."

"Easy does it. I didn't mean anything by it. I just wasn't sure if you were up to it. Sometimes things get a little harsh during an investigation, but of course, you're welcome to come if you want."

"I don't want to. I need to."

"Right, I understand. Let's go."

Chapter 19

AS PETER'S EYES slowly opened, he looked at the ceiling and noticed things were different than the last time he had awoken. The lights were a little brighter, and the dank, musty odor was gone. In fact, the air was fresh and clean. He turned his head slowly to the side and immediately noticed that the terrible throbbing was gone. Now it was just a dull ache. He then realized he was in a soft bed with fresh linens and a plush pillow. He wasn't tied up. He saw two glasses on the bedside table, one filled with water, the other with what appeared to be orange juice. Condensation on the outside of the glasses indicated that the liquids were chilled. There was also a pitcher of water and a large bowl of fresh-cut fruit with a fork next to it.

He was leery, but he was famished. Without further thought, he sat up and reached for the juice. After a quick sniff and a tiny taste of the sweet, cool liquid, he succumbed to his body's demand for nourishment and drained the glass. The juice did little to relieve his severe thirst, so he drank the glass of water just as quickly. His stomach growled as the liquids reminded him of its emptiness. Peter reached for the fruit and began consuming it as if he hadn't eaten in days, which, for all he knew, might be true. He ate chunks of melon and berries as fast as he could chew them. As he neared the bottom of the bowl, his pace slowed, having somewhat quelled his ravenous appetite. He surveyed his surroundings as he speared the last chunk of melon. Most of the room was filled with gym equipment; he realized it was brand new, expensive stuff. There was also a chair and large screen television. There were no windows. He looked to the side and saw an open door to a bathroom in the corner.

Peter slowly swung his legs off the bed. He thought about the straps that had held him down the last few times he awoke. He took a moment to study his legs. There were no marks from the restraints. He checked his wrists—nothing visible there either. Had he dreamed it? Slowly he stood up. He was a little wobbly, but not enough to be concerned. He walked to the room's main door and tried to turn the knob. Locked, of course. He walked to the bathroom, switched on the light, and walked to the toilet. His eyes wandered as he relieved himself. In the center of the large bathroom was a big whirlpool tub. Not the kind found in a luxurious bathroom, however. This was a portable one, used for sports training. Peter was mystified. *Where am I? Who is holding me? Why are they giving me good food and a comfortable bed? What's with all the exercise equipment, and the tub? What the hell is going on?*

He walked back toward the bed, then thought, *I can't lie down anymore. Hell, I might as well try out the equipment.* He turned, but as he was passing the TV, he glanced at it and stopped dead in his tracks. On the screen was: GOOD MORNING PETER. GLAD TO SEE YOU'RE FEELING BETTER. I HOPE YOU ENJOYED YOUR BREAKFAST.

"Who are you? Where am I?" he yelled.

As more letters began to appear on the TV, he read: AT THE MOMENT NEITHER OF THOSE QUESTIONS MATTER. YOU ARE SAFE AND YOU CAN TRAIN FOR YOUR UPCOMING OLYMPIC EVENTS WITHOUT INTERRUPTION. PLEASE FOLLOW THE SAME WORKOUT REGIMEN YOU DO

WHEN YOU ARE WITH YOUR TEAM TRAINERS. THE EQUIPMENT HERE IS THE FINEST AVAILABLE AND YOU WILL BE FED AS MUCH NOURISHING FOOD AS YOU NEED. AFTER WE ARE DONE COMMUNICATING, WE WILL PLAY CONTINUOUS VIDEOS OF THE ST. MORITZ RACE COURSES ON THE SCREEN. THE SKI SIMULATOR BEHIND YOU IS SIMILAR TO THE ONE YOU USE AT ALLSPORT BUT BETTER. YOU CAN VIRTUALLY RACE THE ST. MORITZ DOWNHILL, SLALOM, GIANT SLALOM AND SUPER G ON IT. IF YOU USE THE SIMULATOR AND TRAINING EQUIPMENT YOU WILL BE IN GOOD SHAPE TO WIN THE MEDALS YOU ARE EXPECTED TO WIN.

As he read the typing, Peter could feel his rage percolating, then began to surge. His sinewy body tightened and began to tremble. The fair, freckled skin on his face turned Crayola red. "Who the fuck are you? Why am I locked up? Let me out of this fucking place now!"

PLEASE CALM DOWN PETER. GETTING UPSET WILL ONLY INCREASE YOUR BLOOD PRESSURE. YOUR HEAD STILL NEEDS TIME TO HEAL FROM YOUR FALL. WE DON'T WANT TO LENGTHEN THE HEALING TIME, DO WE? SIT DOWN IN THE CHAIR NEXT TO YOU AND TAKE SOME DEEP CALMING BREATHS.

Peter's head turned toward the chair. He then quickly scanned the room for a camera. Seeing nothing obvious, he zeroed in on the wall clock and walked toward it. He removed it from the wall and studied it. Although he knew nothing about covert surveillance, he figured if there was a camera, it would probably be visible up close. Finding nothing, he tugged the clock from the wall snapping the attached wires.

Out of the corner of his eye, he noticed more words being typed on the screen. PETER, PLEASE DON'T TAKE THE

ROOM APART. WE HAVE SPENT A LOT OF TIME AND MONEY MAKING IT AS COMFORTABLE AS WE COULD FOR YOU.

His blood continued to boil as he approached a portable stereo sitting on the bureau. He lifted the handle, and with one sharp tug, all the wires tore from the back of the unit, and the speakers crashed to the floor.

He tossed the stereo to the floor as well, then looked at the TV. No more typing. He smiled. Maybe he couldn't escape, but at least they couldn't watch him anymore. His head had begun to throb. He walked over, sat in the chair, and closed his eyes.

When the throbbing finally subsided, he opened his eyes and looked at the TV.

GOOD. GLAD YOU CALMED DOWN. NOW JUST SIT FOR A FEW MINUTES AND RELAX.

Fury bubbled up inside him again. There didn't seem to be any other possible hiding places for a camera. Giving up, he sat back in the chair and leaned his head on the headrest. Looking up, he grinned, then walked to the weightlifting bench and grabbed the long steel bar. He carried it back to the center of the room and, with both hands, swung it toward the ceiling, smashing the smoke detector to pieces. Throwing it aside, the bar clanged loudly as it hit the floor and bounced. He picked up the largest piece of the shattered smoke detector and studied it. Sure enough, a tiny lens the size of a pencil eraser was peeking through a hole in the plastic.

He smiled and sat again with a momentary feeling of relief. His satisfaction waned as he looked back toward the TV.

SO YOU FOUND OUR CAMERA. PETER, PLEASE UNDERSTAND, WE ARE NOT SPYING ON YOU. WE ARE JUST MAKING SURE THAT YOU ARE ALL RIGHT. WE WANT YOU TO BE COMFORTABLE AND REMAIN IN PEAK CONDITION TO WIN YOUR EVENTS.

Once again, every muscle in his body tensed like a compressed spring. He jumped from the chair, grabbed the small end-table next to him, lifted it over his shoulder, and threw it at the TV with all his strength. It smashed through the screen sending the TV careening to the floor. Sparks flew, and a small fire started in the electronic mess.

Smiling again, Peter watched the flames slowly grow. His satisfaction faded when the plastic console started to burn, and he realized that if he let it continue, he'd probably die of asphyxiation in the windowless room. He darted into the bathroom, pulled some towels from their hooks, and ran back to the growing fire. He threw the towels over the flames, but instead of snuffing out the fire, they caught ablaze.

"Oh shit!" He ran to the bed, grabbed the blanket, then ran back and draped it over the mess. It seemed to do the job. Thick, dark smoke billowed from the edges, but at least there were no more flames. The nauseating odor of burning plastic rapidly permeated the upper third of the room. His eyes began to sting. Breathing was getting difficult. Peter dropped to his knees, crawled to the door, and tried again to open it. No such luck. He banged on the door, yelling, "Let me out."

He wondered why they hadn't already sent someone. In his excitement, he forgot that he had destroyed the camera. They wouldn't come to save him if they didn't know he was in trouble. He began to cough, slowly at first, then uncontrollably. Assaulted by dizziness, he could no longer think straight. He tried to crawl back to the smoldering TV. *Should I throw water on it? No, that would make it spread. No stupid, oil fires spread with water, not electrical fires.* His head was spinning, and he was short of breath. Unless he acted quickly, he was as good as dead. Dragging himself toward the door, he reached for the knob with one last surge of energy. Too late—his eyes rolled up into his head, and he passed out.

Chapter 20

WITH HIS WOOL hat pulled down almost to his eyebrows, and his high collared parka zipped all the way up to his lower lip, Reid was barely recognizable. Hunter was just as covered up. They both blended in nicely with the onlookers at the finish line. Although he was used to an onslaught of autograph-hungry fans, this crowd was nuts. But luckily, it was not due to Reid. These were rowdy ski racing fans, and from the look of it, most were probably drunk. Glancing around, he saw flasks of various sizes and colors casually passing from pockets to lips and back, with speed and subtlety.

The sudden clanging of cowbells caused Hunter to jump, as Frederic Bouvier, a Frenchman, crossed the finish line, taking over the lead by two-hundredths of a second and sending his fellow countrymen into hysterics.

Noticing Hunter's reaction, Reid put his arm around her shoulders; he gave Shane his free hand and escorted both women away from the crowd. They walked around the perimeter of the throng, searching for Buck and Jay.

Shane looked at Hunter and whispered into Reid's ear, "She's shaking, let's get her some coffee."

They scanned the area and spotted the same café where Buck and Jay had questioned Dinaso yesterday. The trio made their way over and entered the coffee shop. As luck would have it, Buck and Jay, once again, were using the cafe as an office. They were at a table with ski team coaches David Colodny and Stan Williams.

"I'm telling you it was pure evil," Colodny was saying as Reid and the women approached. "I know he can be cold, but I never thought he could be such a heartless bastard."

Quick introductions were made between Reid, Shane, Colodny, and Williams. Hunter knew the coaches from her many trips to Peter's races.

The men stood and gave Hunter comforting hugs. Jay said, "I know this is a difficult time for you, but believe me, we will find Peter."

"Thank you." Hunter's face scrunched in a curious grin. "Dave, were you by any chance talking about Jarrett Eschmann a second ago?"

"I was. Good guess."

"It wasn't very hard. He and Peter haven't exactly been friends for the last few years. He constantly instigates arguments, and Peter tries to ignore him. It's a miracle they haven't duked it out yet."

Williams and Colodny glanced at each other.

"They fought?" Buck asked.

"No way. I would have known about it," Hunter said indignantly.

"'Fraid so," Williams said. "About a month ago, when they were racing in Telluride, they got into it at the top of the mountain. Jarrett pushed Peter a little too far and threw a sucker punch, and Peter fought back. The start ref had to break them up. It turned out the ref was also a lawyer. Jarrett ended up with a bloody nose and asked the guy if he would represent him if he sued Peter. The attorney laughed and said if anyone had a case it was Peter. Jarrett stormed away, totally pissed off. His racing suit was so full of blood he had to change before he raced. They both got warnings from the Chief of Race. I told them if it happened again, I'd suspend them both. The sport is dangerous enough without distractions like that. If Jarrett didn't have the potential to win, I would have thrown him off the team a long time ago. I've had his poor attitude and big mouth up to here." He held his hand level with his eyes.

"I can't believe he didn't tell me about it," Hunter said, looking both worried and angry. "I've never liked Jarret."

"That makes two of us," Buck agreed.

"Well, I guess that moves Eschmann up to the top of my list for questioning," Jay said as he rapidly typed a note on his phone. "Are there any other racers that have been giving Peter a hard time?"

"No," Colodny said. "Peter is one of the nicest guys on the circuit. He gets along pretty well with everyone."

"Okay, I guess it's time we had a discussion with Jarret," Jay said as he stood.

Colodny spoke into his radio then held it to his ear to listen to the answer on low volume. "You'll have to wait a few minutes," he said. "Eschmann is next on the course," he said, adding to Williams, "Let's go. Love him or not, we need to be there to support him."

Both men rose to leave.

"Wait, where will he go after his run?" Jay asked. "I don't want to question him anywhere near the finish line."

"If he medals," Colodny said. "He'll head to Café La Terrasse with everyone else. If not, he'll probably go back to the hotel and sulk."

"I'd like to meet with him privately after the race. Do you think you could call a quick team meeting at your hotel? Then we can pull him aside afterward."

"Of course," Williams said. "Now though, if you don't mind, we'd like to get out there and see his run."

"Let's all go," Jay said.

Chapter 21

JARRET ESCHMANN CAUGHT more air than he wanted off the Cassure ledge on La Verte piste. He had to stay low off the next jump or there was no way he'd win. He was skiing well.

With Peter out of the way, this race was his. If he won today's Kandahar Downhill, the press would smother him.

"That's right, baby, it's my turn for the spotlight," he screamed inside his helmet.

Mid-scream, he caught the inside edge of his left ski in a rut. Luckily his over-torqued binding did not release, but, still attached, his ski shot out from under him. Fighting to regain control and remain upright, he forced all his weight onto his right ski. Then, with no time for a pre-jump, he skied off the Goulet ridge, and once again, was airborne. His left leg was now sticking out like a tree branch, almost perpendicular to his body. His arms spun fast as he fought hard to correct the problem. He landed, mostly on his right ski, with his left not yet positioned correctly. His weight shifted as gravity yanked at his body. Just in time, his muscular left leg forced its ski into place to handle the strenuous balancing act his body was playing. Relieved, Eschmann let out another whooping yell, then refocused on his run. He had no idea how much time he had just lost. What he knew was that he needed to turn on everything he had in order to finish strong. Half the course was still in front of him. If he skied it perfectly, he would own this race. He tucked tight. His eyes locked on the line he wanted to ski, and with finesse, his skis did as commanded. He pre-jumped the next ledge at the right moment to keep his skis hovering just slightly above the snow. He held his tuck as he flew through the air and landed smoothly.

The temperature at the bottom of the mountain, while very cold, was usually a good fifty degrees warmer than at the top—creating a softer, slightly slower surface. That is, if you considered skiing at sixty miles-per-hour slow.

The slower speed annoyed Eschmann. Outside of his near fall, so far he had skied an excellent run. Slowing down fueled his desire for more speed. His torment made him push himself harder. He needed this win. He began to ski with reckless abandon, and he entered the next turn too fast. Compensating, he dug his edges in with every bit of power he could muster. He carved hard to the right, making the gate, but nowhere near as tightly as he intended. He would have been fine if only the course hadn't dropped steeply from under him as he traversed toward the next gate. He came out of his tuck, and his arms windmilled as he tried to regain his balance in the air. Losing control, his body began leaning backward, and his ski tips rose in front of him. The backs of his skis landed first, causing the tips to snap down hard on the ice.

Once again, gravity was not cooperating as his unbalanced weight shifted onto the right edges of his skis, causing them to shoot in that direction. Miraculously, he compensated and just barely kept himself from crashing into the barriers as he reset his edges for a hard left turn.

The crowds lining the course were yelling out his name. Most were filled with terrified excitement. Near disasters, where racers narrowly avoided high-speed crashes, were the ultimate thrill for spectators.

Eschmann managed to regain control and then skied the end of the course flawlessly. He finished in second place, solidifying his position in the upcoming Olympics. The press was all over him. Finishing the race in second, after a perilous run, sometimes attracted more attention than a smooth first-place finish.

Surrounded by cameras, Eschmann grinned at Frank Arnot, the Austrian who had won the race. Arnot sneered at Eschmann from behind the cameras. The limelight should have been Arnot's, and he couldn't hide his frustration.

Chapter 22

"WHAT THE HELL?" Sal DiGiacomo said to himself, tossing his phone onto the table. His call to Benito, his cousin in Palermo, left DiGiacomo dismayed. Benito said that although La Casa Nostra was not involved with Peter's abduction, there were rumors that the 'Ndrangheta organization might be.

Thoughts swam through DiGiacomo's head. The 'Ndrangheta had made a fortune with kidnappings in the 1970s, '80s, and '90s, but they stopped once their other businesses were bringing in more than enough money. Why would they bother kidnapping an athlete? The one-time financial gain was not worth it. Could someone have a personal reason?

He needed more information. He scrolled through the contacts on his phone and tapped on a name.

Chapter 23

THE US SKI team was not happy about Coach Williams' emergency meeting. They were looking to celebrate their great day on the mountain with a beer or two. Their grumbling voices began to fill the brightly lit hotel conference room as they entered.

All sixteen of them walked down the rows of thinly cushioned folding chairs. Most grabbed chairs at the rear and sides of the room. Some turned their chairs backward and straddled them with their arms crossed, leaning forward on the backrests. The rest slouched low with their tired legs stretched out on the chairs in front of them. Some looked put off and sullen, others displayed an air of casual arrogance.

Williams didn't care as long as they all kept quiet and paid attention. When they were all seated, he began, "Gentlemen, first let me congratulate you all, especially Eschmann and Dukes. Jarret, that was one hell of a run. You were a madman on the mountain. I'm always glad when you finish in one piece. Trucker, you skied a beautiful run. Congrats on the bronze."

"Thanks, coach," Trucker Dukes said.

Williams paused and waited until he had everyone's attention. "Obviously, I didn't call this meeting just to congratulate you. Despite this being a very difficult and emotional day, many of you did an excellent job out there. However, I wanted to update you on Peter's situation. When I'm finished, you can go downstairs to the bar for a beer or two. But keep in mind, I want everyone to keep their celebrating to a minimum. We are not heading to St. Moritz tomorrow as planned. We are staying and training here until we know more about Peter. That means I want you all in the weight room by 10 a.m."

"What?" bellowed a racer.

"Come on coach, give us a break," another said.

"All right, all right, make it one o'clock. You can sleep in tomorrow. But I don't want any heavy partying tonight. If the press sees any of you getting sloppy before Peter is found, they will crucify you and the entire team by default. I promise I will not tolerate any nonsense. If any of you end up in the news with negative publicity, you will not be racing with us in two weeks." He paused to let his statement sink in. "Do you all understand?"

There were a few nods.

Raising his voice, he repeated sternly, "Do you *all* understand?"

"Yes, coach," came from most of the guys.

"Yeah, yeah," was heard from a few.

Williams' body instantly stiffened. In a loud, angry tone, he said, "Look, I'm not in the mood for any crap right now. Your teammate, Peter, who is also a friend to most of you, and America's best chance at multiple medals is missing. He could be dead for all we know—God forbid. If any of you have a problem taking this seriously, let me know right now. Cause if you do, you can leave. I'm serious. Either you show respect for each other and for the team, or you can get the hell out of here."

Silence engulfed the room. Some of the men sat up in their chairs.

"Have I made myself clear?" Williams looked at each member of the team and waited for his response.

"Yes, Coach," replied each skier with a nod as he caught their eye.

Williams winced as his eyes locked on Jarrett Eschmann. Eschmann didn't even bother to pocket his snide smile as he gave the requested response. His eyes and body language divulged his contempt.

It took a moment for Williams' visible disgust to pass. Then, after looking at the rest of his men and convinced that they were taking this seriously, he continued. "At the moment, Peter's disappearance is a mystery. There are a lot of people involved in the investigation. The local police are working with Interpol and Europol. We also have Jay Scott, an American Private Investigator, and his team here. I have no doubt that the FBI will be involved soon. You will all be questioned by one of these official groups over the next day or so. Right now, though, I'd like to bring a few people in to join us." He nodded to Colodny, who walked to the door and opened it. Buck, Jay, Hunter, Reid, and Shane entered the room and sat in chairs lined up behind Williams.

"Most of you know Hunter Clark, Peter's fiancé," Williams said.

"Hi guys," Hunter said quietly.

Most of the team returned looks of concern or anguish. Jeff Edwards, Peter's best friend on the team, walked over to Hunter, leaned down, hugged her, and said quietly, "I'm so sorry. This is all so difficult to deal with, I can't imagine what you're going through. They're going to find him, Hunter, I know it."

"Thanks, Jeff. I appreciate it."

Williams said, "I'm sure you all recognize Hunter's brother, Reid, and his wife, Shane. Peter and Reid grew up together and are very good friends."

Knowing nods filled the room. Everyone remembered learning about Reid getting shot during the Master's Tournament. It had been headline news.

Shane gave a small wave. Reid nodded and said, "Nice race today guys."

Some of the guys thanked him. Others, who hadn't skied so well, either rolled their eyes or lowered their heads.

Williams introduced Buck, who gave a slight nod.

"Now, I'd like to introduce Jay Scott. Mr. Scott is running the investigation along with the local authorities. He has worked with Buck and Reid on other issues over the years."

Jay traded places with Williams at the lectern. "Thanks, Stan." He turned to look at the group of men. "Guys, I'm going to be as brief as possible. Until we find Peter, things will be a little difficult around here. There will be a lot of law enforcement asking you lots of questions and invading your lives. You may get asked to repeat the same information to different officers at different times. I highly recommend you cooperate with them. Their ways, and, well, their view of the law might be different than you'd expect back in the states. If they feel that you are holding back information, they will not hesitate to incarcerate you. You all have better things to do than sit in a French jail. Answer their questions politely, even if they get a little pushy. Some European law enforcement officials have an issue with Americans. Don't give them an excuse to make an example of you." He hesitated, then said, "Everyone with me so far?"

Most of the skiers nodded, some shrugged.

"All right, now let's discuss the media. You know they're going to be all over this. With the Olympics just around the corner, this is world news."

Reid's cell phone rang. "Sorry," he said as he hustled to the door and out of the room to answer it.

Jay continued, "As I was saying, this is going to bring on a media circus. Some of you may see it as an opportunity to give the world a glimpse of your face or your name. Don't be lured into their web. Chances are the result will be negative publicity. Some of the press will probably spin this thing way out of proportion. Please use your heads when you speak with them. I would also prefer that you don't engage in social media discussions about this. Facebook, Instagram, and Twitter are all going to blow up with nonsense about it. Please don't fuel the firestorm."

A skier raised his hand.

Jay pointed at him. "Go ahead."

"Sorry to interrupt, Mr. Scott, but many of us have a pretty big fan base on social media. I wouldn't dare post anything to harm the investigation, but I don't want to alienate my fans either. Lots of them are already asking questions. Is there anything I can post? Not to be pushy, but is there any news at all about Peter's disappearance? Like, what really happened?"

"I wish I could tell you. But, we don't want to jeopardize the investigation."

"Okay, I get that," another racer said, "but I'm getting barraged online too. Can we post something simple, like, 'Our hearts and thoughts are with Peter. It's a difficult time for us all. Thanks for your concern'."

"Yes, that's a perfect response," Jay said. "But no more than that, please."

Many of the skiers nodded.

"Okay," Jay continued. "The last thing I want to mention is that starting tomorrow, my investigators and I will be coming around to speak with each of you one-on-one. Our questions will be fairly routine. We need as much information as we can get. Please think about any incidents or discussions you have had with, or about Peter, or maybe something you overheard about him, anything at all. As foolish as you might feel about mentioning something unimportant, everything has the potential to be relevant. You never know which tiny bit of information could save a life in a situation like this."

Hunter gasped.

Everyone turned toward her. She was bent over in her chair with her face in her hands.

Jay cringed, then turned and said, "I'm sorry, Hunter."

Hunter looked up, wiped her eyes, and took a deep breath. "Don't be, Jay. Please don't start watching what you say because of me. I don't want to interfere with your investigation." Looking from Jay to the team, she said, "If you feel that my being in the room is going to hinder your answers or cause you to hold back, please let me know, and I'll leave. I can handle this." Shane reached over and squeezed her hand.

The looks on the faces in the room showed that Hunter's statement had impressed everyone. She was tough. Her statement was courageous, but her fragility was also evident.

Jay gave her a nod, then turned back toward the group. "Well gentlemen, I'm done for now. I look forward to meeting with you individually." He turned toward Williams and motioned for him to return to the lectern.

Williams wrapped up the meeting, and the team filed out of the room with Eschmann at the rear of the pack. Some of the guys shook Jay's hand as they walked by. Most shook hands with Buck. A few even asked if he could spare some time to discuss the possibility of his representing them. They all stopped to give Hunter a quick hug and say a few kind words.

As the first racer opened the door to leave, Reid walked back into the room. He looked extremely shaken.

Instead of leaving, some of the skiers gathered around Reid. His winning PGA record, as well as his co-founding of the ICSF and AllSport, made him one of those inspiring athletes that leaves even other top sports professionals in awe.

Not wanting to be the center of focus, Reid said, "Guys, as much as I'd love to hang out and talk with you, I need to speak with Jay." Noticing that some of the guys seemed put off, he added, "Can I ask you all a favor? After we find Peter, I'd love to ski with you? I could use a few pointers. I've been skiing with Peter for a long time, but you know how he is. He'd never help someone who might turn out better than him."

Some of them laughed. But most gave Reid puzzled looks. His deadpan expression made it difficult to tell whether he was kidding or not. Could he really think he could become a better skier than Peter?

Reid kept a straight face just long enough, and then he smiled. "It was a joke, guys. I am a decent skier, but I could never compete in your sport. This body," he pointed at his torso, "ain't built for speed. The only things that move fast in my sport are my balls—my golf balls, that is," he added with raised eyebrows.

They all laughed.

As the racers left, Reid looked around the room.

Shane approached him with Hunter close behind. "What's the matter? You look upset."

"Where are Jay and Buck? I need to talk to you all about the call I just got."

"They're with Eschmann. He started giving them a hard time when they asked about his relationship with Peter. They took him into the adjoining room over there." She pointed at a door.

"Come with me," Reid said.

Shane and Hunter followed him, giving each other curious looks. Without knocking, Reid opened the door. Shouts from a loud argument filled the room.

"Fuck you all, you bastards. You think I've got something to do with this? You think I'm that stupid? I'd have to be an idiot to pull a stunt like this."

They were sitting around a flimsy, round, wooden table. Eschmann's face was red with fury. He slammed his fist so hard the table cracked. Jay grabbed the water pitcher before it toppled over. Neither Buck nor the coaches were as quick with the full glasses in front of them. Water spilled everywhere, and a glass rolled off the table and shattered on the hardwood floor.

Eschmann didn't let up. "Of course, I'm the first person everyone is going to look at for this. Peter and I have argued for years. We've never gotten along. Truthfully, I don't care if you find him or not. He's a self-righteous, pompous asshole."

Standing just a few feet behind Eschmann, Hunter ran up and slapped his face as hard as she could.

"Ow. My eye. Dammit." Eschmann turned and faced Hunter. His look of fury became one of embarrassment.

"You son of a bitch," she said, swinging her hand to hit him again.

Eschmann caught her wrist before she connected. "Hunter, I'm sorry. I had no idea you were there."

"Don't say another word to me, you bastard."

He raised both of his hands to shoulder height in surrender. "I had no right to say that. Of course, I want Peter found. They just got me so worked up I lost control. I knew I would eventually be accused, but I guess I wasn't prepared to hear it so soon. I promise I had nothing to do with it."

"Yeah, sure," Hunter said.

"I swear it, Hunter."

"Okay, you two, that's enough," Reid interrupted. "Jarret, you need to leave. I've got to talk to everyone else."

Not listening to her brother, Hunter was still fuming over Eschmann's statement. "Why the hell should I believe anything you say? You've been jealous of Peter for years."

"Hunter, please stop," Reid said, cutting her off. "You need to listen to me." He could tell she still hadn't heard a word he'd said. He raised his voice loud enough to get everyone's attention. "I just received a ransom demand!"

The room went silent. Everyone stared at Reid in shock.

"Oh, no. Who were they? Did they tell you anything about Peter?" Buck was full of questions.

"Jarret," Jay said. "Leave the room now."

"So, I'm off the hook, right?" Eschmann asked.

"We'll see," Jay said. "Just get out of here, for now. But understand, I do not want a word of this to leave the room. If I find out that you have uttered even a word …" he let his voice trail off and just stared at Eschmann.

"Is that a threat? First, you *accuse* me, then someone else calls in a ransom demand, and now you *threaten* me?" Seething, Eschmann stood, pointed his finger inches from Jay's face, and said, "Listen, pal …"

Jay sprang from his chair, grabbed Eschmann's wrist, and twisted it in such a way that he went down on his knees, then fell to the floor on his stomach. Jay eased down on him with one knee centered on Eschmann's back, then squeezed a pressure point near Eschmann's collar bone.

Eschmann bellowed in pain. Everyone around the table winced. Cool as ice, Jay said, "Jarrett, don't mess with me, or the pain you're feeling now will feel like child's play. When I let you up, I want you to walk out of this room without another word. Don't even turn around to look at us. If I hear that you have mentioned anything you've heard in this room, you will regret it. Understood?"

"Get the fu-"

Jay added more pressure. Eschmann's face contorted as he tried to hold back a scream. The groan that came from his mouth was sickening.

Williams jumped from his chair. "Jay, please stop. I need him to race."

Jay decreased the pressure. "Do we have an understanding?"

A barely audible, very defeated, "yeah," passed through Eschmann's lips. It came out as more of a moan than a word.

Jay released him. Eschmann slowly stood, turned, and left the room.

Buck grinned and raised a brow as Jay took his seat.

"Sorry about that," Jay said nonchalantly.

"He had it coming," Reid said.

"Damn right he did," Colodny said. "I just wish it had been me who took him down. That was amazing."

Jay shrugged. "Guess we all have our talents." He paused in thought. "Talk to us, Reid."

All eyes were on Reid as he looked around the table. "You all heard my phone ring during the meeting, right?"

"Of course," Jay said.

"When I answered, at first, there was no one on the other end. Then a weird voice asked if it was me on the phone."

"What was weird about it?" Jay asked.

"It was kind of mechanical. You know, like computerized."

"Was it like a mechanically distorted human voice?" Jay asked. "Or, was it computer-synthesized?"

"I don't know. I guess it sounded like a distorted male voice."

"Tell me exactly what was said, word for word," Jay said.

Reid thought for a moment, then said, "First he asked, 'Is this Reid Clark?' After I said yes, he said, 'If you want Peter Buckar back unharmed, you need to follow my directions.' Then I asked why he was calling *me*. He said, 'Because you are good friends with Peter. Because he is engaged to your sister, and because you can pay five million US dollars in ransom quickly.' I was too stunned to say anything at that point, so he asked if I was still on the phone. When I said yes, he said, 'Good. Now write down these instructions.' I told him I had to find something to write with and go someplace quiet where no one else was around. I asked if he would call me back in twenty minutes. He cursed me out and warned me not to tell anyone about the call. Then he reluctantly agreed to call back." Reid looked at his watch. "He should be calling soon."

"Well, now we just wait for the call," Jay said. "I'm going to record it. Hopefully, we can run a voice analysis later. Reid, can you put the call on speaker?"

"Yeah, but don't you think that might piss him off? It annoys the hell out of me when someone puts me on speaker."

"Tell him you're typing his instructions on a laptop, and you need both hands." Jay turned to the others. "Obviously, we will have to be absolutely …"

Jay was cut off by the ring of Reid's cell. Reid placed the phone on the table, looked at Jay, took a deep breath, and pushed the speaker button.

"Hello."

"Reid Clark?"

"Yes."

"You sound different. Am I on speaker?" the computerized voice sounded agitated.

"Yes, you are."

"What the hell? I told you not to tell anyone about this call. Now you have me on a speaker? Are you an idiot? I thought you cared about Buckar. This call is over."

"No, wait, don't hang up. Please. No one else is here. I have you on speaker so I can type your instructions on my laptop. I need both hands."

"Laptop? What's the matter with a pen and paper? Too simple for you?"

"Look, it's what I've got. Does it really matter?"

"No."

"Then why don't you just tell me what you want?"

"I want five million dollars, American currency, all in large denominations so that the bundle is easy to carry. Got that?"

"Yes."

"Good. Tomorrow I want you to put the cash in a backpack and …"

"Tomorrow?"

"Yes, tomorrow."

Jay scribbled a note and held it up. It said: Tell him you need a few days. There is no way we can get that much cash that fast.

"There is no way I can get five million that quickly. I can get the money, but, I doubt there is that much US currency sitting in any of the Chamonix banks. I will need more time."

The following silence was nerve-wracking. Reid looked wide-eyed at Jay and mouthed, 'Did he hang up?'

Jay raised his index finger to his lips.

"Dammit, Reid!" yelled the kidnapper, causing everyone, except Jay, to flinch. "Five million is a drop in a bucket for you."

"I'll get you the money. I just need some time."

"Don't play games with me. Not if you want Peter back, alive."

"How do I know he's alive right now?"

"You'll just have to take my word for it."

"Take your word for it?"

"You know what, I'm getting tired of this. You want him back, come up with the money. I'll even give you an extra day. Expect my call tomorrow night to confirm our meeting. I want you and only you, to bring the money up in the first tram of the day to the Aiguille du Midi. At the top of the tram, you will go through the ice tunnel to the top of the Aiguille du Midi ridge. There, you will put on your skis and …"

"Put on my skis?"

"Do you think this is a joke?" the caller snapped. "Look, if you want Peter back, just shut up and do as I say. When your skis are on, I will call you with further instructions."

Feeling he had already pushed the caller to his limit, Reid remained silent.

"Are you still with me?"

"Yes."

"Do you understand my demands?"

"Yes. But I ..." Reid was surprised that they assumed he could ski.

"I will call you tomorrow evening. If you tell the police or involve them in any way, Peter dies." The kidnapper hung up.

Not a word was uttered around the table. Instead, everyone's eyes scanned one another until they all landed on Jay.

Jay's look was intense. He drummed his fingers on the table, then spoke, "Okay, we have work to do. Buck, you and Reid need to get the cash. All hundred dollar bills, if possible. Will you need help?"

"No," Buck said.

"If we get larger bills, like thousands, they'll fit in a smaller backpack, right?" Reid asked.

"They stopped printing thousand dollar notes sometime in the 1960s. No one used the big bills all that much," Jay said. "The largest denomination in print now is a one hundred."

"Really?" Reid said, reaching for his wallet. He pulled out a few credit cards, and behind them were two folded bills. He unfolded two one-thousand-dollar bills and held them up. "I've been carrying these for years. Are they any good?"

Both coaches' eyes widened. None of the others showed any surprise.

"Sure they are," Jay said. "They're collector's items. Probably worth more than their face value." After a brief pause, Jay continued, "All right, next on the list, Stan, you or David need to get Reid fitted with ski equipment." He turned to Reid with a worried look on his face. "You can ski, can't you?"

"Yes."

"He's very good," Shane said.

"Good," Jay said. "Okay, the problem is not just getting our hands on the physical cash, but finding a way for you to ski with that much bulky weight on you. We are going to need 500 $1000 bundles of 100 dollar bills. That's a lot to carry."

Jay turned to Shane. "You and Hunter need to buy a backpack. There has got to be a sporting goods store nearby. Get a big one with a metal frame. The type used for hiking. Okay?"

Hunter and Shane nodded.

"Let's all get back together at one o'clock tomorrow afternoon. That should give you plenty of time to work on your assignments. I have to assemble a team to protect Reid." He looked at Reid. "I also want to size you for a protective vest and helmet."

Reid nodded. As uncomfortable as it was, body armor had saved his life when he was shot. He had argued about wearing it back then. This time he liked the idea.

"Okay, enough for now. Let's get out of here. We all have work to do," Jay said.

Reid looked at his watch. "I need to get something to eat. Does anyone else want to grab something quick for dinner?"

Buck and Shane nodded.

"I need to call Pompard," Jay said. "He needs to know about this immediately. Hopefully, he has a money scanner so we can record the serial numbers on the bills. If not, we'll have to get a bank to do it. And I need him to get you a vest. I want you in hard armor this time. Last time we used soft body armor so you could swing a golf club with it on. I'm less concerned about your comfort this time. I want you in a level four vest."

Reid shrugged. "What's level four?"

"Better protection. It'll stop an AP round."

"AP?" Shane asked?

"As I said, it's better protection. Let's just leave it at that," Jay said.

Shane looked at Reid with widened eyes.

Reid's shoulders rose as he shook his head. "We'll be down in the restaurant if you want to join us when you're done. Hunter, come with us. You need to eat."

"I'll come, but I'm not very hungry." An air of melancholy now surrounded her.

Reid walked over, put his arm around her shoulder, and gave her a squeeze. "Come on, sis, everything's going to be all right. We're gonna get him back."

Her face melted into pain and despair. She closed her eyes, and tears began to flow. Reid wrapped his long arms around her. "It's gonna be okay," he whispered into her ear. She allowed herself a few more tears then fought to stop. She nodded and slowly pulled herself from Reid's grip. In between sniffles, she murmured, "Thanks." Then she turned and said, "Sorry guys," as she wiped her eyes with her sleeve.

"Don't be silly," Jay said.

"I know how tough this is," Shane said, handing her a tissue.

"I'm okay, let's go," Hunter said a little choked up.

"Are you guys coming?" Reid asked, looking at Williams and Colodny.

"No," Williams said. "I think it would be best for us to get back to the team. I want to make sure that none of them are shooting their mouths off to the press, especially Eschmann. I don't trust him to keep quiet."

Jay nodded. "Smart. When and where should Reid meet up with you to get his ski gear?" he asked, looking at Colodny.

Colodny looked at Reid. "I'll meet you downstairs in the lobby first thing in the morning? Let's say six-thirty? We'll head over to one of our equipment rooms." He turned to Jay, "Skis, boots, poles, and a helmet, right?"

"Just skis, boots, and poles. I'll get him a ballistic helmet from Pompard."

Colodny gave a thumbs up.

"I'm going up to my room and ordering from room service," Jay said. "I have a bunch of calls to make. Then I'm going to hit the sack. I'm exhausted, and I want to head to the mountain first thing in the morning to scout it out with a few of my men. Good night, all."

Reid walked with Jay to the door and quietly asked, "So, what are AP rounds?"

"Don't worry about it. Go enjoy dinner and get a good night's sleep."

"Just tell me, so I don't have to Google it."

"Armor-piercing."

"Oh, great," Reid moaned quietly.

"You see. There are some things you're better off not knowing."

"Yeah, I guess."

Jay patted him on the shoulder. "You've been through this before. You're going to be fine."

"From your lips to God's ears, my friend."

Jay nodded and opened the door. "Good night."

Chapter 24

DRENCHED IN SWEAT, Peter strained through yet one more squat. The pads of the squat machine pressed hard on his shoulders. The searing pain in his quadriceps after his third set of repetitions, while extreme, wasn't even close to the burn he usually felt near the end of a downhill race.

A deep breath in, a forced exhale. Instead of locking the rack and taking a break, he pushed himself for another three squats, finishing each with an enormous grunt.

Grimacing, he pushed the locking mechanism in place and stepped off the platform. Sapped of energy, yet invigorated, he grabbed a towel from a nearby wall hook and mopped the rivulets of sweat from his face. Done with the strength building heavy weights, he crouched, pulled the pin from its hole in the weight stack, and reinserted it a few holes higher. It was time to work on stamina with lighter weights and more repetitions. The more he punished his legs now, the less pain he'd feel as he neared the end of the next racecourse.

After three more sets of squats at a lower weight, he moved away from the machine, stood up straight, locked his knees, and slowly bent at the waist till his palms pushed flat against the floor. Holding the same position, he reached his long arms around the backs of his knees and pulled tight until his forehead touched his shins. As he held the hamstring stretch, his mind wandered, once again. *What the hell is going on here? I'm locked in a room who knows where, working out like it's just another day. This is crazy.*

Releasing his grip, he slowly stood, took a step toward the bench, and sat. He picked up the damp towel again, and holding one end, slung it behind his neck and caught the other end with his free hand. Gripping the ends of the short towel, his fists rested on his chest. He looked around the room one more time then shook his head, baffled.

Chapter 25

AFTER A LONG, anxiety-filled day of prepping for the ransom drop, Reid and Shane lay in bed looking at each other.

"I can't stand this," Shane said.

"I know."

"No really. I'm so scared I think I'm going to be sick."

"Yeah, I'm feeling a little queasy myself."

"You don't have to do this, you know. Jay can have one of his guys do it in your place."

"Are you serious?"

"Of course I am. You're not an investigator or a bodyguard, and unlike Jay and his team, you've never been a Navy SEAL. You're a professional golfer, you're my husband, and more important than that, you're our son's father."

"You're right, and you know that I take each of those responsibilities very seriously, but we're talking about Peter's life here. I know you feel that I have a choice, but I don't agree. I would never forgive myself if I let someone else do this in my place, especially if something went wrong."

"I understand, and although I wish I could, I know it would be futile to try to change your mind. Let's just get some sleep."

"I wish," Reid said.

"Yeah, me too." Shane reached for her iPad, turned it on, and began reading.

Reid forced his eyes closed for about two minutes, then gave in and reluctantly reached for his iPad too.

***

Hunter was waiting in the hotel lobby wearing her parka and holding her hat and gloves when Reid stepped from the elevator at 5:48 a.m.

"Good morning," Reid said.

"Is it?"

"Rough night, huh?" Reid said. "Me too."

"At least I finished the book I've been reading."

"How was it?"

Hunter's nose wrinkled as she looked upwards with squinting eyes, "You know what? I have absolutely no idea. Seriously, my mind is a blank. This is all so damn difficult to deal with, I can't even think straight."

Reid nodded. "I understand. Shane and I were up all night too. I thought I was going to throw up."

"At least you only thought it."

"Really?"

As Hunter bobbed her head, Colodny walked through the lobby entrance and approached. "Mornin'. Ready, Reid?"

"Sure." Reid turned to Hunter. "I'll see you in a little while. Why don't you go up and hang out with Shane after your walk."

"What? You thought I came down this early to go for a walk? No, I'm coming with you."

"No, you're—"

"Stop. Don't even say it. I am coming. I will stay out of the way. But there is no way I'm staying here while you're out there trying to save Peter's life. I need to be there when you get him."

Reid looked at Colodny, who shrugged.

"Okay, let's roll," Reid said.

***

Blinded by the glaring sunlight, Reid lowered his tinted goggles down over his eyes from their perch on his bulletproof helmet. The helmet was surprisingly comfortable except for the protective neck-curtain that hung from the sides and back. The curtain covered the gap between the helmet and the vest, making turning his head very awkward. The built-in wireless communication system would make taking the kidnapper's call easier, and it would allow him to communicate with Jay.

Despite the partly cloudy morning, the snow reflected and intensified the rising sun's glare. Reid didn't even notice the minus twenty-one degrees Celsius temperature.

When the kidnapper called late the previous night, Reid had been ready for his instructions. He now stood in a field of snow on top of the mountain, waiting for the next call. Light-headed, he needed to get accustomed to the high altitude, as well as being on skis again. It had been a while, and the extra 100 pounds on his back didn't help. Although he was confident in his abilities, his nerves were frayed. He hadn't had much sleep. Getting the money took longer than anyone thought, and so did packing it.

Shortness of breath, nauseating dizziness, and eyes still getting accustomed to the harsh glare were an overload on his senses. He felt lightheaded and barely heard two rapidly approaching snowmobiles behind him. As he began to turn toward the noise, he heard one of the machines backfire, or so he thought. A crushing blow in the center of his back slammed him forward, gasping for air. His ski boots were locked into the bindings on his skis, causing him to twist as he fell. Landing face down, he struggled hard to catch his breath in the deep snow.

Powerless to stop his attackers, they easily yanked the backpack off his back, and he felt a searing pain go through him. He now realized what sent him face down into the snow was a gunshot. Reid could barely move his arms. He desperately needed oxygen as his last breath had been expunged from his lungs upon the impact of the shot. He'd had the breath knocked out of him many times from blows to his sternum but never from behind. He turned his scattered thoughts to the chatter of voices coming through his speakers. Unable to comprehend a word, he focused on a consistent low-pitched sound he was hearing. *What is that? Another engine? Jay?* Slowly it dawned on him that it was a long, agonizing moan, emanating from deep within his core as he expelled the last bit of air still held in his lungs. "I can't breathe," he groaned, hoping Jay was listening.

The next sound he heard of more approaching snowmobiles provided a little relief. Help was on the way. Fighting his overwhelming pain, he struggled to turn his head to the side and saw two snowmobiles race by, each with a driver and passenger, and a skier being towed by a rope. The passengers and those in tow carried automatic rifles.

As Jay's team passed Reid, they opened fire upon his assailants. Reid watched, dumbstruck. His dire pain was held at bay by surging adrenaline. *This is insane,* he thought. *Like watching a Bond movie, only it's real.*

***

Jay and his team fired their weapons continuously as the engines of their powerful sleds wailed loudly in chase. The unchanging direction of the assailant's machines as they headed directly for the edge of the upcoming cliff had everyone perplexed. They were going much too fast for a last-minute turn. Jay watched curiously as the two snowmobiles launched over the edge.

Jay arrived at the edge just in time to see the snowmobiles crash into the boulders below. He watched from above as Reid's attacker's parachutes burst open, slowing their freefall. One chute opened into a billowing, rectangular canopy. The other rider was not so lucky. Maybe it was due to the extra weight of the money-filled backpack dangling from a clip near his waist, or possibly it was from the bullet holes in his chute, but whatever the reason, his parachute opened in a twisted, lopsided, rectangular figure eight. It began to spin slowly, then quickly picked up speed. It was soon rotating so fast that the man attached was being whipped round and round, in a wide, sweeping arc.

At first glance, the man whose chute had opened correctly seemed to be dropping at a normal pace. Then, as Jay focused his binoculars, holes in the parachute became evident. The skydiver's rate of descent was being greatly enhanced by large tears in his bullet-hole riddled chute. Despite the ripstop nylon, the increasing speed was widening the tears. Alas, he was caught in a deadly vicious cycle; every inch he dropped caused the holes to enlarge, which in turn, increased his speed, ripping the chute even faster.

As Jay watched from the edge of the cliff, he lifted his radio and redirected the approaching chopper. "Forget about the assailants, they're doomed. Go get Reid."

A minute later, watching from a distance, Jay was somewhat relieved that Reid refused to be placed on a stretcher and was slowly climbing aboard the chopper with only a little help from his rescuer. Yet, grief and guilt gnawed at Jay. Once again, Reid had been shot on Jay's watch, and Peter was still missing.

"Thank God for that vest," Jay said to himself, with his communication system turned off.

Chapter 26

IRRITATED AND ORNERY, Reid could not get comfortable in his hospital bed. Laying on his back was out of the question. Lying on either side hurt like hell. He was tired of lying on his stomach, but he had no choice. The vest had saved his life. The bullet hadn't punctured his skin, but the force of it had badly bruised his back.

Shane grimaced as she said, "It's a raised blood-red welt surrounded by a ring of black that fades into deep purple and slowly to a puke-ish green-yellow." She delicately replaced the sheet over him.

"I guess I'm glad I can't see it," Reid whispered. "Even talking hurts like hell."

"I'm beginning to think I married a human target. Not only have you been shot twice, but now you literally have a target on your back. Seriously, it looks like a tattoo."

There were two light knocks on the door, "Come in," Reid whispered, too softly for anyone except his wife to hear.

"Come in," Shane repeated, reaching for Reid's hand to quiet and comfort him.

Buck and Jay entered. Buck placed a paper bag on the rolling tray table next to Reid's bed. "There are a couple of croissants in there."

"Thanks," Reid whispered.

"How are you feeling?" Buck asked.

"I don't think I'll be swinging a golf club anytime soon."

"Can I look?" Jay asked, reaching for the sheet. Pressure from the weight of the blanket that had been covering Reid earlier had been too much to bear.

"Yeah, but be gentle, please."

"Let me do it, Jay," Shane said.

Jay pulled his hands back and gave an understanding nod.

Shane slowly lifted the top edge of the sheet high and away from Reid's back and gently lowered it onto his legs.

Buck let out a whistle, "Whew, that's mean-looking."

Even Jay shuddered a little.

"Lovely, huh?" Shane said.

"Well, sorry to use a cliché, but you should see the other guys," Jay said.

"Tell me," Reid said with some excitement and a grimace. "Ow." Shane took his hand, again.

"Well, to start with, they were not very smart. They told you to put the money in a backpack, and then they shot you in the back, right through it. Who the hell would put holes through money that they are stealing? Why they felt they needed to shoot you in the first place still baffles me. I mean two guys with guns versus one unarmed man. Like I said, not too smart.

"Anyway, you'll like the rest of this. One guy's parachute was filled with holes from our gunfire. He dropped fast and landed on some high-power electric wires. Charred human flesh really stinks," Jay said, fanning his hand in front of his nose.

"That's gross," Shane said.

"You got that right," Jay murmured.

"What about the other guy?" Reid asked quietly.

"Ah yes, the spinner." Jay was having some fun. "His chute opened in somewhat of a figure eight. It spun and whipped him around in a big arc. He slammed face-first into the cliff. It cracked his helmet and didn't do his face much good either. It crushed his nose, broke all his front teeth and his jaw. Then, he fell like a rag doll the rest of the way, bouncing off rock after rock. His body was a twisted heap when we got to him. Both of his legs are broken. One's a bloody, compound fracture. His left arm is broken, his shoulder is dislocated, and a bunch of his ribs are cracked. He's lucky to be alive."

Jay looked at Shane. "Here's the hard news. Pompard and I had a few words with him before they sedated him. Sorry to say this, but it looks like they had nothing to do with Peter's disappearance, just opportunists trying to cash in."

"I want to talk to him when he wakes up," Reid said quietly.

"We'll see," Jay said.

"Bullshit. Ow." Reid winced.

"Shhh," Shane said. "Take it easy, honey."

"Don't tell me to take it easy," he whispered bitterly. "This is the second time I've been shot. I never got a chance to speak with the first shooter. I'll be damned if I don't get my chance with this one."

"Okay, okay," Jay said. "I had no idea you were harboring these feelings, but I understand. I'll take you to him when his sedation wears off and he can talk."

Reid's nod was barely perceptible.

There was another knock on the door. Buck opened it enough to see Hunter and Peter's parents. All three were sniffling and wiping red, teary eyes as they solemnly entered.

Hunter approached Reid, and as she bent to kiss him, she placed her hand on his shoulder. He scowled and let out an awful moan.

Hunter jumped back, horrified. "Oh my God. I'm so sorry." She covered her face with her hands and started to cry. The added emotion of guilt had pushed her over the edge.

Shane hugged her, peering over Hunter's shoulder at Reid. He returned a look that confirmed he was in pain but okay, best to take care of Hunter, who could not stop sobbing. Shane led her to a chair near the window, knelt beside her, and held her hand.

As Hunter's tears began to subside, Dan and Carole Buckar walked to Reid's bedside. They both knelt to be face to face with him. Carole took his hand in hers and said, "Hunter told us what you did for Peter."

"Reid, we are so sorry this happened," Dan said.

"It's okay," Reid said quietly. "I'll be all right. Really, I will. Nothing's broken. I will be fine." Carole squeezed his hand, and Reid softly added, "Look, everyone, I do not want this to become about me. You all need to concentrate on finding Peter. Dan, Carole, do you guys know Jay Scott? He's standing behind you."

After introductions, Jay brought the Buckars up to speed on the investigation.

When Jay finished his explanation, Dan Buckar crossed his arms and said harshly, "So, ultimately, what I'm hearing is that we have a ton of people looking for him, but we still have absolutely no idea where he is."

Carole reached for her husband's arm. "Easy, honey."

Dan pulled his arm away from her. "Easy? Are you kidding me? Our son was kidnapped, and nobody has any fucking idea where he is. I don't know much about kidnapping, but I do know that time is *not* on our side. Every day, make that every minute that goes by decreases our chances of finding him alive."

Carole's hand covered her mouth. She was fighting back tears. In a trembling voice, she said, "Please don't say that. I know it's true, but negativity won't help. It just gets everyone upset."

Hunter's tears were flowing again.

"Upset? Do you know what gets me upset? Wasting precious time, that's what." Dan stormed toward the door.

"Dan, stop. Where are you going?" Carole asked.

"To look for our son before it's too late. I can't just wait around hoping for the best." He put his hand on the doorknob, then turned and looked at Carolee. "You can come with me, or you can stay here."

Carole hesitated, and Dan left the room. She turned to the others and stoically said, "I'm sorry!" Then she walked out the door.

Shane broke the following silence. "He's right. You should all go."

"Yes," Reid whispered. "Don't stay here on my behalf. Go find him."

Chapter 27

THE FIGHT ON the snowy street in Chamonix had been quick but brutal. People in the street stopped to stare in horror as two top skiers looked set to kill each other.

Jeff Edwards, the quietest and most mild-mannered member of the US ski team, had been walking back from his late afternoon workout when he passed by Vilhelm Dinaso being interviewed on the street by a television reporter.

Edwards stopped dead in his tracks as he heard Dinaso exclaim, "Upset? No way. It is the same as if he crashed and couldn't race because he was hurt. Now the Olympic downhill Gold is as good as mine. Of course, it was always mine, anyway. Dead or alive, it doesn't matter to me. I would still beat him."

Besides being one of Peter's closest friends, Edwards was America's top slalom racer. Peter and he had been training side by side every day for the past few years. The two ate nearly all their meals together when the team traveled.

Hearing Dinaso's remark caused something within Edwards to snap. He charged Dinaso, yelling, "You asshole." Edwards was five inches taller than Dinaso, so when he lowered his head, it slammed into Dinaso's face, breaking his nose. Blood spewed everywhere. After crashing to the ground, Dinaso reached for his nose. The sight of his own blood-covered hands fueled his rage. He jumped to his feet and immediately spun into a roundhouse kick. The steel toe of Dinaso's boot connected with the side of Edwards's head. His neck twisted, and he lost his footing on an icy patch on the street. He dropped to the ground, and the back of his head slammed against the pavement.

The TV camera had recorded the fight. As the camera zoomed in on Edwards's limp body, it was clear there was no movement. A small crowd was forming around Edwards. A middle-aged, gray-haired woman knelt next to him and took his wrist in her hand.

"He needs a doctor," she yelled. "I can't feel a pulse."

Gasps of shock ricocheted throughout the crowd.

Shrill whistles sounded as two officers pushed through the throng. "Move aside," one said while the other radioed for an ambulance.

Crouching, one of the officers took hold of Edwards's wrist, waited a moment, then moved his hand to Edwards's neck. He stood and asked, "Did anyone see what happened?"

"He kicked him," a man said, pointing at Dinaso.

Dinaso turned to walk away.

"Stop. Don't take another step." The officer walked briskly to Dinaso. "Place your hands behind your back. You are under arrest."

"Arrest? For what?" Dinaso asked sarcastically.

"Murder."

The onlookers gasped.

"Murder? Are you crazy? We just had a stupid little fight."

The officer looked at his colleague, who was still kneeling next to Edwards. Blood was trickling from Edward's head into the snow. "Any pulse?"

The officer shook his head. "He's gone."

"Turn around and put your hands behind your back."

"This is absurd. It was self-defense. Look what he did to my face."

"I see," the officer said as he placed cuffs on Dinaso. "He broke your nose, so you killed him. This is what you call self-defense?" He clamped the cuffs tight.

"Hey, what the hell? That hurts."

Dinaso's father, who had been standing next to him, smacked his son in the back of his head. "Shut up! Keep your damn mouth closed until I get you a lawyer."

The arriving ambulance sounded off short siren blasts that parted the now massive crowd. Word of the incident was spreading rapidly. Soon additional officers arrived to keep onlookers at a distance.

Joining the crowd were several ski racers from various countries. Edwards had been well liked on the circuit, and as word spread of his demise, skiers started following Dinaso as he was led to a police car.

"What did you do, you asshole?"

"You son of a bitch."

"Things weren't bad enough around here?"

"Why the hell did you kill Edwards?"

The police stepped back as the skiers surrounded Dinaso and began shoving and punching him. As the senior Dinaso pushed them away, he yelled, "Leave him alone. Officers, help!"

As the aggression of the skiers and the crowd escalated, the officers began to push people aside. After the ambulance departed, Dinaso was shoved into a police vehicle, but the crowd remained, everyone talking about the tragedy.

Stan Williams and Dave Colodny came running from around the corner of a building and quickly approached some of their racers. "We heard a racer was hurt," Colodny said, addressing Rod Kaufman, the closest American skier nearby. "Who was it?" asked Colodny.

"You don't know?" Kaufman asked. He turned his head toward his fellow racers anxiously.

"Know what?" Williams asked. "What is with the look, Kaufman? What happened?"

Kaufman stiffened and stared at his coaches silently. His Adam's apple moved up and down as he swallowed hard.

"Well?"

"Coach, uh, I don't know how to tell you this."

"Just spit it out!" Colodny looked at the others curiously. Their stunned faces worried him; some were wiping tears from their eyes. "Will someone please tell us what the hell happened?"

"Jeff Edwards is dead, Coach," blurted out a shaky Ethan Silverman.

"What are you saying? That's ridiculous," snapped Colodny.

"I'm not joking. I saw it. Dinaso was talking trash about Peter, and Edwards went at him, and then Dinaso kicked him in the head. Jeff fell hard onto the street and wasn't moving. The cops said he was … dead." Tears flowed down Silverman's cheeks. "They just took him away in an ambulance, and the cops arrested Dinaso."

The news struck a blow to Williams, who exclaimed, "Oh my God." His eyes welled up, and he repeated, "Oh my God." His team was more than just a group of racers to him, they were family. Each racer was like a son to him. And now he had lost two.

Tearing up himself, Colodny placed a comforting hand on Williams' shoulder. He managed to take in the fact that several TV news reporters were walking towards them, their cameras rolling. "Ethan, Rod, take Stan back to the hotel. In fact, all of you go with them. Make sure the cameras do not film him. And don't say a word to the press. We will meet up … later. I need to …" Colodny was having trouble getting the words out clearly. "Take him to his room or to the bar, whichever he prefers. I have to find Jay Scott. He needs to know about this."

Chapter 28

NEWS OF THE fight and Edwards' subsequent death traveled through Chamonix as rapidly as an avalanche of fresh snow. In every bar, restaurant, and café throughout the famous ski town, quiet discussions about the dead American skier and his missing friend could be overheard.

But there was one conversation, though, that had a different tone than most.

Two couples sat in a dimly lit, corner booth of a busy restaurant. They were dipping chunks of bread into a bubbling fondue pot. Antique wooden skis adorned the darkly stained, reclaimed barn board walls.

"This changes everything," one of the men said in Ukrainian. His long, blond hair was pulled in a tight ponytail, and a wispy soul patch covered a small spot just under his bottom lip. The lower half of a dark tattoo peeked from under the sleeve of the black t-shirt that hugged his muscular arm. Skinny, black jeans and black leather boots added to his menacing air.

"Of course it does. People are going to be totally confused. The wagers will be all over the board. We will make a fortune," the other man said quietly, a tiny smile forming at the edges of his mouth.

As the man with the ponytail lifted a speared chunk of bread from the heated pot and brought it to his mouth, a glob of melted cheese dripped onto his shirt. "Shit, I hate this stuff," he growled as he threw the fondue spear onto the table. The woman seated next to him tensed and began to wipe the gooey stain off his shirt with her napkin. The more she wiped, the worse the mess became. "Stop, you idiot. You're just making it worse." He grabbed her wrist and flung it off him. His muscular torso dwarfed her petite frame. A tear trickled down her cheek.

"Tears again?" he seethed. He stood abruptly and grabbed his leather jacket, and stomped off.

Chapter 29

HIDDEN BEHIND TREES, vehicles, and neighboring homes, thirty armed officers, mostly in raid gear, surrounded the house. They had remained out of sight until Pompard radioed the command, "*Allons. Allons!*"

Guns drawn, they rushed from all directions, smashed open all three entrance doors with high-impact, forcible entry devices, and stormed the house.

A swift, room-by-room search for Peter revealed nothing. The house was empty. Pompard yelled out a very discouraged, "*Claire*!"

Once outside, Pompard approached Jay. With frustration etched on his face, he kicked a metal trash can as he walked by it.

Jay's mood was no better. Intense hope had been crushed by the letdown of just another worthless lead.

False leads not only wasted valuable time, but they also wreaked havoc on the psyche of the search teams. Similar to many arsonists, the miscreants who called in these leads frequently positioned themselves nearby so they could watch the activity they caused.

Jay quickly discussed this possibility with Pompard, and they assembled a team to question the many onlookers and surrounding neighbors. The call from the informant had been made from a cell phone, and although they had not been able to trace its location, they did get the number. Jay told Pompard to position his men around the perimeter of the small crowd of onlookers and for the men to try to look as if they were packing up after the failed house raid.

Jay punched in the informant's number. The caller had said that Peter was being held in the house at the address they had just searched. Jay looked at Pompard still in front of him. "Ready?"

Pompard nodded.

Jay pressed the dial button, and the entire police team dropped what they were pretending to be doing and watched the crowd and listened. A cell phone chirped.

"That's probably our culprit," Jay said.

As the team rushed toward the sound of the phone, a man started running and knocking into people as he went. By the time he broke free of the crowd, two of Pompard's men were upon him. The closer officer dove and grabbed the runner's legs, tackling him fiercely to the ground.

The officers hauled the mid-height, thin, young man up, cuffed him, and dragged him to Pompard. Blood poured from his mouth, through his scraggly, dirt-filled beard, onto his shirt and open jacket. The fall had cracked one of his front teeth and knocked another out completely.

Pompard's rage peaked as he recognized the man. "Juneau, you bastard!" He clenched his fist and cocked his arm, ready to punch.

Jay grabbed Pompard's fist at its crest. "Don't. The media will bury you."

Pompard lowered his fist. He took a step forward, put his face inches from the bloodied man's face, and hissed, "I hope you enjoyed the show, you prick. Because this was your last one. Now you're going to rot in jail." He turned to his men. "Get him out of my sight."

Jay gave Pompard a moment to cool down, then said, "What was that all about?"

"He's been a pain in my ass for years. Mostly petty crimes. He's been in and out of my jails like they're his personal hotels. Last year he set off a hotel fire alarm just to watch the excitement it stirred. Didn't even use a glove. We lifted his prints from the pull station lever." Pompard shook his head and rolled his eyes. "He's an idiot, but the courts haven't been able to keep him behind bars for more than a few months. Until now, that is. Now, he's done."

"So, you don't think he has anything to do with Peter?"

"*Non,*" Pompard said in disgust.

Chapter 30

HORNS BLARED. IRATE drivers yelled obscenities in various languages. Skirmishes erupted as bumpers bumped and the traffic back-up grew. Every vehicle leaving Chamonix was being searched. With the Kandahar races over, and the Olympics only ten days away, most of the ski teams, as well as their families and fans, were in route to St. Moritz, the posh ski resort town in Switzerland and home of the 'Free Fall,' the steepest start of any downhill race course in the world.

Team Austria's custom bus had broken down, and due to a lack of available replacement vehicles, they were temporarily using an old school bus. They were next in line to be searched as the police rummaged through a Mercedes sedan. Whatever was found in the backseat of the Mercedes caused the police to slap handcuffs on the driver and his female passenger. An officer got into the vehicle and drove it to the side of the road. Two other officers began searching the contents of the trunk. A suitcase was yanked out and unzipped. It was so overstuffed, some of the plastic bags of white powder slid out onto the ground. The massive amount of drugs was going to put the couple behind bars for a long time.

Just as the bus was being waved forward to the checkpoint, the rear door swung open, and an Austrian racer in his red and black team jacket jumped down and started running. Hanging from his shoulder was a worn leather satchel. His getaway would have been easy if the vehicle two cars behind hadn't been an unmarked police SUV. As the skier ran by the side of the vehicle, the officer in the passenger seat swung his door open. The resulting thud of flesh and bone against metal and glass dropped the skier to his knees.

The officer stepped out of the vehicle and looked down. Some of the contents of the skier's open satchel had fallen out.

"What do we have here?" the officer asked as he picked up a small bottle of amber-colored liquid and a zip-lock bag containing a neatly bound bundle of syringes.

Dazed from hitting his head on the door, the skier looked up and said, "*Meine medizin.*"

The officer nodded. It was a potent anabolic steroid. He nudged the satchel with his boot, and similar bottles fell from the bag. A quick look inside revealed an impressive assortment of pills, vials, and more syringes.

The officer put on gloves, returned the spilled contents into the satchel, and placed it on the floor in front of his seat. He turned to the fallen young man who was still dazed from his fall. "You don't look very good. Why were you running?"

The officer in the driver's seat said, "What's the problem?"

"It looks to me like we have a racing doper who got spooked by the search. I'm pretty sure this bag is full of steroids."

The dazed skier made an unsuccessful attempt to stand, but it seemed the egg-sized lump on his forehead was causing some imbalance. He looked up at the officer and mumbled a few incoherent words.

The officer reached down and said, "Come on."

After a momentary look of defiance, the skier reached for his hand.

A quick, sturdy yank by the powerful officer brought the skier to his feet. The sudden movement was more than the skier's scrambled brains could handle. He began to fall, grabbed the car door, then bent over and vomited on the officer's black boots.

Jumping back, the officer hit his elbow hard on the door-frame. "Ow! Damn it!" he yelled, reaching for his elbow.

As the skier raised his head to apologize, he coughed and heaved again, this time covering the officer's chest and legs with another vile mess. With his back against the vehicle, the officer had no way to avoid the repulsive onslaught. Fuming, he pushed the skier away as his own gag reflexes kicked in, and he struggled to refrain from vomiting.

He grabbed the skier's arm, shoved him into the back seat, and slammed the door shut. After looking down at the hideous mess on his clothes, he said, "Unlock the rear door." His jacket, shirt, and pants were disgusting. Luckily, as an undercover officer, he kept extra clothes stashed in the storage area. He carefully removed his brand new expensive leather jacket that was now a slimy mess. He grabbed a shirt from his canvas duffel, glanced at the cars waiting in line behind him, and his chin fell to his chest. Then, having no choice, he practically ripped off his shirt and stood in his white undershirt while being scrutinized by the line of waiting traffic. Some of the onlookers honked. The officer's patience had long since evaporated. Without further thought, he kicked off his boots, dropped his pants, and quickly pulled on a clean pair of jeans. He threw the dirty items in the trunk, grabbed sneakers from his bag, and slammed the rear door closed. In just his socks, he walked to his still open door, carefully stepping over the putrid puddle. He sat and yanked his door shut.

His partner knew better than to say anything. He just opened his window. The rank odor in the vehicle was enough to make anyone gag.

After a moment of uncomfortable silence, the driver looked at his furious partner and said, "You calm enough to talk?"

"Yes."

"Okay, so now we have a new problem to deal with. Obviously, we can't go anywhere." He gestured toward the surrounding traffic. "And I'm not going to just sit in this stinking car, waiting to get through. As far as I see it, we have two possibilities, we can lock him in the car and go look for his coach on the bus. Or, we can call it in."

"If we call it in, we're just going to have to bring him back to the station. I don't want to be pulled off Buckar's search, do you?"

"No way!"

"Okay, let's go find the coach."

After they opened their doors, the driver leaned down, pushed a button, and lifted a lever at the bottom of the dashboard. A thick bulletproof glass shield rose behind their seats up to the ceiling, and the rear doors locked. From the inside, the locks were redundant as the rear doors had no internal hardware. Even Houdini would have had trouble exiting the vehicle. As the officers got out, they both looked at the skier sprawled out in the back. "Why do you think he threw up?" the driver asked.

"Head trauma, I guess. Did you see the lump on his forehead? I didn't mean to hurt him, I just wanted to stop him. I guess I overdid it," he said with a shrug. "C'mon let's get this over with."

As they approached the bus entrance, one of the two uniformed officers near the door said, "Henry, Jean. What are you doing here?"

"We were waiting in the traffic just behind the bus, and we had a little incident," Henry, the driver, replied. "Where is the coach of this team?"

"Why?" the other uniformed officer asked.

"We've got one of his racers locked in our vehicle. We stopped him after he jumped out of the bus's back door and ran.

He was attempting to avoid the search. It seems he's the team's pharmacist. He's got enough steroids in his bag to supply an army."

"Damn," the second officer said, looking dismayed.

"What's the matter?" Henry asked.

"I'm just disappointed that ski racing has stooped to that level."

"Ski racing and every other sport, it seems," Henry said. "Is the coach on board?"

"Yes. Give me a minute. I'll go get him, so we don't disrupt the search."

The officer stepped up into the bus and returned a minute later with a tall, wiry man in a dark blue parka and a red and white knit hat.

The coach stepped to the ground. "You want to speak with me?"

"Have you noticed that one of your team members is not on the bus?" Henry said.

With a look of doubt, the coach said, "No. They're all here. I took attendance when we left the hotel earlier. Why?"

"Because we have one of your men locked in an SUV behind the bus."

"That can't be."

"Come see for yourself."

"No," the coach said, turning to get on the bus. "I'll go take a headcount. I'm telling you, they are all here."

Henry reached for the coach's elbow and said, "And I'm telling you, you're wrong. Just come with us. It'll be much faster."

The coach sharply pulled his arm from Henry's grip. "Please keep your hands off me, officer."

Henry backed off quickly. "Just minutes ago, my partner and I saw one of your skiers jump out the back door of the bus, just as it was about to be searched. We apprehended him, and he's now in our vehicle. He has what appears to be a bag full of steroids and possibly some other drugs."

The coach's eyes opened wide. "I hope you are mistaken."

Without another word, Henry, Jean, and the coach walked back to the SUV. The coach took a quick look in the backseat, and outrage swept across his face. He grabbed the door handle and yanked. The locked handle snapped from his grasp loudly without budging the door.

Jean walked over, opened the front passenger door, and reached for the satchel. As he turned and lifted it toward the coach, he said, "Take a look at this before you speak with him." Jean opened the leather bag revealing the contents.

The coach looked then started to reach in.

The officer snatched it away. "Non, this is going to the lab."

"Let me at least look before you take him away," he said, peering at the vials and syringes. He asked the officer to raise the bottle so he could read the label. The syringes didn't need close inspection.

"You have no way of knowing they are his," said the coach.

"He jumped from that door." Jean pointed toward the bus. "Carrying this bag, and started running. I can't imagine he would be making a run for it if this belonged to someone else."

The coach shrugged.

"There are more drugs in the bag as well. Here, take a look." Jean pulled the bag open further, giving the coach a clear view.

Looking in, the coach shook his head slowly. "Shit, I can't believe this." He looked up at Jean. "Can I speak with him?"

"Yes. We would like you to confirm his identity. Walk to the rear window, and I'll open it. I just want you to know that I think he has a concussion, and he smells pretty bad."

The awful smell of vomit coming off the young man was overwhelming.

Chapter 31

"DAMN IT!" DIGIACOMO shouted as he hurled his phone in a fit of anger. The phone smashed to pieces as it hit the wall, making yet another dent in the pine paneling. His second conversation with his cousin, Benito, revealed things that Sal could hardly believe.

He turned to Joey, his *consigliere*, who was already removing a brand new, prepaid phone from a stack of them on the closet shelf. "Son of a bitch. Benito thinks this was a family thing. The father of an Italian racer is a *soldato* in the 'Ndrangheta organization. His kid hasn't won a medal this season, and the father is always mouthing off, blaming Buckar. That's fucking ridiculous. There's nothing worse than a sore loser. Right?"

Joey pulled the new phone from the box without responding.

"Come on," DiGiacomo yelled. "Hurry up."

"I'm trying," Joey said under his breath, "If you'd stop throwing the damn things so often …" Joey caught a glimpse of DiGiacomo's heinous stare.

Few things scared Joey "Batman" Bertone as much as DiGiacomo's menacing stare. Joey's nickname stemmed from both his love of baseball and his handiwork with a bat on people. Yet, while he was ruthless, he wasn't nearly as coldblooded as DiGiacomo had been in *his* prime.

Without another word, Joey lowered his head, avoiding DiGiacomo's eyes while he anxiously worked on the phone. He removed the SIM card and battery from the broken phone and installed them in the new one as DiGiacomo tapped his knuckles impatiently on the arm of his chair. As soon as the phone was ready, DiGiacomo grabbed it and searched for the number he wanted to call.

"Dante, it's Sal. I need some quick research." He listened. "No, you'll have to cancel your trip. This needs to be done now. I need you to go to Calabria. Find out if the disappearance of Peter Buckar, the American skier, was a 'Ndrangheta thing." He listened again. "I know. You need to be discreet. I don't want to start a family war. Just find out what you can. If they are involved, I want to know if Buckar is alive or dead. If he's alive, I want to know where he is." Once again, he listened. "*Grazie.* Be quick and be quiet. Contact Vincenzo when you get there, he'll help you. I'll let him know you're on your way. Call me as soon as you know anything." Sal hung up.

He quickly searched for another name on the phone and tapped it. "Jay, it's Sal. Call me as soon as you can."

After ending the call, Sal looked at Joey. "You don't think they'd kill him, do you? I mean, come on, it's the fucking Olympics, they're like sacred. This has to be outside the family business. Since when does a guy get whacked for anything other than money or revenge? If Buckar is dead and it was a hit, there's no way it was sanctioned."

"You know things are done a little differently in the old country, Boss. Especially by the 'Ndranghetas," Joey said.

"Yeah, but I have a hard time believing that anyone would condone a hit just so an Italian racer can win a race."

"You said it yourself. Many Italians are as fanatical about ski racing as they are about soccer. Plus, lately, I've been hearing that a lot of *soldato* in Italy are getting trigger happy. Who knows if it was approved or not, but I could see this being a family job."

Sal stared at Joey for a moment, then slowly began to shake his head. "No, Joey, I don't even want to think that way. Buckar's gotta be alive. It'd make me sick if he's dead. Nobody has the right to kill a world-class athlete like him."

Sal noticed Joey's doubtful look. "What's the look for?"

"Nuthin'"

"Don't give me that crap. What was the damn look for?"

Joey shrugged. "You almost offed Buckar yourself. You went as far as giving the order, and then you retracted it. I had to go stop Tommy V. before he whacked him. Did you forget about that?"

"How the fuck could I forget it? That was different. Buckar spoke out against me. No one does that, especially in public. He embarrassed me on live TV."

"So why'd you stop the hit?"

"Cause when I thought about it, I realized that Buckar's got bigger balls than most of my guys. He's tough enough to ski like a crazy sonofabitch, and he's got enough heart to stand up to me. Not the smartest thing a guy can do, but I had to respect him for it."

"If you say so."

"What, you don't agree?"

"I don't know, boss. Seems to me, if I embarrassed you publicly, you'd put a bullet in my head without a second thought."

DiGiacomo raised his brow. He contemplated Joey's words for a second and nodded. "Maybe you're right, but then you're not about to win a bunch of Olympic gold medals for your country, are you?"

"Ha! That's for sure."

The phone rang. DiGiacomo looked at the screen, and answered, "Hi Jay. You're not gonna believe this."

Chapter 32

JAY ENDED HIS call, and then looked at Reid and Buck. "That was DiGiacomo."

"I figured," Buck said.

"He's been talking to his friends in Italy. He thinks the mafia may be responsible. A father of one of Italy's racers is connected. He may have put a hit out on Peter in order to give his son a better chance in the Olympics."

"What? That's insane," Reid said, wincing. He was lying on his side. His bruise still prevented him from lying on his back. But he couldn't stand being on his stomach any longer. The pain meds were making him nauseous, so he had stopped taking them. Which meant even his slightest movement caused severe pain. Even speaking was painful.

Buck looked at Reid. "You sure you don't want a painkiller?"

Reid's nod was barely perceptible.

Buck shook his head. "I really think you'd be better off. It hurts just watching you." Buck lifted the tiny, paper medicine cup from the tray nearby and offered Reid the pill in it.

"Shane said the same thing just before she left earlier," Reid whispered just before putting the pill in his mouth and swallowing it. After drinking from a straw in the cup Buck held close to him, Reid said, "Do you really think the mafia would kill him, Jay?"

"No, I don't. If they were going to kill him, they would have done it in the hospital. They wouldn't have gone through the trouble of moving him. Hopefully, if it is a mafia thing, they'll just hold him until after the Olympics, then let him go. Truthfully, it all seems pretty far-fetched to me. I just wish we knew more."

"Well, don't waste your time here," Reid said. "Go find him."

"You want me to stay?" Buck asked.

"No. I think I'll try to get some sleep."

"All right, feel better. We'll be back later."

Just as Buck and Jay opened the door to leave, Shane returned.

"Hey, how are you holding up?" Buck asked.

"I'm okay. How's my human target?"

Jay sighed.

"He's in a lot of pain," said Buck. "I got him to take a pill. He asked us to leave so he could get some sleep."

Shane nodded. "I picked up a couple of books to read to him. It should put him to sleep in no time."

"What books?" Jay asked.

She held them up. "*The One Man* and *The Boys In The Boat.*"

"I loved *The Boys In The Boat*," Buck said. "Good choice. Reid will like it."

"All right," Jay said. "Let's go. We have work to do."

Chapter 33

HOLDING A TIGHT, mid-air tuck after pre-jumping the last ridge of the downhill course, Peter landed near the bottom of the steep drop with enough time to set the inside edge of his right ski for the approaching, hard, left turn. He was totally in the zone. His run so far had been flawless.

Resuming his tuck, his thighs burned as he soared down the final descent and across the finish line. Turning in a hard, snow spraying arc and stopping at the end of the corralled finish area, his adrenaline rush was explosive.

What an amazing run! he thought. *If only it was real instead of on this damn simulator.*

After releasing his ski boot from the bindings on the simulator, he stepped away. His emotional high from virtually skiing a near-perfect run vanished as he looked at his surroundings.

He still had no idea why he was in this room or who was holding him. His captors had yet to speak with him or show their faces. All communications had been through the television. His meals were either delivered through a slot in the door or waiting on the table next to him when he awoke. They removed his dirty dishes and soiled laundry while he slept. The clothes would be cleaned, folded, and stacked neatly on a chair near the door when he woke up.

They informed him that if he kept training and eating right, everything would be fine. They wouldn't say anything more, regardless of how often Peter asked questions.

While awake, anxiety and tension consumed him. His thoughts swung between fear for his life and anger at being held captive.

Until the past few nights, he had looked forward to sleeping, as it was the only time his brain seemed to set aside his torment. But a repetitive nightmare had begun to wake him each time he fell asleep. He dreamt that he was Kathy Bates' hostage in the movie, Misery, in which Bates tortures James Caan while he's strapped to a bed. Peter jolted awake each time Bates raised the sledgehammer to smash his feet. It took a few minutes for his heart rate and breathing to return to normal. Tired as he was, currently, sleep was not his friend. Once Bates and Stephen King were purged from his mind, his thoughts would return to who was holding him and why.

They obviously have a lot of money, he thought. *This room is so big, the house must be enormous, and all this high-end equipment had to cost a fortune.* He thought about the prices of the lateral ski trainer, the elliptical, the exercise bike, the treadmill, and the multifunction weight training machine. Losing count, he thought, *and all those together can't be anywhere near the price of that simulator.*

He had never trained on anything quite like it. The simulator's hydraulic platform moved in conjunction with the video, as well as Peter's bodily activity. Automatically adjusting high-speed fans simulated wind resistance as Peter skied down the virtual racecourse.

As upset as he was with his whole situation, he figured fighting it would be foolish. If he was going to be confined, why not make the best of it. Things could be worse than eating well and training hard. But, if the opportunity arose, he would escape and run for his life.

So far, no such opportunity had presented itself. As he sat and began unbuckling his ski boots, his thoughts meandered. *Hunter must be devastated. Her, my folks, Buck, Reid … they all probably think I'm dead. How long has it been anyway*? With no windows or a clock, he'd had no way to keep track of time. *How long have I been here? How long was I in that dingy room with the rats?* Just the thought of it sent a shiver through him.

Was it days? Weeks? No, probably not weeks. There was no intravenous feeding tube in me when I woke up the first time. Or was there? He looked down at his forearms and slowly rubbed them. The inner crook of his left elbow had a small red mark. Was *the red mark from a needle? Damn, maybe they were drugging me intravenously.* He rubbed the spot with his right thumb.

Maybe I have been here for a long time. He looked up at nothing in particular, deep in thought. He couldn't remember much. *I'm pretty sure I crashed in a race. Yea,* he thought, *it was the Kandahar. Oh my God, that means the Olympics must be very soon. Or, did I miss them already? No, if these guys wanted me out of the Olympics, they probably wouldn't have all this equipment here. They obviously want me to keep working out. They probably want me to race somewhere and soon.*

He sighed heavily with his head hung low. Like every professional ski racer, Peter lived for the Olympics. His one shot to really make a name for himself. *Why did all this happen now?* The more he thought about it, the more distraught he became. Missing the Olympics would be his ultimate letdown. Exasperated, Peter lay down on the bed. His mind began to run away with thoughts. *Years of hard work and preparation all down the drain. Will I ever see Hunter or my family again?* His eyes welled up, and tears began to moisten the pillow. Tough as he was, every man has his breaking point. He covered his face with his hands as his tears escalated to chest-heaving sobs.

Chapter 34

"EIGHT NEW LEADS have been called in, all anonymous," said Chamonix police chief, Pompard, to Jay.

Pompard's small office was sparse. A wooden desk and chair, two metal file cabinets, and a few pictures on the wall summed up the décor. Buck stepped up to look at the pictures. One was of Pompard with some of his officers, another was of him in a tuxedo with his bride, and the last was of him on skis next to another gentleman. Buck looked closely at it and smiled.

"Ah," Pompard said. "You recognize Jean Claude Killy."

"Of course. He dominated alpine skiing many years ago. He was a true champion."

"Around here, he's a legend."

"Knock it off. That legend won't help us find Peter," Jay grumbled.

"Let's not get too ornery, Pal," Buck said.

Jay sighed. "Sorry, I'm just aggravated by those false leads. I don't mean to take it out on you."

"I understand."

"What did I tell you? The minute this thing hit the papers, the whackos slither out from under their rocks. Now we have to figure out how to prioritize the leads. This investigation is complicated enough, and now these idiots call in just for kicks. Such a waste of valuable time."

"You want me to pull the men together for a meeting to-night?" Pompard asked.

"No, let's wait until tomorrow evening. Let everyone work their leads. Bringing them in now will just break up their momentum."

"Agreed. So what have you learned so far?" Pompard asked.

They brought each other up to speed. Then, after discussing the improvement of Reid's condition after the shooting and the fate of his attackers, Jay handed over a picture of the woman who had been stalking Peter.

"She's attractive," Pompard said, staring at the picture. "Disturbing, but attractive."

Jay nodded. "I look forward to questioning her as soon as we find her."

"I will have this posted immediately," Pompard said.

"Good," Jay said. "Her eyes give her a bit of a crazed look. Maybe she's nuts enough to kidnap a top skier out of a hospital?"

"You really think so?" Buck's face looked dubious.

"I've seen stranger things. If she's nutty enough to follow him around for however long she's been at it, she just might be crazy enough to want him all for herself."

"Now, *that* is disturbing," Buck said. "Sounds like the makings for a horror movie."

"If you think about it, Reid's death threats, Bob's murder at AllSport, and now this, all seem more like a movie than reality. I've told you, Buck. When I retire, I'm going to write a series of novels based on my investigations."

"I'll be happy to help," Buck said. "But for now, as you said, let's just focus on the task at hand."

"Touché."

Pompard's phone rang. "*Allo.*" After listening for a moment, his head slumped. "Oh, come on. This is absurd," he moaned. He looked up and shook his head. "All right, call Arturo. Tell him we need some of his officers to help patrol the streets. We can't afford to pull our teams off the search. Call me back with an update." After hanging up, he looked at Jay. "The tension throughout Chamonix has heightened. There was another fight. A bunch of locals went after some Swiss guys."

"Anybody badly hurt?" Jay asked.

"No, just a broken nose. I'm bringing in more officers to patrol the streets. We have to put a stop to this nonsense."

"You need people? I can make some calls."

"No, I can get enough help from the police in our neighboring towns."

Jay nodded.

"Let's get this picture copied and circulated." He picked up the picture, stood, and took another look at the woman's face. "There's something about this woman's face. She looks familiar."

"Really? You think you know her?" Jay asked.

"No, I just think I've seen her. I'm not sure where." He studied the picture. "Ah, let's just go. I want to talk to our latest arrest, the Austrian skier, about his steroids."

"Steroids?" Jay asked.

"Yes. We've been busy. At one of our checkpoints, my men caught an Austrian skier with a sack full of drugs. It seems most are steroids. He had vials of liquid, syringes, and some pills. He's not saying much. So far, all we know is that he's been supplying them to a few racers. Some Austrian, some Swiss."

Jay sighed. "Even skiers are juicing now? That's disappointing. Where is he?"

"Downstairs, in a cell. Right next to Dinaso."

"Good. How long will Dinaso be locked up?"

"He won't be here long. I'm sure his lawyer will argue for self-defense."

"Since when is kicking an unarmed man in the head with the steel toe of a boot self-defense? It may not have been murder, but there's no question about manslaughter."

"I guess we'll see how it unfolds. He's not saying a word until his lawyer arrives."

"Let's go have a chat with them. Maybe between us, we can get some information from one or the other."

"I could see Dinaso wanting Peter out of the way," Pompard said. "But steroids? Do you really think there could be a connection between them and Peter's abduction?"

"Let's go find out," Jay said.

***

Lenhard Wolff, the Austrian racer and keeper of the steroid bag, was sitting on a metal chair at a table in the center of a small interrogation room. The red lump on his forehead had grown.

Pompard followed Buck and Jay into the room and gave the thick, soundproof, metal door a hard shove behind him. After it closed with a loud clank, Buck took in their surroundings. Dull beige paint covered the concrete block walls. Where the beige had chipped away, there were layers of blue, and brown. The room was bare except for a large, two-way surveillance window. The three men took seats across the small table from Wolff. A uniformed officer stood a few feet behind him. Wolff placed his handcuffed wrists on the metal table with the look of a pleading puppy.

"You want those removed?" Pompard asked.

"*Ja*," he said, holding up his hands toward Pompard.

"Not so quickly," Pompard continued. "First, you need to answer some questions."

Wolff's look of hope faded. "What do you want to know?"

"Let's start with the drugs. Who are they for?"

"Me."

"*Monsieur* Wolff, you want the cuffs off, yet you lie on your very first answer. You're familiar with the tactic known as 'good cop, bad cop,' *oui*?"

Wolff gave a slight nod.

"Well, I'm the good cop here. Although, if you would prefer, I'll introduce you to my American counterpart, Monsieur Scott."

Jay gave Wolff a menacing stare.

Wolf flinched then directed his full attention to Pompard.

"Your cooperation will determine the level of leniency regarding your possession charges," Pompard said. "*D'accord*?"

Wolff took a deep breath and nodded.

"Tell you what, Mr. Wolff" Pompard continued. "For every answer you give me, I will ratchet your cuffs one click. For each answer I like, I will loosen them one notch. For each answer I do not like, I will tighten them a notch. Answer enough questions properly, and the cuffs will come off quickly."

Not receiving any response from Wolff, Pompard said, "Are you ready?"

"Ja."

"Who were the drugs for?"

"Me and a few other skiers."

"Names, please. I need names."

Wolff bit his bottom lip as he stared at Pompard. Closing his eyes, as if in shame, he quietly mumbled a few incoherent words.

"Louder," Pompard demanded.

"Jurgen Prock and Frederic Seifert."

"That's much better. I take it both are your teammates?"

Wolff let out a deep sigh. "Prock is. Seifert is on the Swiss team."

Pompard leaned over and placed a key in the handcuffs. He held both strands of one cuff and turned the key. After loosening two clicks, he removed the key. "Let's continue."

Wolff shrugged.

"While I'm sure there are many other names you could give me, I think we'll take a different direction for a moment. I've recently heard about some other skiers who use steroids. If you want the cuffs completely off, tell me what you know about Marcel Deluca."

"I don't think he uses."

"No? Okay, how about Thierry Lynn?"

"Ja, he uses."

"And you supply his drugs?"

"No."

"Come on, Lenhard. You want the cuffs off? Tell me the truth."

"That is the truth. I only get the stuff for myself and a few others. Do you think I'm the only source for the entire racing community? I promise you I am not."

Pompard just stared into Wolff's eyes for a moment.

"I swear, I'm telling the truth."

With a slight nod, Pompard said, "Okay, tell me about Jarrett Eschmann."

"No."

"What do you mean, no?" Pompard said irritably.

"No, *was* my answer. Eschmann is not a user."

"Oh." Pompard leaned over and loosened the handcuffs another notch.

"I thought you said a notch for every good answer. I have answered many more questions than that. Take them off already." Wolff held his wrists toward Pompard.

"They'll come off when I'm ready to take them off. Tell me about Peter Buckar."

"Buckar is a bastard," Wolff mumbled.

"Why?"

Wolff lowered his head, avoiding eye contact.

"Lenhard, talk to me. Does Buckar use steroids?"

"Ha! No way!" Wolff exclaimed aggressively. "He wouldn't touch them if you paid him." He winced and raised his cuffed hands to the lump on his forehead.

"What's wrong, Lenhard? Why are you so mad at Buckar?"

"Forget it."

"No, that's not how this works. Tell me what is behind your attitude toward Buckar?"

Despair crept onto Wolff's face, but his lips remained sealed.

Pompard grabbed Wolff's right arm and quickly tightened the cuff past the point of comfort. As he reached for the left arm, Wolff pulled his hands away. "Stop, I'll tell you."

Pompard waited while Wolff seemed to be building his courage. Again though, not a word.

"Okay, enough." Pompard stood quickly, knocking over his chair. He placed his fists on the table, knuckles down, and leaned over to glare into Wolff's eyes. "Tell me, now," he seethed.

"He threatened to turn us in," Wolff stammered, quickly leaning back and pulling his cuffed hands away.

"Who threatened who?"

"Buckar did. He threatened me, and …" Wolff's voice trailed off.

"And who?"

"Rodier. My teammate, Max Rodier. This is going to sound much worse than it is. It's going to sound like I had something to do with Peter's disappearance. I swear I had nothing to do with it. Someone told Buckar that Max and I were dealing steroids. He approached us in our hotel room just last week. He was very mad.

He blamed us for ruining the sport. He went on and on, saying that skiing should remain clean and steroid-free. What he didn't realize was that he was partially to blame. He's unbeatable. No one else has a chance when we're racing against him. He's like a machine. There aren't many people in this world who can control their bodies like Buckar. He's incredible."

Wolff stopped speaking.

"Don't tell me you're done," Pompard said.

Wolff looked at him, drew in a deep breath, and slowly shook his head. He closed his eyes and grimaced. After another deep breath, he said, "He threatened to blow the whistle on us. He said if we continued to supply the drugs, he'd tell the police, the Olympic Committee, even the media."

Pompard glanced at Jay and Buck. He then slowly turned his head back toward Wolff. "Okay, Mr. Wolff, tell us, where is Peter?"

"I have no idea. I told you, I had nothing to do with it."

Jay slammed his fist on the table, making a thundering noise. "He threatened to turn you in, and you expect us to believe that you just let him walk away!"

Wolf closed his eyes tightly, and again, he put his hands to his forehead. "My head is killing me."

"Tell us the truth!" Pompard demanded.

"I am telling you the truth. Buckar scared the hell out of me. All I know how to do is ski. I live to ski, and I ski to live. As long as I can make a living at it, I'm a happy man. If Buckar told anyone that I was selling steroids, my skiing career, and, as far as I'm concerned, my life, would be over. So I had to quit. I told Max that I was done. Max was annoyed with me for backing off so easily."

"Has Max continued to supply or say that he planned to?"

"I don't know. We didn't talk about it after that. He knew I was done with it, and he didn't bring it up again. It was only a few days ago."

"So why did you jump off the bus and run?"

"Are you kidding me? I just told you how I feel about skiing, right?"

Pompard nodded.

"Do you think my coaches would allow me to remain on the team if they knew I was selling steroids?"

"*Non.*"

"So what was I supposed to do? The bus was about to be searched. It's not like I could just throw the bag out the window in the middle of the traffic. I didn't have time to think it through. I figured I could go dump it someplace and then just get back on the bus."

"Why did you even have the bag on the bus? You just said that you quit dealing drugs."

"I didn't know what to do with them. I figured if I threw them in the trash at the hotel, a janitor would find them, and people would start asking too many questions. I was scared, so I held on to them, hoping I'd find the right time and place to get rid of them."

"Too bad it didn't work out that way."

Wolff shrugged.

"So, tell me about your friend Max."

"What about him?"

"How long have you known him?"

"I guess about ten years. He's been on the national team for two years, but we've competed against each other for a long time. We've only recently become friends, though."

"Does he have much money?"

"No, not really. His family is not so well off, but we don't need much as long as we're on the team. They cover pretty much whatever we need."

"Is he a good skier?"

Wolff nodded. “One of the best.”

“Is he expected to do well in the Olympics?”

Wolff squinted a little. “Wait a second. Where are you going with this?”

“It’s pretty simple, Lenhard. It sounds to me like your friend Max is much better off with Peter out of the way for two reasons.”

“There is no way Max kidnapped Peter. He’s … he’s not smart enough.”

“Not smart enough?”

“The truth is, he’s a complete idiot. The team often jokes that it’s probably why he’s such a great downhill racer. He’s not smart enough to be scared.”

The guard behind Wolff let out a quick laugh.

“Okay, we’re done for now,” Pompard said. He looked at the guard, “Please take him back to his cell.”

As the guard lifted Wolff’s arm, Wolff said, “Hey, what about the cuffs? You said if I …”

Pompard cut him off. “Remove the cuffs when you put him in his cell.”

The guard nodded and led Wolff from the room.

Pompard looked at Jay. “So?”

Jay rubbed his chin and said, “We need to speak with Max Rodier immediately.”

Pompard nodded.

“What is your gut telling you about Wolff?”

“My gut?” Pompard asked, confused.

“Your instinct.”

“Ah,” he said, nodding. “Wolff is probably not involved with Peter’s disappearance. But this steroid business may have something to do with it.”

“I agree.”

Pompard nodded. “Do you want me to have someone question Rodier, or do you want to do it?”

"I'll deal with him. I'm a little suspicious. Rodier may be dumb, or, he may be dumb, like a fox."

"What does that mean?" Pompard said.

"He may not be as foolish as Wolff thinks he is. Maybe he's clever enough to use being dumb as a cover."

"Hm," Pompard said with a nod. "Well, if you agree, I'll interview Dinaso and go get an update from my team while you speak with Rodier."

Jay rose from his chair, "That's fine with me. Dinaso is probably just a hothead. Terrible that he happened to kill another racer, but I doubt he's got anything to do with Peter. I'll call you right after I talk to Rodier."

Chapter 35

"YOU KNOW WE'RE going to make millions, right?" The man with the ponytail stood by the window, taking in the spectacular view of Mont Blanc. Appropriately named White Mountain, due to its perpetual snowfields and glaciers, its peak reaches 15,777 feet above sea level. His long hair, still wet from his shower, was soaking the neck of his white, terry cloth hotel bathrobe. His phone was tight to his ear. He listened, turning to look at his sleeping girlfriend. The white comforter covered only the lower half of her naked body. As she breathed, the slight rise and fall of her mid-sized breasts brought a lustful gleam to his eyes.

"I know," he responded. "We've already discussed this. There has never been big gambling money in ski racing, but that's changing right now." He narrowed his eyes in frustration. "Look, how long have we been working together? How much have you earned as a bookmaker from my inside information?" He waited, then continued, "Exactly. Now, I need you to continue spreading the word. Call all your clients and get them in on this. Tell every bookie you know about it. The more you help this thing grow, the more you'll make. Your take can be huge, but only if you help make it work. I want a betting frenzy on this." Listening again, he grimaced. "Of course I know what I'm doing!" he yelled, waking his girlfriend. "Look, if you want a piece of the action, just shut up and make the fucking calls!" He hung up, turned, and stared out the window at Mont Blanc's peak, the *Aiguille du Midi.*

He looked at his phone again, scrolled through his contacts, and tapped the screen. When the phone was answered, he repeated his previous conversation, but this time he spoke in Mandarin.

Stabbing the end-call button aggressively after his quick conversation, he looked out toward the mountain again. One by one, he slowly cracked his knuckles while staring at the powerful sight. A sly smile began to break through the rigid tension etched on his face. The smile disappeared immediately when he heard the girl's sleepy voice, "Who were you talking to?"

He turned, stepped toward her while untying the sash on his robe, and let it fall from his naked body. As he climbed on top of her, he said, "A friend. No one you know."

Chapter 36

BEWILDERMENT LIT UP Max Rodier's face as two police officers hauled him off the bus. Jay had decided not to wait until the team arrived at the Olympic Village to interrogate Rodier. Instead, once he found out that the bus had recently passed Milan, Italy, he studied the route from Milan to St. Moritz on his phone. He asked Pompard to call the police captain in Lecco, a small Italian city on the southeastern shore of Lake Como, and request that officers stop the bus and escort Rodier to the Lecco police station.

Pompard remained in Chamonix to interrogate Dinaso and continue the search for Peter. Jay and Buck boarded a helicopter to fly to Lecco.

***

The quick flight to Lecco was rough. The turbulent, alpine winds had tossed Buck around like a martini in a cocktail shaker.

Waiting for Rodier in the Lecco police station's small interrogation room, Buck tried to drink water from a flimsy, paper cone cup. His nerves were frayed from the flight, and his hand trembled. He took sips as he and Jay waited.

Eyes wide and face wrought with fear and confusion, Rodier was ushered into the room by two officers who forced him into a seat across the table from Jay and Buck.

After introducing himself, Jay said, "So, Max, obviously, you know what we want to talk about."

"No, I don't." Rodier's left eye twitched repeatedly as he spoke. His English was okay, but his Austrian accent was so heavy, he was difficult to understand.

Watching him closely, Jay tried to bait Rodier by saying, "We want to offer you a deal."

Rodier squinted suspiciously. "A deal?"

"Yes. You see, we know all about the steroids, and we are willing to let you off the hook if you tell us what you've done with Peter Buckar."

"What the hell are you talking about?"

"Cut the crap. We know he threatened to rat you out. So, if you don't want this jail to be your new home, you better tell us where he is."

"How the hell should I know where he is?" He stared at them for a moment. "Wait a second. This all came from Wolff, didn't it? That son of a bitch is setting me up to take his fall." His fists clenched, his eyes bulged, and his cheeks turned beet red, heavily contrasting his pale skin.

"Please, tell me more," Jay said.

"More?" he seethed. "How about this for a scenario; you caught Wolff, that little wimp, as he ran from the bus earlier today. We all saw it as he ran into the police vehicle. It was the funniest thing I've ever seen." He looked up. "Hm, let's see. So how did it go from there? How about this; you questioned him about the drugs he was carrying, then, low and behold, he started talking about Buckar. Then, after he told you all about Buckar's threats, he added me to the story. I bet he told you I was his partner in his little steroid business and that I was going to get revenge on Buckar for threatening to out us." After a moment of silence, he asked, "Well, am I close?"

Jay and Buck gave each other curious looks then Jay turned to Rodier. "Either it's all true, or the two of you rehearsed your stories."

"True? Ha! You don't know who you're dealing with? Ask anyone on the team; Wolff is the biggest freaking liar in the world. The whole racing circuit knows it. I'd bet the prick could beat a lie detector test if you gave him one. He's a lying, steroid-dealing bastard, and he'd love to pin it all on me."

"Why?"

"Lots of reasons. First, he's asked me to help him with his business many times and hates that I won't do it. Second, he blows all the cash he earns from the drugs and is always asking me to loan him money. And finally, he hates that I'm a better racer than he is. When we were younger, he used to beat me all the time, but not anymore. I have gotten much better than him, and he can't stand it."

"So you aren't his business partner?" Jay asked, keeping a straight face.

"Absolutely not! Even if I did use the shit, which I don't, I wouldn't be dumb enough to sell it."

"Come on, everyone could use more money. Last I checked, skiers on the circuit don't make much until they get an endorsement." Jay said.

"All I need to keep me happy is the opportunity to ski every day. The team provides everything I need. If I ski well enough, which I am doing lately, the bigger money will come. I'd be crazy to jeopardize what I've got. How many people get to make a good living doing what they love?"

"Not many, I guess," Jay said. He turned toward Buck. "We're hearing that a lot lately, aren't we?"

"It's pretty common in the world of professional sports," Buck said. "Most of my clients make more than they know what to do with, and they're all doing what they enjoy most. I just wish most of them knew how to stay out of trouble. It seems to follow lots of pro athletes around. In many cases, it's due to earning too much money, too quickly. That can be dangerous."

Buck and Jay looked back toward Rodier.

He looked at them and said, "I'm not in that league. I'm fine with the money I earn."

"Well, Max …" Loud banging on the door startled the three of them. Jay stood, walked to the door, and opened it just enough to see out while blocking the view in.

The Austrian coach and the team manager were standing in front of the officers who had brought Rodier in. One of the officers shrugged and apologized for allowing them to get by.

"Where's Max? We need to leave now," the manager snapped.

"You'll get Mr. Rodier back, if and when I say so," Jay said calmly.

"What? Who the hell are you, anyway?" The manager's eyes widened. "And what gives you, an American, the right to question an Austrian skier?"

"Look," Jay said. "I don't want any trouble with you or anyone else. You obviously know that Peter Buckar is missing, and I'm here to find him. I'm working with the local authorities, and we have permission to question anyone we need to. So, I suggest you back off and wait until I am finished with Rodier. Unless that is, you want to be questioned as well?"

"How much longer will you need him?" the coach asked.

"I believe I'm almost finished."

The manager nodded and asked, "What can you tell us about Lenhard Wolff? We haven't heard anything since he was arrested. We heard about the drugs, but now you're questioning Rodier about Buckar's disappearance. Does Wolff have something to do with that too?"

"Sorry gentlemen, I am not at liberty to discuss that. I'm sure you will be informed of Wolff's situation soon. And I will let you know more about Mr. Rodier as soon as I'm done questioning him. Now, if you'll excuse me." Jay took a step back and closed the door. He walked over, faced Rodier, crossed his arms, and said, "So, Max, I'm confused. Here I have two possible suspects in the kidnapping of Peter Buckar, and all I know for sure is that one of you is lying. I can usually tell when someone is lying to me. But, in this situation, while I have my doubts about your sincerity regarding the steroids, I don't really care about them. What I want to know is what you've done with Peter?"

"I told you, I had nothing to do with Buckar's disappearance."

"No, Max, you never said that. Instead, you created a very convenient smokescreen. Your little speech was about Wolff's story concerning your involvement in the steroid business. And while maybe you're not involved with that, I'd say that the only way you knew exactly what Wolff told us was that either it really happened, or the two of you made it up together. So, which one is it?"

Rodier stared at Jay for a second, then lowered his head and let out a big sigh. "We didn't make it up. Buckar came into our room the other day and threatened to turn us in to the police. But I swear I was never involved with steroids. I have never used them or sold them. Lenhard wanted me to help, but I refused. The whole situation made me so angry. I mean, there I was being threatened about something I wasn't even involved in. I was furious. I don't like the idea of steroids in ski racing any more than Buckar does. I told him that. Besides, since I'm innocent, I have nothing to worry about, right?"

Jay had been keenly watching Rodier's facial expressions and body language. He saw nothing that made him doubt Rodier's words. Maybe the guy was too naive to understand how difficult it is to prove your innocence when others are lying about you. "Okay, Max, here's the deal; my only concern is to find Peter Buckar, and right now, I don't have enough reason to keep you detained for that. You are free to leave. Go, get back on your bus, but don't think for a minute that you're off the hook. You are going to be watched. You won't know by whom, but we will be watching. If you're involved in any way with Buckar's disappearance, we will know the minute you contact your colleagues. I couldn't care less whether or not you're using or selling steroids. Go train for the games. Just know that the minute you make a mistake, we will be all over you. Now, get out of here."

Rodier's eyes shifted from Jay to Buck and back to Jay. Then, without another word, he stood and left the room.

"Now what?" Buck asked.

"I'm fairly certain he's telling the truth, but to be sure, I'm going to put someone on him. This is the first thing we have heard about Peter that could prove to be a motive. I'm going to use one of my men instead of Pompard's. I want to give Rodier just enough room to regain his confidence. Then, if he is involved, we'll be ready when he makes contact."

"I've never seen you so unsure about possible suspects, Jay," Buck said.

"Sure, you have. In our past dealings, there were so many possible leads, I had difficulty narrowing down the list. This case is the same. The possibilities seem endless. It's the reason we have to move quickly. The more time we give them, the poorer our chances are for a clean recovery."

Buck winced. "He can't be dead, Jay. I won't allow myself to even think that way."

"I'm sorry, my friend, I realize that Peter is more than just a client to you."

Buck nodded. “He is. He’s like family.”

“We’ll find him. I promise.”

Buck sighed. “We better. For now, I’d like to head back to Chamonix. I want to go check on Reid.”

Jay nodded. “Sure, let’s go.”

Chapter 37

REID GRIPPED THE handrail as the hotel elevator neared the lobby. He looked at the mirrored wall and thought, *at least I don't look as bad as I feel*. His first night out of the hospital was miserable and mostly sleepless. He had gotten out of bed before sunup and dressed without waking Shane. He figured some fresh air and a quiet walk through Chamonix couldn't hurt. The medication he was taking dulled his pain, but he still needed to avoid any quick movements. Knowing that it would be a long time before he'd swing a golf club again was even more upsetting than his discomfort.

The elevator slowed to a stop, and Reid turned from the mirror just as the doors opened. He gasped and instinctively jumped back in fear, slamming into the back wall of the elevator. He scowled from the pain as he stared, petrified, at the face of the biggest dog he had ever seen. The massive animal's eyes were locked on Reid's as it slowly entered the elevator. Reid tensed, ready to be mauled. The pain in his back was unbearable. In an agonizing voice, he quietly moaned, "Good puppy. Please don't eat me."

The creature stopped with his face inches from Reid's crotch and looked up with its huge, droopy eyes.

"Grady, come!" said a jovial American voice from just outside the elevator. As the dog's owner stepped into view, his eyes widened at the sight of Reid with his back pressed against the elevator wall.

"Grady! No!" The owner, a thin man with a dark beard, leather vest, and matching fedora, quickly grabbed the dog's collar and pulled him away. "I am so sorry. I promise he won't hurt you. Oh my God! You're Reid Clark. Wow! I apologize. I was talking to someone, and I didn't realize Grady had wandered off. Oh my God," he repeated in a panicked voice. "You're in pain. What did he do to you?" Aggressively the man pulled Grady's collar, and the docile dog backed away even further.

The owner quickly stepped in front of his dog and asked, "Are you hurt? He didn't bite you, did he? He's never bitten anyone. Oh, no. Mr. Clark, I am so sorry. Here, let me help you." Reid winced as the man took his arm. He immediately removed his hands. "I'm sorry. What's the matter? I barely touched you. Did Grady do this to you?" The man's expression and tone were filled with concern.

Still in extreme pain, Reid quietly said, "Don't worry. It wasn't the dog. I was already injured." Reid's eyes swept a quick glance at the vacant lobby. "Please just help me to a chair."

The man very tentatively placed one hand on Reid's elbow. Slowly he led him into the lobby and helped lower him into one of the big armchairs by the fireplace. Only one step behind his master, Grady walked up to Reid's chair, sat and looked him in the eye, then gently lowered his huge head and rested his chin and many folds of dark jowl on Reid's leg. Reaching to pet the dog's short brown hair, Reid said, "Hi Grady."

Grady's sleepy-looking, silver-dollar-sized, black eyes continued to stare up at him.

"How much does he weigh?"

"225 pounds," the owner said.

"Wow! What does he eat for breakfast? Little kids?"

"Yeah, and sometimes pro golfers."

Reid laughed and winced again.

"Are you all right?"

"No, not really. I had a really bad fall on the mountain a few days ago. I just got out of the hospital yesterday."

"Must have been some fall?"

"Yeah, a real yard sale. By the way, what's your name?"

"Jon Badal."

"Nice to meet you, Jon."

"You too, Mr. Clark, although I'm sorry about the circumstances."

"There's nothing to be sorry about, and please, call me Reid." He turned toward the dog. "So, the gentle giant here is Grady?"

"Yup."

"I've never seen a dog this big before. What breed is he?"

"English Mastiff."

"He is so well behaved."

"Yeah, he's a great dog. He's a big part of our family. No pun intended."

Reid smiled. "I can see why. But it's got to cost a fortune to feed him, and cleaning up after him can't be much fun."

"It's no worse than changing a baby's diaper, and some things are worth the trouble."

Grady seemed to know they were talking about him. He lifted his head from Reid's leg and licked his hand. Rather than the slobber Reid had expected, Grady's huge tongue felt like dry sandpaper.

Reid scratched the top of the dog's head and received an adoring look. "Hey, I came down to go for a walk. Will you and Grady join me?"

"Sure, we were headed out too. You sure you're up to it?"

"I'm alright. If I have a problem I can always ride Grady, right?"

"Uh, probably not," Badal said.

Reid smiled. "Can I hold his leash?"

"Do you really think that's a good idea? You're obviously still in pain."

"I'm fine. Besides, he seems pretty easy going to me."

"He is," Badal said, handing the leash to Reid. "But listen, you need to give it back to me if we pass anyone wearing dark sunglasses and a baseball hat."

"Really?"

"For some reason, as gentle as he is, he sometimes gets excited when he sees people with sunglasses and baseball caps. He freaks out a little when delivery guys wearing them come to our door at home."

Reid looked out the lobby window. "It's pretty cloudy out there. We probably won't see anyone with sunglasses." Turning his head toward the dog, he added, "Ready Grady? C'mon pup."

Walking through the lobby, Reid asked, "How old is he?"

"Almost four, why?"

"I was just wondering if he was still growing," Reid said with a shrug.

Badal's eyes widened. "No, he's as big as he's going to get. Thank God."

After walking down the block, Reid patted Grady on his head. "You know what Grady? You're the perfect companion for me. Everyone we pass looks at you and barely notices me. I love it."

"Funny," Badal said. "It's the opposite for me, he brings me so much attention. I enjoy it, though. People are usually a little scared to approach him at first, and then, they fall in love with him."

"I can relate to that," Reid said with a sly grin.

"Yeah, I can see that," Badal said with a smirk.

Reid smiled. "I could use a cup of coffee. How about you?"

"Sounds good. There's a café around the corner."

As they rounded the corner, a man in a black leather jacket, with a red Ski-Chamonix cap and sunglasses, was exiting the café less than five feet away. Grady stopped and let out a fierce growl. The man flinched, spilling his hot coffee and dropping his cup. His face contorted with fear.

"No, Grady!" Badal ordered as he grabbed the dog's collar

Grady growled again, then barked but did not approach the stranger.

"It's okay, sir," Badal said. "He's very gentle. He won't harm you. Please, let me buy you another cup of coffee."

"Just keep that monster away from me." The man's heavy Slavic accent was evident even through his clenched teeth. His eyes remained locked on Grady as he sidestepped by with his back against the building. Once he passed them, he increased his pace.

Reid continued to watch as the man hustled away. Just before he reached the corner, he turned his head quickly and glanced back at them, causing his ponytail to swing out from the bottom of his baseball cap.

"Pleasant fellow," Reid said.

"Grady brings out the best in some and the worst in others. Go ahead and get your coffee. I'll stay here and keep my friend out of trouble."

"What would you like?"

Badal reached for his wallet. "I'll take a café au lait, and could you get Grady five eggs?"

"Five?" Reid smirked. "How does he like them?"

"He's not very picky. Scrambled, fried, whatever." Badal offered Reid fifteen Euros.

"No, I've got it."

"Thank you."

Badal wiped the light layer of freshly fallen snow off a nearby bench and sat with Grady lying near his feet.

Chapter 38

MANY OF THE smaller hotels in St. Moritz Bad were quite charming. Danielle Maldonado, one of Pompard's Lieutenants, noted how the rustic little wooden bridge she was crossing added even more character to the chalet-style hotel it led to.

Her earlier interview in Chamonix with Dan Miron, one of Peter's teammates, had provided what sounded like a strong lead. He told her that Canadian racer, Claude Bouchard, had attended school and raced with Peter at Burke Mountain Academy in Vermont. Miron said Peter and Bouchard had been friendly but also fiercely competitive, and, as it turned out, their rivalry eventually reached beyond the slopes. Bouchard had started dating Peter's college girlfriend, Joanne Chase, immediately after Peter had broken up with her.

Chase, who also trained at the Academy, had been in love with Peter and had expected to marry him. In their senior year, Peter decided that Chase was distracting him from reaching his full potential as a racer. He broke her heart when he told her, "I'm sorry, but I need to focus completely on my skiing. I can't do that with you in my life." Chase never quite got over being dumped, and she held a grudge. She quit skiing and followed her passion as an artist. Her specialty was paintings of sports figures. She often traveled to races with Bouchard to paint scenes of the racers as they skied.

Peter had seen Chase at a few races but kept his distance after seeing one of her paintings of him. While most of her work was very realistic of the racers, her portrayal of him in this piece was extremely distorted, bordering on deranged. One eye was grossly oversized and bulging, the nose was crooked and off-center, the random teeth in the large, wide-open mouth were jagged and cracked, and the chin was long and pointed. Chase made sure there was no question about who the painting was of by accentuating Peter's dirty blond hair and freckled complexion.

After Maldonado heard about Bouchard and Chase, she wondered if the couple might be warped enough to think that Chase's more flattering paintings of Peter might fetch more money if he were dead. Or, maybe his disappearance was Chase's revenge. Or, could Bouchard be resentful of Peter's winnings, or possibly even of Chase's continued interest in her ex-boyfriend.

Maldonado knocked on their hotel door. Seconds later, a beautiful brunette opened it. Her jeans, t-shirt, and untucked, unbuttoned flannel shirt were spattered with a rainbow of paint stains. She had opened the door with one hand, while the other held a wooden paintbrush, glistening with green paint.

"Can I help you?"

Maldonado showed her badge. "I hope so. I'm Lieutenant Maldonado. I'm looking for Joanne Chase."

"That's me."

"Very good. I'd like to ask you and Mr. Bouchard a few questions about Peter Buckar."

With a nod, Chase said, "We kind of expected someone to come around. Please come in."

"Expected someone?" Maldonado asked as she followed the painter into the room. An easel stood near the window. A slalom course gate flag with interlocking circles in blue, yellow, and black was painted just off-center on a snow-covered race course. A green semicircle was waiting to be finished.

"We have company, Claude. Lieutenant uh …"

"Maldonado," she repeated.

Chase walked to the easel and looked at her canvas. Claude Bouchard stopped typing and looked up from his laptop computer. "Hello, Officer."

"It's Lieutenant, Mr. Bouchard."

Bouchard smiled. "Very well, Lieutenant. No disrespect intended."

Maldonado gave a slight nod. "Mr. Bouchard, Miss Chase, I hope we can make this a quick visit. I'm sure you want to hit the slopes or the gym or whatever your team is doing today, Mr. Bouchard." She walked to a chair. "May I?"

"Sure, make yourself comfortable, but, as you said, this needs to be very quick. I have to be on the mountain soon. As Joanne already mentioned, we kind of figured someone would be coming to ask about Peter."

"May I ask why?"

"Are you kidding? Joanne, Peter, and I have history. We all went to college together. Peter and I have been good friends for years, and yet, we have always been very competitive with each other. Joanne dated him during school and, well, although she and I have been together for quite a while, she's been pissed at him ever since he broke up with her."

Maldonado looked at Chase, who shrugged, then resumed painting.

"Why are you still so mad at him?"

"I'm not."

"No? Then, why the distorted painting I heard about? And why have people told me otherwise."

"Because they're busybodies. People should mind their own damn business."

"What about the painting?"

"Oh, all right already. I painted it after Peter and I spoke one day. He was so happy with his life it just pissed me off. He ripped out my heart when he left me. I was totally in love with him, and he just walked away. Part of me never got over it. I mean, I really love Claude." She looked at Bouchard and smiled. "But, when someone hurts you as badly as Peter hurt me, the sting never completely goes away. The three of us had always been very close. So, when Peter ended things, it felt kind of natural for Claude and me to hook up."

Bouchard stopped typing, looked up from his laptop, and gave a wry smile.

"How did Peter feel about it?"

"At first, he wasn't happy, but he got used to it."

"How do you know he wasn't happy about it?"

She chuckled. "He went a little nuts the first time he saw us kiss. He asked how long Claude and I had been intimate, implying that we had been fooling around behind his back. He stopped his tirade very quickly when I reminded him that it was he who had broken my heart, not the other way around."

"What was his reaction to that?"

"He knew I was right. He just stopped yelling and stormed away. He apologized to both of us later."

Maldonado nodded. "All right. So, tell me about your paintings."

"What about them?"

"You paint a lot of them, right?"

"Enough to make a living."

"They sell pretty well?"

"Yeah. The racer's families, friends, and fans buy most of them."

"How much do you get for them?"

"Depends on the size. Anywhere from $800 to $3,500."

"Not bad! Do you keep a big inventory?"

"I always try to have about fifty or so available, mostly of the top skiers. I keep half of them in my loft at home and sell them through my website. I also have a bunch displayed in galleries at high-end ski resorts. That's where they sell the best, along with the ones I display at races."

"Have you sold many paintings of Peter?"

"Sure. The top racers all sell well."

"How many paintings of him do you have currently?"

Chase walked to the desk, picked up her iPhone, swept her finger slowly across the screen while counting to herself. "Sixteen."

"Can I take a look?"

"Uh, yeah, I guess. Here." She held the phone toward Maldonado.

"Look here instead," Bouchard said, placing his laptop on the coffee table. "You can see them better on my laptop. I have Joanne's website up. You'll see her whole inventory."

Maldonado walked to Bouchard and looked at his computer screen.

"Just push this button to scroll to the next picture," Bouchard said.

Maldonado clicked through all the pictures. "You're very talented."

"Thank you," Chase said.

Looking at the screen, Maldonado asked, "What's this file at the bottom of the screen? The Vigilante?"

"One of my manuscripts. I write novels," Claude said.

"Really, what kind?"

"Crime thrillers, mostly."

"Anything published?"

"Yeah, sixteen, so far."

"Wow. How do you find time to write so many books while you're on the racing circuit?"

"It's difficult, but I have no choice."

"What do you mean?"

"Well, I love skiing, but my true passion is writing. I need to write, it's when I feel most fulfilled and happy. I'm going to race for as long as my body allows it. Then, I'm going to write full time."

"Do the books make you much money?"

"They do okay, but the business is tough. Some authors have to scratch and claw their way to success. My books sell pretty well in Canada, where I'm fairly popular as a skier. I guess if I won more races, I'd sell more books, eh?"

"I guess. Maybe now with Buckar out, your chances are better, no?"

Bouchard's look became contemplative. He rubbed his chin through his short beard. "I like where you're going with this, Lieutenant. You're making Joanne and me out to be quite an interesting couple. Or, should I say, a couple of interest?" He raised his hands to shoulder height and made air quotes with his fingers as he finished his sentence.

"Why do you say that?"

Bouchard sniggered. "Why indeed. I'm a crime novelist. I twist situations in my books just like you're doing here. Let's see, so far you have Joanne stockpiling paintings of Peter that will sell for millions if he isn't found. And now you have me, a racer and thriller author, who will sell more books as I win more races because Peter isn't competing. It's good stuff, the perfect red herring."

"Red herring?"

Bouchard rolled his eyes. "Ah, forget it. I'm getting tired of this nonsense. I need to suit up and get out on the mountain. Have a good day, officer." Bouchard closed his laptop, stood, and walked past Maldonado toward the bathroom.

"Excuse me, Mr. Bouchard, but I'm not done yet, and frankly, your arrogance is beginning to annoy me. You see, in my thinking, quite often arrogance coincides with guilt."

Bouchard turned and faced Maldonado. "I like that. Arrogance coincides with guilt. I think I'll use that in my current manuscript. How would you like to be a character in it?"

"What?"

"I use real people's names all the time. It's a whole lot better than making them up."

"Mr. Bouchard, I don't care about your novels at the moment. And if you don't start taking me seriously, I will be happy to bring you in for further questioning."

"Take you seriously? Give me a break. I ..." Bouchard looked at Chase. "Make that *we* ... had nothing to do with Peter's disappearance. Ask whatever you want. We have nothing to hide. If you don't mind, I'm going to suit up while you talk to us?" He glanced at his watch. "I need to get out of here."

"Go ahead and get ready. I'm going to leave with you."

Bouchard removed his yellow, one-piece racing suit from the hook on the bathroom door and began putting it on.

"Ms. Chase, I'd like you to email me the pictures of your paintings that are on your phone."

"Why?"

"Because I'd like to show them to some of my colleagues. That's not a problem, is it?"

She glanced at Bouchard, who was standing in front of a mirror, tying a red bandana on his head.

"I'm not sure I like the idea of emailing my entire portfolio to anyone."

"They're on your website for the entire world to see, no?"

"Most of them."

"Is there any reason to hide the others?"

"No, I guess not."

"Then I'd appreciate it if you'd email them to me now, while I'm here."

Chase sighed, shook her head slightly, and finally said, "Oh, fine!" She put her paintbrush down and pulled the phone from the breast pocket of her loose flannel shirt. "What's your address?"

"dmaldonando at—"

"Spell it please," Chase said, cutting her off.

"D M A … Let me enter it," she said, walking toward Chase with her hand out.

Chase looked as if she were about to argue, then handed over the device.

She entered her address, handed the phone back, and said, "One last thing, tempting as it may be to leave town to avoid further questioning, neither of you should go anywhere."

"As we mentioned," Bouchard said, coming out of the bathroom in his ski outfit. "We have absolutely nothing to hide. We will both be here until just after the closing ceremonies." He put on his dark, wraparound, reflective shades. "Now, Lieutenant, if you're ready, I'll walk you out."

"Ms. Chase, did you send the pictures?"

Chase smirked, then looked at her phone and tapped on the screen. "Yes."

"Thank you. I'm sure we'll be speaking again very soon."

Chapter 39

THE INCESSANT WHISTLING of wind passing through the micro vents surrounding the wood-burning stove was driving Swiss racer Anton Wyss crazy.

Sitting in the lobby of the Hotel Schlafen Sie Gut in St. Moritz, he tried to vanquish the irritating sound from his mind. After an annoying few minutes, he slammed his fists on the arms of his chair, closed his eyes, and shook his head. *Damned noises, they're everywhere*, he thought. He had left his room earlier because his roommate's snoring, combined with the relentless howling winds, had destroyed his hopes of getting any sleep. A sleep-deprived alpine ski racer is bound to make costly mistakes on the slopes.

He stood and walked to the floor-to-ceiling windows. Outside, bright spotlights pierced the darkness like lasers, illuminating two tall flag poles. On one, the bold white cross and red background of the Swiss flag fluttered and snapped in the bitterly cold wind. An Olympic flag whipped about just below the gold ball at the peak of the second pole. The five colorful interlocking rings resembled haphazardly bouncing balls.

Wyss sighed. *Exercise would be a good distraction right now,* he thought as he stared at the flags. *It's way too windy and cold for an outdoor run. Maybe an hour on a treadmill or exercise bike will clear my head.*

The Olympic Games should be the most exciting event of his life, but they had ruined it all for him. His family should be here, ready to root for him in his pursuit of gold. Instead, he had made absolutely sure they didn't come. They were so upset, they pleaded with him relentlessly, not understanding why he held his ground. But he wouldn't, actually, he couldn't, tell them why he was so adamant about their not coming. He couldn't tell them about the threat he had received or about the fact that regardless of the world's expectations, he wouldn't be taking home any medals. Because if he did, *they* had promised harm would come to his family. Although he didn't know who *they* were, they had proven that they were very serious. They had verified it by killing his dog, Kira. Ruthless bastards! Wyss had adored Kira, his beautiful White Swiss Shepherd. Her unconditional love and affection had made even his toughest days more tolerable.

Wyss had been leery after receiving the threat. The note was left in his workout bag while he was at the gym a few weeks earlier, back home in Verbier. No one had seen who left it. It warned that if he won an Olympic medal, someone in his family would die. It also said that he must compete, and it must appear to the world that he is going for the gold, as expected. If he faked getting hurt in order to avoid the competition, the result would be the same. *The bastards,* he thought again. *Threats against me I can handle but not against my family.* They also warned that informing the police would bring about the same conclusion. The note finished by stating that they would provide proof of their seriousness the following afternoon. Wyss had been distraught, but what could he do?

The next day he stayed at the gym late, consumed with fear. By the time he returned home, it was dark. His parents met him at the door with tears in their eyes. They told him that they had found Kira dead in their backyard earlier in the day. The veterinarian had yet to determine the cause of death.

Wyss's emotions had run amok. An immediate flood of devastation and terror had hit him hard. How could anyone kill a defenseless dog? Their message was clear and strong. If they would do this just to prove the seriousness of their intentions, they probably wouldn't hesitate to kill someone in his family.

He was sickened by the thought but felt he had no options.

Standing by the hotel window, Wyss recalled how hard he had worked during the last four years. And for what? Just to lose all of his Olympic races? Making a fool of himself in front of the world disgusted him. He was a winner, a champion at heart, until now, anyway. Now he had to make sure his performance was flawed. Even worse was that he had to make his loss look unintentional. He could not make any blatant mistakes that would give away the fact that he was deliberately screwing up. *That,* he could handle. The worst it would bring about were questions as to why he had done it. Throwing his races, while ethically wrong, might make the world question his moral integrity, but not his ability to ski. He had worked so damn hard, both physically and mentally. He was ready to prove that he was the premiere alpine skier in the world. But no, his time for glory was being senselessly taken from him. Stolen by criminals, just as if it was money or jewelry. Taking this from him was tantamount to removing his heart and soul.

Looking at his reflection in the hotel window, Wyss watched his tears stream down his cheeks. They couldn't do this to him. He wouldn't let them. No one would make a fool of Anton Wyss. *No one!* He turned abruptly and walked from the lobby with determination in his step. He was torn, but he knew there was only one solution.

He went back to his room and quietly opened the door so as not to disturb his roommate. He found his backpack by his bed, kneeled, and carefully rummaged through it until he found what he was looking for.

Until this moment, he hadn't been sure if he could do it, but now he realized he had no other choice. He would not be made a fool of in front of the world, nor would he put his family in jeopardy. He was disgusted with what he knew was his only alternative. He felt weak as he clenched his fist around the small plastic vial and stood.

Ever so quietly, he walked to the bathroom and slowly closed and locked the door. Filling one of the plastic tumblers by the sink with tepid water, he avoided his reflection in the mirror, fearing it might weaken him and prevent him from doing what he must. He unscrewed the cap on the amber bottle, and after a brief hesitation, poured a bunch of pills into his mouth. He gulped them down with some water and repeated the task, emptying the bottle. Then, he looked at his reflection, not quite sure of what he expected. What he saw frightened him. His tears had dried, only to be replaced by dark, empty resignation. Head hung low, he turned, went into the bedroom, found a notepad and pen, and returned to the bathroom. Sitting on the cold tile floor with his back against the wall, he placed the pad on his bent knee and began to write.

To my family, friends, teammates, and country,

I am so sorry to let you all down, but I was left with no choice. I received a threat that if I won an Olympic medal, a member of my family would die. They proved that they were serious by killing my beloved dog, Kira. They wanted me to ski badly enough to lose my races without making it obvious that I was intentionally losing. If you know me

well, you know that I could not do that. Winning an Olympic medal has been my life's goal ...

Wyss wrote until his eyelids grew heavy and his hand became weak. Starting to lose consciousness, his body slowly slumped to the side, and his eyes closed.

Chapter 40

THE DEVASTATING NEWS spread rapidly despite attempts by the Swiss ski team to keep the situation under wraps.

By mid-day, most people throughout the Olympic Village had heard about the attempted suicide, but very few knew anything about Wyss's note. If the information he wrote was true, the threat he had received might be connected to Peter's disappearance.

Jay and Pompard flew from Chamonix to St. Moritz as soon as they had heard. On the way, Pompard had contacted his old friend, Dieter Lang, a detective with the St. Moritz *Kantonspolizei.* Jay agreed that working with a local officer could help.

Lang met them at the hospital entrance, where Pompard filled him in on their investigation so far.

"*Mein Gott,*" Lang said. "What a mess. Kidnapping, street fights, extortion, and now suicide. It is such a shame. The Olympic Games used to be revered by everyone. Now they are just another event filled with crime, violence, and greed."

"It has become the way of the world," Jay said.

"Ugly, but true," Pompard added with a sigh. "At least it was only an attempted suicide."

Lang nodded.

"By the way," Pompard said. "I called the police captain in Verbier, Wyss's hometown. He sent a team to guard his family."

"Good," Jay said.

"Can you imagine working as hard as these athletes do to prepare for the games, only to be threatened or kidnapped at the last minute? These ruthless bastards are going to beg for mercy when I'm finished with them," Pompard said with his jaw clenched. "It all just makes me so damn mad."

Jay grinned and raised his brow.

"I'm looking forward to getting my hands on them, too," Lang said.

Jay laughed. "Okay then, so we're all feeling the same way. Let's go speak with Wyss."

Walking toward Wyss's hospital room, they saw two men sitting in chairs beside the door, watching them approach.

The man sitting closest to them was hunched over with his elbows on his knees and his chin resting on his closed fists. The dark blue hood of his sweatshirt covered his head. A sullen voice emanated from under the hood. "Who are you?"

"Police investigators," Jay answered, avoiding long introductions. "May I ask the same of you?"

"I'm Mark Weisbarth, Anton's slalom coach," he said, pushing off his hood. His thin, chiseled face needed a shave.

The other man scooched back in his chair, straightening from his slouch. "I'm Jon Stein, one of the team doctors." He looked at them through crystal blue eyes as he tugged his sweater away from his ample gut with one hand while pushing his tousled, blond comb-over into place with the other.

"How is he doing?" Jay asked, gesturing with his chin toward the door.

"We got him here quickly enough so that most of the meds were still in his stomach when they pumped it," Stein said. "He'll be all right, it will just take some time for the drugs to clear out of his blood."

"I was told we had an officer guarding the door. Where is he?" Lang asked.

"He went to the bathroom," Weisbarth said.

"Is Wyss awake?" Pompard asked.

"Yes," Weisbarth answered. "We were in the room when he woke up a couple of minutes ago. A nurse came in and asked us to step out for a little while."

Pompard shot Jay a tense, untrusting look. Jay quickly, yet, quietly opened the door and peered in.

"I told you to give me a few minutes," the nurse said with her back to the door. Jay watched suspiciously as she adjusted the pillow, making Wyss more comfortable.

"How long before we can speak with him?" Jay asked.

Not bothering to turn around, the nurse said, "I will let you know as soon as the doctor says it's okay. Now, if you don't mind, please step out and close the door. He needs rest."

Jay kept his head in the room for another few seconds watching the nurse in her blue, flowered scrubs. *She must be legit*, he thought. *If she were here to kill him, she would have done it right away.* He backed out, pulled the door, leaving it open just enough to watch, and gave Pompard a shrug.

"Is he coherent?" Pompard asked.

"Not sure," Weisbarth answered.

"Did anyone say how long it might be before we can talk with him?" Jay asked.

"The doctor said it shouldn't be too long, but I don't know whether he meant hours or days."

"We're not going to wait very long. We need to speak with him soon," Jay said.

"I hope you can," the coach said as he stood. "I'm going to get some coffee. Anyone want some?"

"I'll take a cup, thanks," Pompard said. "Black, please."

Weisbarth nodded and began walking away.

"Wait, Mark, I'll join you," Stein said.

"This has to be very tough on them," Pompard said once they were out of earshot.

Lang sighed heavily. "It's tough on our whole country. Everyone loves Anton. He's a national hero."

The hum of the harsh, fluorescent lights sounded like a swarm of bees quietly buzzing overhead as the men waited impatiently for permission to enter the room.

Finally, the door opened, and while looking at her watch, the nurse said, "You can come back in and speak with him now." She looked up from her wrist. "Wait a minute. Who are you? Where are the team doctor and the coach?"

"They're getting coffee," Lang said. "We are police officers. We need to speak with Mr. Wyss."

"I'm sorry, but he's not ready for questioning."

"Ma'am, this is a matter of life and death, not just for him, but possibly for many others. We just need a few minutes," Jay said forcefully.

She looked at the three men, then glanced into the room at Wyss. "Well, it goes against my better judgment, but since you say other lives may be at stake, I'll allow it. He needs rest. Be quick, and please do not agitate him."

"Of course not. Thank you," Pompard said.

The men entered the room along with the nurse. Wyss's slightly open, glassy eyes followed them as they approached.

"Anton, can you hear me?" Lang asked quietly in German.

Wyss's nod was barely perceptible.

Turning toward Pompard, Lang asked, "Do you speak German, or should I do the talking?"

"English is fine," Wyss quietly slurred.

Pompard nodded. "Thank you, Anton. I am Police Captain, George Pompard. I know you need rest, so I'll be quick. I'm going to ask you a few questions that may help save lives here at the Games. Before that, to put your mind at rest, police officers are on their way to guard your family as we speak."

Wyss smiled weakly.

"We read your note, and we understand your predicament. It must have been very difficult for you not to tell anyone about the threat."

Wyss tried hard to speak.

"Take it easy, Anton. If it's easier, just blink once for yes and twice for no. Would you prefer that?"

He nodded very slightly and blinked once.

"Very good. Do you know who threatened you?"

Two blinks.

"Do you have any idea where they are from?"

Two more blinks.

"Did you see them?"

Wyss strained to speak again. "No," he said with some effort.

"Where did they leave the note?"

"In my bag at the gym."

"Did anyone at the gym see them?"

He shook his head slightly.

"Where is the note? Can we see it?"

"I burned it after they killed my dog," he said, very quietly.

"Why?"

"I don't know, I was scared. I wasn't thinking straight."

"That's understandable. I'm very sorry to hear about your dog. Was that meant to show that they were serious?"

Wyss nodded and seemed to be gaining some energy. "Their note said that I would get proof the following day. That's when they killed Kira." Tears trickled from the corners of his eyes, and his chest heaved under the hospital sheet.

"What did they want you to do?" asked Jay.

"Throw my races without making it look intentional."

Jay nodded. "Did they say why?"

Anton blinked twice and teared up.

"Okay, that's enough," the nurse said as she walked to Wyss's side. "He needs to rest."

The men backed away from the bed.

"Yes, Madame. Thank you for allowing us to speak with him. May we come back later?" Pompard asked.

"After he's had some rest."

"May I ask him one more question?" Jay requested.

The nurse looked at Wyss and sighed. "One more."

"What language was the note written in?"

"German."

"Thank you," Jay said as they were leaving the room. When he reached the door, Jay turned and asked, "Was it handwritten or typed?"

"Typed."

"Okay, thanks, Anton. Get some rest. You're going to need all your energy to win the gold."

Wyss looked at Jay curiously. Then, slowly his face brightened. Jay's message was clear.

Outside the room, Pompard asked, "You think it's smart for him to race?"

"Now that we know about the threat, we can make sure that he and his family have round-the-clock protection. I'm sure they'll be coming to watch him, now that the cat is out of the bag."

"What?" Pompard asked.

"It's just a saying. It means that people know about the secret."

"American sayings," Pompard mumbled with his head shaking.

Jay chuckled.

"Jay, why did you ask whether the note was written or typed?" Lang asked.

"Because if it had been handwritten, chances are the person who wrote it speaks the language it was written in. It's not a lot of help since that person might speak and write various languages. But a clue is a clue."

"But, since it was typed on a computer, it doesn't help much because anyone can use a word processor and the internet to translate anything these days," Lang said.

"That and the fact that Anton burned it," Pompard said.

"Right," Lang said with a shake of his head and a quick chuckle.

Jay rubbed his chin, looking contemplative.

"What's on your mind?" Pompard asked.

"Tell me what you think of this idea. We immediately put covert security teams on Anton and each of his family members. Then we let the media know that Anton is still going to race. In fact, we go one step further; we have Anton give a statement. He'll explain to the media that although he hadn't intended it to work this way, his failed suicide attempt has allowed him to go for the gold because now that the police know about his situation, they can protect him and his family from the people who threatened him."

"Hmm." Pompard nodded. "It might draw them out."

"It'll depend on how smart they are and how badly they want him out of the competition. They'll expect us to put protection on the family and Anton, so we'll have to put some guards here at the hospital and a team outside the family's house or hotel room. We'll keep the visible teams light, so the perps don't feel too intimidated. Then, if they try to get to Anton or the family, we'll have larger, covert teams ready to take them down."

"I like it," Pompard said.

"Good," Jay said. "And if we get them, chances are, we'll get Peter too."

"You believe it's all connected?" Pompard asked.

"Don't you?"

"Yes, it's doubtful that two unrelated factions are pulling similar stunts with Olympic skiers."

"I agree," Lang said. "Coincidences are rare in our line of work."

"Very," Jay said. "The question is who is behind all this and what do they hope to gain by taking out two skiers?" Jay rubbed his eyes. He was tired.

"Dieter, George has already asked the Verbier police to provide the family protection," Jay said. "But will you call too? They might act quicker if the request comes from a fellow Swiss officer."

"Of course, I will."

"Good. Make sure they understand what we're looking for. We want visible protection that's light enough for the perpetrators to feel that they can get past them without much trouble. Then, we want undercover teams ready when they make their move."

"Right," Lang said. "Then, after I call Verbier, I'll set up our people here. We should position a uniformed man right here at Wyss's door, and another at the main entrance. Then, I'll place undercovers in various hospital worker's uniforms throughout the building. We need people at all the entrances, including the emergency room and the loading dock. Obviously, we'll need a few up here, too. One should be positioned over there." Lang pointed. "Behind the counter at the nurse's station."

"Good," Jay said. "Let's go find the head of hospital security and coordinate all this."

***

On the way out of the building, Jay said, "Dieter, can you give us a lift to the Olympic Village? We can discuss how we're going to handle the press on the way."

"Sure. My car is out front. Maybe you both should come to the station and meet the chief. He'll need to okay the manpower, and I know he'll want to be involved."

"Why don't you ask him to meet us at the Olympic Security Offices," Jay said. "We might as well brief him and Fisher at the same time."

"Who is Fischer?" Pompard asked.

"Christoph Fischer. He's Chief of Olympic Security. We're getting pulled in too many directions with this mess. We need all the help we can get, and Fischer has a small army at his command."

"Do you know him?" Pompard asked.

"No. But he's got a good reputation."

"I do," Lang said. "He's a decent guy, as long as things are done his way."

"I know the type," Pompard said.

A quick laugh slipped from Jay.

"Did I say something amusing?"

Jay shook his head and grinned.

"What?" Pompard asked.

"You *know* the type? Who are you kidding? You *are* the type."

"Maybe a little," Pompard said through a crooked smile.

"Sure, just a little," Jay said with another laugh.

Pompard shrugged.

With his phone at his ear, Lang said, "Okay Captain, we'll meet you at Fischer's office in about twenty minutes."

Unable to contain himself, looking at his phone, Pompard spoke before Lang finished his sentence., "Here we go. One of my detectives just asked me to call him. His text is vague, but I think he has information about that woman who's been stalking Buckar." He tapped on his screen and raised his phone to his ear.

Chapter 41

JAY POUNDED ON the table. "We've had so many leads, but we haven't learned a damn thing yet. We need something solid, and we need it soon."

Chief of Olympic Security, Christoph Fischer and St. Moritz Cantonal Police Commander Speiser stopped drinking from their mugs of steaming coffee as they listened to Jay's explanation.

They were sitting around a table in Fischer's office, located within the Olympic Village's Security enclave. These double-wide trailers located in the northeast corner of the Olympic Village were jam-packed with state-of-the-art electronics, manned by a slew of Information Technology specialists.

"We need to work together on this," Jay said. He looked at Speiser. "Commander, if you can take the lead on the Wyss situation, that would be great."

"Of course." Speiser's air of distrust eased as he stroked his closely trimmed beard.

"Good. Detective Lang can fill you in on what we've learned so far."

Jay turned to face Fischer, "So, now that you know where we stand with our search for Buckar, you see why we're asking for your help. Without it, I'm afraid we'll be too late."

"Too late?" Fischer asked.

"He's been missing for a week now. Do I need to say more?"

"A week? I guess I've been so busy setting everything up here, I didn't realize how much time had elapsed. Of course, I will devote a team to Buckar. But, understand, my primary responsibility lies in keeping the Olympic Village and venues safe for everyone. There will be millions in attendance."

"I know, Christoph. May I call you Christoph?" Jay asked.

"That's fine," he said with a disregarding shrug.

"Good, and both of you, please call me Jay." He looked from Fischer to Speiser and back. "I know that you've got your hands full already, but if I didn't feel that Peter's disappearance was an Olympic issue, I would not be asking for your help."

"Given the timing of the kidnapping, I agree. Somehow it must be tied to the Games," Fischer said. "Tell me what you need."

"Excellent. I'm very happy you feel that way."

"You look surprised."

"I guess I am. We heard that you like things done your way, or else."

"Hmm, I wonder where you heard that." Fischer shot Lang a wide-eyed, sarcastic look. "I know I had that reputation when I ran my department, but it's different here. There is no room for pride or ego at the Olympics. There are way too many lives at stake. Why don't you tell me what you've come up with, so far?"

"George, why don't you begin," Jay said.

Pompard pulled his cell phone from its belt holster and slid his finger across the screen. "Our search of Chamonix turned up nothing. We continue to investigate every lead that gets called in, but so far, they have all been worthless, at least as far as Buckar is concerned. One anonymous call led us to a large meth lab in a warehouse. While it had nothing to do with Buckar, we arrested twelve people and seized around thirty kilos."

Fischer's brow wrinkled in thought for a moment, then he said, "Street value is probably around a million and a half. Impressive."

After quick nods, Pompard continued. "Before Jay and I left Chamonix, my men brought in an Austrian ski racer named Leonard Woolf, who was caught with a bag full of steroids. When Jay and I questioned him, he told us that Buckar had threatened to blow the whistle on him and his business partner, a teammate named Max Rodier, if they didn't stop selling the steroids to other racers. Rodier of course denied everything when we questioned him. We're holding Woolf in one of my cells, and Jay has guys tailing Rodier. If Buckar threatened them, maybe they grabbed him so he couldn't turn them in."

"They're women," Jay said.

"Who?" Pompard said, sounding surprised that Jay interrupted him.

"You said I have guys tailing him. They're women."

"And your point is?" Pompard asked.

"Just clarifying," Jay said.

Speiser said, "Do you really think that two small-time steroid dealers would take Buckar hostage?" He shook his head. "No, it would be too difficult, and what would they gain? If it was them, my guess is they would just kill him."

"I can't see these guys killing anyone," Pompard said.

"I agree," Jay said.

Speiser shrugged.

"There have been two other arrests during vehicle searches since we left Chamonix," Pompard continued. "One for drugs, one for weapons. We found two Frenchmen, both high as kites, in an old Jeep with two kilos of heroin. The other bust was two couples in a Mercedes. I think they are Russian. They had a couple of Pernach automatic pistols and an old Kalashnikov. All the serial numbers were filed off."

"Could they be Russian mafia? The OTs-33 Pernach is the Russian mob's preferred gun, isn't it?" Fischer asked.

"You never really know with the Russian mafia," Jay said. "They change their favored guns almost as often as their underwear. Besides, the Pernach is popular these days, and, as you know better than I do, there are a lot of goons in Eastern Europe. There are probably as many wannabe mobsters as there are real ones. George already has Interpol and Europol checking organized crime possibilities, and I have a friend looking into it too."

"A friend?" Fischer asked, frowning.

"Just someone I trust."

"Connected?"

"Uh-huh," Jay said.

"You Americans never cease to amaze me. A police officer with a friend in the mafia." Fischer's head shook. "I just couldn't do it."

"Well," Jay said with a harsh edge. "I am not a cop. I own a private security company, and although I may do business a little differently, my goals and beliefs are in line with most police officers I know. Being in the private sector allows me some liberties. While I do not approve of organized crime of any type, I have found that sometimes using a friend with connections on the other side of the law can help solve a case. Solving crimes and protecting innocent people is my job, and I will do whatever it takes to protect my clients. And besides, Sal helped me solve a case at the Olympics in Australia."

Fischer nodded. "I read about that when I was doing my research for this job. It was an issue with a gymnast, right?"

"It was."

Fischer scrunched his face. "And, if I recall correctly, kids helped with that case, no?"

Jay smiled again. "That's right. I'm sure you know of Reid Clark?"

"Of course, I do. You think there's someone on this planet who doesn't?"

Jay shrugged.

"Oh, now I remember," Fischer continued. "It was Reid's son who helped stop an assassin from killing a gymnast. Must be a tough kid."

"He is. And smart, too. Very smart."

"How is his father? I heard about him getting shot during that ransom drop."

"He's doing okay. Thank God he was wearing body armor again. He's been shot twice now, and both times vests saved his life."

"I remember the first time. It was years ago, during the Masters tournament, wasn't it?"

Jay nodded. "Yes, it was on the eighteenth hole at Augusta."

"That really shocked me."

"You and the rest of the world."

"Who expects a golfer to get shot? I mean a football player, or basketball, or American football, sure, they're always getting into trouble. But a golfer?"

"Yeah, I know."

"Amazing. Will he be here? I'd like to meet him."

"Yes. He told me he was leaving Chamonix right after the memorial service for Jeff Edwards. He should arrive soon."

"Memorial Service?" Speiser asked.

"Yeah, Jeff Edwards was a teammate and a good friend of Buckar's. He was killed during a fight with a Swedish ski racer," Jay said. "Peter's abduction has stirred up emotions in a lot of people. Tempers are flaring badly. The fight got out of hand, and Edwards got kicked in the head. The Swede didn't mean to kill him. In fact, I feel a little bad for him."

"What?" Speiser said. "A skier killed a fellow racer by kicking him in the head, and you feel bad for him?"

Jay put his palms out defensively. "It's not the way it sounds. George, would you show him the video? The fight was recorded by a nearby TV camera that had been filming an interview between a journalist and the Swedish racer. Someone posted the video online."

"Here, look." Pompard offered his phone to Speiser. "It's gone viral. There are over a million views already."

Speiser watched and said, "Hmm, it's different than I had imagined. I had pictured him kicking the guy while he was down on the ground. While it wasn't exactly self-defense, I can see why he did it. I might have been mad enough to do the same thing."

"That's how I felt," Jay said.

"The Swede's name isn't Dinaso, is it?" Fischer asked.

"Yes, how did you know?"

"He's on a watchlist I was given for the Games."

"That's interesting," Jay said.

"Agreed. There are about twenty names. Some are athletes or their family members, some are known troublemakers that frequent big sporting events, and there are a few other people of interest."

"I hope you'll share that list with us."

"Of course. I'll email it now." He picked up his phone, asked for their email addresses, and typed. "All right, it's sent."

Each looked at their phones and acknowledged receipt. After scrolling through the list, Jay said, "I'm going to forward this to my team, okay?"

"Sure. The more eyes on it, the better."

"I'll do it too," Pompard said.

"Same here," Speiser said.

After sending his email, Jay looked at Fischer. "So, obviously, you've already checked out everyone on this list. Is there anyone on it you like for the abduction?"

"Yes, there are two guys we should speak with, besides the Dinasos." Fischer peered at his phone. "Yury Filipov, a Russian multi-millionaire who owns a few companies. A lot of his wealth comes from the gambling industry."

The men nodded.

"And the other is Itsuki Manaka. He was a politician in Japan, until his corrupt ways got the better of him. His name jumped out at me when I first looked at this list, but I wasn't sure why. It didn't take much digging to find that along with other shady activities, he tried to bribe Olympic skating judges at the Games when they were in Japan."

"Sounds like he would fit in well with the old FIFA regime," Pompard said. "What a mess that was."

Fischer nodded. "It seems crime has found a home in the world of sports."

"They've been entwined for a long time," Pompard added

"Can we please just concentrate on the issue at hand?" Jay said.

"Right," Fischer said. "The Opening Ceremonies are just three days away. Time is not on our side."

As Pompard looked at his phone, his face soured.

"What is it?" Jay asked.

"I just got a text from one of my detectives, clearing his suspect. It's so frustrating. We've had a lot of good people working on this case for days, and so far we have absolutely nothing. It just bothers me."

"Me too," Jay sighed. "But we need to push through our frustration. Chances are the answer lies in our hands already. While we've hit a lot of dead ends, we've narrowed the list down quite a bit. We just need to stay focused and work our way through the rest of the leads."

"Of course. I'll shake this off. It just gets to me sometimes."

"Oh, come on, cut the crap," Fischer said. "We all feel that way once in a while, but there's no time for it right now."

Jay watched Pompard's expression flash from angst to fury, then, just as quickly, to acceptance. Fischer may have been harsh, but he was right.

"I know—" Fischer was silenced by the chirp of his phone. His eyes widened when he glanced at the screen. "I need to go." As he stood, there was a loud knock and the door opened. Henry Seiler, one of Fischer's captains, hastily approached. "I saw the text," Fischer said. "Let's go."

Lang's and Speiser's phones buzzed also. After reading their emails, they looked at each other and stood.

"What is it?" Jay asked.

"Online chatter revealed a possible terrorist cell," Fischer said. "Follow me. We'll talk on the way."

"Lang, ride with me," Commander Speiser ordered.

They all hustled outside. Speiser and Lang took off in Speiser's truck, and the others piled into Fisher's waiting SUV.

As Fischer's driver pulled onto the street, Fischer said, "Henry, give us the details."

"There are two men in a small motel about ten minutes from here, in Samedan. Sasha said there wasn't much information in the chatter, but ISIS was mentioned."

"What does this Sasha cover?" Fischer asked.

"I thought you knew her. She's one of our best Intelligence Specialists," Seiler said. "She should get credit for spotting this."

"Fine. What's the current situation?"

"I sent a team ahead as I came to get you. They're surrounding the motel now."

"Good. Who is the lead?"

"My son, Thomas."

Fischer nodded. "Have him find out whatever he can from the motel manager before we get there."

"Already done. There are two rooms with a pair of men occupying each. The rest of the rooms are filled with families or young couples, and there's one older couple. Granted, it could be anyone, but the online chatter said it was men. So, I figured they should be checked first. The men in one room are Middle Eastern and have been there for about a week. The manager thinks the other two are French and just arrived a few days ago. The Middle Eastern guys have had the Do Not Disturb sign on the door since they arrived, and the staff has only seen them leave once."

"Okay, do we know how many rooms there are and what the building looks like? I don't want to take anything for granted. We need to check every room."

"Here's an image from Google Earth." Seiler handed Fischer his phone and said, "It looks like a typical two-level motel with ten rooms on each level."

After a quick evaluation, Fischer said, "Besides the teams who will enter the two rooms we suspect, I want two officers ready to enter every other room, and I want another ten in the back of the building. Contact the EU Counter-Terrorism Coordinator and have them bring in an EOD team and get snipers on as many surrounding rooftops as possible. Make sure everyone on-site stays out of view. I don't want to spook these guys if they are out for a walk or something and come back while we're setting up." After a moment of thought, Fischer added, "Position plainclothes officers a block away in every direction to keep us informed of any approaching people."

Seiler nodded as Fischer returned his phone.

"Can you think of anything I haven't covered?" Fischer asked.

"No sir," Seiler said as he dialed the dispatch desk to give Fischer's orders.

Fischer looked at Jay. "Am I missing anything?"

"I've never dealt with terrorists. But it sounds like you've got everything covered."

Minutes later the driver parked the SUV around the corner from the motel.

Fischer looked at Jay. "Don't get offended, but I prefer you sit this one out. It could get messy."

"No offense taken. You guys have fun. My job is to find Peter, and I'm pretty sure these punks have nothing to do with his disappearance."

As they stepped from the vehicle, they saw Speiser and Lang running toward them. "I've got more teams on the way," Speiser said through heavy breaths. "Those that are here already are surrounding the motel. We need to—"

Fischer held up his palm, cutting Speiser off. "Commander, please just listen to me for a minute."

"What?" Speiser barked. "This is my jurisdiction."

"Look," Fisher cut him off again. "You don't know my strengths, and I don't know yours. So instead of debating who was going to run this takedown, I reached out to David Froelich, EU's Counter-Terrorism Coordinator. He will be here shortly to take the lead."

"How the hell did you get him here so fast?"

"Don't underestimate the power and importance of the Olympic Games."

Twenty minutes later, with everyone in position, Froelich had his Squad Captain give the Go signal. Teams entered every room of the motel simultaneously. Two Anti-Terrorist Specialists crashed through the door of the Middle Eastern men's room with Fischer, Pompard, and Speiser at their heels.

Through his raid helmet's face shield, Fischer saw one of the two men, who were both in beds, reach under his pillow. After two quick steps and a dive, Fischer was on top of the man, pinning him, face down. The business end of his pistol was pushed hard against the terrorist's temple. Half the terrorist's face was pressed into his pillow. His one visible eye was staring at Fischer eerily, seemingly filled with hate more than fear. An anti-terrorist team member yanked the terrorist's arm from under the pillow. Fischer looked at the man's empty hand.

"Damn, I could have sworn he was reaching for a gun," Fischer said quietly.

On the other side of the room, the second terrorist rolled from his back to the edge of the bed and reached to the floor for a vest lined with explosives. Pompard leaped, slamming his knees into the terrorist's back hard enough to make him drop the bomb. The muted sound of cracking bones and the terrorist's agonizing grunt confirmed that a rib or two had been broken. Handcuffs were slapped in place.

The terrorists were no longer a threat.

Fischer lifted the first terrorist's pillow and smirked at the sight of a Glock 19.

A peek under the bed revealed another explosive vest. After his quick evaluation of the vests, a Bomb Squad member yelled, "Mother of Satan. Everyone out now!"

"That's a hell of a command!" Pompard said with a nervous grin.

"And that was a terrible pun. Mother of Satan is the name terrorists use for triacetone triperoxide, or TATP," Fischer said as they hurried from the room. "It's one of the most unstable explosives known. Did you see all the nails, screws, and ball bearings in the vests? Those bombs were powerful enough to have taken out a large crowd. Thank God those assholes won't get the chance to test my bomb detection systems in the Olympic Village."

"You have doubts about your systems?" Speiser asked as they walked back toward their vehicles.

"No. I'm just glad we stopped them here."

"Nice job, gentlemen!" they heard from behind.

They turned and saw David Froelich, the European Union Anti-Terrorist Coordinator, approaching with his team. All were wearing snug-fitting, dark blue, quarter-zip, pullovers.

Then, from further down the street, behind them, a long, curly-haired woman yelled, "Hey boss, stop for a second."

Froelich and his team turned. Counter-Terrorism was embroidered in bold white letters on the back of their pullovers. Bulges from handguns were obvious at his team's waistlines, but not at Froelich's. Always curious, Fischer scanned Froelich up and down, noticing a protrusion on the inside of his right ankle. *Hmm, a southpaw*, Fischer thought.

After Froelich's quick discussion with the curly-haired woman, he turned toward Fischer, Pompard, and Speiser and said, "Clean work back there. My team was impressed. I just wanted to shake your hands and let you know that we'll handle the interrogation."

Jay and Lang had just joined the group from a different direction in time to hear Froelich's statement.

Pompard shot an annoyed look at Froelich, then glanced at Fischer and Jay.

Jay motioned for Pompard to relax.

"You're okay with him handling the questioning?" Pompard's anger flared.

"We've got enough to deal with already. Terrorism is his game," Jay said, gesturing with his chin toward Froelich.

Fischer nodded.

Pompard's lips fluttered as he blew off a little steam. "You are right." He turned to Froelich. "Sorry, I just got caught up in the moment."

"Perfectly understandable. I would have been surprised if one of you hadn't after that apprehension. I'm sure your adrenaline is overflowing."

"You got that right," Pompard said. He inhaled and expelled another deep cleansing breath.

"You can use my interrogation rooms," Speiser offered, looking at Froelich.

"Thanks, but we have other plans."

"Please press them for information regarding any other terrorist cells that might be in the area," Fischer said. "I need to keep the Games safe for everyone."

"Of course, and I'll keep you informed."

"Thank you." Fischer reached to shake Froelich's hand.

Chapter 42

FISCHER STARED INTENSELY through the tinted rear passenger window of the SUV on the ride back to the Olympic Village. His right forearm was on the door's armrest, his fist continuously clenching, releasing, and re-clenching.

"Relax, Christoph," Jay said. "You just took two terrorists off the streets. Take a breather."

"Relax?" Fischer shot back. "All I can think about is how many more of them might be out there getting ready to kill innocent people at the Olympics. I'll relax when the Games are over. These bastards scare the crap out of me."

"Me too," Jay said.

After a quiet moment, the blaring horn from a yellow Ferrari made them all flinch as it pulled out from behind their SUV into the oncoming lane and raced by.

"*Fils de salope*!" Pompard yelled.

The Ferrari cut quickly back into their lane, almost hitting the SUV's front bumper and narrowly missing a head-on crash with an oncoming truck. Obviously, the Ferrari driver had no idea he had just passed a police vehicle. It looked like any other black SUV with dark, tinted windows.

The officer driving sped up and switched on the siren and flashing lights in the grill. At first, the Ferrari increased its speed, then it slowed, pulled to the side of the road, and stopped. The SUV parked just behind it.

"Anyone care to teach the asshole a lesson?" the driver asked.

"Damn right!," barked Pompard, opening his door.

"We don't have time for this," Fischer said calmly. "Close your door, and let's go."

As they pulled away and passed the Ferrari, Pompard said, "I could use a drink."

Chapter 43

THE OLYMPIC VILLAGE was abuzz. Athletes had been arriving for weeks to train and see the sights. While St. Moritz is always extravagant, the Olympic Games brought with them an added air of excitement to the glamourous town. Throngs of spectators from around the world were there to see and be seen. The shops and restaurants were packed. The uber-wealthy were known to spend endless amounts of Euros in St. Moritz, yet, the Games promised a considerable uptick in the regularly thriving economy of the high-end stores, restaurants, and hotels. Even the lower-end Inns were jammed with overcharged patrons. Similar to Cannes and Monaco, the Olympics are like a playground for socialites, royalty, and celebrities. Many aren't the slightest bit interested in the sporting events. For them, it's more about extravagance and indulgence. For others, it's all about partying. While Olympic festivities are not as outrageous as Mardi Gras or Rio's Carnival, the nightlife in the Olympic Village had its own caliber of excitement. Most private gatherings were not considered dangerous, yet the guest lists at many parties were synonymous with a Who's Who of the world's most powerful and wealthy. Fischer knew these events were tantamount to a terrorist's wet dream.

Weeks prior, he had circulated a letter he had written and signed along with David Katz, the president of the International Olympic Committee.

Dear(name),

If you are planning to attend the upcoming Olympic Games, and we hope you are, please know that we are doing everything within our power to provide an enjoyable and safe experience for all.

There are those, like yourself, that we believe might require an extra degree of security. It will be extremely helpful if you keep us informed about where you are staying and any private gatherings you plan to attend. This information will be kept private and will help us provide better security and a safer environment for you and your group.

Thank you for your cooperation.

We hope you enjoy the Olympic Games.

Sincerely,

David Katz	***Christoph Fischer***
President IOC	*Chief of Olympic Security*

Thousands of copies were delivered to people of importance around the globe. The email account that was set up for replies filled quickly. Fischer knew that many of the wealthiest recipients of the letter traveled with their own security teams and that some of them would feel safer without the added attention his officers might bring. There were also those who thought they knew better than everyone else and believed that they could hide in plain sight. While Fischer didn't agree, he couldn't force protection on anyone, even if he felt it was somewhat selfish of those who declined his offer. After all, the more his team knew, the better his chances of providing a safe environment for all.

Fischer already had his plate full, keeping the Games safe. The addition of the Buckar issue was an extra serving he just didn't need.

Chapter 44

THE HIGH-SPEED body-slam forced the man hard against the wall. Two guys near the man who had been hit tried to restrain him from retaliating. With his adrenaline raging, he threw one of them down on the ice. The following skirmish was inevitable as men pushed and shoved each other aggressively.

Another street fight? No, not this time. This was the Russian hockey team's practice session.

"Don't be an ass, Dmitri," said the man who had been thrown against the boards. "Coach said no hard checking until the Games begin."

"It was instinct, Fyodor. Don't be a pussy. I barely hit you!"

"Yes, but when I'm told there will be no hitting, I don't expect to be hit. And besides, you don't hit like an ordinary man. You're like a fucking freight train." He laughed, skated over to Dmitri, and put his arm over his comrade's shoulder. "I'm glad we're on the same team. I feel sorry for our competition."

Fyodor and their surrounding teammates joined in his laughter. As the group dispersed, Fyodor gave Dmitri a hard shove, knocking him to the ice.

"What the hell?" Dmitri yelled as he scrambled back to his feet, threw his gloves off, and started toward Fyodor.

"Oh, don't be a pussy," Fyodor said with a big grin as he skated backward, away from Dmitri.

The rest of the team laughed, and as Dmitri realized he was being played, he nodded and smiled.

Behind the rink's glass wall, their coaches sat on cold, hard benches and watched. When Dmitri had hit Fyodor, the head coach stood, blew his whistle, and yelled, "*Prekrati!*"

The coaches knew their players well enough to know that Dmitri's hit was no big deal. It was just his way to get everyone's adrenaline flowing.

Most of the seats in the arena were filled. It was only a practice session, but Russians loved their hockey team passionately.

The noise level and commotion throughout the arena had spiked with Dmitri's hit. There's nothing like a little violence to get a hockey fan's blood flowing, that and a stiff shot or two of vodka. People in the stands were alternating between drinking and chanting, "Dmitri, Dmitri."

Russian fans liked Fyodor for his scoring ability, but they absolutely loved Dmitri's aggressiveness on the ice. When he hit a competitor, the crowds cheered. When his gloves came off, and he squared off mano-a-mano with his foe, his fans went berserk.

"Yes, we will make a lot with hockey too, but I want to steer the big money toward skiing." The man with the blond ponytail was seated in the stands talking into his phone.

"I know it's never been done be—" The loud crack of Fyodor's slapshot, the blast of the siren as the puck hit the back of the goal, and the roar of the crowd caused the blond man to stop talking. "What," he yelled into his phone a moment later. "Wait a second, I can't hear a word." He waited for the noise to decrease. "Look, the beauty of this deal is that there has never been any real money bet on skiing, but the fantasy gambling business is bringing in money from a whole new breed of gamblers. People who have never gambled before are betting millions. We can maneuver this any way we want. All we have to do is set the reward money high enough, and the bets will come." He listened. "What do you mean you don't know? You need to grow a pair!" The crowd erupted again as a shot deflected off the goalie's stick. As the noise died down, he said into the phone. "I'm telling you, this will make us a fortune." He listened. "Vlad … Vlad … are you there? Dammit," he said loudly as he shoved the phone in his pocket. He looked at his girlfriend sitting next to him and the couple next to her. "Let's go."

"But we just got here," she said. "I want to watch for a while. At least let us finish our beer."

He sneered at her. "Do what you want. I'm leaving."

As he walked away, she looked at their friends, her head shaking and her lips pursed tight, then she looked back in his direction. "Where are you going? I thought we were going to watch them practice, then go for dinner? Come back. Just stay till we finish our beer. Then, we will all go."

He continued down the aisle, side-stepping past people in the seats.

"Misha, please," she begged.

At the end of the aisle, he turned and started up the stairs without looking back.

Chapter 45

PETER THOUGHT ABOUT the dream he had just awoken from. He'd been standing on the top step of the podium as a gold medal was placed around his neck, and the Star-Spangled Banner played.

His mindset had changed. When his captors originally revealed that they intended for him to race in the Games, he was confused and furious. Since then, despite his injury-induced persistent headache, he thought, *why not get in the best shape possible, and go for the damn Gold. They can take away my freedom, but they can't steal my dreams.*

His newly found resolve made him smile. *That virtual machine may not be the same as skiing on a real race course, but, in some ways, it's better. I have no distractions. I can work out and train all day and night. Things could be worse.*

On his way to the bathroom, he noticed a new message on the TV.

"GOOD MORNING, PETER. WE HAVE A TREAT FOR YOU TODAY. ONCE YOU ARE DONE WITH BREAKFAST, PLEASE GO OUT THE DOOR OF YOUR ROOM AND WALK DOWN THE HALLWAY TO YOUR LEFT. GO

THROUGH THE DOOR AT THE END OF THE HALL. THERE YOU WILL FIND A RUNNING TRACK AND A SWIMMING TANK. THERE IS A SWIMSUIT, TOWELS, AND RUNNING GEAR IN THE BATHROOM. GO CHANGE, AND WHEN YOU COME OUT, THERE WILL BE AN OMELET WAITING FOR YOU. WE FIGURED YOU COULD USE SOME PROTEIN BEFORE YOU SWIM AND RUN. ENJOY!"

Peter hustled into the bathroom and saw a bathing suit, robe, t-shirt, running shorts, and socks all neatly folded in a pile with sneakers on top. After relieving himself, he quickly threw on the t-shirt and sneakers. His only thought was to escape. Wearing boxers, the t-shirt, and sneakers, his anxiety was now amped to the max. He ran from the bathroom to the room door, grabbed the handle, twisted, and pulled. His sweaty hand slipped from the locked door. "Shit!"

Completely let down, he shuffled over and sat in the chair across from the TV.

Just as he knew it would, new text was being typed:

"WE'RE GLAD YOU'RE SO EXCITED ABOUT SWIMMING AND RUNNING, BUT WE WANT YOU TO EAT FIRST. SO WHY DON'T YOU GO BACK INTO THE BATHROOM AND TAKE YOUR TIME CHANGING, SO THAT WE CAN DELIVER YOUR EGGS. THEN, AFTER BREAKFAST, THE DOOR WILL BE UNLOCKED, AND YOU CAN HEAD OUT FOR YOUR ACTIVITIES. AND PETER, TEMPTED AS YOU MAY BE TO ESCAPE, PLEASE UNDERSTAND, THE EXIT DOOR YOU WILL SEE AT THE END OF THE HALLWAY TO THE RIGHT, IS LOCKED, AND THERE IS NO OTHER WAY OUT. SO, LIKE BEFORE, BE GOOD, GET YOUR EXERCISE, ENJOY YOUR NEW ACTIVITIES, AND YOU WILL BE READY TO RACE IN

THE GAMES IN A FEW DAYS. IF YOU TRY TO ESCAPE, WE WILL HAVE TO RE-THINK ALLOWING YOU OUT OF YOUR ROOM TO SWIM AND RUN—SO, PLEASE COOPERATE!"

Peter's jubilation had once again turned to extreme disappointment. He sat for a minute to let his adrenaline dissipate. He was at their mercy, and he hated it, but if he did what they suggested, maybe he really would race in the Games. *Hell, I can last just a few more days. At least now I know the time frame!* Not knowing how long he had been there and when the Olympics were going to begin had been causing him a lot of torment. How could he know how to prepare his body if he didn't know the timing? He needed a couple of days to completely relax his legs before a race. He typically worked his legs hard, and then a couple of days before a race, he would just stretch them and get them massaged. The looser he was in the starting gate, the better he raced. *Well, since I obviously can't get a massage, I may as well go for a swim—and maybe I'll find a way out of here.*

Chapter 46

READING -9 DEGREES Celsius on the thermometer near the door of Fischer's trailer office, Jay thought, *of all days for me to forget my gloves.* His fingers were so cold he felt like they might break off as he turned the doorknob. He rubbed his hands briskly together after putting down the cardboard coffee cup tray and the paper bag he had brought onto Fischer's desk.

Fischer lifted a cup and took a sip. "Ah, cappuccino, thank you. And breakfast, I hope?" he asked, pointing at the brown bag.

"Zopf," Jay said. "I tried it yesterday, and I'm hooked. I figured you could use some Zmorge."

Fischer smiled as he took the warm, braided loaf of bread from the bag and pulled a German KM2000 combat knife from his drawer.

"Not a fan of Swiss Army knives?" Jay asked with a smirk.

"Not when it comes to slicing a masterpiece like this," Fischer said as he cut a thick slice, speared it, and offered it to Jay. "You better be careful with this stuff, it's addicting."

"Thanks for the warning, but I think you're too late."

"Oh, I'm so sorry," Fischer said with a grin.

With a smirk, Jay said, "Don't worry, I'm not sorry at all." He took a bite and closed his eyes with a look of bliss.

After swallowing a mouthful, Fischer said, "I'd like you to join me for a talk with Yury Filipov and Itsuki Manaka, the two men of interest I told you about who are on my watchlist of potential troublemakers."

"Why do you need me?" Jay asked. "We have a lot of leads to cover. It might be better if we split up and each work with our own teams. I mean no disrespect, Christoph."

"None taken. After we speak with these two men, I agree, we should go in different directions. We'll get more accomplished, faster. But I like the way I've seen you handle people, and I have a feeling that one of these guys might be our man, or at least be able to shed some light for us."

With a curious tilt of his head, Jay asked, "Is there any specific reason for that feeling?"

"Not really. Just instinct."

"Okay. I follow my gut instincts all the time. Why not yours."

"Good."

They left Fischer's trailer and boarded his SUV.

"Luckily, they're both staying at the same hotel," Fischer said.

"Really?"

"Yes. It's a popular hotel. Could just be a coincidence."

"You don't really believe that, do you?"

"I don't know."

Jay nodded.

It took some time for the driver to navigate through the traffic in St. Moritz. The streets were mobbed with crowds of tourists, media, and athletes. Staring out the window as they drove toward Badrutt's Palace Hotel, Jay glanced at Lake St. Moritz. He couldn't believe what he was seeing. People on skis, being towed at high speed by galloping horses. "What the hell are they doing out there?"

"They're practicing for the skijoring races."

"Skijoring? Never heard of it. Looks difficult."

"I haven't tried it, but they say it's extremely difficult. I've done some dangerous things but getting towed on skis behind a racing-thoroughbred horse, that's not for me."

"I can see why. It looks a little crazy."

"They're on a straightway. You should see when they turn. That's when it gets crazy."

"I'll bet."

Fischer nodded as they turned into the entrance of the hotel driveway.

As they entered the hotel, one of Fischer's men, who had been sent ahead, was waiting near the entrance. He approached and said, "Manaka's not here, but Filipov is. He's swimming laps."

"Where's the pool?" Fischer asked.

"This way."

As they walked, Fischer asked, "Where's Manaka?"

"He's at the figure skating venue with his wife and another couple, watching a practice session."

Shoes wet from the snow, Fischer skidded as he stepped from the entrance rug near the door onto the marble floor of the grand lobby. His arms shot out, and his body twisted, yet he managed to remain upright.

"I'll give you an eight. Awkward, yet graceful," Jay said with a grin.

"Shut up."

Both men smiled.

They passed a small group of tourists, sitting on couches in front of a tremendous, arched, stone fireplace. The crackling blaze warmed the entire room. Continuing down a wide hallway, they walked by a crowded restaurant, then stopped in front of French doors with *SPA* etched into the frosted glass windows. Fischer's officer slid a hotel key card through the reader, waited for a green light, then opened one of the doors.

A tall, muscular man and a very fit woman were standing behind the counter. Both nodded at the officer as he led Fischer and Jay by. The officer had obviously done his homework. Passing a glass-walled exercise room, they saw two women on treadmills and a man stretching on a floor mat. Continuing down the hall, they passed a few doors. Two were slightly open, exposing dimly lit rooms. Quiet, soothing music and subtle, relaxing scents floated from the doorways as they hurried by.

Jay breathed in deeply. "Jasmine?"

"And vanilla," Fischer said. "I could use a massage right about now."

Jay nodded as they continued briskly toward the frameless, glass, French doors at the end of the hallway. Another swipe of the officer's hotel key card caused the doors to slowly swing open. A harsh burst of chlorinated air greeted them. The tremendous indoor pool area was surrounded by floor to ceiling, glass-paneled walls, providing a gorgeous view of the snow-covered Alps. A rock formation, trees, and a small waterfall on one side of the pool added to the natural, outdoor feeling. A low opening at the bottom of the glass panels at the far end of the room allowed swimmers to pass through to the half-round, outdoor section of the pool, where a thick layer of steam lingered just above the heated water.

But for the soft babbling of the waterfall, the room was very quiet with only three inhabitants.

Two men sat at a poolside table, smoking cigarettes despite the numerous *No Smoking* signs. Another man was swimming.

Fischer and Jay watched as the lone man in the pool turned at the far end to swim another lap. His bald head parted the water smoothly as he swam powerfully in their direction.

Jay took a neatly folded towel from one of the stacks piled high on a table near the entrance. He walked to the edge of the pool that the man was approaching, and crouched.

The two smokers simultaneously stood. One, a short, beefy guy, loudly said, "Hey, you, by the pool. Who are you? What do you want?"

Fischer walked toward the men with his badge displayed.

Jay glanced and saw the two men approaching, and then he quickly refocused on Filipov.

Jay unbuttoned his cuffs and pushed his shirt and sweater sleeves up to his elbow. As Filipov was swimming up to the wall, Jay reached to tap his shoulder, but he missed, and instead, his hand brushed the side of Filipov's head.

Filipov abruptly stopped swimming and lifted his head from the water. After quickly removing his swim goggles with one hand, he rubbed his eyes with the other, then looked at Jay through intense, steel-gray eyes. "Who the hell are you?" he asked in Russian as he stood in the waist-deep water. For a man in his late 60s, Filipov was in impressive, physical shape.

"I apologize for disturbing you, but I need to ask you a few questions," Jay said in English as he flashed his ID toward Filipov.

Filipov turned quickly toward his men, who were now sitting in chairs by the pool, at the opposite end of Fischer's gun.

Filipov's subtle reaction told Jay volumes about the man. Many men would have yelled, and aggressively jumped from the pool. Others might cower in fear. Filipov just turned his head and locked eyes with Jay.

"I'll repeat my question. Who the hell are you?" Filipov had switched to English. His look and words were as cold as the long, dagger-like icicles hanging from the gutter just outside the windows.

"Jay Scott. I'm working with the Chief of Olympic Security, Christoph Fischer," he said with a nod in Fischer's direction. "Along with the police and Europol, we're investigating the disappearance of American ski racer, Peter Buckar."

"What do you want from me?"

"Just a moment of your time. We have some questions for you. Why don't you come out of the pool so we can talk." He offered the towel he was holding.

"I know nothing about Buckar's disappearance. I have nothing to tell you. Good day, Mr. Scott." Filipov turned and began to lower himself into the water.

Jay's anger flared. He didn't want to jump in the water. Without further thought, he swung the towel hitting Filipov's shoulder.

The muscles in Filipov's back and shoulders tightened. He spun around, reached for the edge of the pool, quickly bounded out, and stood face to face with Jay.

"You have some nerve," Filipov seethed through tightly clenched teeth.

"You gave me no choice. I don't want to get physical, nor do I want to argue. I just want to talk. Why don't we go sit."

"We can talk right here. Make it quick. I want to continue my laps."

"I'd like Mr. Fischer to join us. Let's just go sit with him and talk like civilized men."

"Civilized? You slap me with a towel, and your friend has a gun pointed at my men. You call this civilized?"

"As I said, you left me no choice. I'm sure your men left Mr. Fischer no choice either."

"Tell him to put the gun away. Then, I'll come sit."

"Tell your men not to pull their guns out when he puts his away, and you've got a deal."

Filipov took a deep breath and let it out while staring into Jay's eyes. Obviously, he wasn't used to complying with another man's demands. He nodded slightly, turned toward his men, and said, "He's going to put his gun away. Leave yours where they are."

His men nodded.

Fischer holstered his pistol.

Filipov turned back, once again staring into Jay's eyes.

Jay stared back and offered the towel, once again. This time Filipov took it. A bit of detente?

Walking toward Fischer, Filipov turned his head to Jay, "Thanks for the *wet* towel," he said, emphasizing wet.

"Whose fault is that?" Jay said with a smirk.

Jay figured that Filipov's attempt at humor was more about conveying a message than it was about being funny. If he could joke at a time like this, he obviously wasn't worried about their upcoming discussion. It seemed he was already trying to prove he had nothing to do with Peter's disappearance.

Filipov draped the towel over his muscular shoulders, and the three men sat at a poolside table with Filipov's men sitting at an adjacent table.

"So, gentlemen, let's keep this conversation short. I want to get back in the pool. I need to work off all the excellent food I have been eating here in St. Moritz."

"Tell us what we need to know, and you'll be back in the water in no time," Fischer said.

"That might be a problem," Filipov said.

"Why?"

"As Mr. Scott has informed me, you're here to get information about Peter Buckar's whereabouts."

"That's correct," Fischer said.

"Sorry to let you down, but I can't help you. I had nothing to do with it, and I have no idea who does."

"Why should we believe you?" Jay asked.

"Because I'm an honest man."

"Okay then, that's good enough for me," Jay said.

Fischer's head jerked toward Jay, giving him a bewildered look.

Following a chuckle, Jay said, "C'mon Yuri, you're honest? Really? Which of your businesses is the honest one? Drugs or gambling?"

"I have made most of my money in technology. I have invested some of that money in other businesses. A couple of those businesses have partial ownership of yet other businesses. The minute I learn that any business I own is involved in anything illegal, I sell my shares and get out. I will never have anything to do with drug trafficking. If you've done any research, you know that I lost my daughter to drugs. She overdosed on heroin when she was twenty-one. The whole idea of it nauseates me."

"I'm sorry. I had no idea," Jay said.

Fischer nodded. "I read about that. I'm very sorry."

Filipov stood. "I wish I could help you find your man. I really do. He's one of the best racers I've seen, probably one of the best ever. I hope he's okay. Good day, gentlemen." He started walking away.

"Yuri," Jay said. "Please come back and sit. We are not done yet."

Filipov turned his head. "Come on. This is ridiculous. I'm telling you, I've got nothing for you. I'm innocent."

"Then you have nothing to worry about by continuing our discussion. Come back and have a seat."

He walked back. "You know, you're becoming a real pain in my ass. I'm here on vacation to watch the Games. I really don't need this." He sat in the chair. "I'll give you five more minutes, then I'm going to finish my laps."

"Fair enough. Let's talk about your gambling business."

"Fine. Last I knew gambling wasn't illegal. I own one small casino and a small percentage of four others."

"Must be profitable."

"They do okay."

"How about online betting?"

"I have a small share in that too."

"How about the new online fantasy gambling sites?"

"Too new for me, but they seem to be catching on. I have my people looking into it. It all depends on how they will be regulated. The owners are claiming that they are not gambling sites at all. They say they are contests. And that they don't need to follow gambling regulations. Sounds like a bunch of nonsense to me."

Jay nodded.

"Why do you care about my gambling business anyway? It's not like there's any real money being bet on the Olympics."

"I'm just curious. The fantasy sites seem like they might be bringing new blood, so to speak, into the industry. I was wondering if you knew anyone who owned, or invested, in one?"

"No."

"Would you mind making some calls to your associates? One of them might know someone."

Filipov gave Jay a shrewd, contemplative look. "What's in it for me?"

Jay shook his head. "Really? How about saving the life of an innocent human being. Or, how about keeping the Olympics a safer place. Or how about …"

Feigning boredom, Filipov crossed his arms and rolled his eyes.

"Okay, I'll tell you what, if you come through with something that helps us find Peter, Christoph and I will each owe you a big favor. That my friend could be of serious value to you one day."

Now nodding, Filipov said, "I'll see what I can find out."

"Very good. Here." Jay handed Filipov his business card.

Filipov stood and said, "There is one guy I know of who is new to the gambling business. I don't know him, but I know he is very corrupt. He's been making offers to buy casinos, and he's being very pushy about it. He's already pissed off a couple of my comrades in the business. I'll make some calls and let you know if I hear anything worthwhile"

"*Spaseeba*," Jay said.

"*Pazhaista*," Filipov answered as he handed Jay's card to one of his men.

Exiting through the heavy glass doors, Jay turned just in time to see Filipov dive into the pool. Along with the no-smoking signs, there were no diving signs all around the pool area. And, just in case a hotel guest didn't understand the print in German or English, there was a picture of a diver with a bold red X through it. Jay shook his head, thinking, *Arrogant bastard. He won't call.*

As the door closed behind them, Fischer said, "Waste of time, huh?"

Jay nodded. "Probably!"

Fischer looked at his phone, then back at Jay. "I hope you'll join me in speaking with Manaka over at the skating venue. It's a short ride."

Jay looked at his watch. "Sure, let's go. But let's make it quick."

Chapter 47

PETER GLANCED UP at a clock on the wall of the warehouse. He had been running for an hour. It was time for a short rest, some stretching, then a swim. After changing into the swimsuit, he climbed into what looked like a very long hot tub. The water was cool, and although the tub was long, it wasn't long enough to do laps. He waded to the end of the tub, where there was a thermostat dial, a large button, and a plastic emblem that read in English: Endless Pools. He pushed the button, a motor rumbled, and water began to flow, creating a current that ran the length of the pool. Peter thought, Hm, *this should be interesting. Reid has one of these in his house at AllSport, and he loves it. How bad could it be?* He snickered, thinking, *well, that is, as long as I don't drown.*

It took a little getting used to, but after a couple of minutes of swimming against the current at a nice slow pace, he began to feel comfortable with the process.

Peter was not a big fan of swimming or running, but after being holed up in that God-forsaken room for however many days, the new activities felt like a little bit of freedom. He might as well enjoy the feeling for as long as he could. Grueling as they were, running and swimming got his body moving in ways it hadn't in days, and besides, the cool water was refreshing.

After a few more minutes, his arms began to feel weak and rubbery. Never a quitter, he continued pulling against the current. Soon he could barely lift his arms to take the next stroke. *Wow, my upper body strength sucks,* he thought. Then, as he pressed on, the pain began to subside. He smiled, realizing it wasn't weakness, he was just using muscles in his arms and shoulders in ways they weren't conditioned for. *When I get out of here, I should add swimming to my routine,* he thought. *Damn, I'm going to be sore tomorrow.*

Then he smiled again, thinking, *Hmm, I just made plans for the future. At least my subconscious believes what these bastards keep telling me.*

Chapter 48

149 KM/H FLASHED REPEATEDLY on the big red digital speed display as the bobsled rocketed toward the next banked "S" turn on the solid ice race course.

Gus DiBetta and Alfonse Brunelli had been walking down the mountain on the steep concrete steps next to the bobsled run. They stopped at a large concrete platform near a few spectators to watch as another four-man sled whooshed by. Feeling the rush of wind, DiBetta said, "Wow, I've always wanted to ride in one of those."

Brunelli nudged DiBetta with his left elbow just enough to get his attention.

"What?" DiBetta said, turning toward his colleague.

Brunelli raised his finger to his lips and tilted his head in the direction of the men standing to his right.

DiBetta looked past Brunelli. The man with the blond ponytail was speaking loudly into his cell phone. He either didn't care who heard his conversation, or he figured chances were good that those standing nearby didn't understand Ukrainian.

DiBetta, who was fluent in Ukrainian, listened closely. "Yes, I said bobsled. This sport is crazy. It'll bring in a lot of money ... No, skiing, hockey, and bobsledding are enough. I don't want to distract from our main goal. Skiing must be the main contest … Yes, we will offer a prize big enough to entice even those who've never gambled before … Yes, I'm sure. Alexi said the bets are coming in steadily already, and when we increase the prize money to one million, word will spread … We have to keep it simple! New gamblers will only place bets if it's very easy. Are you with the programmer now?… Good, I will clear the extra prize money and the bobsledding with Alexi, and then I'll call you back. Get the programming done for the bobsled. I want you to be ready to upload it as soon as Alexi gives the go-ahead … Yes, just add the bobsledding and raise the skiing prize. Keep the bobsledding contest simple, just like the others. Prize money will be paid for gold, silver, and bronze, and any combination of the three … Yes. Just be ready … Okay. Before I hang up, tell me, how's our man doing? … Good, I'll call you back soon."

DiBetta couldn't quite make out the man's last sentences due to the racket of another bobsled soaring by. Speed blurred the white sled, but the bold word Ukraine and its blue and yellow flag were unmistakable. DiBetta saw 153 blinking on the digital speed display, then glanced to his right. A wide smile stretched across the blond man's face. He pulled a flask from his jacket, knocked back a swig, then turned and started walking down the long flight of stairs.

DiBetta and Brunelli followed at a distance. A few seconds later, the man stopped at the next platform, walked toward a flagpole, and leaned against it. He took another pull from his flask and removed his phone from his pocket. Although there were other spectators on the platform, the man was standing alone. DiBetta and Brunelli could not get close without him noticing.

"What was he saying on the phone?" Brunelli asked.

"Something about online Olympic gambling, especially on skiing. Sounds strange, but I guess people would bet on it."

"You think so?"

"A fast sport with high risk is a good formula for gambling. Maybe he's on to something big, but I wonder if it could have anything to do with Buckar's disappearance."

"Probably not."

DiBetta scrolled through the contacts on his phone.

"Who are you calling?"

DiBetta raised his forefinger as he brought his phone to his ear with his other hand.

"Jay, it's Gus. We're at the bobsled track about to go speak with a few Italian racers who are here watching … I just wanted to let you know that we overheard a strange conversation a guy was having on his cell in Ukrainian … Yes, I had a Ukrainian girlfriend for a while, so I had to learn it. It's similar to Russian, so it wasn't too difficult … Uh-huh, Russian, French, Spanish, a little Greek, some Mandarin, and, of course, English and Italian." Gus listened and laughed. "Sure, Jay. Pay me enough, and I'll go wherever you need me to." He listened and chuckled again. "Right. He was talking about betting on skiing, hockey, and bobsledding. He said skiing would be their biggest … he used the word contest. He told his guy to get their programmer ready to upload everything to their website. He wanted to add bobsledding and raise the prize money for the skiing contest to one million … I agree, I've never heard of online betting for skiing, but if you think about it, there may be an opportunity to make some serious money. I know Italians love ski racing, I'm sure most people throughout the Alps do too … Yes, that's what Brunelli and I thought. I doubt it's connected to Peter, but who knows … No, I'm not sure. He could be Ukrainian, he could be Russian … He has a long blond ponytail and some hair below his lower lip … No, not a beard, I think it's called a soul patch … Yes, he was speaking loudly, like he had nothing to hide. He didn't care who was listening. I doubt he would do that if he was involved with Peter … Yes. Just before he hung up he said he was going to call someone named Alexi to get his approval on some gambling changes … I don't know. We followed him, and now he's on the phone again, but he is standing by himself, so we can't get close enough to listen … Yes, he's still talking. You want us to follow him? … I know. We're running out of time … Okay, we'll go speak with the Italians instead … Okay, talk to you later."

DiBetta hung up and turned to Brunelli. "You heard, right?"

Brunelli nodded.

"Let's head down to the bottom quickly. I hope Lupinacci is still there."

After a few minutes of walking down the steep stairs next to the track, another sled raced by.

"I'd rather be in one of those than hoofing it down these steps," Brunelli said.

"That would be awe …" DiBetta stopped mid-word as the bobsled careened hard into the ice wall of the track. The driver oversteered, and they hit the other wall. The sled rolled onto its side and slid toward the next banked turn. Then, it slid up the embankment and hit the boundary at the uppermost edge of the track. Having lost its momentum, the bobsled flipped into the air and dropped ten feet, like a lead weight, landing upside down on the ice.

DiBetta and Brunelli ran, bounded over the wall and down onto the track. Both men fell as their feet hit the ice. Brunelli landed hard on his elbow while DiBetta hit the back of his head. Without a thought about their own wellbeing, they got up and moved as quickly as they could, slipping and skidding toward the overturned sled. As they got close, Brunelli fell again, grunting loudly.

"You all right?" DiBetta asked.

"Just go help them," Brunelli groaned.

DiBetta turned and moved gingerly toward the bobsled. Two medics were already trying to right the sled. DiBetta bent down to help, and the three of them managed to roll it, along with the three men still inside, onto its metal blades.

The rear man, of the four bobsledders, had already pushed himself out the back of the sled and was lying on the track. DiBetta helped the number three man slowly untangle himself from the heap and slide over next to his teammate on the ice. The number two man was slumped over the driver's back and was not moving. A medic placed his fingers on the man's neck and said, "He's alive, but we're not moving him until we get a stretcher."

Two more medics were already carrying a backboard over the wall onto the track. The medic working on the men in the sled spoke to the number two man but received no response. He then asked the driver if he was all right.

"I can't move my shoulder, but I'm okay. How's Mateo?"

"We'll know soon. We'll get him off of you as quickly as we can."

The medics with the backboard asked DiBetta to move aside. He stood and slowly backed away. A quick look around revealed two other medics putting a neck brace on the number four man. The position three bobsledder rose to his feet and rubbed his face. DiBetta noticed that the man looked very unsteady, so he approached to offer help. As he got close, the man's eyes rolled up in their sockets. DiBetta was close enough to catch him as he collapsed and slowly lowered him to the ice. A nearby medic quickly crouched to help. DiBetta stood and scanned the entire scene, shaking his head slowly in dismay. Off the track he saw another medic putting Brunelli's arm in a sling. DiBetta climbed over the wall and walked to them.

"How bad?" DiBetta asked.

"Don't know yet. How is he?" Brunelli gestured toward the bobsledder that was getting placed onto the stretcher.

"Don't know that yet, either. He's alive. Which is a miracle after that crash."

Brunelli nodded.

"Why don't you go with him," DiBetta gestured toward the medic. "Get your arm checked out. I'll go talk to the Italian skiers."

"No, I'll be okay. I'm coming with you."

Surprised at Brunelli's statement, the medic said, "Sir, You really need to come with me to get x-rays. I'm fairly certain your arm is broken."

"That's all right. I'll get it checked out later. Thank you for your help."

"I'm sorry, but I must insist."

"Insist? Look, I'm fine. Don't worry about it. Gus let's go. We don't have time for this."

"Sir, it is not an option. We've been given strict orders not to take any chances during the Games. If someone gets hurt, they must go to the hospital."

"Give me a minute," DiBetta said, pulling out his phone. "What's your name?"

"Rudolf, why"

"Just give me a second." DiBetta tapped on his phone and put it to his ear.

"Jay, it's Gus again. Are you with Fischer? … Good, can I speak with him? … Hi Christoph, we had a small dilemma at the bobsled run. We stopped to help out with an overturned bobsled, and one of my men got hurt. He's okay, possibly a broken arm, but the medic who is helping him insists on taking him for x-rays. He says he is required to take him to the hospital, that it's one of your rules. I'm sure it's a liability issue, so do me a favor, tell the medic it's all right to let us go … Okay, thanks, here he is."

DiBetta handed his phone to Rudolf, who said hello and listened. His demeanor instantly changed. "Yes, sir … Okay, sir … Bye." He handed the phone back to DiBetta.

"So, are we okay to go?"

"Of course. I'm sorry I held you up."

"You were doing your job," Brunelli said. "And I thank you for that."

"Just do yourself a favor and get that arm x-rayed soon."

"I will. Thanks again."

As the two men turned to head down the mountain, they saw medics lifting the stretcher over the wall from inside the race course. They walked toward the medics, and as they got close, the man on the stretcher gave them a slight nod.

"I'm glad you're okay," DiBetta said to the bobsledder.

"Thank you."

"How is your teammate?"

The loud wail of sirens drowned out his answer as two ambulances approached.

DiBetta noticed a television reporter and cameraman pushing through the onlookers toward the bobsledder on the stretcher.

The reporter inched his way closer, and after speaking into his microphone, reached out and put the microphone close to the bobsledder's face.

"Go away," yelled the medic who was carrying the rear of the stretcher.

Ignoring the warning, the reporter pushed his mic closer to the athlete.

"Dammit," Brunelli said as he took a step in the reporter's direction. DiBetta quickly reached for Brunelli's good arm and stopped him.

"Let me go."

"We don't have the time for this. Let them deal with the reporter," DiBetta said, gesturing toward two approaching security officers.

Brunelli nodded with a sigh.

They turned to leave, and DiBetta's heart sank when he saw the second stretcher being loaded into an ambulance with a sheet covering the body from head to toe.

Brunelli's eyes were already moist as DiBetta quietly said, "Let's go."

Chapter 49

IN THE BACK seat of the SUV, on their way to the skating venue, Fischer was handing Jay's phone back to him as it rang.

Jay answered the call, listened, and said, "Okay, thanks. Might as well head to your next lead. I'll talk to you later."

Fischer stared at Jay, waiting.

"Two of my guys found the stalker. Actually, she found them. They were near the finish line of the slalom course, questioning one of the American coaches when she approached the coach, asking about Peter. After escorting her from the crowd, they questioned her, and to make a long story short, they cleared her."

"Are they absolutely sure?"

"I don't second guess my team, Christoph. I only employ those whose intelligence and intuition are worthy of my complete trust. I hire the best and reward them accordingly. So, to answer your question, yes, they're sure."

"Fair enough. In terms of reward, what are we talking?"

"When the Games are over, I'll be happy to discuss it with you."

"I'd like that, thanks."

Jay turned to his phone and read through his emails until the vehicle stopped near one of the rear entrances to the skating rink.

A female officer from Fischer's team was waiting. She was attractive, with long, wavy, dirty-blonde hair. Her expression was stern, but Jay was sure her big brown eyes sparkled a little, and there was just a hint of a smile as she firmly shook his hand.

As she led the two men through a maze of hallways and escalators inside the skating facility, Jay thought she looked similar in age to him. On the rear right side of her head, her hair had narrow streaks dyed in the colors of the Olympic rings. Her military-style black boots and semi-tight uniform were kind of sexy. Jay couldn't peel his eyes from her. Fischer grinned the second time he caught Jay staring.

Jay saw the smirk on Fischer's face and shrugged.

Finally, they entered the arena and followed her down two flights of concrete stairs that led to the first tier of seats. The VIP section. She stopped and gestured toward an aisle, where there were a few unoccupied seats and two Asian couples sitting just beyond them. Luckily Manaka was the closest of his group to the aisle.

Fischer motioned for Jay to enter the row first then followed him. Jay made his way toward the seat next to Manaka and sat. Manaka glanced and gave Jay a nod. He was a slight man who barely filled out the seat. He smelled of cigarette smoke.

Jay leaned his head slightly toward Manaka and quietly said, "Mr. Manaka, my name is Jay Scott, and sitting next to me is Chief of Olympic Security, Christoph Fischer. We would like a quick word with you. Shall we talk here, or would you prefer to walk someplace a little more private?"

Turning his head slightly toward Jay, without taking his eyes off the skater on the ice, Manaka said, "Your ID, please."

Jay looked at Fischer, who handed over his leather ID wallet. Manaka studied the badge and identification card for a moment, then, after he said a few words to the woman next to him, he turned to Jay, handed him Fischer's ID and said, "I'll come with you."

They walked up the steps and into the closest corridor. Once they were out of earshot of anyone, they stopped and turned toward each other.

"How may I be of help, gentlemen?"

"We're investigating the disappearance of American skier, Peter Buckar," Jay said. "And we're wondering if you have any information that may help us."

"Why would I know anything about it?"

"Mr. Manaka, we know about your past issues bribing Olympic judges."

"Ah, I see. So a foolish mistake I made years ago to help my niece makes me a suspect now in the disappearance of another athlete. Well, gentlemen, sorry to disappoint you but I have no information about this problem of yours. So, if you don't mind, I think I'll head back to my seat." He turned and took a step.

"Mr. Manaka, please come back. We are by no means done."

Manaka turned and looked at them. "That is where you are wrong. I am here to enjoy the Olympics with my wife and friends. I know nothing about the missing American skier. So unless you have a warrant, please leave me alone." He turned and continued to walk away.

Fischer looked at Jay. "Should I call to get a warrant?"

"No, we don't have the time. Just have your people trail him. Tell them to stay close enough to hear his conversations. It's going to piss him off, but too bad. Just like Filipov, he's too arrogant for my liking."

"Agreed."

"Let's go. I need to reach out to my team."

Fischer nodded.

When they stepped back into Fischer's SUV, Jay said, "By the way, when this is all over, I'd like the name and number of your officer, that is, if she's single."

Fischer smiled. "Her name is Florjana Kastrati. She goes by Flo. I met her when I was working on a case in Albania. She's one of my most dependable officers. I wouldn't have thought she was your type."

"Neither would I until fifteen minutes ago. I've barely looked at another woman since my wife died."

"Oh, I'm so sorry," Fischer said.

"Thanks. So, tell me about Flo. There's something about her. She's pretty, with a tough flair. Is she nice?"

"Find out for yourself," Fischer said with a smirk.

"Gee, thanks."

Both men smiled.

Chapter 50

STEAM ROSE FROM the Miami streets after the twelve-minute downpour. The rain had brought welcome relief from the sweltering, midday heat.

Joel Rebah and Stuart Mann had luckily entered Hector's KO, a gym owned by boxing champion Hector Vasquez, just before the skies had opened up.

Jay had pulled Rebah and Mann off another assignment. Not only because they were his best team but also because they knew Vasquez from a previous AllSport investigation.

While Rebah and Mann rarely displayed their skills in public, they were both former Navy SEALS. Their tight, sinewy bodies were as lethal as the weapons they carried. Their subtle confidence was underestimated by some of the gang members who stared them down and mumbled to each other as Rebah and Mann walked by them in the gym.

A quick survey of the brightly lit facility revealed four boxing rings. In the closest ring, the one surrounded by gang members, two shoeless, gloveless fighters were throwing kicks and punches, MMA style. The heel of one man's foot connected hard with the jaw of his opponent. The kick would have sent most men to the mat. Not this guy, though. His head snapped back, then, after reaching for his jaw and moving it a little, a crazed look consumed him, and he attacked. Hoots and hollers engulfed the room, reaching a crescendo as the fighters landed simultaneous kicks to each other's heads. They both dropped to the mat with loud thuds. Neither man moved.

Eyebrows raised, Mann looked at Rebah and said with a grin, "That was cool! I've never seen a double KO."

"Nor have I," Rebah said as they continued by an empty ring.

Approaching the third ring, Rebah was about to ask one of the men standing nearby about the whereabouts of Hector Vasquez when Mann reached for his arm, stopping him.

"What do you think that's all about?" Mann asked, gesturing into the ring.

An older Latino man, probably around seventy, in loose-fitting, shiny, red, boxing shorts and a black tank top, was shuffling his feet and doing his best to raise his right arm to punch a practice pad. The pad was held by an attractive young woman wearing tight black shorts and a bright blue sports halter. The guy's feet moved slowly with the unsteady hobble of a much older man. His arm and fist shook badly as he hit the pad.

"Would you look who we have here," an approaching voice bellowed from behind Rebah and Mann.

They turned to face Vasquez. His accent, a rhythmic mélange of both Miami and Brooklyn Latino, made them smile. "If it ain't Joel and Stu, the dynamic duo from AllSport. What do I owe for the pleasure of your visit to my gym, gentlemen?"

"So, you remember us, Hector?" Rebah said.

"Remember? How could I possibly forget? You two are the best fighters I've ever seen. And mind you, I've been in the ring with some champions."

"You certainly have, I've watched all your fights," Rebah said, looking back toward the old man in the ring.

"I'm honored to have such a highly esteemed fan. I see that you are intrigued by my father."

"Your dad, huh?"

"Yeah. He has Parkinson's. Boxing is great therapy. The program is called Rock Steady Boxing. My sister, Angie," he nodded toward the girl in the ring, "works with him and about eight others who suffer from the disease. It's helping some of them a lot. My wife works with them too."

"That's amazing," Mann said.

"I'm glad you're impressed, but tell me, why are you here?"

"Can we talk someplace private?"

"Sure, follow me."

He led them past an area where a mixture of heavy bags, speed bags, and double-end bags were hanging. Some were in use, others idle. One heavy bag was being worked by an older woman with a long, gray, braided ponytail. A younger Latino woman was coaching her loudly, and somewhat aggressively.

"That's Pauline." Hector nodded toward the older woman. "She could barely walk when she first entered the gym a little less than a year ago. She shuffled her feet, and her hands shook constantly. She's a really sweet woman and very smart. She owns four big art galleries between South Beach and Palm Beach. She started getting frustrated as her Parkinson's got worse and made it difficult for her to travel between them. She heard about Rock Steady and came to check it out. My wife and she took a liking to each other. They work together three times a week, and, well, you can see the results. She's come a long way." They looked at the two women just as the older woman threw a decent round of punches, hitting the bag slowly, yet squarely, with each.

"Wow, that's amazing. Is that your wife working with her now?"

Hector nodded. "Yup, she's the best thing that ever happened to me. She keeps me in line and helps me run this place."

"You're a lucky man, Hector," Mann said. "She's beautiful."

"Yeah, there's that too." Hector grinned. "C'mon, let's go have this talk."

They walked by a huge, incredibly realistic mural of Hector in one of his championship fights.

"One of Pauline's artists painted that."

"Nice," Mann said.

They followed him down a carpeted hallway at the rear of the gym. They passed a weight room, a couple of restrooms, and a kitchenette, before stopping at an old, heavily varnished, solid oak door. Vasquez turned the brass doorknob, and they entered his lair. The fact that he hadn't used a key spoke volumes to Rebah. With a gym full of assorted thugs, and other characters, Vasquez was either tremendously feared or extremely respected. Most likely, it was a combination of the two and enough so that he knew no one would dare enter his private office unless invited.

"Please sit. Do either of you want coffee or tea?"

"No thanks," Mann said.

"Water, juice, or how about a protein smoothie? I'm going to have one if you don't mind." He opened a refrigerator, removed a large glass pitcher, and placed it on the blender base on the adjacent counter. He pushed a button and let the blender do its job for about 15 seconds.

Rebah said, "Very fitting."

"What?" Vasquez asked.

"The word Ninja on your blender."

Vasquez smiled. "They sold out of the boxer model, so I ordered this."

"Cute," Mann said sarcastically.

"Bad jokes are my specialty, Stu. Ask anyone, especially my wife."

Rebah laughed. "Now that's something we have in common."

Vasquez pulled three glasses from a shelf and poured equal amounts of the thick green liquid. After handing Rebah and Mann each a glass, he took his own and sat in the high-back, leather chair behind his desk.

"Salud!" he said, raising his glass.

"Salud," Mann & Rebah responded together.

"So, gentlemen. Let's skip the pleasantries. I know you didn't come all this way just to say hi."

"True," Rebah said.

"Then why?"

"Obviously, you know the Winter Olympics are about to begin in Europe."

"Of course."

"And you probably know that Peter Buckar was expected to win a bunch of gold medals for the U.S."

As soon as he heard Peter's name, Vasquez twitched, he crossed his arms, and his entire demeanor changed. "*Was* expected? Why do you use the past tense?"

"He was kidnapped," Mann said.

Vasquez chuckled a little. His face momentarily became very serious, then he erupted in another short burst of laughter and settled down again. Then, it happened once more. This time he took longer to stop. "Sorry guys, but this is killing me. I mean after that righteous bastard blew the whistle on me for something I didn't even do, what do you expect? He was kidnapped, I love it. Karma is a wonderful thing."

Vasquez took a deep breath and slowly let it out. "So, you think I had something to do with it?"

Rebah shrugged.

"C'mon guys take a look around." He swept his arm in a big arc. "You see the trophies and belts. You know what they mean, don't you?"

"Why don't you tell us," Rebah said.

"They mean I don't give a crap about Buckar, or anyone from my past, for that matter. Excuse me—I mean anyone from my past that meant me harm. Reid, Buck, and you guys were always good to me, and I appreciate that. If it weren't for AllSport, Reid and Buck, I would never have accomplished what I have. In fact, I'd probably be dead. Gang life is a bitch. That's why you see so many gang members in my gym. I try to help as many of them as I can. It's hard to envision it when you grow up on the streets, but I try to show them that if they work at it, there is a better path in life than the one they're on. Fighting for a title is much better than fighting to stay alive. A lot of them look up to me, so I try to give them the opportunity to break free and make an honest living from fighting. Like I said, I know how lucky I was to be given the opportunity, so I'm just trying to pay it forward."

"That's commendable. I'm impressed, Hector. Really I am, but I hope you also understand that I need you to convince me that you had nothing to do with Peter's disappearance."

"C'mon, Joel. Why would I bother? What he did to me didn't affect my career. Not at all. Sure, I was pissed at him when it happened, but it wasn't something to hold a grudge about. I don't even think I threatened him back then. I guess you might say I had already become a changed man by that point. I left my violent side out on the streets when I left gang life. AllSport, or, more specifically, Reid Clark, taught me to re-channel my violent ways. He helped me focus on what was important. I used to enter the ring, ready to knock the shit out of my opponent with a frenzy of punches. I was in constant movement all over the ring. My coach called me 'the blur.' Not anymore! Now I focus on making every punch count, with just enough movement to make sure my opponent can't do the same. My mom says I'm maturing. I think it's more like I'm conserving my energy as I get older. Whatever it is, it's working."

"That's an understatement," Mann said.

Rebah nodded, yet his expression revealed some doubt. "As I said, I'm impressed with all this, but the Hector I remember is still bottled up in there somewhere." He gestured toward Vasquez's body with his hand. "As I've heard, you can take the guy out of the gang, but you can't take the gang out of the guy."

"Where the hell did you hear that BS?"

"Actually, I just made it up. But I still say it's true. Maybe you forget where Stu and I came from. It's the same for a SEAL, you can take the man out of the SEALS, but you can't take the SEAL out of the man. Not completely anyway."

"You're wrong, my man. If you think back to when I first came to AllSport, I was volatile. If my altercation with Faxton happened back then, there's no doubt that I would have killed him. But it didn't go that way, did it? I had already changed by that time. Not only didn't I waste him, I did everything I could to avoid him. So, you see, maybe there's some SEAL left in you guys, but there's no street gang left in me. None at all."

"Okay, let's say that's true. Tell me how you feel about Peter's kidnapping."

Vasquez looked at Rebah but didn't say anything.

"Silence, huh? So, you are still harboring some ill will. Maybe he deserves this. Maybe it's retribution. Right?"

Vasquez shook his head slowly. "Wrong again. Fact is, I was silent because I was trying to figure out how to express my feelings without sounding like an overly compassionate fool."

"Try us," Rebah said.

"Okay. Here goes." Vasquez looked up at the ceiling, obviously gathering his thoughts. "Thinking back, Peter really did nothing wrong. I mean, he only ratted me out because he thought he overheard some really bad stuff. I'm pretty sure if I heard one side of a conversation about drugs, weapons, and murder, right now, I would probably take it to the cops too."

"Really?"

"Yeah. I have no room for that kind of stuff in my life anymore. I have zero tolerance for needless violence and death. This world is crazy enough, what with all the freakin' terrorism and shit out there. If I can stop something bad from happening on my turf, then shame on me if I don't."

"If that's how you really feel, then you've come a long way, Hector. Congratulations."

"Thanks. It does feel pretty good. I truly feel like I'm making a difference here."

"It sure seems that way."

"I would offer help with finding Buckar, but I have no connections in Europe. It's a shame, though. The guy is an incredible athlete. I may be able to take a beating in the ring, but flying down a mountain at crazy speeds like he does, that takes cojones."

"Yeah. I guess we all agree with that," Mann said.

Rebah stood.

"So we're good here?" Vasquez asked.

"We're good, my friend," Rebah said, reaching out and shaking Vasquez's hand.

"Are you guys hungry? Let's break bread together before you leave, for old times' sake. I'll have them rustle up some paella for lunch at my friend's restaurant around the corner, in Little Havana. You'll love it, and it will give you some time to meet my wife. What do you say?"

"We're on borrowed time, Hector. The longer it takes to find Peter, the worse his chances are. The opening ceremonies are only a couple of days away, and Jay still doesn't have a solid lead. It's not looking very good at this point. Jay needs us in St. Moritz as soon as we can get there."

"Okay," Vasquez said. "I'll tell you what, after lunch, I'll have my driver take you to the airport. What time is your flight?"

"We haven't booked one yet."

"Oh. That makes sense. You didn't know what you'd find out here. Right?"

Rebah nodded.

"Okay, give me your credit card. I'll have my assistant book your flights while we have lunch."

Rebah looked at Mann and snickered at his pleading eyes.

"Did I say something funny?" Vasquez asked.

"No, Hector, it's not you. It's Stu. The man is driven by his stomach. He's always hungry."

"Come on, dude," Stu said. "You know how much I love Paella."

Rebah pulled out his credit card and handed it to Vasquez. "Okay, we'll join you. Thanks."

"Great. You want to fly first class, right?"

"Business class is fine."

"What? No way, brother. Okay, how about this? As a token of good faith and maybe to help convince Jay of my innocence, I'll fly you guys to St. Moritz in my jet. It'll save you a lot of time, and I'll score some points with my wife. She'll get a kick out of watching the Olympics."

"Really?" Rebah asked.

"Dude. What's the sense of making it if you don't enjoy it a little? Sound like a plan?"

"Are you kidding? It sounds excellent. Thank you."

"No problem, *mi hermano*. Besides, we could use a break. We've been working way too hard lately. Now, let's go round up the troops and get a bite to eat."

"The troops?" Rebah asked.

"My wife, my sister, and my mom and dad."

"Your mom is here too?"

"Yeah. She does my bookkeeping. It's better to have someone you trust handling the money. Plus, it keeps her mind off Dad's problems."

"Hm," Rebah said. "Well, I look forward to meeting them all."

"Me too," Mann said. "That and the paella."

Vasquez laughed.

As they were walking out of the office, Rebah said, "I'll be right with you guys. I need to give Jay an update." He looked at the time on his phone as he hit the dial button and said, "He's probably having dinner now."

He put the phone to his ear and waited a few seconds. "Hey, it's Joel."

Chapter 51

JAY SLID HIS phone back in his pocket and picked up his fork. "Sorry for the interruption. That was Joel Rebah with Stu Mann."

Reid, Buck, Shane, and Hunter knew Rebah and Mann, but Dan and Carole Buckar did not. Jay quickly updated everyone about their discussion with Vasquez.

They were seated in a private dining room in Kostlich, one of St. Moritz's many Michelin starred restaurants. While Jay knew he didn't have the time to sit through a long meal, he felt it was important to spend some time with Peter's friends and family. Hunter and the Buckars were entitled to know how the investigation was going. Reid and Buck were not only like family to Peter, they were footing the bill for Jay's services.

"Besides my team, we have the local police, Europol, Interpol, and Olympic Security working on finding Peter. We're also getting some help from an unofficial source. We are searching round the clock, and we won't stop until we find him," Jay said, looking at Hunter.

"What do you mean by unofficial source?" Dan Buckar asked.

"He's connected."

"As in the mafia?"

Jay nodded.

"What the hell is that all about?"

"Mr. Buckar, I've been in this business for a long time. I have friends throughout the world who help me with certain cases. I know it sounds strange, but sometimes it helps to get information from the other side of the law. My contact may uncover things within the mafia that law enforcement can't. I trust him completely. He's helped me solve a few very complicated cases in the past."

"Buck and I can vouch for that, Dan," Reid said.

Buck nodded.

Dan Buckar shrugged. "I guess I don't care how you do it, as long as you find him."

Carole Buckar was dabbing her tears with a tissue. She stopped and took a deep breath. Then, she gently placed her hand on top of her husband's and entwined her fingers with his.

Jay looked at his phone. "Folks, if you don't mind, I need to go make a call. I will keep you all apprised of anything new."

"Before you go, I'd like to run something by you," Reid said. "I've been thinking a lot about the possibilities. The one ransom request we've received was fake. It seems to me that since we haven't gotten another by now, this is probably not about money, right?"

"That's probably correct," Jay said.

"If it's not about money, then chances are it's only about keeping Peter from racing."

Jay shrugged.

"And if that's the case, then whoever has him probably means him no harm and will hopefully let him go once the Games are over."

"Are you asking if I agree with that?"

"Well, no, not exactly. I guess I just want to lift everyone's spirits. We've all been trying hard to remain positive, but it's been getting more and more difficult as time passes, especially now that the Opening Ceremonies are tomorrow. I just wanted to explain how I've been staying upbeat."

Jay nodded.

Reid continued, "If Peter is in the hands of someone from within the ski racing world, that's probably good. I mean, skiing is not like horse racing or boxing, where nefarious people often try to rig the outcomes. Right?"

"I don't know about that," Jay said. "But I agree that you all need to stay positive. Don't give up hope for a minute. Our investigation is reaching out in many directions. I'm confident we'll get a solid lead very soon. Keep your faith. We're going to find him." Jay stood. "But right now, I have to go. The French police have a lead."

Jay walked from the private dining room with Buck at his heels. After closing the door behind him, Buck said, "Hold up a second." He joined Jay where the short hallway opened into the main dining area. With his back toward the dining room, he asked, "Did you mean what you said in there?"

"You know as well as I do that the longer he's missing, the worse his chances get. But we need to keep everyone in that room back there upbeat. We have an army looking for Peter. We'll find him. Hopefully alive!"

"Hmm." Buck sighed.

"Come on, man, don't get down. Go back in there with a good attitude. You need to stay positive for …" Jay stopped midsentence. He was staring into the main dining room.

"What's wrong? What are you looking at?" Buck asked.

"Don't turn around. I want you and Reid to do something for me. I have to go. But as I leave, I want you to watch me. There's a guy with a blond ponytail sitting at a table with three other people. I will nod my head in his direction as I walk by him. I want you and Reid to sit at the bar till he leaves, then I want you to follow him."

"Who is he?"

"I'm not exactly sure, but earlier today, my guys overheard an interesting phone call up on the mountain. The caller spoke Ukrainian and had a blond ponytail. The conversation was about gambling on skiing, which is a little weird, considering what Reid just said back there. I doubt it has anything to do with Peter, and I have no idea if this is even the same guy, but it's worth a shot. I want you guys to follow him, but be as discreet as possible. Hopefully, he'll lead you to wherever he's staying, and I'll take it from there. Okay?"

"Of course."

Jay looked at his watch. "I have to go. Be discreet and be careful." He gently squeezed Buck's shoulder.

"Discreet is my middle name," Buck joked.

"I'm serious, Buck."

"I know you are. No worries. He won't even know we're there."

Buck watched as Jay made his way between a few tables and turned his head slightly as he passed one. Buck saw a fair-skinned man in a tight black shirt with a blond ponytail. He was sitting and laughing along with another guy and two women.

Buck turned and walked back into the private dining room. After a moment's hesitation to collect his thoughts, he said, "Sorry to break up the party, folks, but Jay just gave Reid and me an assignment. We have to leave."

Questioning looks from everyone at the table made Buck laugh. "Okay. I guess you'd like more of an explanation."

"That would be nice." Shane's sarcasm overflowed.

"Bear with me, this is somewhat convoluted. Jay saw a guy seated in the restaurant that he thinks is the one his men overheard earlier today, having a questionable conversation."

"Wait, that sounds odd," Hunter said. "How would Jay know who his guy overheard if he wasn't there during the conversation?"

"His men said the guy had a long, blond ponytail."

"Is he Russian?" Reid asked.

"Jay said he spoke Ukrainian, which I think sounds similar to Russian. How did you know that?"

"If it's the same guy, I witnessed a brief encounter with him and a dog a couple of days ago while I was taking a walk."

"A dog?" Hunter asked.

"It's a long story that's not worth the time. So, what's our mission?" Reid added with a tinge of excitement.

"Your mission?" Shane laughed.

"Yeah, that's if he chooses to accept it," added Hunter, with a chuckle.

"Which of course he will," said Buck interrupting them. "Enough with the comedy. Reid, we need to tail this guy when he leaves."

"What?" Shane said, turning toward Reid. "Honey, you're not going to do this. The doctor said no sudden movements."

Reid shrugged, slid his chair back, and stood.

"So, you are doing it. I thought I married a golfer, not James Bond. This is absurd."

"Come on, don't get upset," Reid said.

Shane, let her chin fall to her chest and held one hand up with her palm facing Reid. "Go, just go. But, please be careful."

"I will."

Dan Buckar stood.

"Don't get up," Buck said. "Stay here and relax. Order dessert. There's no rush."

"I'm coming with you," Dan Buckar said.

"Please stay here. We need to be discreet."

"I'm sorry, Buck, but it's my son we're looking for. I'm coming."

"Me too," Hunter said as she stood. "Besides, this way we can split up in teams and cover both sides of the street. Then, if he suspects one team, they can drop back, and the other can keep tailing him."

"Hm. That's a good idea, Hunter." Buck said.

"Very," Reid agreed.

"Okay, let's plan this," Buck continued. "First and foremost, we all need to stay safe. We have no idea who we're dealing with. Reid and Hunter, you leave first and walk across the street. Make believe you're window shopping while you keep an eye on the door."

Reid and Hunter nodded.

"Dan, you and I will go sit at the bar and order drinks. We'll follow the guy out when he leaves. Our job is to follow him to wherever he's staying and then report to Jay. That's it. No heroics. Agreed?" Buck looked at Dan, Hunter, and Reid, getting a nod from each.

"Hold up just a minute," Carole Buckar said as she rose from her seat and began putting her coat on. "You guys are missing one possibility. What happens if he gets into a car or a cab instead of walking to wherever he's staying?"

"Another good point," Reid said, looking at everyone.

Carole took charge. "Shane put on your coat and come with me. We're going to get a cab and have the driver wait. Then, if the guy gets in a car, we'll follow."

"What will you tell the driver?" Reid asked.

"That we're waiting for our husbands," Shane said. "But, I'm sure these will convince him not to care what we're waiting for." She removed two 100 Swiss franc notes from her purse and raised them.

As Reid and Shane hugged, the Buckars did the same.

"Please be careful, James." Shane's tone was sarcastic, but her look was extremely serious.

"Of course, Moneypenny," Reid said with a smirk.

Hunter and Buck were waiting at the door as the others approached.

"You guys go ahead," Buck said. "Dan and I will head to the bar as soon as you're all outside. Don't be obvious, but look left as you walk out through the dining room. He's sitting at one of the center tables with another guy and two women. Don't stare, just glance to get a sense of what he looks like." Then, looking at his phone, he added, "Before we separate, I'm starting a group text so that we are all connected and know what's happening. I have everyone's number except yours, Carole."

Carole gave him her cell number as the others waited anxiously.

"Okay, I just sent you all a text. Just reply, yes," Buck said.

Reid checked his phone last, then looked up and said, "All right, let's go." He pulled his hat and glasses from the inner pocket of his jacket.

***

A few minutes later, everyone was in position, and the waiting began.

"It's cold," Reid said. "I wish I wore a heavier coat."

"Yeah," Hunter said, "and I'd do anything for a hat and gloves."

"Want my hat?"

"No, all we need is for someone to recognize you. I'll be okay."

"Maybe there's time to stop in a store to buy you a hat and gloves for each of us. I'm starting to shiver."

"Me too," Hunter said. "But we shouldn't chance it." She looked at her phone. "We've been out here for twelve minutes. They'll probably come out soon. The guy was drinking coffee when we walked by him."

"Drinking coffee? I didn't notice. You're a natural at this sleuthing stuff."

"No, I'm just detail-oriented."

Reid looked at his phone. "Wow, it's seven degrees out." Phone in hand, he crossed his arms, tucked his hands into his armpits, and hugged himself tightly.

"I guess we drew the short straws. Must be nice sitting at the bar or in that van." Hunter nodded toward the parked taxi that they saw Shane and Carole get into, halfway down the next block.

"Could be worse. At least we found a bench."

Their cellphones buzzed with a text from Buck: *He's coming out.*

"Here we go," Reid said.

"Yup," Hunter said hesitantly.

"You okay?"

"No. Not really. But at least I won't think about the cold anymore."

The man and his friends exited the restaurant and began walking along the crowded sidewalk. Business was brisk in the many brightly lit stores.

Luckily, the guy's six-foot-four height and long, blond hair contrasting against his black leather coat made him easy to keep an eye on.

The foursome stopped at the first store they came to and gazed through the window at a dazzling assortment of jewelry.

Reid shifted his eyes just enough to see Buck and Dan backtrack a few quick steps into the shadow of the restaurant's recessed doorway.

Watching the ponytailed guy was somewhat comical. While his friends remained glued to the jewelry store window, he'd obviously had enough. At first, he looked up into the night sky. Then, he looked toward his group, shook his head, and began walking away.

Reid lost view of the guy's friends in the crowd as they dashed after him. Shifting his eyes and regaining sight of the man's ponytail, Reid said, "Good thing Ponytail is tall."

"Ponytail, easy name," Hunter said. "I like it, and it's a whole lot better than calling him, the guy. It's a good thing they didn't go into that store. It's too cold to wait out …"

Ponytail and his crew entered a cigar store.

"Damn." Hunter let out a tiny groan, and she rolled her eyes.

Reid grinned.

"What, you're not cold anymore?" Hunter asked.

"Of course, I am, but the timing of your statement was perfect."

"Whatever."

"Don't get mad at me," Reid said.

"Oh, shut up."

Reid chuckled again as he typed on his phone.

"What are you writing?" Hunter asked as her phone buzzed.

Text from Reid: *Ponytail and crew are in the cigar shop.*

Hunter grinned at Reid as their phones both buzzed.

Text from Shane: *So you named the guy, huh, James?*

Text from Reid: 😆

"Real cute, James," Hunter said.

"Shut up!"

The couples finally left the cigar store, each with a stogie ablaze. Their smoke billowed like four chimneys alternately spewing blue-gray plumes.

Reid typed another text: *Just follow the smoke signals.*

Hunter shook her head after reading his text.

"Come on, that was funny," Reid said with a chuckle.

"Nope. Not even close."

Reid shrugged. "Oh, well."

Sure enough, the trail of smoke was easy to follow as the group continued down the block, stopping at each window. After placing their smoldering cigars on a brick windowsill, the foursome entered a leather goods store. Fifteen bitterly cold minutes later, they emerged with shopping bags. After relighting their cigars, they moved on. The further they walked from the center of the shopping area, the thinner the crowd became. After waiting for a traffic light, they began crossing the intersection toward Reid and Hunter's side of the street.

Walking slowly about ten feet from the corner, Hunter reached for Reid's hand and stopped him. "Wait here to see which way they walk."

The group stepped onto the sidewalk and began walking directly toward Reid and Hunter.

"Uh oh." Hunter flinched.

Reid put his arm around her shoulders and led her to the window of the art gallery they were in front of. Then, instead of passing behind them, Ponytail and his ensemble huddled up right next to them and gazed at the artwork.

Hunter tensed as Ponytail positioned himself aside her brother.

Reid pointed and said to Hunter, "I like that one of the mountains, don't you?"

Hunter took his cue. "Yeah, kind of, but I like the ones of the skiers better. Wait, that's Pe …" Hunter stiffened and abruptly stopped talking.

Reid glanced at her. She was upset. He followed her eyes and saw various paintings of skiers. Then, he saw one of Peter in a slalom race. Luckily, Hunter was holding her feelings in check. Reid was unsure of what to do. Questions flooded his head; *Did Ponytail notice the painting? Did he notice Hunter's reaction? Will he remember me from our encounter with Grady, the dog, or will he recognize me from the PGA? If he recognizes me, will he put two and two together and realize the connection between Peter and me? Does he even have anything to do with*

Peter's disappearance? Holy cow. There are way too many questions. But really, thought Reid, *what are the chances?*

"Hey, don't I know you?" Ponytail asked.

Great, he reads minds too, Reid thought, doing his best to remain calm. He turned his head slightly without facing Ponytail directly. "Who me? No, I'm sorry. I don't think so." Then, he turned and looked at Hunter through wide eyes.

She shrugged and returned the look.

"I know!" Ponytail exclaimed. "You were with that guy and his huge dog at the coffee shop. I thought that monster was going to eat me. He made me spill my coffee all over myself. That was you, wasn't it?"

"Oh, yeah. Grady gave me a scare too. Then, I found out he's just a gentle giant. He wouldn't harm a flea if it bit him."

"If you say so," Ponytail said, looking at Reid. "Why do you look so familiar? I feel like I know you."

"Probably because he's famous, you jerk," said the woman standing next to the guy. "He's only like the best golfer in the world. Right, Mr. Clark?"

Reid shrugged and smiled. What choice did he have? His cover was blown.

Ponytail's girlfriend and the other couple moved closer to Reid.

"Can we get a picture with you?" the second woman asked.

Suddenly the two women were at his sides, their arms entwined around his back and smoke from their cigars curling upwards into the crisp night air. Realizing how ludicrous the whole situation was, Reid smiled weakly for a few quick pictures and then signed a small signature booklet that the second woman had pulled from her orange Hermes Birkin handbag.

"Uh, you better get going," Ponytail said. "Your girlfriend already went in. Sorry."

"It's okay, she's my sister, and she hates attention. Did you see where she went?"

Ponytail pointed into the gallery where Hunter was speaking with a professionally dressed woman.

"Thanks. Enjoy the Games." Reid gave a quick wave as he reached for the handle on the heavy glass door. *Damn,* he thought. *That couldn't have gone any worse. Why the hell did I say she was my sister? If Ponytail is behind all this and he Googles me, he'll see the connection to Peter.*

As he stepped into the gallery, his phone buzzed repeatedly. He pulled it from his pocket and looked at the screen.

Text from Shane: *What was that all about?*

Text from Buck: *WTF?*

Reid typed: *No choice, they recognized me. I guess Hunter and I should drop off the trail.*

He put his phone back in his pocket, and just as he joined Hunter, it buzzed again.

Text from Buck: *No, don't stop. Now they think you're just out shopping. Stay back but stick with them.*

"We need to go," Reid said to Hunter, cutting off the woman she was speaking with.

The tall, thin, Asian woman's face hardened as she crossed her arms. Clearly, she was not used to being interrupted. Her look and her attire, a dark gray pinstriped pantsuit and white satin blouse, were all business.

"Don't be rude," Hunter chastised.

"Sorry," Reid said to the woman as he gently took Hunter's arm. "We really have to go." He shot Hunter a distressed look and flinched his head toward the door.

"Wait a second," the woman said, looking back and forth between a painting on the wall and Reid's face. "You're … you're … Oh, Mr. Clark, could I get you to sign that? Please," she begged.

Reid and Hunter looked at the painting of Reid with his fist clenched in victory on the eighteenth hole of Augusta National.

"I promise I'll come back and sign it, but we really need to leave right now."

"Please don't forget, Mr. Clark," the woman said in defeat. "It would mean so much to me."

Reid turned his head back toward the woman as he and Hunter were walking out the door. "Don't worry, she won't let me forget."

Hunter turned and added, "He's right, and thank you. I'll be back tomorrow."

Walking down the sidewalk, looking for Ponytail and crew, Reid said, "Why are you going back there tomorrow?"

"I want to buy that painting of Peter."

"Good. I'll buy it for you, but let's work with the owner of the gallery, instead of that woman. We'll probably get a better deal."

"That woman *is* the owner."

"Oh. Well, that explains why she wanted my signature so badly." He looked briefly at Hunter, who was avoiding eye contact.

"You okay," Reid asked gently.

"It's nothing."

"Really? What's wrong?"

"I was just upset to see the painting of Peter. He looked so vital, so alive. I can't take much more of not knowing where he is."

Reid put his arm over her shoulder as they walked.

"Okay, where are they?" he asked after a moment.

"I see smoke way up there," Hunter said as she pointed toward the end of the block.

"Oh yeah. I see them. Let's move up a little, but not too close, in case they turn back. I don't want to end up in another awkward situation."

"Now that you're practically buddies with them, what's the difference?"

"Buddies? Are you kidding me?" Reid said with some anger.

"Of course I am! Down boy."

"Sorry, this whole thing is just starting to get to me."

"Me too. I'm just trying to keep things light."

"Hm. I guess if you can keep that attitude, I should be able to do the same."

"Good. Now let's go get those bastards." Hunter's tone had turned serious.

"Whoa! Easy girl. What happened to keeping things light? We're following them on a hunch. They may have nothing to do with Peter."

"Yeah, well, I want to find out already. Let's go!"

Reid squeezed her shoulder, and they quickened their pace. A few people stared as Reid passed.

"I'm glad no one is making a fuss over me."

"I guess there are enough other celebrities here to keep your normally ogling fans distracted."

Then they heard, "Wow, Reid Clark just walked by! Did you see him? Let's get his autograph."

Reid groaned quietly.

"Just make it quick," Hunter said.

Reid forced a welcoming smile as the young couple hurried from behind him, directly into his path.

Holding out a folded piece of paper and pen, the girl asked, "Could we please get your autograph, Mr. Clark?"

"Of course." He took the paper, but noticing wet ink on the girl's fingers, he pulled his ever-present Sharpie from his pocket.

Reid's feigned smile remained, but his inner demeanor sank as a father and daughter, as well as another couple, queued in front of him. Without small talk, he signed a small Olympic flag, a turtleneck shirt, and a baseball cap. Relieved to be finished, he pocketed the Sharpie, looked at Hunter, and said, "Done. Let's go."

She shook her head and gestured in front of him. Reid turned, ready to apologize and explain that they had to go. Two men were waiting, arm in arm "*Il tuo atografo per favore,*" one said, pulling a t-shirt from his shopping bag. Reid signed it and gave it back, only to be handed a mock Olympic gold medal to sign. He signed the ribbon as the other guy removed his rainbow-colored scarf and held it out toward Reid.

"Nice scarf." Reid signed it, adding, "My wife has the same one. It's from MoMA, right?"

Hunter discreetly nudged Reid with her elbow.

With a smile, the guy wrapped the scarf around his neck and repeated, "Moma?" He looked bewildered. "*Non capisco.*"

"*Grazie*, Reid, *grazie*," the other man said as they turned and walked away.

"MoMA, really?" Hunter said.

"What? It was a Museum of Modern Art scarf."

She shook her head. "Gay pride."

"Oops. Well, they look the same."

"Kind of."

"I wasn't disrespectful, was I?"

"No. You were fine. Let's go."

Reid looked up ahead. "I don't see them. Do you?"

"You're the tall one. I can't see anything."

Their phones buzzed.

Text from Buck: *Hurry up. We're at the intersection in front of you. They're getting in their car. Run. Discreetly. But, run!*

Hunter followed as Reid quickly cleared the way through the crowded sidewalk. They arrived at the corner and looked around.

"Where are they?" Hunter said. "Was he talking about a different intersection?"

"I don't know."

"Reid, Hunter. Over here," Buck whispered loudly from the van that Shane and Carole had been waiting in.

They ran, jumped in the van, and closed the door. The driver pulled away and drove toward Ponytail's car. He slowed the van about six car lengths away and waited for the big, black Mercedes sedan to leave its parking spot. Then, he began to follow at an inconspicuous distance.

All eyes were riveted on the Mercedes. The air in the van was thick with anxiety.

"What the hell was with all the autographs?" Buck asked.

"You're really going to bust my chops about that? You, of all people? You want me to piss off my fans like I used to do in the old days?"

"No, you're right. But time is of the essence now."

Happy to change the conversation, Reid turned to Shane and said, "So, what did you tell the driver?"

"The truth."

"Really? How'd you bring it up?"

"Ask Carole."

All eyes fell on Carole.

"Shane and I spoke with him while we were waiting. Luca is a nice man."

The driver smiled.

"When he's not driving this cab, he's usually out skiing with his son and daughter. He's a big fan of ski racing and has been looking forward to the Olympics since they chose St. Moritz as the host city. When I explained what happened to Peter, Luca said he'll do whatever he can to help. His daughter races slalom on a junior team, and his second cousin races luge on the Austrian Olympic team. And, by the way, Luca lived in the States for a few years when he was younger. He speaks English very nicely."

"I'm guessing you gave him the money you showed us before?" Reid asked, looking at Shane.

She nodded.

"Luca, thank you for helping. I will pay you an additional bonus at the end of this ride."

"Thank you. It is my pleasure, and honestly, I find it very exciting."

They followed the Benz to the outskirts of St. Moritz, leaving the bright lights and crowds behind. They drove through a well-manicured community of large homes. Then, past a poorly lit neighborhood of smaller homes. The next street they turned onto was the last one in the residential area. The Mercedes pulled to the side of the road, stopped, and the headlights went off. It was a quiet street. Cars passed by, but not many.

The van remained at a safe distance. They waited for the foursome to exit the Mercedes, and waited, and waited.

"What the hell are they doing?" Dan asked.

"Good question," Buck said.

"Do we have to just sit here?" Carole asked. "Can't we go talk to them?"

"And say what?" Dan blurted obnoxiously.

"I don't know? How about, where the hell is my son?" As she said it, she broke into tears.

Shane reached over and patted her forearm.

Dan leaned forward from the rear seat and placed his hand on his wife's shoulder. "I'm sorry. I shouldn't have snapped at you. It's getting to me too."

She put her hand on his. "It's all right. The stress is just so hard to deal with."

"It sure is," her husband said quietly.

"Buckle up everyone," Luca said. "They're on the move." As he pulled the van from its parking spot, they all heard the blast of a horn and screech of skidding tires. Luca had cut off an oncoming vehicle, and instead of stopping, he stepped on the gas, making sure he positioned the van in front of the oncoming vehicle, with no cars between the van and the Mercedes. He opened his window and gave the driver he had cut off an apologetic wave. The other driver's response was not quite as respectful.

"Sorry if I scared any of you. I just didn't want that car between us, and the Mercedes."

"No worries, Luca," Reid said. "You're obviously the right man for this job."

The Mercedes was far enough ahead that the sounds of the near accident did not seem to have any effect on them. The van fell back on their trail. A few minutes and a few turns later, they were driving through an industrial area. They passed a couple of run-down automobile repair shops, one with a sputtering, neon sign dangling from one of its top corner chains.

The slow, steady drive continued, stop sign after stop sign, turn after turn. But now, with very few other cars driving by, the fear of being noticed by Ponytail and his ensemble heightened.

"I'm not sure if I should turn off the headlights. Dim as the streetlamps are, they're good enough for me to see without our lights on. On the other hand, if they've already noticed us behind them, turning our lights off wouldn't be good."

"Right," Buck said. "Keep them on, but stay back. We'll just have to hope for the best." Luca, the driver, put more distance between his vehicle and the Mercedes.

Before Buck finished his statement, the brake lights of the Mercedes glared, and it pulled into a brightly lit driveway. The van's distance at a quarter-mile away made discerning the location impossible.

No one said a word as Luca pulled close to the sidewalk and turned off the lights. Once again, they waited. Up ahead, the car's brake lights remained bright.

After another minute ticked by, Reid said, "Why do you think they keep pulling over? You think they're doing drugs or maybe something else?"

"Something else?" Shane said. "Like what?"

Reid shrugged.

"Wait, you can't be thinking. That's just gross. Get your mind out of the gutter?"

"Eww," Hunter added.

Luca, Buck and Carole laughed.

"Don't put words in my mouth," Reid said defensively. "I wasn't thinking sex. Maybe you should get *your* mind out of the gutter."

The discussion ended abruptly as the Mercedes backed out of the driveway. Everyone remained silent, hoping the car would not switch directions and drive back toward the van. Luca and Buck breathed loud sighs of relief as the car continued in its original direction.

Keeping the headlights off, Luca pulled the van from its spot and drove toward the driveway that the Mercedes had been parked in. He pulled the van's right side wheels onto the wide driveway and stopped, giving everyone a chance to look around. It was a gated entrance to a multi-building warehousing facility with an unmanned guard shack. The chain-link gate was closed. Buck entered the address into his phone, as he had done at the last place the Mercedes had pulled over.

Reid saw Buck typing and asked, "You don't think these were just random stops?"

"No idea. No one got out of the car, so they probably are random, but I'm sending them to Jay just in case."

Buck looked up through the windshield. The Mercedes was a long way down the street. "Don't lose them."

"Don't worry," Luca said, stepping on the gas with the headlights still off. As they got closer to the Mercedes, snow began to fall. Light flakes swiftly became a heavy storm. Although Luca was used to driving the 4-wheel drive van in all conditions, visibility was decreasing rapidly. He switched on the headlights and drove faster to maintain a visual on the Mercedes. Maneuvering on the snow-covered road was not a problem for Luca. The challenge was getting close enough to keep an eye on the Mercedes without being seen by its passengers. Luckily, the car turned onto a busier road, so it was not just the two vehicles anymore. But now there was a new problem: it had begun to snow. Within minutes the storm had increased to near white-out fury. Following a car on slick streets can be tricky. Besides maintaining control of the van, Luca now had to watch out for other skidding vehicles. To the inhabitants of St. Moritz, driving in severe weather was commonplace, but the Olympics brought many less capable motorists to the area.

Chapter 52

SITTING ON THE edge of his bed after showering, Peter was tying the lace of his sneaker when he heard a commotion outside his door. Although he had no idea what time it was, his stomach was telling him it was time for food. Without the luxury of a clock or windows, the only way he had been able to keep any track of time was by his regularly scheduled meals. Since his last meal was lunch-like, he assumed it was now dinner time. The shouting grew louder. *This is strange,* thought Peter, *and alarming.* What if the shouting was about him? As usual, two men wearing black ski masks entered his room.

The first time he saw the masks, it scared the hell out of him. But, like everything else, he had grown accustomed to them. As long as they brought his meals, they could wear suits of armor if they wanted.

But when he looked at them today, he froze. Instead of carrying his tray of food, they had guns in their hands.

He drew in a deep breath and tensed up as they rushed toward him.

"Stand," one of them yelled in English with a Slavic accent.

Peter remained where he was, more due to shock than defiance.

One man reached for Peter's arm and aggressively pulled him up. "We're not going to hurt you, but we need to leave. Right now!"

The man who grabbed his arm turned slightly and gripped his other arm. He stood behind Peter, pulled his wrists together, and held them tightly while the second man reached into a black cloth bag and removed a set of handcuffs and an eye mask.

"Wait!" Peter yelled. "What the hell is going on?"

"Just cooperate, and you'll be fine."

Peter squirmed as the cuffs were placed on his wrists. "Ow. Come on, loosen them up."

"Stop moving so I can put these on you." The mask and the black cloth bag were dangling from the man's fingers. "Then, I'll loosen the handcuffs."

Knowing that fighting would be futile, Peter relinquished. He allowed the second man to stretch the elastic band of the eye mask over the back of his head, then adjust it to fit snugly on his face. The darkness was agitating, but at least there was a tiny bit of light coming through the lower-left edge of the mask. Next, he felt the soft black bag brush against his hair, his forehead, his nose, and finally his chin. All light was now extinguished. The complete darkness was terrifying. Peter's nerves began to twitch, and his mind shifted into overdrive. *Terrorists place black bags over their victim's heads before they behead them. Wait, that's not right. It's the terrorists who wear black bags, so they're not recognized on TV.*

Anxiety ridden, Peter could barely breathe as he was led from the room. Fear, confusion, and disorientation ransacked his mind as he was forced to move quickly through the first hallway.

"We have to run," yelled one of his captors.

Things instantly became chaotic. Running blindly without the balance of his arms was insanely difficult. Being pushed and pulled by his captors made it even more harrowing.

The situation became ridiculous when the man on his left side tugged Peter's arm without warning. Somehow Peter managed to make the left turn without falling, until the man on his right clipped Peter's legs with his own, and fell. Falling forward, with his arms cuffed behind him, Peter could not brace for impact. He did a face-plant with his nose smashing directly into the man's knee, and emitted a grunt. The pain was intense, from both the re-jarring of his head and his now badly broken nose.

He attempted to stand, but complete disorientation in conjunction with his bound wrists made it impossible. He was roughly helped to his feet and pushed forward.

"We must hurry!"

Doing his best to put one foot in front of the other, new sensations crept into Peter's darkened world. Extreme pain and nauseating dizziness were now accompanied by the salty, metallic taste of blood coming from his nose. To top it off, the smell of gasoline had somehow made it through the bag and past the swollen membranes within his nostrils.

"You have to move him faster," said a gruff, new voice to Peter's left. "Get out of the way. Let me do it."

"No, I've got him," argued the man next to Peter.

"I said, move away! We don't have time for this."

The hand that had been gripping Peter's upper arm released it. Then, he felt a hand push through the tight gap between his biceps and his back. The cuffs made moving his arms backward difficult and painful. The man forced his own arm further across Peter's back and clamped his hand, tightly gripping Peter's armpit. Aggressively he began moving Peter forward.

"Ow, stop," Peter yelled. "You're going to rip my shoulder out of its socket." The added pain mixed with the now overwhelming gaseous odors escalated Peter's nausea.

"I'm sorry, but there is no other way," the man said.

Unable to refrain, Peter's body convulsed as he vomited.

The man yanked his arm from the tight channel between Peter's arms and back. "Untie the hood," the man yelled.

As Peter bent forward to retch once more, hands untied the black bag, allowing vomit and blood to spew from the bottom.

"Go get another bag and meet us at the van," screamed the man next to him.

"Where from?"

"The office."

"But it's already on fire!"

"Just get it," the man yelled as he bent down and quickly lifted Peter over his shoulders in a fireman's carry.

Peter puked again, and the black bag fell to the floor. Vomit ran down the man's back and pant legs as he moved quickly toward the nearest exit.

They say that the loss of one sense sometimes enhances another. At the moment, Peter's senses were being attacked from every angle. Blinded by the sleep mask, his sense of smell had sharpened enough to notice the faint odor of gas. Then, his ability to smell all but vanished as swelling prohibited him from breathing through his nostrils. His sense of taste was fouled by the putrid assault of vomit, bile, and blood. That left hearing and touch. While nausea, pain, and confusion were wreaking havoc on his mind, he knew that amidst all the yelling and shouting, he had heard one of the men say that the office was 'already on fire.' And now, in addition to the pain from being carried roughly on top of someone's shoulders, he felt intense heat!

The guy carrying him had to be powerful, as Peter was no lightweight. Peter grimaced as the guy's shoulder dug into his ribs. As he bounded up a staircase, each jarring step felt like an uppercut punch to Peter's ribcage. He held his breath and stiffened his core, attempting to fight the pain. The unmistakable sound of a door's crash-bar being hit gave Peter hope that the rough ride was almost over. The blast of cold air and pelting snow on his bare arms was a welcome feeling.

The man carrying him, slowly placed Peter on his feet. Then, he felt a warm, moist cloth cleaning his face, avoiding his covered eyes, and thankfully his tender nose.

"I'm putting a water bottle to your lips," said one of the men. "Rinse your mouth."

Peter rinsed and spat, twice, then gulped what was left in the bottle.

"I'm going to remove the cuffs so we can change your shirt. We need to hurry."

After helping him into a clean shirt, one of the men apologized as they put another cloth bag over his head. They then helped him climb up into a vehicle leaving the cuffs off and giving him a few blankets to wrap up in. He heard the door shut and felt the vehicle begin to move.

Chapter 53

LUCA WAS NOW following the Mercedes on a wider two-lane road near the outskirts of town. The Mercedes had picked up speed.

"If they go any faster, keeping up will be dangerous," Luca said. "They're already driving way too fast for these conditions." As he said it, the Mercedes shifted lanes to pass the car in front of it.

"Look at him, he's crazy." As Luca said it, the Mercedes fish-tailed, and the driver overcorrected, sending the rear of the car into a slide. The car that the Mercedes was passing moved over just enough to avoid being hit. Then, through the heavy snow, they saw headlights from an oncoming car rise over the crest of a hill just ahead. "Oh no," Luca shouted, unable to contain himself, as the Mercedes smashed head-on into the oncoming vehicle. Luca pumped his brakes, reducing the van's speed. As the rear began to slide, he steered into the skid, preventing a full spin. Then, still pumping the brakes, he corrected a skid in the opposite direction. Finally, the van slowed enough so that he could safely drive around the mangled heap of cars in the middle of the road.

As he was passing the wreck, Luca glanced in the rearview mirror. "Uh oh."

He stepped hard on the gas pedal, fishtailing again as they sped up. "Hold on," he yelled as the van's rear bumper clipped one of the cars lightly.

Bewildered and frightened, everyone turned to see what had caused Luca's reaction. An SUV that was now in a very fast side-ways skid, slammed into the two cars. The high winds muffled the sounds of crunching metal, plastic, and glass.

"Oh my God," Hunter yelped.

"Wow. Good job avoiding that, Luca," Shane said.

Luca let out a sigh. "Thanks. I'm going to pull to the side here."

As he took his foot off the brake, two more vehicles crashed into the pile.

"Oh my God," Shane exclaimed. "This is horrible."

"What should we do?" Hunter asked.

"Let's go see if we can help," Carole said.

"That could complicate things if Ponytail is our guy," Buck said. "Give me a minute. I'll ask Jay. In the meantime, Luca, please start driving. If we're here when the police arrive, they might not let us leave."

Buck's call was quick. He explained everything, gave Jay the addresses of the two stops the Mercedes had made, as well as the location of the crash. Then he listened for a few seconds and said, "Okay, bye."

"He's going to check out the two addresses, and he's sending a team to check on the accident. He wants us to go back to the hotel."

"What? No way!" Hunter said.

"What's the matter?" Reid asked.

"If Peter is at one of those places, we should be there when they find him."

"The only thing we'd do is get in the way," Reid said. "We have no idea why they made those two stops. Chances are it had nothing to do with Peter. Let's go back to the hotel and let the pros do their jobs."

"You go to the hotel," Hunter said. "I'm going back. I want to be there when they find him. So, either take me back or let me out."

"Hunter, listen, Reid's right," Shane said. "We'll just be in the way."

"Luca, please pull over," Hunter said a little louder than necessary as she pulled the lever on the van's door and slid it open.

"Close the damn door," Reid snapped.

"I'm going with her," Carole said.

"Me too," Dan added.

Luca had braked as soon as the door opened. He pulled the van to the shoulder and stopped as quickly as possible without skidding.

Reid shot Buck a quick questioning look, and Buck nodded. Hunter already had one foot on the ground.

"Hunter!" Reid snapped. "Get back in and close the damn door so we can go back."

"To the hotel?"

"No, to whichever address Jay and his team are heading first. All we need is for the three of you to get lost and die of hyperthermia."

Hunter shut the door. "Thanks for being so understanding," she said with disgust.

The following awkward silence was finally broken after Buck read Jay's text and said, "Luca, head back to the neighborhood where the Mercedes first stopped."

Luca nodded and looked up at the rearview mirror. "I see flashing lights at the crash."

"Good," Buck said, turning to look.

"Should I turn around here, in the middle of the road, or should I continue the way we're headed and take a longer route?"

"Do you think you can turn without getting hit?"

"I guess so. But it's illegal to do this. I need more than just my fare to risk so much."

Shane immediately reached into her purse and handed him two one-hundred Swiss Franc notes. Luca nodded.

"This could be dangerous," Buck said. "Is everyone okay with …"

"Just do it, already," Hunter said belligerently.

"Hunter," Reid said. "Calm down. We've agreed to do what you want, but you can't make decisions that may put others in jeopardy. It's just not fair."

"I'm sorry. I'm not thinking straight."

"It's okay. We all understand," Carole said. "I'm sure we're all feeling the same way. I know I am."

Reid looked around. "Everyone okay with turning here?"

There were no objections.

"Go ahead, Luca."

The snow was falling harder now. Visibility was only a couple of car lengths. Luca looked back over his shoulder, then, forward, then, back again. "Hold on," he said as he hit the gas and turned the wheel.

The tires spun, grabbed hold, then spun again as Luca coaxed the vehicle around. With the van now halfway across the lane and almost perpendicular to the road, Luca mumbled, "Oh shit."

Lights from an oncoming vehicle became visible through the deluge of falling snow. Luca pumped the brakes, but the result was a wider skidding turn that would place the van at a terrible angle, just in time for impact. Luca pressed the gas pedal, committing them to turn in front of the oncoming vehicle. The unmistakable sound of a truck's air horn trumpeted through the gusty wind scaring the hell out of them all. Everyone cringed and braced themselves as Luca spun the wheel and hit the gas just enough to help slide the van into the lane ahead of the truck. The truck's headlights swayed as it skidded toward the van. Luca straightened the van and applied more pressure to the gas. As the truck got closer, it skidded just enough to the side that they all could see its shape and read the writing on it.

"Oh my God. It's a gas tanker," Shane shrieked.

Gasps filled the van.

The truck driver had regained control and was slowing down as Luca was speeding up. The vehicles were going to collide, the only question was how hard? The van was still gaining speed as the truck hit it directly from behind. The van lurched forward and slid sideways. Once again, Luca steered into the skid, and with a nimble combination of brakes, gas, and steering, he kept the van from sliding off the road and down the adjacent embankment. The truck driver was not as lucky. The tanker had spun completely around and was skidding backward toward the narrow shoulder. They all watched in horror as it passed over the edge, flipped onto its side, and slid out of sight.

Luca clutched his heart and gasped, "Oh my God! I have to stop. Oh my God!"

"Luca, take a deep breath and calm down, but please keep going," Buck said. "We can't stop now. Time is of the essence."

"I'm sorry, but I need to stop. I feel like my heart is going to jump out of my chest."

"Slow down and breathe deep. I'm feeling the same way, but at least the truck didn't explo—"

The massive blast rocked the night. A brilliant, fiery flash penetrated the heavily falling snow. The flickering afterglow from the burning tanker cast an eerie glow. Luckily, the steep hill had contained the force of the blast, preventing it from reaching the van.

"Oh my God!" Shane said as Reid reached to grasp her hand. "That poor driver!"

Dan Buckar had reached forward over the back of his wife's chair and was hugging her from behind. She crossed her arms over his and cried.

"We have to check on the driver," Luca said anxiously. "I can't believe I caused this." He began to hyperventilate.

"Luca, this was not your fault," Reid said. "If anything, it was ours. We pushed you to do this. Stop the van and catch your breath. And here, this might help." He handed Luca another two-hundred Swiss franc note.

"Okay, everyone," Buck said a little aggressively, trying to quiet everyone down. "Here's the deal. I feel as badly about this as you all do, but what's done is done. If we stop to check on the driver and the police arrive, chances are they'll keep us here all night. Hopefully, the driver jumped out of the truck before it blew up. But, regardless, there's nothing we can do to help him."

"Look, there's an emergency vehicle coming already," Luca said anxiously.

They all turned and saw flashing lights heading their way.

"Luca, are you okay to drive?" Buck asked.

"I guess so."

"The police will help the truck driver more than we can. So please just start driving."

Luca shifted into drive and began moving as the oncoming police truck got closer. The driver shined a spotlight on the van. Then, he stuck his arm out his window with his palm toward the van.

"He wants us to stop," Luca said.

"Then stop," Buck said. "I'll speak with them. I may need you to translate."

"Okay."

As Luca braked, another tremendous explosion burst from the truck. The police vehicle sped up and drove by them toward the burning tanker.

"I guess I should keep going, right?" Luca asked.

"Yes, continue," Buck said.

An uneasy silence filled the van as they drove slowly toward the multi-car pileup. The near-miss with the colliding cars, getting hit by the truck, and then the explosion had all been way too much for everyone to handle.

As Luca drove on the shoulder, slowly passing the accident and several emergency vehicles, they received blank stares from those standing nearby.

Two stretchers were being loaded into ambulances. While they couldn't see the condition of the people on them, there was a lot of blood on the sheet covering one. A quick count revealed an additional five vehicles had piled into the first two, making for a huge mass of twisted debris. Besides the two people on the stretchers, emergency technicians were working on another who was still on the ground. Crimson-stained snow surrounded the injured person's head of long blond hair.

As the van crept forward, Reid quietly said to Buck, "Did you see the guy on the ground?"

Buck nodded. "Lots of blood and long, blond hair. You think it was him?"

"I couldn't tell. At first I thought so, but it was tough to see. It may have been a woman."

Buck shrugged.

The van passed the last of the emergency vehicles, and Luca edged the wheels back onto the snowy road from the shoulder. The line of headlights from cars stuck behind the accident seemed endless. Slowly they passed car after car. Then, through the swirling snow, they saw flashing lights coming directly toward them in their lane. As the flashing lights quickly got closer, it became evident that the approaching emergency vehicle wasn't slowing down. Unless Luca acted swiftly, it was going to hit them head-on.

"Hold on," he yelled as he spun the steering wheel toward the shoulder, skidding and sliding, as the huge red truck just missed them.

Already anxious, the blast of the truck's horn scared the hell out of them all. Squinting due to the bright flashing emergency lights and heavy snowfall, Luca saw the word FEURWEHR written in bold letters on the side of the passing vehicle.

The van slid to a stop at an angle. Three wheels were on the shoulder, and one was still on the road. Luca leaned his head back on the headrest and expelled a loud sigh of relief. "I can't believe we almost got hit by a rescue vehicle. How ludicrous? It's like he didn't even see us."

He then bent forward, leaned his crossed arms on the steering wheel, and rested his head on the back of his hands. He let out another big sigh, then flinched as he looked at the dashboard.

"Luca, are you okay?" Reid asked.

"I guess so. Embarrassed, but okay."

"Embarrassed, why?"

Luca reached and flipped the headlight switch on.

"He didn't see us because our lights were off. I guess I turned them off at one point, hoping to see better in all the snow, and with all the excitement, I forgot to turn them back on." Luca buried his face in his hands and said, "I can't believe it. I could have killed you all. I'm so sorry." He shook his head slowly with his hands still covering his face.

"Sorry? Luca, look at me," Buck said sternly.

Luca looked into the rearview mirror with watery eyes.

"Snap out of it. Take a quick look at us all."

Luca's eyes roamed side to side in the mirror.

"You want to know why we're all alive? It's because of your excellent driving. If anyone else was at the wheel, we would probably be dead by now—twice! We've been pushing you to do things no driver should ever do, and you have been doing a great job."

Luca blinked a few times and wiped his eyes with his sleeve. He gave Buck a slight nod.

"Now, take another deep breath and get this van moving. I just received another text from Jay. Teams have already checked out the houses near the first stop the Mercedes made. They're searching the industrial park now."

As Luca passed the last of the cars in the line of traffic, he increased the van's speed. After all the flashing emergency strobes, explosions, and bright headlights, the sudden darkness had a very welcome, calming effect.

"Can you please help me with the directions?" Luca asked, looking at Buck through the rearview mirror.

"Sure. I figured you knew them."

"No, I just followed the Mercedes earlier without paying much attention to the roads."

"Here." Buck held his phone to Luca. "The directions are on it."

Luca quickly removed his phone from the dashboard mount and replaced it with Buck's. A little while later, they turned onto the road where the Industrial Park was located. The GPS showed the entrance was a little over half a kilometer up the road. Despite the twisting, unplowed road, Luca accelerated. None of the passengers even flinched as the tires spun. Luca had proven himself behind the wheel. As they rounded the first turn, they saw an orange haze in the snowy sky. The faint sounds of sirens grew louder as they drove. Making the final turn, Luca immediately had to slam on the brakes. Once again, the van began to slide. The skid wouldn't have worried anybody if the van wasn't heading directly toward two police cars barricading the road.

"Oh, not again. Hold on!" Luca ordered.

As they braced themselves, the van made impact. Reid's painful grunt made everyone grimace, but luckily no one else was hurt.

"You all right?" Shane asked.

"I'll live," he groaned through clenched teeth.

The officers inside each police car bounded from their vehicles and quickly approached, yelling at Luca to get out.

Luca followed their orders along with Buck and Reid. Buck had dialed Jay and had his cell phone at his ear.

The officers questioned Luca while Buck quickly explained the situation to Jay. Leaping flames and fire trucks were visible through the property's boundary fence and trees. Toxic smelling fumes permeated the air.

After listening to Jay, Buck held his phone out to the officers. "Your captain would like to speak with you."

With an odd look, one of the officers said, "My captain?"

"Please, just take the phone."

Skeptically the officer put the phone to his ear. "*Hallo.*" He listened for a moment, raising his eyebrows. "*Ja Kapitan,*" he said. He listened more, nodded multiple times, and said, "*Ja.*" He then pulled the phone from his ear, handed it back to Buck, and said in English, "Follow me."

He began walking briskly toward the entrance of the Industrial Park.

"Officer, please wait," Buck said loudly enough to be heard over the wail of sirens, bullhorn amplified voices, and random explosions.

Buck motioned for everyone in the van to join them.

"Who are these people?" the officer asked. "I was told to bring you and your friend."

"It's a long story, Officer. Would you like me to call your captain again and clear it?"

The officer looked at the group, gave a resigned shrug, and said, "Just follow me."

As the group weaved around all the emergency vehicles, Hunter said, "I'm so scared."

Reid put his arm over her shoulder, and Shane reached for her hand. "Me too," Reid said. "Try to stay tough, sis."

"Yeah," she sighed. "Sure."

They increased their pace to keep up with the officer. Walking through the park's entrance, the officer saluted a colleague who was manning the gate.

Suddenly, they all heard a loud motor and turned to see headlights coming toward them. Snow rooster-tailed behind the wheels of an approaching all-terrain vehicle. Jay skidded to a stop next to the group and yelled loudly enough to be heard over the noise of the ATV's engine. "Follow me. We'll talk over there." He pointed at the open garage door of a warehouse across the parking lot, then drove away, wheels spinning.

They entered the big empty building and stomped the snow off their shoes. Fluorescent lights blazed throughout the cavernous structure. Red elements glowed inside heating units that hung from chains near each overhead door. Three firemen were walking the interior perimeter of the warehouse, opening and closing doors as they went. The group huddled below one of the heaters.

"Okay," Jay said loudly. "For the sake of time, I'm going to get right to the point. It looks like Peter was being held here."

Hunter, Dan, and Carole gasped. Dan and Carole reached for each other's hand. Reid gave his sister's shoulder a squeeze.

"They were keeping him in that warehouse." Jay pointed through the garage opening to a smoldering building next to one that was still aflame. "The fire in the building on the left was extinguished, but not before it spread to the one next to it. The one that's burning now is filled with containers of combustible chemicals. The good news is there's no evidence that anyone was hurt. We're thinking that something spooked them into setting the fire and leaving the facility in a rush. It looks like it only started a couple of hours ago. When you guys stopped earlier to get the address of this place, were you on foot or in a vehicle?"

"We were in a van," Buck said.

"Did you pull into the driveway, close to the guard shack?"

"Yes, we were pretty close. Why?"

"There's a surveillance camera on the shack facing the driveway. Whoever has Peter probably saw you pull up. There are tons of cameras all over the place. There's viewing equipment still in the building, but it looks like they took the recording device with them."

"So, do you think he's alive?" Hunter asked.

"Yes, I do. It appears that they were treating him well, too."

"How do you know?" asked Peter's mother.

"There are weights, a lifting bench, and what looks like a ski simulator in the room. There's also a swimming tank and running track in a different part of the warehouse. The kitchen was stocked with healthy food. It seems they wanted him to stay in shape. But we have no idea why."

"So now what?" Reid asked.

"Now that we know he's in this area, all our teams will concentrate the search here. As I told you before, between Fischer's team, the local police, Europol, and my team, we've got plenty of manpower. We'll find him."

"I don't mean to be negative," Buck said. "But what if they flew him out of here on a chopper?"

"We're watching the skies, and we've got teams knocking on doors throughout the area. So far, nothing."

"So, what's the plan?" Reid asked.

"Roadblocks, vehicle searches, the usual. Now that we know approximately what time you were here earlier, we can set better parameters."

"As you can see," Jay motioned with his chin to the firemen in the rear of the warehouse. "We're searching every building. Hopefully, we'll find more surveillance cameras and someplace to view the video. We're also talking to the people who manage the property about the guard shack cameras and hopefully other gate cameras. Chances are they're all viewable online. Then it will depend if the feed is live only, or if they're recording it too. Hopefully, we can get a video of the vehicle they left in and maybe even see who we are dealing with."

"And what about Ponytail?" Buck said. "At least we know where he is. Do you know how badly he was hurt? Reid and I think we might have seen him lying in the snow as we drove past the accident. Whoever it was, looked pretty bad."

"Ponytail, huh. That's appropriate."

"We got tired of saying the guy with the ponytail," Buck said.

"Works for me," Jay agreed. "It *was* him that you saw, and yes, he's in bad shape. He wasn't wearing a seatbelt and his airbag did not deploy. A bunch of his ribs were broken when his chest hit the steering wheel before he went through the windshield. It's a miracle he survived. He's still in a coma. Hopefully, we'll get a chance to speak with him when, or I guess I should say, *if* he comes out of it."

"This all seems so crazy," Buck said. "Why would they take Peter in Chamonix, then bring him here and make sure he trains and stays in shape? It sounds like they want him to race. But why? I mean, as much as the thought of it sucks, I understood why someone would want him out of the Games. Allowing another racer to medal at least makes sense. But taking him, then letting him race. I just don't get it. The Opening Ceremonies are tomorrow, and the downhill is two days after that. It makes no sense."

"None of this does. But right now, our job is to find him," Jay said. "I want you all to go back to the hotel. Get some rest. I'm going to stay here for a while to see if we find any video. After I review it, I'm going to the hospital. Hopefully, I can speak with one of the people that were in the car with Ponytail. I'll call you as soon as I have anything worthwhile to tell you."

"I'm going to stay here," Hunter said. "I want to be close when you find him."

Dan and Carole Buckar glanced at one another. "We're staying too," Dan said.

"I understand how you all feel," Jay said. "But if you stay here, it just gives me one more thing to worry about. Besides, it's too cold, too dangerous, and quite frankly, you'll be in the way. Please go back to the hotel so I can concentrate on finding Peter. I promise the minute we find him, I will have someone ready to bring you to him."

Dan and Carole nodded. It took a moment for Hunter to accept with a long face and a slight shrug.

"We may need a ride to the hotel," Buck said.

"Just have the driver who brought you here take you?"

"That will depend on how bad his van is."

"Why? What happened?"

"We skidded into two police cars that were barricading the road when we got here."

"Was anybody hurt?" Jay asked.

"No."

"Okay. Well, check with the driver. If he can't take you, I'll get you a ride."

Buck turned toward the group. "Did anyone get Luca's cell number?"

"I did," Carole said, reaching for her phone. "Calling him now.

After a quick conversation with Luca, she said, "Looks like we need a ride. They're towing the van. I told Luca to stop by the hotel sometime during the next few days so we could thank him properly."

"Good," Buck said. "He deserves something for his help. We'll take care of him after we find Peter and the games are over."

"We should get him a new van," Shane said.

"If it's his, I agree," Reid said. "If it belongs to a taxi company that he works for, their insurance will cover the damage, and we'll do something else for him."

"Okay all," Jay said. "Your rides are here."

A big, four-door pickup truck, and a rescue vehicle with oversized, knobby, off-road tires, pulled into the warehouse and stopped near them. Feuerwehr was painted in bold white lettering on both red trucks.

"You sure they can spare these?" Reid asked.

"Yes. With the fire in control, there's more than enough manpower and vehicles here already. They haven't found anyone so far, and most of the buildings are vacant anyway."

"That's probably why they chose this facility," Dan said. "Less chance of getting noticed by busybodies."

"Agreed," Jay said. "Okay, everyone, get out of here. I've got work to do. I'll let you know the minute we come up with something."

***

As the trucks departed, Jay jumped on the ATV and drove back to Fischer's SUV, but Fischer was nowhere in sight. Jay pulled out his phone and called him.

"Where are you?" he asked when Fischer answered.

"In the management office in building one. Come over. We're watching video clips that you'll want to see."

"Stupid question. Where's building one?"

"It's near the main entrance. Just follow the building numbers."

"I'm on my way!"

"Hurry, Jay. I need you to take the lead on this. I've got to get back to my office. The Opening Ceremonies are tomorrow. I've got a million things to do."

"Okay."

Jay hopped back on the ATV and took off. He looked at the building to his right, then to his left, and the one next to that. *What the hell,* he thought. *No numbers? That's ridiculous!*

He saw two firefighters on the other side of the parking lot and sped toward them. Visibility, especially without goggles, was lousy. He had covered about half the distance to the firefighters when the ATV slammed into something under the snow. The machine bucked hard, sending Jay flipping over the handlebars. Luckily, the deep snow cushioned his fall as he landed on his back.

Shaken but unhurt, he wasted no time as he sprung to his feet and remounted the ATV.

He stopped next to the firefighters and killed the engine.

"*Bist du en Ordnung*?" a fireman asked.

"*Sprichst du Englisch*?" Jay asked.

"Yes."

"I'm fine. Just dumb of me to go so fast when I couldn't see."

"Yes, it was. Are you sure you're okay? I can call for a medic."

"I'm fine, thanks. But I need to find building number One. Do you know where it is?"

The fireman looked up and pointed to the top corner of the building they were next to. Jay looked up and saw a big white 14 against the light brown bricks of the building.

"Ah. Danka! I couldn't see the white numbers through the snow."

Jay drove away. He slowed down as he approached the corner of the next building and looked up. Squinting and shielding his eyes from the wind-driven snow, he saw the number 16 and groaned. He spun the ATV around and cranked the throttle to its maximum. As he drove by, he gave the firemen a wave.

Without bothering to check any more numbers, he continued to the end of the road and saw an exit sign with an arrow pointing to the right. He made the turn, drove toward the exit, and entered the parking area of the last building.

He crossed the empty parking lot, slowly drove up the snow-blanketed steps leading to the main entrance, and stopped on the landing below the final few stairs. After killing the engine, he climbed off the quad, looked up to confirm it was the correct building, then dashed up the remaining steps and yanked on the handle of the locked glass entrance door. Rather than waste any more time, he called Fischer.

"I'm at the front door. It's locked."

"Go around the right side of the building. I'll meet you at the door closest to the rear."

"Okay. I'll be there in a minute."

Jay took a few steps then rethought leaving the ATV on the steps. He ran back to it and rode down the steps and around the building. As he made the turn, he saw a red emergency vehicle, an SUV, and a small economy car, all parked at the far end of the building. His face now stung from the pelting snow. He'd had just about enough of the ATV. Fischer was holding the door open when Jay got there.

He followed Fischer into a large office where he saw the backs of four people sitting at the far end of the room, in a row of chairs at a long, wall-mounted desk. They were all studying a series of video monitors built into the wall above the desk.

A guy turned his head and gave Jay a quick nod. He was one of Pompard's men that Jay had met at the hospital.

"I'm sorry, I forgot your name," Jay said.

"Jacques Ferrer. I'm one of Pompard's detectives."

"Yes, of course," Jay said, nodding.

"And these young ladies are Shruti, Sydney, and Lily," Fischer said. "They work for the company that owns this office park. Girls, this is Jay Scott."

The three girls turned and said hi.

One looked older and maintained a serious expression. The other two, who were obviously twins, smiled.

"Shruti, please show Mr. Scott what you just showed me," Fischer said.

"Sydney, bring up cameras nine and ten. Lily, three and four," the older girl said.

The three young ladies clicked on different photos on their monitors.

"Please run the video of the group leaving the building," Fischer said.

"Already loaded. Expanding it now," Shruti said.

A picture enlarged on one of the monitors on the wall above her. She moved her mouse and clicked the 'play' arrow. Jay watched as a closed black door on the outside of a beige brick building appeared on the screen. A floodlight lit the door from above. Snow was whipping at a forty-five-degree angle, impeding the view. After about eight seconds, Shruti said, "Okay. Watch closely."

The black door opened outward, and two armed men exited. One had a dark beard. Both wore dark knit hats and carried automatic machine pistols. As they walked out of the camera's view, another man with a gun came through the door, stopped, and held it open.

"He's going to stand there holding the door for a moment," Shruti said. "Then, your man will be coming out. He's being carried by another man." Shruti moved her mouse and clicked. The second monitor above Shruti showed the first two men who had walked out, now opening the doors of a big SUV.

Movement in the first monitor brought Jay's eyes quickly back to it. Another man came through the doorway with someone on his shoulders in a fireman's carry. Jay watched as the man stopped and lowered the person he was carrying down to his feet. Jay's worry about why the man was being carried, was somewhat assuaged when he saw him standing on his own accord. His height and build were similar to Peter's, but the heavy snowfall made facial recognition impossible.

"Can you give me a closer look at his face?" Jay asked.

"A bit," Shruti said while adjusting, spinning, and clicking her mouse buttons. "These aren't optical zoom cameras, so the digital zoom is not very strong."

As she adjusted the view, the resolution decreased as the man's face grew on the screen. Despite the picture's graininess, Jay could see that it was Peter, and that his eyes were covered by a black mask. There was a dark smudge leading from Peter's nostrils to his chin and another on his cheek.

"Is that blood?" Jay asked.

"I think it's a combination of blood and vomit," Shruti said.

"How can you tell?"

"You'll see in about seven seconds."

Jay watched intensely as the man leaned and shifted his feet. He looked very unsteady. Suddenly, he bent over and vomited.

The man who had been carrying him grabbed Peter's handcuffed arm to prevent him from falling but held him at a distance, staying clear of Peter's discharge.

After Peter finished throwing up, the man helped him walk to the SUV, where the two other men uncuffed him, cleaned him with towels, and helped him change into a clean shirt. *That's a good sign,* thought Jay with some relief. *They're treating him with consideration. His death is not imminent.*

Then, two more men joined them. One put a black sack over Peter's head, and they placed him in the vehicle. Once they were all inside, the truck drove away.

"Okay, now look at Lily's screen," Shruti said.

Jay looked at the backs of the two other girls. The one to the left slowly raised her hand.

The monitor on the wall above her showed views from four cameras. One showed the chain-link entrance gate and the driveway leading to it from the street. Another was from the guard shack into the industrial park. It showed a roundabout in the road that split off in four directions. The right and left roads looked like they continued around the outskirts of the park. The view of the far road that left the circle leading away from the camera and through the middle of the industrial park, was partially blocked by a big, floodlight lit fountain in the center of the roundabout. The fountain was off, and its round base was piled high with a dome of snow.

Headlights slowly became visible as a vehicle approached from the oncoming road. The closer the vehicle got to the circular intersection, the more the fountain blocked the view. Then, as the SUV made its way around the island and turned toward the exit, the camera caught the full view of the front bumper.

"Damn! No plate!" Jay said, glancing at Fischer.

"Keep watching," Fischer said.

Jay's eyes returned to the monitor just as another picture on Lily's screen showed the SUV closely as it passed by. The camera was angled directly at the darkly tinted driver's window and rear passenger window. The combination of falling snow and darkened windows made for poor visibility of the inhabitants. As the truck continued through the open gate, Jay stared at the gate and driveway camera view. Unsurprisingly, the rear license plate was also missing. He watched the SUV make a right turn onto the street.

"At least we know their direction," Jay said.

"Okay," Shruti said. "Now take a look at Sydney's screen."

Sydney's monitor had a split view. The left picture was of a dark, snow-covered road bordered by the fence that surrounded the industrial park. A wall of tall trees set back from the road about ten feet on the far side of the street created a boundary between the adjacent residential neighborhood and the industrial park. Two narrow off-shooting roads cut openings in the tree line further down the street.

Headlights appeared and quickly grew larger and brighter as the vehicle approached the camera. A brief moment later, the rear of the vehicle appeared in the second picture, shrinking as it drove away from the camera toward an entrance to a highway.

"Damn, a highway. They could have gone anywhere," Jay said.

Sydney raised her right hand in a tight fist, quieting Jay immediately. She ticked off the seconds by raising her thumb, then forefinger, then each of the other three fingers, one by one. Then, she dramatically pointed at the screen just as the vehicle turned left onto a side street leading into a neighborhood.

"Nice timing," Jay said.

Lily and Sydney gave each other big smiles. Shruti rolled her eyes.

"So, they turned into a local neighborhood instead of getting on the highway. That's good," Jay said.

"Yes," Ferrer said. "We already have over a dozen teams searching those neighborhoods."

"Very good. At least we know he's alive. If, in fact, that was him. And, although he was unbalanced, it looked like he's in decent physical condition. His tipsiness and nausea could be from anything—abuse, drugs, lack of food, or sleep. Who knows. But they were treating him humanely in these videos anyway."

"I feel terrible about this, but I really must go," Fischer said. "I need to be back at my command post finalizing things for the Opening Ceremonies."

"Where's Pompard?" Jay asked.

"He's out with the search teams. He left as soon as he saw this video," Ferrer said. "He asked me to wait and take you to join him."

Jay gave a slight nod. His face revealed the utter frustration he was feeling.

Looking at Jay, Fischer said, "I know Jay. We're all feeling it. None of this seems to make any sense. At least we know he's close. All we can do is keep searching and hoping for the best."

Jay sighed and shook his head while looking at Fischer. "That's not enough for me in this case, Christoph. Buck and Reid are practically family to me, and Peter is like family to them. In fact, he will be soon. This case is very personal for me. Having no idea why these bastards are holding him and playing this … this game, is tearing me up inside. So, you see, hoping for the best is not an alternative for me. I need answers. More than that, I need to bring Peter back to his family—my family!"

The room fell silent. Ferrer lowered his head. All three of the young women turned in their chairs and looked at Jay with sad yet understanding eyes. Fischer walked to Jay, hugged him, and quietly said, "I understand, my friend."

As Fischer let go, he said, "You know you have my full commitment to help find him," Fischer said. "I have and will continue to supply as many men and resources as I possibly can."

"You have been a tremendous help, Christoph, and I appreciate it. You better go. The safety of a lot of people is in your hands."

Fischer nodded. "Thank you for understanding. Please keep me informed if you find him."

"Of course."

Fischer looked toward the girls. "Ladies, thank you for coming in and staying so late to help us." He put on his Olympic Security jacket and reached into his pocket. He pulled out a small stack of tickets, walked to the girls, and handed one to each of them. "These are for tomorrow's Opening Ceremonies." Looking at the twins, he added, "Here's two more for your dad and your uncle. Please tell them we said thanks for helping us. And tell them I will be available if they need any help dealing with their insurance company about the fire claim on the buildings."

"*Vielen dank, Herr Fischer,*" the eldest girl said.

"Bitte schon."

***

"They're searching over on Vietta Saluver in Celerina," Jay told Ferrer after hanging up from a quick conversation with Pompard.

Ferrer entered it into his phone and flipped his right turn indicator on before stopping at the next light.

"On second thought," Jay said. "I think we should head to the hospital. Maybe we can get an address from one of Ponytail's friends."

Ferrer nodded and switched the turn indicator to make a left turn. "It's worth a try. The hospital is only a few minutes from here." The moment the light turned green, Ferrer stepped on the gas. Wheels spun before grabbing the slippery road. The vehicle lurched forward, fishtailed, then straightened, just missing the parked cars lining the street.

"*Verdammt,*" Ferrer yelled.

"Whoa!" Jay said. "A little excited, huh?"

"Frustrated."

"Yeah, me too."

Chapter 54

HUNTER LEANED BACK in her uncomfortably stiff seat and raised her eyes to the starless sky. Light snow fell as the procession of athletes made their way through the stadium. Hunter's heart was as overcast as the sky. Peter had not been found during last night's search, and Hunter's sullen attitude was shared by many athletes and fans. While one missing athlete would not prevent the Opening Ceremonies, it cast a pall over what was usually a colorful display of ceremonial grandeur.

Looking to her left, Hunter saw Carole Buckar dabbing her eyes with a moist tissue. She reached for what she still hoped was her future mother-in-law's hand and gave it a squeeze. Carole turned her head, and their mutual grief reflected in each other's eyes.

***

Hours after the Opening Ceremonies, the Buckar and Clark families sat in Reid and Shane's suite at the hotel, doing their best to comfort one another. Sadness and tears increased as hope slowly diminished.

"He's gone. I know he is," Hunter said as her sniffles once again became sobs.

"Please don't say that," Carole begged. "I refuse to lose hope."

Trying to refrain from crying, Hunter's breathing was erratic as she said, "I'm sorry, I'm trying to stay positive, but it's getting so difficult. My hopes remained strong until the Opening Ceremonies, but for some reason, now that they're over, I just can't …" Her tears returned with a vengeance.

"I understand," Carole said. "You know I do. Part of me feels the same way. But I'm fighting it. We need to stay upbeat until they find him. I've been praying for a miracle."

Shane stood and walked to the bar. "Who would like some wine? I'm opening a bottle."

Fighting back tears while trying to control her breathing, Hunter dabbed her eyes with a tissue and joined Shane at the bar. She picked up a bottle of Gran Patron and said, "The hell with wine, who wants a shot of tequila?"

"I'll have one," Carole said.

"Really?" Dan asked, completely shocked.

"Yes, really. I may even have two."

"Wow," Dan said. "Oh, what the hell. I'll take one, too."

"Might as well just line 'em up, Hunter," Reid said.

"You're going to drink tequila?" Shane asked Reid. "I thought even the smell made you gag?"

"Yeah, well. If there was ever a time to make an exception, drinking a shot of tequila to Peter's safe return certainly qualifies."

They all approached the bar as Hunter filled the final shot glass. As they raised their glasses, Carole said, "Wait, what about the salt and lime?"

"You don't need it with premium tequila," Hunter said. "Salt and lime help cover the bad taste of the cheap stuff."

"If you say so." Carole's face filled with dread.

Everyone raised their glasses.

"To Peter," Reid said.

"To Peter," they all repeated loudly. Then each threw back their shot.

Chapter 55

THE COVERING OVER his head muffled the conversation between the two men in the front seats of the vehicle. They spoke rapidly in what sounded like Russian to Peter, but he didn't really know. He thought they sounded nervous, or maybe excited, but again, he had no way to be sure.

"Peter," someone next to him said.

The sound of his name pronounced in American English with only a slight hint of a foreign accent caught him off guard. He turned his head toward the voice.

"As you may have guessed, today is your lucky day. Your downhill race is due to begin in a little over an hour. That will give you plenty of time to reach the starting gate and inform your coach that you are ready to race. We will be texting him as soon as you leave this vehicle, so hopefully, he will have your equipment ready.

"We're going to drop you off at the base of the mountain with the outer cover removed from your head, but your eyes will remain covered. I'm going to put a baseball cap on you to hide your eye mask. Keep the visor low, and keep your head down so no one will notice the mask. When we tell you to, I want you to count slowly to ten. Then, and not a second earlier, I want you to remove the eye cover and go straight to the lift. I'm sure you know the mountain well enough to know that you'll have to switch lifts on the way up. You should make it to the start gate well before the first racer begins his run. Then, it's up to your coaches to get you ready. Hopefully, they can get you an early start time."

"Wait. You want me to race today?" asked Peter, stunned.

"Silence!" the man demanded. "If you remove the eye covering before ten seconds, or if you cause any commotion, I'm afraid we'll have to take action. If that occurs, believe me, you will not be racing today or ever again."

The man let a couple of seconds pass, then asked, "Do you understand?"

Peter responded with a slight nod.

"I said, do you understand?" the man repeated, giving Peter a nudge.

"Yes, dammit," Peter growled as he shoved the man. "Keep your damn hands off me."

"Very good. A little feistiness might just help you win."

Peter was mad, but at the same time, curious. "How much did you get?"

"What do you mean?"

"Ransom. How much?"

"Funny that you ask. We thought about asking for ransom. But that's not what this is about."

"Then what?" Peter asked in surprise as the vehicle stopped.

"It's time for us to part ways, Mr. Buckar. My colleague will take it from here. I wish you the best of luck in your quest for gold."

Peter felt the covering being removed from his head and winced as it brushed against his nose. He heard the door open to his right and welcomed the blast of icy air. Stimulated by the sudden chill, his muscles tensed. As he stepped from the vehicle, his first thought was to yell and run, but he felt a hand grip his shoulder.

"Say one word to anyone, and you're a dead man. Now be quiet and come with me," a man said quietly, with a heavy accent.

They walked about ten steps and slowed to a stop. Peter heard the sounds of people in the surrounding area. There were various conversations and a burst of laughter.

His anxiety was soaring. More than anything, he wanted to rip off the eye covering and finally get a look at his captor. But he knew if he did, they'd follow through on their threat. He took a deep breath and slowly let it go.

"Remember, we're watching you. Don't play games with us. Just get yourself to the top of the course and win that medal. Okay, start counting, slowly!"

Peter heard the vehicle's motor race and the wheels spin.

Ten, nine, eight, he counted to himself. *Damn, is someone really watching me, or should I take this stupid eye cover off now? No—you're so close, you idiot, just keep counting. Five, four, three, two, one.* He pulled the eye cover down to his neck, grimacing as it rubbed against his sore nose.

Bright light stung his eyes. He squinted, spun around, and saw three SUVs driving away in different directions. Which one were they in? Damn, there was no time to do anything about it anyway. He had to get to the top of the race course as quickly as possible.

He turned back toward the mountain. Thoughts were wreaking havoc in his head. *Should I report this? Should I contact Stan? I need to call Hunter, and Mom, and Dad! Is someone really watching me?*

He started running toward the lift. *Why is there no line? Is the chairlift running? Wait, they don't open the mountain to the public during the Olympics. Do they?*

Swimming in confusion, everything around him was blurred. He ran past a small group of people, directly into the path of two rapidly advancing snowmobiles. One of the machines veered, just missing him. The other rider had to turn his sled so hard it slid sideways and rolled, throwing the rider directly toward Peter. The man tumbled, stopping practically at Peter's feet. He stood quickly and faced Peter, bright red with anger.

"Why don't you watch where ..." The man stopped mid-sentence. "Wait ... you're ... Peter Buckar! Where did you come from? How did you get here?"

Peter looked at him, wondering where to begin. The emblem on the man's jacket read *Olympic Security.*

"They just dropped me off."

"Who did?" asked the man who had been riding the other sled as he quickly approached on foot.

"The idiots who kidnapped me. Look, there's no time to talk about it. Can you please take me up to the start of the downhill run?"

"Of course, but are you feeling well enough to ride on the back of my sled?"

"Yeah, why?" Peter asked.

The man gestured with his hand toward Peter's face and awkwardly said, "Well, your face. It doesn't look so good."

"I'm okay. Can we just go?"

"If you say so. Help me flip this thing back onto its skis," he said, reaching for the handlebars of the overturned snowmobile.

Peter grabbed the sled at the rear and helped roll it over.

The man boarded the machine and said, "Climb on. By the way, my name is Mathias. I am with Olympic Security. We have been looking everywhere for you. I am glad that you're okay."

"Thank you, Mathias."

"Alberto," Mathias yelled to his colleague. "Call Fischer and let him know we've got Buckar."

Once Peter was aboard. Mathias yelled, "Ready?"

Peter latched onto the rear hand grips and yelled, "Ready!"

As Mathias pushed the sled to its limits up the unforgiving, bumpy trails, Peter's forearms began to ache from gripping so tightly. Unlike the driver, Peter couldn't see the upcoming ridges and mounds in time to use his legs as shock absorbers, hence his death grip on the passenger handles.

Midway up the mountain, Peter's mind was reeling with thoughts. *Thank God I'm free.* It was a heady feeling that he would never take for granted again. *I can't believe I'm actually going to race. Oh my God, I haven't studied the course. Will the IOC even let me race? I need to get off this snowmobile. I need to stretch. I need to meditate. I need to see the course before I ski it.*

The screaming engine of another snowmobile startled Peter, snapping him from his thoughts as Mathias' colleague passed them.

Minutes later, after a final steep incline, they reached the Piz Nair cable car mid-station, where the downhill race course began.

Peter got off the sled, thanked Mathias, and was practically attacked by some of his teammates. Try as he might, he could not hold back his tears.

As word spread, racers from other teams joined in the welcoming melee.

"So, tell us, Buckar, where the hell have you been?" someone bellowed behind him.

Peter turned and saw Gustav Weber, a burly Austrian racer pushing his way through the mob.

"Where have I been?"

"Yes, Peter, that's what I asked. They say you were kidnapped, but suddenly you show up just before the race, completely unharmed. Well, maybe except for a couple of shiners and a crooked nose," said Weber with a sneer.

Peter hadn't looked in a mirror since he had fallen. He thought, *My nose hurts like hell, but crooked? And black eyes too? Great!*

"Are you accusing me of something, Gustav?"

All the other racers started in on Weber.

"Shut up, Weber!"

"Cut the crap, Gustav!"

"Excuse me, men," Coach Williams ordered, making his way through the crowd. "There's no time for this nonsense." He walked up holding Peter's racing suit, stopped directly in front of him, and just stared for a second. Then, he pulled Peter into a hug and said, "Thank God you're okay. Go inside and suit up. Colodny is waiting to stretch you. We'll talk after that. Meanwhile, I will call Hunter and your parents. They've been doing nothing but looking for you along with Reid, Shane, and Buck."

Peter's eyes lit up at the mention of Hunter's name. He had missed her so much his heart ached.

"And Peter," Coach Williams said as he walked away, "It's good to have you back."

"It's good to be back, Coach."

***

Peter was lying on his back in a small room in the Piz Nair mid-station being stretched by Coach Colodny when Williams walked in and asked, "So, are you really ready for this?"

"Hell yeah, Coach!"

"His legs are like rocks," Colodny said. "Seriously. I have spent a lot of time stretching these legs. I know them well. They are bigger and stronger than I've ever seen them. That machine must have been something special. We should get one for the team."

"What machine?" Williams asked.

"I was telling him about the equipment they had me training on. The virtual racing machine was amazing. I feel like I've been skiing this course daily now for …" he thought for a moment. "Wow, I have no idea how long I've been gone."

"Eleven days. They took you from the hospital while you were still unconscious from your crash in the Kandahar."

"Damn. I don't … oh, never mind."

"What?"

"Coach, I can't even remember being in Chamonix."

"Well, you took a hell of a fall. It was a miracle that you didn't break anything."

"Yeah, nothing but my head."

"Well, there's that."

They both grinned.

"Look, we can talk about all this after your run. I'll have a video of the course in your hands soon."

"Really? How'd you manage that?"

"With some help."

"What does that mean?"

"Man, if you only knew how many people have been involved with your disappearance. You've been headline news throughout the world. The FBI, Interpol, Olympic Security, and Jay Scott and his team have all been looking for you."

"Wow!" After a moment, Peter added, "Who is Jay Scott?"

"I figured you knew him. He's Reid's and Buck's security guy."

"Oh, that's right. Hey, speaking of Reid and Buck, do they know I'm here?"

"Of course. Buck was my first call after being told you were on your way up here. They'll be at the finish line with Hunter and your parents."

Peter smiled.

"Actually, Buck was my second call. I called the IOC first to ask for clearance to have a drone shoot an aerial video of the course. They agreed that the only way it would be safe for you to race was if you watched a video before your run. Dave Kane is downloading it now. Luckily he didn't have an early start time. I never would have thought that drone of his could be so useful."

"Wow, I can't believe he's taking the time to do this before he races the Olympic downhill. That's nuts."

"He didn't even think twice when I asked him," Williams said. "You've got some good friends on this team. They were all very worried about you."

"I guess I owe Dave, big time."

Williams nodded. "He should be here any minute."

"Excellent."

Williams let a moment pass, then said, "Peter, look at me."

Peter turned his head. "What?"

"I need you to look me in the eye and tell me whether you're really up to this or not."

"Are you kidding?"

"Do I look like I'm kidding?"

"Coach, not only am I up to it. I'm in the best shape I've been in in a long time."

"I'm not talking about physical strength. If you're going to ski, I need to know that your head is totally in the game."

Peter nodded. "I'm all here, Coach. Focused and ready. Don't even try to keep me out of that start gate."

"What about those black eyes and your nose? It looks like they broke it."

"They didn't do it. I fell as we were running out of a burning building. My hands were cuffed behind my back, so I had no way to brace my fall. I'm okay."

"Burning building? Handcuffs? I can't wait to hear the rest," Colodny said. "But for now, we should end this conversation and get you stretched and focused."

"You're right," said Williams as his phone rang. He answered, listened, and said, "Yes, he's here, and he looks good." After listening more, he said, "Of course, I'll tell him."

Putting the phone away, he said, "Jay Scott doesn't want you talking to the press until he speaks with you. They are going to be all over you after your race."

As Peter nodded again, Dave Kane entered the tent and handed him a video tablet. "Peter, it is so good to see you here, ready to ski. I hope the video helps. It's crystal clear." He pushed the button, and Peter could see the image of the video ready to start.

"Thanks, Dave."

"No problem, my man. I'm really glad you're okay. I'll see you in a little while. I've got to get ready for my run."

"Kill it, man."

"That's my plan, brother!"

As Kane was leaving the tent, Peter said, "Hey, do me a favor. Would you ask Jarrett to come in?"

Kane, Williams, and Colodny all turned toward Peter with confused looks.

"What's with the faces?" Peter asked.

"You're kidding, right?" Colodny said.

"No. Why?"

"Really? Maybe because you can't stand Eschmann."

"I have no problem with him. We may argue once in a while, and I may not like how jealous he gets, but I respect him as a racer. If there's anyone who can help me figure out the right line on this course, it's him. We may not see eye to eye, but, on skis, we're very similar. He's a smart skier. He's aggressive without being reckless. I admire his racing style, and while I've never admitted it before, I have learned a lot from watching him race."

Leery expressions on the three men had transformed to looks of shock.

"Hmm. Nothing like a good concussion to change a man's views," Kane said, turning and continuing his walk to the exit. "I'll go find him."

"Please hurry," Williams said. "Peter is number sixteen."

Increasing his pace, Kane acknowledged with a quick thumbs-up as he left the tent.

"How did you convince them to keep my position?"

"Actually," Williams said. "It was your friend here," he nodded toward Colodny. "He never lost faith that you'd show up. He convinced the race committee to reserve your starting spot. His argument was simple. Keep your spot so that if you showed up, you'd have a fair chance, based on your World Cup ranking, and if you didn't show, just skip over you as they would with any no-show."

"Thank you," Peter said, looking very closely into Colodny's eyes. Peter was still lying on his back with Colodny over him, pushing Peter's outstretched left leg toward his torso.

"You're welcome," Colodny said, a little choked up. "I did my part. Now it's time for you to do yours. Do us proud, buddy."

"I'm gonna give it all I've got."

"What are you giving all you've got?" Eschmann said obnoxiously, as he entered the tent. "Ah, look at you, getting stretched in private. And you," he looked at Colodny, "I should have known you'd be working on your pal here. You haven't stretched me since …"

"Come on, Jarrett, why don't you finish your sentence, or are you too embarrassed?" Colodny said.

"Fuck you."

"Cut the crap, guys. Whatever you're talking about can wait," Peter said.

Eschmann and Colodny gave each other one last sneer, then they turned toward Peter.

"Wow, looks like they worked you over a little. Are you all right?" Eschmann asked.

"Yeah, I'm fine, thanks. Jarrett, you and I have had our differences, but I hope you can put them aside for now. The truth is while we may argue and fight, I know with me it's because I see you as a bit of a threat."

"What? You seriously think I'd lay a hand on you?"

"No. Not a physical threat. A threat to my ranking, a threat to my medal count. You're the only guy on the team who I feel can beat me anytime we race together."

"I wish," Eschmann said, softening up a little.

"Well, stop wishing for it, and focus on it. It'll happen. Maybe even today."

"Dude, if I don't beat you today, I should quit racing altogether. You haven't been on skis since the Kandahar. I'm surprised they're even letting you compete."

"That's why I asked for you. You've studied the course. Obviously, I haven't. They allowed Kane to video it with his drone. I need you to watch it with me and give me your thoughts."

Doubt instantly creased Eschmann's face. "You're going to trust me to be honest?"

Peter smiled. "Dude, even though we haven't gotten along over the years, we know how each other thinks."

Eschmann gave a slight nod.

"I think we both agree that a win is only meaningful if it's a fair win," Peter said. "If you beat a competitor because he's hurt or any other unfair reason, it isn't a righteous win. Many say a W is a W, no matter what. That's not me, and I know it's not you."

Eschmann smirked and laid down on his back, on the floor, next to Peter. Their shoulders touched.

"What are you doing?" Peter asked.

"Start the video," Eschmann said. "We don't have much time."

Peter lifted the tablet. "We could sit over there." He gestured toward a bench.

"Nah, this is perfect. This way Dave can keep stretching you, and possibly me a little too?" Eschmann looked at Colodny with pleading eyes.

Peter and Williams laughed. After a moment, Colodny smirked and gave a slight nod.

Peter tapped the video icon. Before long, the two men were chatting like old friends, pointing at different parts of the video, and sharing their thoughts about every turn and jump on the course.

Williams watched and listened for a minute, then caught Colodny's eye and gave him a look of sheer amazement. Colodny returned a slight shrug. For years both coaches worked hard to keep peace between these two men, and here they were, side by side, giving each other tips on how to win. As Colodny was simultaneously pushing Peter's right leg and Eschmann's left, Williams began walking out.

"All right, guys, obviously I'm not needed here. I've got to go hike up those damn steps to check on your teammates. I hate those stairs, all 187 of them."

"At least you don't have to climb them in ski boots," Eschmann said.

"Lucky me." Williams let out a quick chortle as he walked by and snapped a picture of them with his phone. "No one is going to believe this."

After Williams left, the skier's discussion continued while Colodny stretched them for another ten minutes.

"Okay, that's enough, men," Colodny said. "Peter, you need to suit up. Your helmet, goggles, gloves, and boots are in the bag over there." Colodny pointed near the entrance. "I had Mikaela bring up five pairs of your boards. She's waiting out near the rack to help you choose a pair."

"Thanks, Coach."

Colodny gave a simple nod.

"Nobody does all that stuff for me," Eschmann complained. "It's probably because you're such a kiss ass."

Peter's eyes went wide, and Colodny yelled, "What the hell is the matter with you?"

Eschmann laughed.

"What are you laughing at?" Peter asked, unamused.

"I just wanted to push his buttons," Eschmann said, gesturing toward Colodny. He looked back toward Peter. "Dude, you might be a pain in my butt, but you're definitely not a kiss ass."

Peter rolled his eyes. "You are such a jerk."

"That's an understatement if I ever heard one," Colodny said, grinning.

"Get over it, gentlemen," Eschmann said, getting up.

"Jarrett, thank you!" Peter said.

"No problem, brother. Go lay down a solid run."

"You too. Hope to share the podium with you."

"You will. I'll be the guy looking down at you."

They both smiled as Eschmann left the tent.

Chapter 56

ABOUT THIRTY MINUTES later, Peter's time had finally come. He planted his poles in front of the start gate and slid the tips of his skis forward, past the steep ledge. He stood at the edge of the starting platform with the front of his skis suspended horizontally out over the forty-five-degree drop. The start official pulled the hinged wand into place just in front of Peter's shins. All the crazy thoughts that had been fluttering through Peter's mind during the previous two weeks instantly vanished. What mattered right now were just the next two minutes.

The referee warned, "Ten seconds!"

Peter tingled with anticipation as he focused on the vertical drop directly in front of him, known as the *Free Fall*! The steepest start of any downhill course in the world.

The digital clock started its countdown, beeping as each second ticked by; five, four, three. Racers could go anytime during the five seconds.

On two, Peter pulled hard on his poles and threw his weight forward. The backs of his skis raised high in the air as he exploded through the gate. After a fierce, speed-gaining shove with his skis and poles, he began his descent down the insanely steep, icy chute in his tightest, aerodynamic tuck.

Within seconds he was skiing at over eighty miles per hour. Adrenaline surged through him like it was being injected by a firehose. He shut out all thoughts except the task at hand. His mind was already two turns ahead. The exhilarating rush was enormous.

As he entered a banked left turn, his speed amplified the gravity pulling him hard toward the snow. He fought the compression with his legs, expecting the typical burn in his thighs, but he felt no discomfort whatsoever. Maybe a week and a half of concentrated weightlifting was exactly what he had needed. He had worked harder while captive than he would have otherwise, mainly because there was nothing else to do.

Just before the edge of the upcoming steep drop, he rose from his tuck, drove forward and down with his arms, and sucked up his knees, lifting his skis from the snow to pre-jump the ridge at the perfect moment. He held his tuck as he sliced through the air only a couple of feet over the icy surface.

After a smooth landing, he immediately shifted his weight to the inner edge of his left ski to pre-turn the next gate. Fighting gravity, he held his edge and stayed tight to the gate, which helped him avoid a ski chattering, time-consuming sideways slide around the steep fall-away turn. The newly found power in his legs probably just shaved a tenth of a second off his time. "Yes," he said to himself.

***

The television commentators weren't even trying to contain their excitement and confusion as they yelled into their mics. It wasn't enough that they had just announced to the world that Peter had inexplicably appeared, ready to race, but also that it looked like he was in excellent physical condition. "If he skis the second half of the course as well as he did the first, he is going to take over the lead," exclaimed an elated American TV announcer.

Although alpine ski racing is not one of the most popular spectator sports, this was the Olympics, the proving ground for the world's greatest athletes. Bragging rights of entire nations were on the line. Word of Peter's racing spread like wildfire as sports commentators and news reporters interrupted shows to break the news of Peter's return to the slopes. Photographs and videos of Peter racing in earlier competitions were being posted and shared on every social media platform on the internet.

One of the videos was of Peter's earlier release from the SUV. It showed Peter being escorted from the vehicle and then standing in the snow, with a mask over his eyes. Then, it scanned the area, including the adjacent parking lot, where the dark SUV was driving away. It then showed Peter pulling the mask from his eyes, starting to run, and almost getting hit by the snowmobile. The final clip showed him mounting the sled behind the driver and racing away.

***

With two-thirds of the course behind him, Peter had only three big turns to go. The first turn was another high-speed fall-away left. The steep drop immediately after the turn was treacherous. The boundary fence had already stopped an earlier racer from sliding into the trees after his fall. By this point on the race course, most of the skiers would be fighting the pain caused by a buildup of lactic acid in their leg muscles. Peter knew many of them would be making calculated decisions to hold back a little on the turn. His legs were still very strong. If he could attack this turn with fervor and maintain just enough control to hit the final two jumps without crashing, he might just medal. He tightened his tuck and held it a little past the safe point, then he opened just enough to set his edge for the turn. As he cut hard around the gate, the ground dropped from below him faster than he'd expected.

Flying, his arms wind-milled wildly. He knew he was in trouble. He was catching way too much air and was going to land at precisely the spot where he should be pre-jumping the upcoming ridge.

"Oh my God," cried out television broadcast ski analyst Lindsey Vonn. Few people knew the perils of ski racing predicaments as well as Vonn, who had recently retired from her ultra-successful ski racing career. "He took that turn way too fast. No way he can prepare for the next jump. This is gonna be really bad!"

Peter's skis landed on the ice without a moment to spare. With no time to regain his stability, he used all his strength to steady himself for the upcoming ridge. Without a pre-jump and way off his intended line, he sailed high and long, arms thrashing to maintain balance. The only thing that would keep him from skiing off the course upon landing, was an immediate hard right. If he couldn't make the turn he was done, and at the speed he was moving, his fall was going to be bad.

"Oh no," shouted Vonn. "This is going to be ugly!"

Peter landed with almost no room to maneuver his turn. He leaned to the right, digging the inside edge of his left ski into the ice with everything he had. Turning just enough to avoid the crash nets, his left arm brushed against them as he flew by. The netting grabbed at the small cone-shaped basket at the end of his pole and tugged his arm just before he cleared the boundary. Miraculously he remained upright, grimacing from pain as he yanked his pole back into position. He was ready for the next steep drop.

"He's like a machine. He's unbelievable!" Vonn exclaimed.

Peter skied the last turn and the final steep drop flawlessly before crossing the finish line. He turned hard, spraying snow onto the boundary wall that separated the finish corral from the spectators. He stopped, closed his eyes, and stilled his mind. All he heard was his own heavy breathing. All he felt was the rapid beating of his heart. He was completely unaware that this would be his last peaceful moment for quite a while. When he finally opened his eyes, he saw the massive crowds were cheering. Raising his eyes to the big screen, he saw his time, 1:58.73. Pole in hand, he raised his fist high and pumped his arm. It felt good to be back on top, even if it might be just for a short time. There were still forty-two skiers left to race. For now, he savored the moment and breathed a sigh of relief. It was over. No more threats. He was a free man now. He began to look for Hunter and his parents.

He searched along the boundary but couldn't find them. As his eyes passed the press area, he saw hundreds of camera lenses pointed at him. He knew he should take off his skis and hold them high, as his endorsement agreement succinctly spelled out. *Too bad! They'll just have to understand this time.*

Scanning the crowd once more to the left, then to the right, he thought, *Where are they?*

He noticed a poster with *Peter* in big, bold letters. *Ah, finally,* he thought. His eyes traveled below the sign expecting to see Hunter, but instead, it was a middle-aged woman. He saw another poster with *Buckar is Back!* and yet another with *Welcome Back Peter*! They seemed to be cropping up everywhere. *How could they have known?* On closer inspection, he saw they were all handwritten. *That explains how new signs are created the moment a racer crosses the finish line.*

Emotions overcame him as he heard his name chanted, not only by American fans but everyone in the crowd, regardless of their home country. Tears streamed down his face. All he wanted at the moment were hugs from his fiancé and his parents. He looked one more time at the crowds and waved, doing his best to smile.

Bill Brotherton, an American racer who had skied earlier, ran to Peter, hugged him, then took him by the arm and led him away.

"Where are you taking me?"

"To your family. I figured you needed a little help finding them. That was one hell of a run," Brotherton said.

Peter's eyes roamed the crowd in the direction he was being taken. His heart almost leaped from his chest as he saw Hunter being helped over the boundary in front of the security tent.

"Thanks, Bill," Peter shouted as he pulled free of Brotherton's grip and ran toward his future bride.

Peter dropped his skis and poles, then removed his helmet as they ran to each other. Their embrace elicited loud cheers from the crowd.

"I was so scared. I thought I'd never see you again," Hunter said in his ear as they held each other tightly.

"I know! The only thing that kept me going while being held captive were thoughts of you."

After a long hug, Hunter said, "Although I never want to let you go, you better go to your parents."

"Where are they?"

"Back where I crossed the boundary."

"I didn't even see them. All I saw was you," he said, still holding her.

"Just go."

Peter ran and vaulted over the small wall, ski boots and all. Tears flowed as his parents rushed towards him, followed by Reid, Shane, and Buck. Cameras clicked incessantly. Viewers throughout the world watched as TV cameras filmed the emotional reunion. Even the television announcers were sniffling.

"I'm so glad you're back," Reid said as he looked at his friend. "You probably don't care at the moment, but after Buck works his magic, you're going to earn millions from all this."

"Hmm. I hadn't thought about that. Silver lining, huh?"

"Exactly! Now, you better head over to that podium. You have a lot of fans here who want to see you standing on top, even with those black eyes."

"Are they that bad?"

"Well, they ain't pretty, and your nose is a little crooked. Does it hurt much?"

"I guess I was so focused on the race, I forgot all about it, but now that we're talking about it, yeah, it hurts."

"You've always been such a baby."

"Shut up." Peter chuckled as he pushed Reid away.

"You better go, brother. Your medal awaits you."

"Not yet it doesn't. Let's just hope I'm still on the podium after the last racer crosses the line."

After another hug from Hunter and his mom, Peter walked to the podium. The crowd's chanting had grown louder. "Buckar, Buckar." Overwhelmed by the whole scene, tears stung his eyes as he waved.

As Peter climbed to the third platform, Croatian Ivan Bakulic patted his shoulder, shrugged in acquiescence, then stepped down from the bronze level.

Lost in thought as he watched the other two skiers maneuver to their respective levels, Peter flinched when the crowd gasped. He turned and looked up at the huge video screen. He couldn't tell who it was, but a racer was tumbling uncontrollably down a steep grade on the course. One ski came off and whipped away to the side. The other detached and rocketed into the air, flipping continuously as it soared. It finally landed, vertically, like a spear, just missing the racer's torso and eliciting another outburst from the spectators.

Peter cringed. Watching another racer crash was always difficult.

Shifting his eyes, he noticed that the mid-course time comparison between Riku Nylund's and his own was still displayed. Nylund, Finland's top skier, had been faster by three-tenths of a second before he fell. While Peter certainly hoped he was okay, he didn't mind that Nylund was out of medal contention.

Peter had competed against Nylund for years. While they weren't exactly friends, Peter liked the guy. Similar to most of the racer's, his concern for Nylund would linger at least until the medics revealed his prognosis.

At the moment, though, worrying about Nylund's medical status took a back seat to Peter's anxiety about remaining on the podium. Nylund was out of contention, but Arnot, Eschmann, and a slew of others had yet to ski. Any racer had the potential to throw down the run of his life at any time, and today, more so than usual, they would all be giving it everything they had.

Skis in hand, Peter stood on the top tier as photographers snapped shot after shot. He glanced at his skis, wondering who Buck would negotiate new endorsement deals with.

As Nylund was helped off the course, the next racer pushed through the starting gate.

Peter watched as Denmark's Markus Lange and, then, Max Schrieber from Liechtenstein each attacked the course. Schrieber's halfway time had only been one-hundredth of a second behind Peter's, but he made two big errors on the second half and finished in fifth position. Lange did not ski well at all.

Peter tried hard to conceal his relief each time a skier crossed the line with a time higher than his own. With all the cameras focused on him, he didn't want to appear petty. *My crooked nose and black eyes are bad enough,* he thought with a chuckle.

He looked in Hunter's direction and caught her eye. Her beautiful smile set his heart ablaze. He smiled, thinking, *wow, absence really does make the heart grow fonder.*

Cowbells and cheers snapped Peter from his thoughts. His eyes shot toward the video screen. He had been so distracted he hadn't realized that Frank Arnot was on the course and he was on fire. His mid-way time was almost a second faster than Peter's.

Peter chewed his lower lip as he watched Arnot sail off a ridge in a tight tuck, flying like a bullet.

Carving one of the final turns, edges chattering on the ice, it looked like the gold was his, as long as he maintained his composure. But Arnot's extraordinary speed didn't allow him the time he needed to prepare for the final jump. Instead, he flew off the crest too fast and at a bad angle. Instead of leaning forward, his weight was back. The tips of his skis flew up in front of him, and his arms spun, prompting another gasp from the crowd.

At the speed Arnot was flying, his crash was going to be awful. Squinting at the screen, Peter held his breath.

With only a fraction of a second to spare, Arnot somehow forced his left ski into place before landing. Then, with an astonishing display of strength, he maintained control as the tail of his right ski hit the snow, causing the rest of the ski to slap down hard under him. It wasn't pretty, but Arnot evaded disaster. He had only one turn left before the steep finish.

As he crossed the line ahead of Peter's time by six-hundredths of a second, cowbells rang, and his fellow Austrians roared.

Sighing, Peter stepped down to the silver platform. The thrill of potentially winning the gold faded, yet he knew that today, after what he'd been through, any medal would be a miracle.

As Arnot climbed on the podium, he squeezed onto the silver platform next to Peter, looked him in the eye, and said, "I'm glad you're here, my brother!"

"Thanks, Frank. That means a lot to me."

"Oh, don't get sentimental on me. Winning the gold just wouldn't feel quite as good without you competing."

"Really?" Peter said.

"Yes. Why?"

"Because I was kidnapped, and I thought you would care about my safety. I thought we were friends."

With his skis in one hand, he hugged Peter with the other. "Of course we're friends. Thank God you're back. You scared the crap out of all of us."

"Yeah, I was a little scared too."

"Ha! You scared? Never!" Arnot turned and stepped up onto the gold platform.

"Hey," Peter said, giving him a swat in the arm with his free hand.

Frank looked down at him. "What?"

"Amazing run, Bro!"

"Thanks. You too."

The cameras clicked wildly as the men bumped fists.

"Let's just hope the rest of these clowns don't ski quite as well," Arnot said quietly. "With Dinaso out, we have a good chance, unless … well, you know."

Peter knew exactly what he meant. Every man yet to race had the skill to win the gold. All they needed was about a minute and forty seconds of absolute focus, stamina, nerves of steel, and maybe, just a little luck.

French racer, Pierre Ausset, was skiing flawlessly as Peter and Arnot looked at the screen. Ausset's quarter-time was highlighted in green. His mid-course lead was even wider. The rest of his run made skiing the downhill look easy. His tuck was tight, his edges held steadfastly, and he pre-jumped every ridge at precisely the right moment.

Peter held his breath as Ausset tripped the finish beam. Peering anxiously at the timing board, his lips puffed, then fluttered with a sigh of relief. Ausset's time was great but not quite good enough to bump Peter from the silver platform.

He glanced up at Arnot, who returned a silly grin with one eyebrow raised.

Ausset nodded and fist-bumped Arnot as he climbed to the bronze platform. He then turned to Peter and embraced him in an awkward ski entangled hug. "Welcome back, my friend. Glad you're safe."

"Thanks, Pierre. Nice run."

"Merci. You too."

"Uh oh," Arnot said. "Turn around, guys. Loopy's hot!"

They looked up at the screen. Italy's Alex Lupinacci was soaring down the course. His mid-course time was better than Arnot's. They watched him carve a tight turn and ski off a ridge like a missile. Then, due to his high speed at the next gate, his edges chattered on the rock-hard ice, and he went too wide to set up properly for the following turn, a fall-away left. Icy ruts on the course grabbed ferociously at his skis and finally won the battle. Just as he was shifting his weight to his right ski, a deep rut threw his left ski out to the side. The timing could not have been worse. He entered the turn on one ski as the course quickly dropped from under him. His body flew straight as the course turned hard left.

Peter briefly shut his eyes. Then, unable to resist, he opened them just enough to see Lupinacci land on his back and bounce. His body flipped twice, and his skis flew off on different trajectories. Screams from the crowd slowly quieted as Lupinacci's body slid the last twenty yards until being abruptly stopped by the safety net. Peter's chin fell to his chest, and the crowd went silent. All eyes were fixated on the video screen in total dismay as Lupinacci lay still. After a few agonizing seconds, Lupinacci's helmet raised from the snow.

Not even realizing he'd been holding his breath, Peter expelled a huge sigh of relief. The crowd went wild as Lupinacci slowly stood and took a couple of unsteady steps while medics rushed to his side.

Wiping a tear, then patting his hand over his heart, Peter looked up at Arnot, who was crossing himself with his head tilted up at the sky.

Peter and most of his fellow racers shared a mutual concern for one another. As competitive as they were, they were also extremely compassionate with each other. When a fellow racer got hurt, they all felt the pain.

There were now nineteen skiers left to race. Yet, now with Lupinacci out of contention, there were only a few that Peter really worried about.

Andreas Strom, a huge, powerful man from Norway, blasted through the starting gate and skied an amazing run from top to bottom.

Photographers caught the faces of Arnot, Peter, and Ausset as Strom crossed the finish line. It was a comical picture with each man's eyes revealing his apprehension differently. Arnot was wide-eyed, Peter squinted, and Ausset's were closed tight.

Ausset's head dropped after he looked at Strom's time. He gave Arnot and Peter a long face and stepped off the podium.

A minute later, Strom shook Arnot's hand, then gave Peter a quick hug, hitting Peter's helmet with his skis.

"Sorry!"

"It's okay. Nice run."

"Thanks, but you're the man today," Strom said, patting Peter's shoulder. "Only you could get kidnapped and win an Olympic medal on the day you're released. You deserve the gold for just getting through it."

"Thanks, Andreas. Let's just hope we're still standing here at the end of the race."

"Yes." Strom nodded and smiled.

Loud cheers as a Croatian racer crossed the line made Peter and Strom turn to view the timing board. Peter's heart fluttered until he saw the finishing time in red. Another sigh escaped his pursed lips. Strom gave him a light elbow nudge.

Their eyes shifted to the new racer on the course. It was Jarrett Eschmann, and he was off to a great start. Every racer wanted the downhill gold, but Eschmann seemed to be throwing safety aside. He was attacking the race course with zeal, bordering on recklessness.

With skis bouncing wildly through the icy ruts at each gate, and arms whirling to compensate for too much air off every jump, he was destined for a spectacular crash. Yet, he managed to defy the laws of gravity repeatedly with awkward twists of his body. If not for his ultra-powerful legs, he would have crashed at least three times already. Each save evoked another gasp from the spectators.

Again, all eyes were riveted on the screen. Peter's heart palpitated with every near fall.

"That crazy bastard just may do it!" Arnot said.

"Yeah, if he doesn't kill himself," added Peter.

"Whether he medals or not," Strom said. "Oh hell, whether he finishes or not, this run is going to become legendary."

"Yes," Arnot said. "It will be used by every coach in the world to show how *not* to ski the downhill. If he finishes, it'll be due to sheer luck."

"And superhuman strength!" Peter said.

They watched in amazement as Eschmann skied off the peak of the last roller and flew high and long, somehow remaining in a loose tuck the entire way. Instead of opening from his tuck to reduce the length of his flight, he held his position and landed down where the incline decreased rapidly. The impact of his landing was too much for his tired thighs. The compression slammed his butt down to his skis, yet somehow his muscular core held the rest of his torso from falling back. Then, with a surge of brute strength, he powered himself almost upright and crossed through the finish beam.

Again Peter held his breath as he peered at the timing board, and again, relief swept through him. Eschmann's insane run, ugly as it was, earned him the bronze platform.

"*Paska*," Strom mumbled as he stepped from the third level of the podium and skulked away.

Moments later, Eschmann stepped onto the bronze platform. He looked Peter in the eye with a crazed expression. Still winded, he gasped, "You were right! It's all about focus. Well, I meditated too. But focus is what it took. I completely cleared my head of everything except the next turn or jump. I mean, of course, I've always known to focus, but this was different. The way you said it earlier, well, something just clicked in my head. You know, like an epiphany. Oh hell, I don't know what it was, but it worked. I've never skied like that in my life."

"I know," Peter said. "And if you keep it up, you're gonna kill yourself. You were completely reckless up there. Winning is great, but you can't risk your life for a medal."

"Hah! You can't be serious. I mean you of all people. The guy that lets it all hang loose in every race. Come on."

"Let's just leave it alone for now. Enjoy the moment. You skied like a lunatic, and it paid off. Nice run!"

"Thanks. It *was* kind of crazy, huh? I thought I was going to buy it a few times up there, but what a rush."

Cowbells signaled another racer finishing.

Peter and Eschmann turned to see that Stefan Renner, another Austrian, had crossed the finish line four-tenths of a second behind Eschmann's time.

As Peter watched racer after racer cross the line, his heart rate increased and slowed with each. His buddy, Trucker Dukes, skied a phenomenal run. All three racers on the podium held their breath as Dukes tripped the beam only three-hundredths of a second behind Eschmann.

With the adrenaline now out of Peter's system, the extreme ebb and flow of his anxiety sapped his energy. He had been so distracted from the moment his kidnappers released him that he never even realized how cold it was or how exhausted he felt. He looked around. Everyone except the racers was bundled from head to toe.

The microfibers of his racing suit offered little protection from the elements.

He looked up at the board. There were twelve racers still to ski. He shivered and thought, *I'm going to freeze to death before this race is over.* He looked in Hunter's direction and caught her eye. He crossed his arms, briskly rubbed his biceps, raised his shoulders, and exaggerated his shivering.

She nodded, turned, and walked into the crowd. A minute later, just as Peter began to wonder if she had understood, she returned to the boundary and raised a finger. Seconds later, a security official climbed over the boundary and approached the podium while removing his jacket. As he handed it over, Peter said, "I appreciate it, but you don't have to do that."

"It's my pleasure. You've been through enough. You shouldn't have to freeze." Then he leaned in close and whispered, "Besides, I may be Swiss, but I'm a big fan of yours." He raised a finger to his lips. "Just don't tell anyone I said that." He shook Peter's hand, smiled, and walked back to the security area.

Peter put on the jacket and looked over at Hunter. He blew her a kiss, then mouthed, *I love you.*

She formed a heart with her hands and smiled.

"You're a lucky man," Eschmann said.

"Yeah, I know. She's amazing."

"I was talking about the jacket."

"Really?"

Eschmann laughed. "No, you idiot. Of course I meant Hunter."

Peter shook his head.

Eschmann grinned. "Just don't get her mad. She hits hard."

Peter looked at him. "What are you talking about?"

"It's a long story. I'll tell you all about it later."

"Are you kidding me?" Peter looked up at the timing board. "Dude, there are four racers left. We have plenty of time. Let's hear it."

"Okay, I am going to make a long story very short. They were questioning me as a possible suspect while you were missing."

"What?"

"Yeah, well, word got out that we fight a little."

"Hmm."

"Anyway, I got worked up and said some stupid stuff. I didn't realize Hunter was standing behind me. Next thing I knew, I got smacked in the face from behind."

"Wow. Really? What did you say to piss her off?"

"I don't remember. But it was about you, and it was pretty mean. There was no question that I totally deserved it."

Peter laughed. It took a moment, but then Eschmann joined him.

"You know what?" Eschmann said. "I'm glad we're both on this podium laughing about it all. You may think I'm full of it, but I was really worried about you."

Peter looked him in the eye for a second, then grinned and nodded. "I believe you."

"Good, because it's true."

"It's interesting how a crisis can change things, isn't it?"

"Yeah." Eschmann leaned toward Peter and wrapped his long arms around him in a bear hug. They were similar in height, so the difference in podium levels put Eschmann's head against Peter's chest.

He rolled his eyes and patted Eschmann's shoulder. "Let's not get carried away."

"Dude, I've been watching everyone else give you hugs. Can't I give you one, too?"

"Cut the crap! You're doing this because you know Hunter is watching, and this is probably making her squirm."

"Wow, am I really that transparent?" Eschmann said as he let go.

Peter looked down at him with a crooked smirk.

The final racer was a third of the way down the mountain when Peter looked up at the screen. He saw that it was his old college roommate, Claude Bouchard. He was skiing fast and smooth, but his current time was no threat to the three men on the podium.

A wave of emotions engulfed Peter as he watched. Suddenly everything around him felt surreal. He thought back. *Just a few weeks ago, my only concern was winning this race. Gold in the Olympic downhill has been my dream forever, and here I am, on the podium. Okay, maybe not winning the gold, but considering what I've been through, silver is pretty damn good. So why do I feel so empty? Could it be that after fearing for my life, winning isn't so important anymore?*

Deep in contemplation, his eyes swept over the massive crowds, then up to the peak of the enormous mountain. Craning his neck, his eyes shifted to the cloud-dotted sky. The longer he stared, the smaller he felt. He took a deep breath and slowly let it purge.

Another poke from Arnot's elbow jolted Peter. Arnot draped his arm over Peter's shoulder as cameras clicked away in front of them.

Peter looked from Arnot to Eschmann and smiled. Overcome with emotion, his eyes welled up. Then he began to laugh as he raised his fist victoriously. Suddenly, he felt arms wrap around him from behind and lift him. *What the hell?*

Arnot held Peter in the air for a few seconds, then lowered him onto the gold platform.

"What are you doing?" Peter asked.

"My time may have been a little faster than yours, but you are the true winner today. I want you to share this platform with me."

Peter stepped down to the silver level and turned to face Arnot. "You're a good man, my friend. The gold is all yours today. I already have plenty to be thankful for, anyway."

"You sure do! A silver medal, a hot babe, and I'll bet your agent is negotiating some huge endorsement deals as we speak."

Peter grinned. "Yeah. But, you know what? Right now, it feels pretty damn good just to be alive."

"I'll bet it does."

***

After a brief ceremony, Peter made his way back to Hunter and his parents. All he wanted was to head back to their hotel, take a hot shower and enjoy a good meal. Photographers swarmed him. Television, newspaper, and magazine journalists were pushing their way through the crowds hoping to get a few words.

As he stood holding hands with Hunter, Buck approached and gave him a big hug. "Thank God you're okay." Buck wiped a tear from his cheek and added, "That was an amazing run. Congratulations!"

"Thanks. Reid said this should all pay off nicely?"

"Very. I've got lots to tell you, but it can wait. I'll give you a small taste, though. So far, Sports Illustrated, Time, People, and Ski Magazine all want interviews as soon as possible."

"Time? Why would a business magazine want to bother with me?"

"Are you kidding? You're big news right now, and better than that, you're *good* news. With so many bad things happening these days, when something good happens, everyone wants to tell the story."

"I can't believe they all want to write about me."

"Well, they do. In fact, most of them want you on their covers. That's not all. The talk shows want you too."

"What? I don't want to do talk shows. No way!"

"I didn't want to do them in the beginning either," Reid said. "But the more you do, the bigger the endorsement checks become. They're worth it, and truthfully, once you get used to them, they're kind of fun."

"Maybe for you. I don't think I'm going to like it at all."

"It's your life, Peter," Buck said. "You can decide when you've had enough. Just give it a try. Okay?"

"You know we're in the middle of the racing season. I'm not going to miss a race because of some interview."

"Of course not."

He shrugged again. "Okay, I guess I'll give it a shot."

"Good," Buck said. "Also, I know you've been told already, but Jay does not want you talking to any reporters until he says it's okay. He is trying to figure out who was behind all this nonsense."

Peter nodded solemnly.

"Once he finds them, though, you may want to send them a thank you note."

"What?" Peter looked at him as if Buck had gone crazy.

"You know I'm kidding. But this whole situation is going to allow me to make sure that you and Hunter have no financial worries for the rest of your lives."

Peter grinned. "Like turning chocolate into fondue, right?"

"What is that supposed to mean?" Reid asked.

"You know, like turning lemons into lemonade. I just tried to give it a Swiss spin. Didn't work, huh?"

"Nope. But, it was kind of cute," Hunter said as she leaned in for a quick kiss.

Peter smiled and said, "Can we go? I'd really like a hot shower and a good meal."

"Not quite yet," Reid said, gesturing for Peter to look back.

He turned and saw a throng of his teammates, as well as racers from other countries approaching.

Peter glanced at Hunter, and she waved him away. "Go. You deserve this."

Cameras clicked incessantly again as Peter was hoisted above the heads of his fellow racers and passed along like a rock star in a concert mosh pit. Chants of "Buckar's back," grew louder and spread throughout the crowd of onlookers.

Peter knew he would have to get over the awkward feeling of being the center of attention. The money might be about to pour in, but it was going to come at a cost. *I guess my days of flying under the radar are over,* he thought.

A couple of minutes later, Peter was lowered to the street and the loud cheering diminished. He smiled as he received hugs and pats on the back from his colleagues.

As his friends dispersed, so did Peter's adrenaline. All of a sudden, he felt emotionally and physically spent.

He walked slowly along the sidewalk with his old friend, Claude Bouchard, reminiscing about their college days. Bouchard's arm was around Peter's shoulders as they chatted and laughed.

"Come say hi to my parents. They'd love to see you, and I'd like to introduce you to Hunter."

"*Tres bien.* I'd like that," Bouchard responded as they walked.

A short distance behind them, a Russian accented, male voice yelled, "Stop!"

Peter and Bouchard paid no heed.

"I said stop, Buckar," the man yelled again.

"He's got a gun!" a woman shouted.

Peter gasped. He and Bouchard stopped abruptly, glanced at each other, and slowly turned. Screams emanated from the people nearby. Some ran while others dove for cover.

A thin, balding, middle-aged man stood about ten feet away with a liquor bottle in one hand and a handgun in the other.

"You bastard," he stammered, pointing the gun at Peter with an unsteady hand. "I lost everything because of you." He raised the bottle to his lips and gulped the clear liquid. He then began to ramble in Russian as tears streamed down his red cheeks.

Peter's heart palpitated. He could barely breathe.

"Please, put the gun down." Bouchard's voice was unsteady as he stepped in front of Peter.

"Get out of the way, or I'll shoot you, too." The man began to sob while he mumbled incoherently.

Four Olympic Security officials emerged from amongst the onlookers with their guns drawn.

"Put the gun down now," an officer said calmly.

Suddenly, the bottle slipped from the distraught man's hand and shattered on the sidewalk. He waved the gun at Bouchard, and shrieked, "Get out the way. I want Buckar. I have nothing left! You hear that, Buckar. Nothing! You wiped me out!"

"Put the gun down now, or we'll shoot!" another officer said loudly.

"Go ahead, shoot me. Do it! I'm done anyway." He then raised the gun with his trembling hand and pointed it at his own head. He closed his eyes as his body shuddered as he sobbed. He fired his gun and collapsed in a bloody mess.

The officers ran to the body.

During the standoff, Hunter, Reid, and Peter's parents had all hurried over. They were being held back by other officers.

Peter fell to his knees. Bouchard put a comforting hand on his friend's shoulder, and Peter looked up into his eyes with a look of dismayed appreciation. "Thank you," he said quietly.

"Anything for you, brother," Bouchard said.

Hunter pulled away from the officer's grip, ran to Peter, kneeled, and hugged him tightly. Together they cried.

The loud wail of a siren drowned out all the other noises as an ambulance approached.

Looking over Hunter's shoulder at the man on the ground, Peter said, "I'll be right back." He walked over and peered past the officer's shoulders at the body. Peter flinched when the man moved. "He's alive?"

The man's face and neck were covered in blood. His blood-drenched hand was cupped over his ear, and a handcuff dangled from his wrist.

Pale as a ghost, completely fixated on the bloody mess, Peter stood in place, wobbling a little.

An officer rushed over and placed his steadying hand on Peter's elbow. "Are you all right, *Herr* Buckar?"

"I think so." Peter looked at the officer and took a few deep breaths. "Thank you."

"Of course. Captain Fischer wants us by your side until we know more about this man."

"I'll be right over there." Peter pointed toward Hunter. "With my fiancé."

"Just wait, I'll take you to her in a moment."

Peter nodded, then gestured to the man on the ground. "How is he, and how did he have a gun here?"

A paramedic pulled the man's hand from the side of his head, and another began wrapping him with bandages. Peter gagged at the sight of the man's missing ear, then turned away and fought the urge to vomit.

The officer saw Peter turn to look again at the bloodied man and said, "He has a Russian Diplomatic ID card. Maybe that's how he got the gun in. But you are right, no civilian should have a gun in the Olympic Village."

Peter shrugged.

"The *dummkopf* shot his own ear off. It looks bad, but he'll be all right. *Herr* Buckar. You don't need to see any more of this."

Chapter 57

WHILE ADRENALINE HAD kept Peter energized throughout the day, the gun incident weighed heavily on him. By the time he got back to the hotel, he was overcome with exhaustion and slept for fourteen hours straight. Then, after a mind-clearing run with Reid, he shaved, showered, and along with Hunter, joined his parents, Buck, and Jay in Reid's suite for dinner. The throngs of reporters that were gathered at the hotel entrance and throughout the lobby, had made the decision of where to eat dinner an easy one.

***

As he twirled an enormous amount of spaghetti onto his fork, Peter's mother asked, "Why don't you just call room service and order your own bowl and let Hunter eat hers?"

With a mouthful, Peter said, "She doesn't mind." Then he turned toward Hunter. "Do you?"

"Not at all," she said with a chuckle. "Enjoy it. Just don't speak with your mouth full."

Peter grinned as his mother picked up a plate from one of the room service carts and placed a porterhouse, large enough for two hungry adults, in front of him.

"Now, will you leave her food alone?" Reid asked.

Peter looked at his steak, smiled, and said, "Maybe."

Jay put down his drink. "I hope you don't mind if I speak while you all eat. I need to leave soon."

"No problem, Jay," Peter said. "What's up?"

He looked at Peter and Hunter. "I'm replacing Fischer's security team with one of my crews. I want to have round-the-clock protection on both of you, at least until we know more."

Hunter lowered her fork. Peter continued to eat.

"So, you think we should still be worried?" Dan asked, looking at his son and trying to hide his worry.

"We still don't know who is responsible for his kidnapping, and considering Peter's newly earned fame, it can't hurt to be extra careful."

"For how long?" Hunter asked unhappily.

Jay shrugged, "Can't answer that right now."

Dismayed, Hunter replied, "Gee, that's comforting. It sounds like I need to get used to this, huh?"

"Hunter, Peter just became one of the most famous athletes in the world. He will be recognized everywhere you go. That fame, along with the financial windfall, can create potential problems."

Peter's fork clinked against his plate as he put it down, giving Jay his full attention. "What kind of problems?"

"Very wealthy people, especially the most famous, often become targets. Financial scammers are always looking for their next mark. The same goes for those looking to break the law for a big score, such as kidnapping, extortion, or blackmail. Since we really don't know who was behind your kidnapping or why they did it, nor much about the guy who pulled the gun on you, we want to be extra cautious, at least for the next few months. Ask Reid. He knows what I'm talking about."

Peter let out a sigh.

"Don't let it get to you," Reid said. "When we get back to the States, it will be easier. It's not going to be so bad."

"Are you kidding me?" Peter said. "It's already a pain in the ass. I mean staying here is nice and all, but I really should be staying with the team."

"I'm sorry," Jay said. "I just can't keep you safe enough overnight in the Olympic dorms. There's way too much activity there, and we don't know who we can trust. Fischer and I both agreed it would be safer for you and less disruptive for all the other athletes if you slept here."

"Yeah," Peter said with a sigh. "I know it's for my own good, and I guess the team's too, but now you're telling me that we'll need twenty-four-hour protection when we get home. I hate this."

"You'll get used to it," Shane said nonchalantly.

"Yeah, it feels a little intrusive in the beginning," Reid said. "But after a while, you'll hardly know they're around." Reid looked at Jay. "Maybe you could have Joel and Stu take over their detail. Shane and I certainly don't need them very often anymore."

Hunter and Peter knew Joel and Stu very well. They had been running Reid's security detail for years and were like part of the family.

"Well, that would at least be tolerable," Peter said. "They're both decent skiers, which would help."

"I'm sure they'll be happy to work with you two," Jay said. "They were supposed to return to a short-term assignment they were on. I'll just have to clear it with their client. He won't be happy to see them go. But I'll make it work."

"Who is it?" Peter asked.

"Jagger," Jay said.

"As in Mick?" Carole asked incredulously.

Jay nodded.

"Wow. That's cool," Hunter said. "They'll probably be bummed, leaving him to protect us."

"Nah," Jay said. "They're both adrenaline junkies. They'll get a kick out of working with Peter and you."

"Not me," Hunter said. "Unless piano playing raises their heart rate."

Everyone laughed.

Chapter 58

PETER WAS SITTING on a thick blue mat in the hotel gym with his long legs stretched in a wide 'V'. He could feel his hamstrings and lower back stretch as he leaned forward. A drop of sweat transferred from the tip of his nose to his knee as they made contact. His phone chirped, and he smiled at Hunter's text. *Now that I have you back, I don't like waking up without you next to me.* What *r u up to—gym, meditating, or coffee?*

He glanced at the time, 5:10 a.m. He typed, *almost done stretching. I'll bring you coffee in 15 mins.* ♥

Funny, he thought as he looked at all the different colored hearts he could choose from on his phone, *I've always hated emojis, and I don't even know why. I need to lighten up.*

His thoughts moved on. *Finish stretching, get coffee, shower, and leave for team meeting by 6:45.*

Of course, Peter wanted to win every race he competed in, but his desire today was stronger than usual. A medal in today's race, after the three he'd won already, would make history. He wanted to be the first male alpine skier to win four medals in one Olympics.

I can do this, he thought as he stood. He tossed his towel in the hamper, pushed the metal bar on the heavy glass door, and gave a quick nod to the two officers who had been assigned to him. He was still overwhelmed at the thought of having bodyguards, but at least they were nice. Four guards were assigned to him every day. The two flanking him now were usually very chatty, but today they were quiet. Maybe it was due to Peter's demeanor. Friends and relatives often had to remind him to smile on race days. He tended to wear a very serious face and barely communicate with anyone until his race was over.

He stopped in the lobby, poured two cups of coffee, then continued to the elevator. As Peter pushed the up button and took a step back, another man joined him and his guards.

The man was Peter's height. Fresh snow had begun to melt from the shoulders of his long, beige overcoat and the brim of his brown fedora. The hat rested low on his head, covering his forehead. Sunglasses and a beard hid the rest of his face. As Peter's eyes moved from the hat down, he noticed a bulge in the man's overcoat pocket.

Peter had been somewhat uneasy since his confrontation with the guy who had threatened to shoot him. Then, as his medal count had grown during the past week and a half, he had become a trending topic throughout social media. While most posts were kind and praising, there was a fair amount of ridicule and even a few threats. Posts blaming him for gambling losses were piling up on Facebook and Twitter. Peter had never been a big fan of social media, and now he avoided it altogether.

The elevator opened, and after a hotel guest emerged, one of Peter's bodyguards stepped in, turned around, and nodded. Peter followed, then the second guard entered and turned to face the doors.

As the man in the overcoat stepped forward, the officer blocked his path and said, “Please wait for the next elevator.”

“There’s plenty of room. I’m a guest here,” the man said with a British accent as he put his hand in the pocket of his overcoat.

The officer quickly drew his gun and said, “Take your hand out of your pocket, slowly.”

The man quickly stepped back. “Are you off your trolley? I’ve done nothin’ wrong.” He slowly removed his hand with his keycard between his forefinger and thumb. “I just wanted to show you my room key.”

The officer took a step forward, still pointing his gun. “Put your hands in the air.”

The officer reached into the guy’s pocket and slowly pulled out a wrinkled, brown paper bag. “Jonas, I need a hand.”

The other officer took the bag and looked inside.

“It’s just a bloody bagel,” the Englishman said, lowering his hands.

“Keep your hands up,” the officer holding the gun said. “Frisk him, Jonas.”

After patting him down, the second officer said, “He’s clean.”

“Bloody right, I am.” He lowered his hands, this time without objection from either officer.

“Sorry for the disruption, sir,” said the first officer, holstering his gun.

The Englishman looked at Peter for a moment, and his jaw dropped. “Blimey! You’re Peter Buckar! Now I understand!”

“Sorry,” Peter said, a little sheepishly.

“No way, mate. You’ve got nothin’ to be sorry about. Not with all the rubbish you’ve been through.”

“Thanks for understanding.”

"Don't be silly, mate. My life is dull as dishwater. This is the most exciting thing that's happened to me since I served in the Falklands. Can't wait to tell the grandkids."

"Okay then, have a good day, sir." The officers stepped back into the elevator.

"Wait," the Englishman yelped. "Can I get an autograph and maybe a photo?"

The officers looked at Peter, who nodded.

Chapter 59

PETER ATTACKED THE gates during his final slalom run of the Games with intensity and precision. He had never skied as well as he had in the past three races. Could he continue this amazing medal streak? Would he be written into the history books?

He stood on the bronze podium, having been bumped down from the silver by Italy's Guglielmo Vitro. Billy, as his American friends called him, kept laughing, and talking, and nudging Peter. It was Vitro's first time on an Olympic podium, and although he was a little annoying, he made Peter laugh. With one skier on the course and two still to race, Peter's eyes were glued to the screen. Buck's earlier words, *win a medal in this race, and your kids kid's kids will be set for life,* played over and over in Peter's head. While financial gains were important to him, Peter's yearning for this medal ran much deeper. Like many overachievers, Peter set an even loftier objective with each goal he tackled. Four medals in this Olympics would be his ultimate achievement.

But suddenly, the thought of making history filled him with anxiety. He stared at the screen as a skier crossed the line three-tenths of a second behind Peter's time. What if it actually happened? What could he possibly strive for next? He had never thought of that before.

He closed his eyes and held his breath, thinking, *Oh my God, there's only one racer left.* Another annoying nudge from Vitro made Peter flinch and start breathing again.

He watched as Anton Wyss blasted out of the start gate, skied smoothly through the first few turns, then zipped through the first tight flush, smacking the four lined up gates aside as he rapidly snaked around each. Wyss had obviously pushed the threats he had received far from his mind. As expected, the cheering from the predominantly Swiss crowd was completely out of control. A glance from the center of the screen to its lower corner made Peter queasy. Wyss's halfway time was half a second faster than his. He entered the second flush and skied it perfectly, then took the next few turns extremely fast. Peter sighed, dropping his chin to his chest and his eyes to the ground. There would be no fourth medal. Wyss was going to beat him.

Suddenly the crowd began to yell. Peter raised his head and saw Wyss skidding to a stop off to the side of the race course.

"What happened?" Peter asked, suddenly very excited and anxious. Could his dream actually be coming true?

"He missed a gate," Vitro said.

"Oh my God," Peter said as photographers immediately rushed over and began snapping pictures of the three men on the podium.

Peter turned and congratulated Vitro and Tom Moore, the American skier, on the gold platform. Despite Moore's attempts to step down to congratulate his friend, Peter, the exuberant Vitro kept unintentionally blocking the path.

"*Grazie, e tu,*" Vitro said. "*Quatro medaglie. Fantastico.*"

"Thank you, Billy," Peter said quietly as a new reality began to sink in. He looked out at a sea of people screaming his name, and a smile bloomed across his face.

Chapter 60

THREE WEEKS LATER. Back in the USA

The early part of the interview had gone well. The television lights were bright, but Peter was getting used to them. Jimmy was easy to speak with and had Peter laughing, even as they discussed the kidnapping.

"So the kidnappers were being nice to you, but you decided to push over the TV in your room and cause a fire that almost killed you?"

"Uh, kind of. It's not like I thought a whole lot about it. It was more of an impulse thing."

"Some impulse." Jimmy laughed. "So, Peter, you race down mountains at speeds over eighty miles per hour, you light toxic electrical fires in small rooms that you happen to be locked up in, and I heard you were pulled over last week for driving your Porsche at a rather excessive speed. How fast was it?"

Peter looked downward and mumbled, "One thirty."

"Wow. Remind me never to get in a car with you."

Peter shrugged. "You're not the first person to say that."

The audience roared along with Jimmy. "I know people say that you're an adrenaline junkie, but it sounds more like a death wish to me."

Peter uncrossed his legs and adjusted from a relaxed position to an upright, rigid posture. His face tightened, and with some irritation, he said, "You're completely wrong. I'm very happy. I love life. I just like to go fast." He looked at his watch.

"I hope I didn't upset you. That wasn't my intention," Jimmy said.

"No, I'm just uptight. My life has changed so quickly." Peter sighed. "I have World Cup races coming up that I need to train for. I now have bodyguards with me twenty-four seven, and my agent has me way overscheduled. It's just a lot to handle, and quite frankly, it's getting on my nerves."

"Phew, I thought it was me."

"Well, maybe a little," Peter said with a grin.

The audience laughed. Jimmy smiled.

"You're an impressive guy, Peter. Not many people could handle the pressure of what you've been through. You get kidnapped, you have a near-death experience, and then, immediately after you're released, you set a new Olympic alpine skiing record." Jimmy turned toward the camera and the audience. "Folks, let's hear it for this phenomenon sitting next to me. Peter Buckar, the first male alpine ski racer ever to win four medals in a single Olympics."

As the theater filled with cheers, Jimmy held up an album, looked directly at the camera, and said, "Stay right where you are. When we come back, Modern Diet is here with us. They will be playing their hit, Karenina. I love these guys! They're so good."

Once the cameras were off, Jimmy leaned over his desk and put his hand on Peter's shoulder. "I really hope I didn't upset you. You were a great guest. I'd love to ski with you one of these days."

"I'm okay. It's not you. As I said, I'm just a little uptight lately. Let me know when you're ready to go skiing. I'll come pick you up in my Porsche."

They grinned at each other for a moment, then both laughed.

Chapter 61

WHEN PETER AND Hunter left the recording studio in midtown New York City, they got into his Porsche and set off for his parent's house. Peter knew his driving pissed off his guards, but so be it. He drove above the speed limit but not so fast that they couldn't keep up in their SUV. He liked watching them in his rear-view mirror when he took the winding turns on the Saw Mill River Parkway at more aggressive speeds than their vehicle would safely allow. Each time, with one hand on the steering wheel, Joel Rebah would hoist his middle finger up to the windshield in Peter's direction. Immediately following that would be a witty text from Stu Mann. Hunter laughed as she read his latest text out loud, "How exciting, we're following a graduate of the Vin Diesel driving school. Take it down a notch, wise guy. A little less fast, a little less furious." She looked at Peter. "Why don't you slow down and give them a break?"

Peter smiled and accelerated a little.

Hunter rolled her eyes.

Peter finally started unwinding after half an hour on the road. Forty minutes later, he pulled into his parent's quiet, suburban New York neighborhood. He parked in their driveway and smiled as he looked up at the old, white colonial house in which he had grown up. While he hadn't lived there for years, it would always feel like home to him.

The last rays of the sun filtered through the dark wooden window blinds in Dan and Carole Buckar's living room.

Jay had called Buck yesterday asking for a meeting with the whole family, as well as Reid and Shane.

Already overscheduled with interviews and TV shows, the meeting request had annoyed Peter. He needed to train for his upcoming races at Beaver Creek. He should have been there already.

"So, I heard Jimmy pissed you off today," Buck said.

Peter rolled his eyes. "It was nothing."

"Yeah, well, when you get edgy and look at your watch while being interviewed on one of the biggest talk shows on TV, believe me, it's something."

"Looked at my watch?"

"That's what they told me."

"Who?"

"The producers."

"The producers called to tell you that I looked at my watch? That's ridiculous."

"Peter, this is the big time. The show is going to be seen by millions of people. The producers of all the shows you're scheduled for are watching everything you do. You may have only been checking the time, but a glance at your watch can have other meanings, like, maybe you're bored or fed up with the interview, or you've just got better things to do. Things like that worry producers. They care about what their viewers, and even more so, their advertisers, may be thinking."

"Wow," Peter said.

"Forget about it for now. We'll chalk it up to inexperience. Just don't do it again. It was my fault, anyway."

"How was it your fault?"

"Because I didn't prepare you. You're one of the most honest people I know, and you don't take crap from anyone. When some-one annoys you, you usually let them know it."

Hunter and Reid grinned. Peter's parents and Shane nodded.

"Really? You're all going to gang up on me? Cut the crap!" Peter said sharply.

"There you go," Buck said with a smile. "Exactly my point."

"What?" Peter chewed his lower lip, reflecting on what he said. "Oh," he added quietly.

"As I said, now is not the time to discuss it. We'll talk before you go on Ellen's show tomorrow."

"Tomorrow?" Peter whimpered. "No way. I need to train, Buck. Why didn't you tell me before?"

"Because they just called me a little while ago. Just do Ellen's show, then I won't schedule anything until you're back from the races in Norway."

Reid laughed.

Buck shot him an angry look.

"What are you laughing at?" Peter asked.

"Forget it," Reid said, grinning and shaking his head.

"He's full of it, huh?" Peter asked. "He's going to book me for interviews regardless of my need to train."

Reid smiled and shrugged.

"All right, both of you, please stop," Buck said. "Peter, I promise I'll respect your training requirements. Obviously, I want you to win."

Reid chuckled again.

"Damn it, Reid. Cut it out," Buck said.

"You've heard all this before, haven't you?" Peter asked, looking at Reid.

Another slight nod from Reid.

"Enough already," Buck said. "As you all know, Jay came here to explain what they've discovered so far about the kidnapping. The floor is yours, Jay."

Jay walked to the stone fireplace and turned to face Peter and his family. "Okay, so this is what we've learned. The whole scheme was the brainchild of a seventeen-year-old Ukrainian boy. He's a computer whiz who spends most of his time hacking into corporate computers throughout the world. He's also a gambler and an avid skier. When he's not wreaking havoc on computers, he helps his father and uncle with their gambling business. By the way, his father is our friend Ponytail."

"Ah, the plot thickens," Reid joked.

"A bit," Jay continued. "Anyway, the kid created and manages their gambling website. A few years ago, he thought up a gambling con. That's what Peter's kidnapping was all about. They took him, making it look like he was gone from the Games for good. Peter's not racing changed all the odds on the races. But, at the last minute, he returns and wins a medal. Since the Ukrainians had marketed the gambling opportunity very heavily, tons of bets were placed, and since no one bet on Peter, the house made a ton of money. Luckily, since they were caught quickly, they didn't have time to hide the money in any offshore accounts, so it was easy to confiscate." Jay's tone changed. "They've tried this scam before. In the previous attempt, they kidnapped a German soccer player, but they bungled that job pretty badly. In fact, the guy they kidnapped was never found, and the kid, his dad, and the other Ukrainians were never caught. Until now, that is."

"Did they kill the soccer player?" Peter's father asked.

"His body was never found. But now that we have all the major players in custody, Europol is hoping to find out. The kid is talking, but, as you can imagine, he's kind of upset by his father's condition."

"Which is?" Reid asked.

"He's still in a coma. If he comes out of it soon, I'll fly over and question him."

"So, Jay," Carole said with a look of concern. "If these guys are possibly murderers, and their entire plan just came apart, do you think Peter is still at risk?"

"Look, I didn't mean to worry you," Jay said. "I only learned about the incident with the soccer player a few hours ago. I have more security on the way. Joel and Stu will have a full team and will stay with Peter and Hunter. Carole and Dan, you'll have four of my best people, around the clock with you, too."

"Oh my God," Carole exclaimed.

"Don't be scared. I really don't think there is much to worry about," Jay said.

With a dismissive look, Carole said, "You keep saying things like that, yet, you keep adding more people to protect us."

Dan placed a comforting hand on her knee.

"I'm sorry if that sounded rude, Jay," Carole said. "But this whole thing is terribly upsetting."

"I understand," Jay said. "I am only adding extra protection as a safeguard. I really don't think it's necessary. The kid gave us the names of four others who were involved in Peter's kidnapping. Besides Ponytail, we've got all but one behind bars already. I'm told we should have the last guy in custody by the end of the day.

"I'm also working with Europol to make sure that no other irate gamblers will try to retaliate like the guy who shot his ear off. Europol is not easy to work with, but I have friends there, and I'm fairly certain I've convinced them that the safest scenario for Peter will be for them to give the money they confiscated back to everyone who placed bets and lost their money on Peter's races."

"How can you tell us not to worry when there are so many open issues?" Hunter asked.

"Come on, babe," Peter said. "Jay is doing all he can. Let's just let him finish so we can get out of here. I need to go to the gym to log in my training hours. Otherwise, Coach Williams is going to get on my case."

Hunter took a deep breath and slowly nodded. "How did you find the Ukrainians, Jay?" she asked.

"With the help of social media and a tattoo. Did any of you see the video of Peter's release that went viral?"

"Are you testing us?" Reid asked.

"Testing? What do you mean?"

"You told us to stay off Facebook and the other sites till you figured all this stuff out."

"Oh. No, what I meant was just don't post anything. But it's good to know you're taking me seriously."

"So, tell us about this video," Peter said.

Jay nodded. "An American girl and her mother had been standing nearby when you were released. When the girl saw you get out of the SUV with a mask over your eyes, she didn't know who you were, but she was curious enough to start filming with her phone. She and her mother posted the video on Facebook and a bunch of other sites. Search for Jackie and Amanda Ricciardi if you want to watch the video."

"Would you spell that?" Hunter asked.

"Just type Peter's name and kidnappers on YouTube. It comes right up," Shane said, holding up her phone with the video running.

"When you watch the video, you'll see three identical black SUVs. Then, you'll see a closeup of an arm reaching out to shut the passenger door on one of the vehicles as it starts moving. If you look closely at the wrist, you'll see a tattoo right where the face of a watch would be." He held up his wrist and patted the spot with his other hand. "You probably can't see it clearly enough on your phones, but the tattoo is of two small dice sitting on top of a poker chip. The kid has an identical tattoo, and so does Ponytail. The others that we have in custody do not have that tattoo, so chances are it was the uncle in the SUV with Peter. While gambling tattoos are common, the writing on the poker chip on all three of their wrists is in Ukrainian.

"Although the scam was the kid's idea, it seems his only involvement was programming the website. His uncle and his father were responsible for everything else."

"I guess you've questioned the others that were in the car with Ponytail when he crashed?" Buck asked.

Jay nodded. "Of course. The man and woman he was traveling with aren't saying much. But Ponytail's girlfriend is telling us everything she knows. He's been abusing her for a long time. She said it was mostly psychological, but I'm pretty sure there was more. She seemed so relieved he was in a coma."

"Wow," Shane said. "That's terrible."

"It is," Peter agreed. "I wonder if he abused the kid too? And what do you know about the boy's mother?"

"Nothing yet," Jay said.

"I still can't believe this whole thing was a teenager's idea," Peter said.

"Well," Jay continued. "I guess when a very smart kid grows up in a twisted environment, he's likely not using his intelligence for the greater good."

"I guess not," Peter said with a frown.

After a moment of silence, Peter said, "Are we done?"

"For now. I will keep the updates coming."

"So, extra security teams are on their way," Dan said. "Otherwise, it's business as usual? No lectures on how we should act or where we can, or can't, go. Nothing like that?"

"No," Jay said. "As I said, I'm pretty comfortable that we have things under control. Peter, you can train and race. Everyone else, just live your lives as you normally do. You'll have to get used to my teams being around. But I think you'll find the peace of mind they provide well worth the nuisance of having them nearby."

Nods of acceptance made their way around the room.

"Okay then," Jay added. "Buck, Peter, and Reid, could we please meet privately for a little while? We need to discuss some business."

"Really?" Peter scoffed.

"Sorry, Pete, just give me fifteen more minutes. Then you can go."

Peter looked at his watch. "Fine, fifteen minutes, but—"

A loud explosion outside rattled the living room windows.

"What the hell was that?" yelled Dan Buckar.

"Everyone get down on the floor now," Jay ordered as he un-holstered his gun and ran to the wall at the edge of the front window.

"It's Joel. I'm coming in, Jay, don't shoot," yelled Rebah as he opened the living room door and ran in, gun in hand.

Jay gave Rebah a moment to evaluate the situation in the room. Then, while peering out the edge of the window, he calmly said, "Put someone at every door, and outside each of the windows of this room. Then search the property inside and out."

"Copy that."

As Rebah was hustling out the door, Jay added, "Tell Stu and Greeny to get in here. I want additional eyes on everyone in this room until we know exactly what's going on."

"Already here, boss," Stu Mann said, rushing into the room, gun down by his thigh.

"Where's Greeny?"

"Upstairs checking rooms. He'll be here in a minute."

"No. I want him outside checking on whatever exploded. Have someone else search the rooms," Jay said pointedly.

"Yes, sir."

As Stu bolted out the door, Reid started to stand.

"Stay down, Reid," Jay said. "I know it's uncomfortable, but I'd like you all to remain where you are. I don't want anyone above the bottom edge of the windows until we know what's going on."

Carole Buckar was sniffling.

"Are you okay, mom?" Peter asked.

Her very pained "Yes," as her tears dripped to the floor, said otherwise.

Peter crawled over and put his arm over her shoulder. "I'm so sorry about all this."

"Sorry? Honey, this isn't your fault. I'm just upset that someone wants to hurt my baby." She awkwardly reached out and cupped his face in her palms.

"Mom, I'm not …"

She slid her fingers over his lips. "You'll always be my baby."

Peter forced a small smile.

Rebah re-entered the room a few minutes later, walked to Jay, and spoke quietly.

Once Rebah was done, Jay turned and said, "Okay, you can all return to your seats. We've scoured the house and the property. For the moment, there are no further concerns. The explosion came from a small device that one of my guys saw as it was thrown from a passing vehicle. It detonated immediately upon landing. Luckily, the only damage was to a couple of the cars in the driveway."

Peter cringed. "One was mine, right?"

Jay nodded.

"Damn!"

"It's only a car," Hunter said.

"Yeah, I know," Peter groaned.

"My guys informed the local police immediately. They're chasing the perp now," Jay said. "I'm going over to question him as soon as they have him in custody. Until we know more, I am assigning round-the-clock teams to each one of you. I will also post teams at each of your homes.

"Peter, you're going to have to change your plans. I won't rule out your upcoming races yet, but I'd like to limit your public appearances for a while."

"That's fine with me, as long as I can keep going to the gym."

"There's a gym in your apartment building, isn't there?"

"Yeah. It's pretty lame, though." Peter sighed heavily.

"You and Hunter can stay here," Carole interrupted. "Your training equipment is still in good condition downstairs. And, if you're here, we'll all have a little extra peace of mind knowing each other is safe."

Peter shrugged and nodded. "We could do that, but the equipment downstairs is old. I guess I can buy some new machines."

"Why doesn't everyone just stay in our houses up at AllSport, until this blows over," Buck said. "Reid, Shane, and I have more than enough room."

"No. We can't impose on you like that," Dan said.

"It's not an imposition at all," Shane said.

"That would be the best alternative until we know more," Jay said. "Protecting you will be much easier if you're all in one place. I've got enough security on campus to cover you all."

"How long is the drive from AllSport to the city?" Hunter asked.

"Why does that matter?" Jay asked.

"Because between rehearsals and performances, I need to be at Lincoln Center five or six days a week."

"By chopper, it'll take a little more than half an hour each way," Reid said.

"I can't take one of your helicopters every day," Hunter said.

"Why not?" Reid asked.

"Because it's too expensive."

Buck laughed and said, "Don't worry, Hunter, you and Peter can afford it." He pulled an envelope from his pocket and held it out toward Peter.

"What's that?" Peter asked.

"While you were at your interview earlier, I was finishing your endorsement deal with Periwinkle Water."

Peter took the envelope and peered in. "Sweet!" he said as he stood and handed Hunter the envelope.

"Oh my God," Hunter said, looking at the seven-figure check inside. "I guess we *can* afford it." She hugged Buck.

"Good. I'm glad that's decided. I want to get you all moved up to AllSport today," Jay said.

"Wait a second, don't I get a say in this?" Peter asked.

"Of course, you do, Bud," Reid said. "But if there's anything I learned when I was dealing with my death threats, it's that although it was me receiving the threats, I needed to keep in mind that my family would simply be collateral damage to these maniacs. Without question, I had to do whatever was required to keep everyone I loved out of harm's way. Even if that meant doing things I didn't want to do."

Peter crossed his arms. "I hadn't thought about it that way. You're right. Okay then, AllSport it is."

Dan stood, walked to the corner of the room, picked up one of his golf clubs, and began swinging it like a pendulum.

"Honey, what the hell are you doing?" Carole asked.

"If we're going to live at AllSport, I am going to work on my game. I've always thought about trying out for the senior tour. This could be my big break."

"Really, Dad? I didn't see that one coming," Peter said with a laugh. "Then, I guess we should get moving. Your legions of fans await."

Acknowledgements:

Some think that novel writing is a lonely endeavor, and there is some truth to that, at least during the first draft of a manuscript. But, once the original story has been completed it takes a team to help make it readable, entertaining, and ready for the world's eyes.

Thank you to all the wonderful people who helped bring Stealing Gold to fruition. As always, my first editor is my best friend for the last 40 plus years and wife for 33, Greer. Without her input and overall help from beginning to end, my characters would never see the light of day.

Then, there are a slew of editors and readers who helped clean and polish my gibberish. It's difficult to put into words how much I value their suggestions, critiques, and ideas. Andy Gillentine, Corey Cohn, Mark Jeffers, Tim Parker, Ken Ettinger, Melissa Libutti, Deica Ruiz, Karen Moore, Sheri Anderson, Steven Peltz, Warren Groner, Aimee Friedman, Cover artist Johnny Breeze, Editor extraordinaire (book doctor) Barbara Chintz, and of course, Steve Himes and his wonderful team at Telemachus Press.

Thank you all from the bottom of my heart.

About the Author

Michael Balkind's novels *Sudden Death, Dead Ball, and Gold Medal Threat* are endorsed by literary greats including James Patterson, Clive Cussler, John Feinstein, Andrew Gross, John Lescroart, Wendy Corsi Staub and Tim Green. He has appeared on ESPN's *The Pulse*, *Sportsnet's Daily News Live*, and has co-hosted *The Clubhouse* radio show. He is a member of Mystery Writers of America. Balkind's novel, *The Fix*, is co-authored with NBC Sports and Golf Channel Host, Ryan Burr. Balkind graduated from Syracuse University and resides in New York.

Balkind's website: www.balkindbooks.com
His author page on Facebook:
Michael Balkind—Mysteries & More
Follow him on Instagram and Twitter: @michaelbalkind

If you enjoyed *Stealing Gold*, be sure to read Michael Balkind's other novels:

Visit Michael Balkind's Amazon Author Page:

CPSIA information can be obtained
at www.ICGtesting.com
Printed in the USA
BVHW031740211121
622171BV00012B/407/J